CW00504745

The Final Twist

The Untwisted Series – Book 5

Alice Raine

Published by Accent Press Ltd – 2017

ISBN: 9781786152541

Acknowledgements

I'd like to dedicate this latest Untwisted series book to all of you readers who have read and become involved in the Jackson Brother's story. Without you reading, reviewing and supporting my work this book would never have happened. I am so overwhelmed with the lovely feedback I have received for this series, so I truly hope that this instalment lives up to all you hoped for.

This book also goes out to my friend Karen W, one of the strongest, kindest, funniest, most inspirational women I have ever met. She also has a wickedly filthy mind, which is no-doubt why we shall forever be friends. She is the inspiration behind one of the characters contained within this story – love you to bits, and can't wait to see you again in June.

As always, a huge thanks must go to my publisher, Accent Press, and all the staff who work tirelessly on producing and promoting my books: Hazel Cushion, Kate Ellis, Karen Bultiauw, Ffion Morris and Joe Moore, to name just a few.

To my editor, Liz Coldwell, thank you for the advice, feedback and your patience with my grammatical errors!

As part of the research process for this book I needed help on several subjects, so thank you to all that came to my aid. In particular, the advice on police procedures was so helpful, so huge thanks to: Sarah-Jayne McIntosh and Sam Berwitz (via your family member) for helping me get the details correct.

Also my trusty advisors and beta readers: Leah Weatherall (who basically became my unpaid PA during the writing of this book!), Grace Lowrie, and Katie Newman – hugs to you girls! As always, your feedback was invaluable in helping me shape the story.

I shall leave you now to enjoy the continuing lives of Nicholas and Nathanial, get a cuppa, or perhaps a glass of wine and hold on tight, because there are a few twists in here that you might not be expecting!

Alice xx

Chapter One

Stella

The sight before me was possibly the most erotic vision I'd ever seen. Nathan stood with his legs splayed wide in that cocksure stance of his. His feet were bare, jeans hanging low from his sinfully trim waist, and best of all, he was topless too. Yum. His stomach muscles were unfairly tight, and contoured into those little bumps and ridges that I loved to run my tongue over, and his biceps bulged just enough to indicate how strong he was underneath his lean figure. There was barely a scrap of fat on him, meaning he was muscular, but not overly so – just about as perfect as a man could get.

I made myself comfy in my seat. My grin widened as I let my gaze drift across the zipper at his crotch, up his happy trail, and over his six pack to where our nappy-clad boy was resting in his arms.

Like I said; it really was the perfect view.

Since dating Nathan I'd learned just how deceiving looks could be, though. Yes, he made a beautiful picture and was handsome as sin, but beneath his handsome façade he was a tortured soul. A tortured soul that apparently only I could soothe. But although we'd had our hiccups along the way, thankfully everything was pretty bloody amazing at the moment.

We were happy. Blissfully happy. Our new home in the Cotswolds should be ready in a month or so, our young son William was healthy and happy, and Nathan and I were solid as a couple.

My gaze softened as I looked at our son nestled against Nathan's shoulder. God, what a sight. It made my stomach all fluttery, but I couldn't quite put my finger on why. I suppose it must be to do with the fact that he had all those imposing muscles, but yet could be so sweet and gentle with his son. Nathan absolutely adored William. He would literally do anything for him, including letting him vomit all over him without a word of complaint while gently rubbing his back and whispering soothing words to him.

After a moment of soppy adoration, I grew greedy as I once again got distracted by my man's fine physique. Finally meeting his gaze, I tensed when I found him glaring at me with a narrow-eyed look of frustration. 'You know it's highly unfair to give me those lusty looks while I'm burping our son?'

Giggling, I tried to look apologetic and immediately failed. I didn't care, either. Nathan was gorgeous, and I would take every opportunity I could get to ogle his ripped perfection, even if that was while he carried out his daddy duties.

He was proving to be a near-perfect dad, but seeing as William vomited after practically every feed Nathan now did the winding topless, which was absolutely fine and dandy by me. As he had his hands full, I decided to live dangerously and taunt my delicious Dom just a little more by giving a carefree shrug. 'I'm not sorry in the slightest.'

Nathan let out a low, frustrated growl and pulled his lips into a tight line. 'Trying to top me from the bottom again, are you? I don't think so, Stella,' he warned, his tone dropping and filling with salacious intent as he began to rub Will's back with more determination, apparently keen to get our boy laid down for his nap.

He often joked that I tried to "top him from the bottom" – meaning that I tried to exert some form of dominance

2

over him – but we were both fully aware that wasn't the case. I liked to tease, but when Nathan really got his Dom side out I didn't stand a chance at topping him in the slightest.

The dip in his tone and the wicked spark in his eye were enough to shut me up and send desire coursing through my veins. Licking my lips, I squirmed in my seat, a move that didn't go unnoticed by Nathan, who snickered his pleasure at my sudden discomfort.

'That serves you right for being a tease.'

Huffing out a flustered breath, I tried to give him my most disgruntled look, but probably just ended up looking like a petulant kid, because Nathan barked out another loud laugh.

'I love it when you get frustrated, baby. Your cheeks flush the most gorgeous shade of pink. It's rather similar to the colour your bottom goes after a good spanking, actually.'

My eyes widened at his salacious words, and I felt my cheeks heat with desire. He was being far too smug for my liking, though. Keeping my eyes locked with his, I laid myself back more comfortably in the armchair and then propped one leg over the arm. I brought my right hand up to gently trace my forefinger up over my belly, dragging my T-shirt up slightly to expose some skin before continuing to rise along the edges of my ribs and finally arriving at one breast.

'Jesus, Stella. Do you want me to accidentally drop William?' His cool composure almost cracked as he watched me, and his heated response to my actions absolutely thrilled me. 'Stop, Stella …' Nathan's voice was gruff and filled with warning, but his eyes were still locked on the movement of my hand. 'We have company arriving in less than twenty minutes for a dinner party.'

He was right. My family would be arriving at any

minute now, so we definitely didn't have time to get ready *and* squeeze in a quickie, but for some reason I felt reckless today and couldn't help but play with him a little more.

Having dragged my T-shirt up higher to expose my breast, I circled my nipple with my fingertip and sucked in an exaggerated breath before rolling my eyes closed and repeating the action, causing Nathan to splutter. 'Enough! We don't have time for your teasing. Not unless you want your mother to arrive and find me fucking you senseless over the dining room table.'

Now that was an image I would struggle to get out of my head all night. He absolutely meant every word, too. Nathan would literally have no qualms about spreading me out on the dinner table and having his wicked way with me, which would certainly give us all something to talk about over the starter, but might give my mum a seizure in the process.

'For one, you know damn well that I am the only one to give you pleasure these days, and, secondly, you shouldn't be doing that in front of William!'

I laughed and shook my head in amusement. Will was way too young to understand what I was doing, and besides, he used to get up close and personal with my boobs on a daily basis until I'd recently stopped breastfeeding, so I really couldn't see the logic to Nathan's argument at all.

I'm not quite sure what had got into me; perhaps I'd had too much caffeine, but I just couldn't stop. I trailed my fingers lightly back down my body, making a show of pushing my hand inside my trousers. Then I traced my damp flesh with a hissed breath. God, I was so aroused already.

'Fuck!' Nathan gawked at where my hand was moving inside my trousers and, much to my pleasure, I saw that his jeans were now straining at the crotch with excitement. Readjusting William over his other shoulder, he turned

4

away with a curse. 'You are going to pay for this later, Stella.'

'I certainly hope so … *Sir*.'

At my blatant invitation, Nathan spun back around, his nostrils flared and eyes glinting with dark pleasure. 'The sooner this bloody dinner party is over, the better.'

Chapter Two

Stella

As they did each year, my parents had spent the best part of January and February in their holiday home in Spain, and so today's visit was the first time we'd seen them since Christmas.

My mother had eyes like a hawk, so I'd been expecting her to notice the commitment ring that Nathan had given me over New Year, but I seriously hadn't expected her to notice it quite *this* soon.

She wasn't even through the bloody front door. One foot was barely over the threshold and her eyes lit up like Christmas tree lights. 'Oh my gosh! Is that an engagement ring?' she squawked, while grabbing my hand and practically tugging me out onto the front step along with her.

'Oh, Stella! It's beautiful!' she cooed, her voice high from excitement as she almost dislocated my shoulder in her exuberance. 'I can't believe Nathan finally proposed!'

Letting out a heavy sigh, I rolled my eyes. I'd been preparing myself for her misunderstanding, but I knew my mum wasn't going to grasp the truth, however I worded it. 'It's *not* an engagement ring, Mum, it's a commitment ring.'

That certainly took the wind out of her sails. Bless her. Pausing, she looked at the ring again, and then back up at me with an expression of complete confusion on her face. 'A commitment ring?'

'Yep. It means we're together in a committed

6

relationship,' I explained briskly, pulling my hand back. Mum opened her mouth to speak again, but I silenced her by waving them into the house. 'Don't stand in the cold, come in. I've just made a pot of coffee.'

As he passed me, my dad looked briefly at the ring, too, and flashed me a reassuring wink. 'It's lovely, poppet.' Which was exactly the type of understated reaction I'd known he'd have. I closed the front door and led them towards the lounge, trying to suppress a grin at how disgruntled my mother currently looked as she trailed behind me. I would place money on the fact that she'd already bought a wedding hat, which was a shame seeing as Nathan and I were not getting married. Ever.

'It's on your ring finger,' she stated, 'And it looks like an engagement ring,' she added petulantly as I got them settled in the lounge.

Holding in my fraying temper, I nodded and gave her a tight-lipped smile. I'd tired of this conversation already. 'Yes, it does, Mum. But it's not,' I stated firmly. 'After his parents' messy marriage, Nathan isn't really a fan of wedlock.'

Thinking of Nathan, I wondered where the heck he was. This conversation was torturous, and I could have really done with his back-up. Narrowing my eyes, I realised that he was probably "hiding". No doubt he'd anticipated this very discussion and was lurking in the kitchen or locked away in his dressing room, picking out which suit to grace us all with today, while I faced the worst of the storm. The bastard.

'Well, if it isn't an engagement ring then perhaps you need to be having words with that man of yours. You have a baby together, Stella, and you're living in sin ...' My mother's tone faded off in apparent revulsion at the idea, which was ironic, seeing as she wasn't even remotely religious. I very nearly laughed out loud. If only they knew

7

exactly *how* sinful Nathan and I could be when we chose … Floggers, crops, cuffs, butt plugs … life surely didn't get much more sinful than our bedroom activities.

'No, Mum, I don't. I love this commitment ring, and I love Nathan, just as we are. I don't need a wedding ceremony to confirm that.' As I spoke, I subconsciously moved my hand to my neck and absently played with the chain there. My collar, of sorts. If anything was similar to a wedding ring, it was this collar, not the commitment ring on my finger, but obviously, I didn't try to explain that to my mum. She'd probably pass out if I gave her the explicit details of what a Dom/sub relationship entailed.

As I thought of my dashing man, the hairs on the back of my neck suddenly gave a little tingle and I turned to see that he was finally joining me in the lounge. As I'd suspected, he had swapped his earlier jeans for a grey three-piece suit and had a bottle of fizz in one hand and some glasses in the other. It seemed he was set on distracting us all with booze, which probably wasn't a bad idea.

As was usual, my breath caught in my lungs when our eyes met and he gave me one of his perfectly practiced panty-soaking stares. God. His eyes really were remarkable. I was so glad he'd learned to share eye contact with me, because, wow, it really was amazing the reaction it caused in my body.

I was now seriously regretting teasing him earlier, because while it had been fun at the time, it had also left *me* wanting more, and as a result I was horny and fidgety and couldn't stop squeezing my thighs together. The corner of his mouth rose slightly, as if he could sense the response in my body, and then, giving an almost imperceptible wink in my direction, he poured some drinks and handed them round. I noticed my mother's glass was the fullest, so either he was trying to gain favour by giving her a generous portion, or he was planning on getting her drunk so she couldn't bombard him with questions about my "not-an-engagement-ring". Knowing Nathan, I suspected it was the latter.

'So, Nathan, Stella has been telling us about this "commitment" ring ...' The way she-over enunciated the word *commitment* caused Nathan's lips to tighten into a straight line and his eyebrows to lower.

'I sometimes wonder why people are so obsessed with weddings and marriage, Susan,' Nathan observed, before sliding an arm around my waist and pulling me close in to his side.

Oh dear. My man did not like being questioned, or put on the spot, and I had the distinct feeling that he would explain exactly how our relationship worked if Mum kept pushing him, but as I went to try to intervene he silenced me with a small shake of his head then looked my mother directly in the eye.

Holding my breath, I waited in anticipation for his next words, knowing that this really could go either way.

'Stella is the love of my life, we have a beautiful son together, and I can safely say that I intend to cherish both of them for the rest of my life. She has a ring on her finger and my unerring commitment ... why do you need a piece of paper to go with it?'

My mother's mouth literally fell open at Nathan's words, as did mine, because, wow, seeing as this was Nathan we were talking about, that was a seriously touching statement he had just made.

'I ... well ... I ...' Mum was totally stumped for words, which didn't happen often, but then she took a sip of her fizz and swallowed hard as if absorbing his reply. 'When you put it like that, Nathan, I suppose I was just being silly and old-fashioned.' Smiling up at him, she raised her glass. 'To happy families, just as we are.'

I'd never expected my mum to back down on the

marriage issue, but it seemed my man had won her over. Just like that. Jeez, his influence obviously extended beyond me to my mother, too. This was all really bizarre, but I wasn't about to let the opportunity go and so quickly clinked my glass with theirs and joined in the toast.

Nathan gently knocked his glass against mine last and then bent to kiss my cheek. 'Just as we are,' he murmured, his low tone adding to my earlier arousal and making me lean into him for support.

Thankfully, we were then saved from any more emotional outpourings or questions by the ring of the doorbell, indicating the perfectly timed arrival of Rebecca and Nicholas.

Today's meal was supposed to have been a birthday gathering for Kenny, with just us, Kenny, Tom – his new boyfriend – and Rebecca and Nicholas. It was intended to be the first time we all met Tom, but my parents had phoned up yesterday to announce that they were back from Spain and promptly decided to gate-crash.

I had phoned everyone to warn them that my folks were joining us, and Kenny had seemed really keen to show off his new man to my mum. But, as Becky and Nicholas joined us in the lounge, I had to laugh when I saw Nicholas standing next to his brother looking almost as uncomfortable with the gathering as Nathan did. The Jackson boys really didn't do parental gatherings very well at all.

I looked at them both, standing there with rod-straight backs as they quietly spoke about something and realised how daunting most people probably found them. It was probably why my mum had been so easily swayed by Nathan's declaration just now. I'd adjusted to their intense stares, relatively brusque social etiquette, and over-the-top possessiveness, but they certainly were an impressive pair, that was for sure.

With their calm confidence, perfect posture, and stunning good looks, the brothers were what most women, and no doubt a large proportion of men, would describe as the perfect catch, but looks weren't everything, were they?

Nathan's and Nicholas's chiselled handsomeness and muscled frames disguised a multitude of hidden issues that the men had had to deal with throughout their lives, but now we were all getting settled, and I thought we might finally be over the worst.

Kenny and Tom arrived. They thrust a bottle of wine into my hands and shoved a huge bunch of flowers at Nathan as we answered the door. The deliberate move made Nathan growl and had Kenny and me in stiches as my man stalked off to the kitchen to get rid of the bouquet.

'Sorry, couldn't help myself. He's just so hot when he's in a strop!' Kenny commented, as he watched Nathan's retreating figure and pretended to fan his face. 'Not as hot as you though, babe,' he added with a grin aimed at his boyfriend as he shyly did the introductions. 'Stella, this is Tom.'

Tom stepped inside and closed the front door behind him before turning to me. 'I've heard a great deal about you, Stella. All good,' he added with a smile as I made a worried face. He held out his hand and gave mine a firm shake as he smiled at me with an almost perfect set of white teeth. I could immediately see why Kenny – Mr Perfectionist himself – liked Tom. He was immaculately dressed, his stubble was trimmed and clearly there because it was meant to be, and his ruffled brown hair made him look far too sinful to be a truly good boy, which had never been Kenny's type.

All in all, he was just about Kenny's perfect man, but I couldn't help worry about my sensitive bestie. He always seemed to pick handsome extroverts who quickly bored of his exuberant personality and moved on because they wanted more of the spotlight for themselves.

I exchanged a cheek kiss with Kenny and grinned at him. 'Happy birthday, Ken.'

'Thanks, Stel,' he replied with a blush as I took their coats and ushered them inside.

'Go on through, everyone's in the lounge.' Watching them go, I couldn't help grinning as they practically skipped inside hand in hand. It would certainly seem that things were going well between the new love birds at the moment. I'd need to pull Kenny aside later and get the full details. What with having William to look after and him seeing Tom at every available opportunity, we'd been getting fewer and fewer chances for catch-ups than we used to, and one was definitely in order.

Mum had always treated Kenny like a second son, so his arrival with Tom totally grabbed her interest. As we watched them all greeting each other, she smiled across at Nathan and me and seemed genuinely over the whole the engagement obsession, thank goodness.

Over the next hour or so, I watched Kenny and Tom together carefully and was thrilled to see that Tom was seemingly perfect for Kenny. He was good-looking, yes, but quiet with it, and had the ideal combination of attractiveness, dry humour, and humbleness, which seemed to balance out Kenny's wild streak almost effortlessly.

According to Kenny they'd been together for nearly four months now; a record for Kenny, who had even confided in me last week that he finally thought he might have found "the one". For his sake, I really hoped he had. They looked great together, and I'd love to see my best mate in the settled relationship that he'd always craved.

Chapter Three

Rebecca

I didn't know Kenny that well, but since becoming so close with Stella I'd met up with them both for several lunches and cocktail nights. Even to me, a virtual stranger, it had been obvious just how desperate he'd been to find himself a boyfriend and leave behind his days of disastrous dates and meaningless flings.

Tom seemed to tick all the right boxes. He was exceptionally charming, and after chatting to him for a while between courses I could see why Kenny had fallen for him. He was smart, handsome, and funny, but in a slightly toned-down way, which seemed to be an ideal match for Kenny's extrovert personality.

Just as there was a lull in our current conversation, I got the distinct feeling that we were being watched. The hairs on the back of my neck rose and tingled, and without looking I just knew that Nicholas was watching me. Turning to scan the room, I smiled when I proved myself right. Nicholas stood on his own on the other side of the lounge, staring across at us.

Smiling at him, I was about to indicate that he should join us, when I noticed his lowered brows and tense jaw. Hmm. It would seem that something had riled my darling husband, and from the glacial glare currently being directed at my conversation partner, I could only think that it was Tom.

Politely excusing myself, I left Tom to go and refill his wine. I wandered over to Nicholas, changing my expression so it mirrored his current look of disapproval. As I reached his side, I propped a hand on my hip and raised an eyebrow. 'Please tell me that you're not jealous.'

His nostrils flared, giving me the answer I needed, but, being stubborn, Nicholas didn't directly answer. Instead, he just rammed his hands into his trouser pockets and hunched forwards, ruining his usually perfect posture.

He looked hot when he was broody like this, all dark and bad boy, but really this was ridiculous. 'He's gay, Nicholas! And you and I are married!' I whispered in amusement.

There was a long moment of quiet between us where Nicholas simply stared across the room at nothing in particular then began fiddling with his wedding ring.

'I know, I know. And I trust you implicitly.' His words sounded almost exasperated as they rushed from his lips. 'And that's why I'm still over here and not grabbing him by his shirt collars and giving him an earful.' Running a hand through his hair, Nicholas let out a long, low sigh. He looked at me with an expression of pure possessive lust on his face.

'You're mine. I know that, but sometimes I still struggle with my emotions. Seeing him with you being all touchy-feely brought out my inner caveman, I guess.'

Expressing exactly how he felt was still relatively new to Nicholas, so his effort at explaining his feelings was a good step. I couldn't really be mad at him. This was a major forward move; he'd vocalised why he was angry, and could see that it was misplaced.

'You wanna drag me off to your cave and have your wicked way with me?' I teased, leaning in close to his neck so my breath must have tickled his skin.

'Yes.' Nicholas grabbed my hand and began to pull me towards the hallway, but I dug my heels in and gave him a wide-eyed stare when he looked back at me.

'I was kidding!' I squawked, unable to believe that even Nicholas would think it was fine and dandy to sneak in a sex session at his brother's house.

'Ten minutes till the main course,' Stella announced as she poked her head in from the kitchen with a smile.

Nicholas nodded, and then leaned in to kiss my neck. 'Perfect. That's plenty of time for what I have in mind,' he growled by my neck. Then, before I could put up any further arguments, he dragged me from the room and directly into the downstairs toilet at the end of the hall, already pulling his suit jacket off as we went.

This is crazy!

Once he'd locked the door, he pounced on me, his eyes dark and full of lusty intent as he skipped my lips and buried his mouth against my neck. He kissed and licked across my collarbone towards my shoulder, sending goose pimples flooding my skin.

A second later he was flicking the strap of my dress down with his tongue.

Blimey.

My dress began to fall down and expose one breast, and the cooler air on my skin finally snapped me from my lusty shock. 'Nicholas! Stop! What if someone hears us?'

I could already tell that my reasonable question was going to go unanswered, because it was clear from the determined expression on Nicholas's face that he was well and truly set on his claiming mission.

'You better be quiet then, babe, hadn't you?' he murmured, dropping one hand to the front of my dress and popping out my other breast.

'Relax, Becky. Enjoy it, sweetheart. It'll be just like that time in the shop changing room, remember that?'

Oh God, did I. It had been incredible. He'd sneaked in and fucked me senseless against the mirrored wall, all while other shoppers tried on their clothing completely unaware

15

of our steamy tryst.

'Just thinking about that day makes you hot, doesn't it?' he muttered against the skin of my chest before he sucked a nipple into his mouth and circled the peak with the tip of his tongue. 'I know it does me.' This final statement was accompanied by him standing up again and thrusting his rock-solid groin against me as he grinned down at me flirtatiously.

Oh sod it. We'd been gone a few minutes now anyway; if anyone was going to notice our absence and jump to conclusions they already would have. I might as well get an orgasm out of it now we were here.

I raised my hands and dug them into the hair at his neck, then pulled his mouth to mine, meeting his hungry growl with a kiss just as demanding.

He dropped one hand to drag my dress up around my waist and dip inside my knickers to find my core. 'Fuck. You're soaked already.'

Yeah, I was. I might have been saying this was an inappropriate time, but that was just the sensible part of my brain being rational. Realistically, I was never going to turn him down, because Nicholas was so hot when he was on a mission like this and it never failed to get me aroused and horny within seconds.

I knew I should, but I didn't care where we were, or who might hear. I just wanted him buried deep inside me.

As if reading my thoughts, Nicholas quickly bent to strip me of my panties then stood again and freed his erection from the confines of his suit trousers. He was so excited that I could already see the shine of pre-come on his tip, but I couldn't bend to lick it off as I wanted because he pressed me back against the wall and kissed me hard. 'No time for that, I'm already close.'

He gripped my right leg, raising it around his waist, and brushed himself across my entrance before pausing and

16

running a hot lick of his tongue across my lips.

'No noise, remember, baby?' The question didn't get an answer because a second later he jerked his hips forwards and buried himself into me in one smooth, hard thrust. The only way I managed not to scream out was to sink my teeth into his shoulder and bite down, but rather than causing him pain, he seemed to get a kick out of my move because he let out a quiet moan of approval and upped the speed of his hips.

Pinned against the wall like this, I didn't have much room to manoeuvre, but I rotated my hips with each of his frantic thrusts and soon felt my climax building. Nicholas was close, too. His jerky moves had lost their usual finesse, but seeing as we needed to be quick that was just fine by me.

His lips found mine again, tongue pressing inside my mouth and stealing my breath as he pinned me to the wall and thrust so hard and fast that I couldn't help but tip across the edge into my orgasm. My body started to clench around him, and my head went dizzy, but he caught my moans in his mouth. Then, as he kissed me deeply, he, too, began to climax, grinding his hips against mine and filling me with his hot release.

Standing together for a few seconds we tried to get our breath back, both of us panting and speechless. Finally, Nicholas eased out of me, flashed me his smug smile, and wiped the damp tip of his cock across my stomach.

'I like the idea of you having a trace of me on your body for the rest of the night,' he murmured. He grinned at my shocked expression, before handing me some tissues.

'It's lucky I have my suit jacket, because my shoulder is soaked,' he remarked, giving me an amused look as he brushed at the wet, circular bite mark on his pale grey shirt.

Oops. Looked like we'd both left our trace on each other.

17

Glancing in the mirror, I saw my flushed cheeks and the twinkle in my eye and I winced. I definitely looked well fucked. How I was supposed to go and face a room full of our nearest and dearest now was beyond me, but Nicholas seemed perfectly at ease. He shrugged into his jacket and helped me straighten my clothes before offering me his hand.

'Let's go and eat, I'm starving.'

My eyes widened at his complete calm as he guided me out of the bathroom. He'd gone from primal caveman to utter gentleman in a matter of minutes. Unbelievable!

Chapter Four

Stella

Nathan had been hilarious so far. Even though he had his brother here to keep him company, he had followed me like a puppy every time I left the lounge. He was so calm and controlled in every other aspect of his life, but put him in a room with my mum and dad and he turned into this nervy, vulnerable creature. It would be quite unsettling if I didn't find it so funny.

I'd just entered the kitchen to get the dessert ready when Nathan burst in after me and let out an audible sigh of relief. Turning with a giggle, I found him leaning on the kitchen counter loosening his tie in a move that would have been incredibly sexy, if he hadn't currently looked so stressed. 'Oh come on, Nathan, Mum hasn't been that bad! She's even dropped the engagement topic since your little speech.'

Nathan nodded and ran a hand over his face before tugging at his shirt cuffs in a way that I knew meant he was agitated about something. 'I know. But after your little display in the bedroom earlier I can barely even focus on conversation.'

Ah, *that* was what he was agitated about. Sex. Made sense, really, seeing as this was Nathan we were talking about. Not to mention that I was also still on a low simmer from my little act earlier, and had been all evening.

Biting my lower lip, I nodded and squeezed my thighs together, because now that he was here, alone with me, I was really starting to struggle again, too. I'd read in a

19

magazine once that sex drives lessened when you had children, but that wasn't the case with Nathan and me. We were still like horny teenagers all the time. That was the last time I would try to get the upper hand by teasing him, though, because this was hellish.

Delayed gratification was definitely not my thing.

'Besides, she might not be talking about your ring any more, but she still keeps staring at it.'

'I think she's just happy that we're so settled,' I said softly, trying to soothe him, but it didn't work, because he tugged at his cuffs again and grunted.

'It makes me uncomfortable.'

Totally confused now, I frowned. 'What does?'

Pausing, he licked his lips and then tilted his head forwards to land me with one of his supercharged low-browed stares. I was the complete and utter focus of his attention, and that knowledge always made me feel a bit quivery. 'Be honest, Stella, you say you're fine not getting married, but is that really true?'

Relaxing my shoulders, I rolled my eyes and put the carton of cream onto the counter. 'Absolutely. Like you said earlier, it's just a piece of paper. I'm perfectly content as we are. Besides, I have this …' I touched the gleaming diamond on my left ring finger. 'Not forgetting this …' I murmured, my voice turning huskier as I reached up and gently traced the collar around my neck.

Nathan's eyes darkened as he watched me play with the delicate necklace. Then, as if he could no longer hold himself back, he strode across the kitchen and dragged me into his arms with a low growl.

'Damn right you do.' He placed a short, hard kiss on my lips and leaned back, looking down at me curiously. 'I've been thinking …'

Whatever it was, he seemed to be quite excited about it, and so I raised my eyebrows in invitation for him to continue.

'Now that you have my ring and my collar I've … I've found myself wanting more.' His statement was puzzling to say the least, because we'd only just persuaded my mum that we were great as we were. I'd changed my name by deed poll to Jackson, and apart from marriage, I couldn't see any other type of "more" we could do. Surely he wasn't suddenly changing his mind?

Seeing my confusion, he brushed a few hairs back from my face and took a deep breath.

'Sometimes in relationships like ours the commitment between a Dom and his sub can be formalised with a collaring ceremony.' My eyes widened further at his words, but I listened intently, my curiosity well and truly piqued.

'I know we don't live strictly by that lifestyle, but it's still a part of us, or certainly it is still a part of me, and I was hoping you might agree to validating us in that way, too.'

I paused, wondering what it would involve. From the title of a "ceremony" it sounded like it might be quite a big thing, but Nathan frowned with obvious worry at my hesitation. 'It would mean a great deal to me, Stella,' he added eagerly.

I would do anything for this man, literally anything, so really that was all I needed to hear for now. The details could wait. 'Of course I will, Nathan.'

With a groan, he lowered his lips to mine and pressed his tongue into my mouth. He kissed me until I was breathless, then proceeded to trail his lips down my neck until he came to the collar. 'Thank you.'

He dropped light pecks in the hollow of my throat then followed the line of the necklace until he came to the delicate skin where my shoulder met my neck. His kisses paused there, and he licked across the skin before sucking. Hard.

21

I was dizzy from his onslaught, so it took me a second to work out what he was doing, but then, as the insistent pulling on my neck became more painful, I let out a yelp and pushed against his chest. 'Nathan! Don't you bloody dare give me a love bite when I have to go back out and face my parents!'

Instead of stopping immediately, Nathan lessened his pressure. He grumbled against my skin. 'Mine.'

'Yes. But you don't need to mark me to prove that. I'm yours, and with all the sodding hickeys you give me I think we've well and truly established that fact.'

'Cheek like that will earn you a red arse, Mrs Jackson. Especially seeing as I'm already wound up from your earlier performance. It's left me with a serious case of blue balls.'

I would have laughed, but his tone was silky and full of salacious intent, so all I could manage was a shocked gasp. Surely he wouldn't spank me in here, while we had a room full of dinner party guests just the other side of the door?

Leaning back, he glanced at my neck and narrowed his eyes. 'Besides, I like marking you. It's one of the reasons I want the collaring. I want everyone to know you're mine,' he murmured, his tone so low and seductive that I actually shuddered in his arms. 'See? You like the idea of it too,' he whispered smugly. Which I did, but just not on my neck when I was wearing a low-cut dress.

'I do,' I admitted with a carefree shrug, 'but I happen to know you wouldn't dare mark me today. Not with my mother in the next room.'

Before I'd had time to get my lusty thoughts back in line I felt myself shifting as Nathan took a firm hold of my hips and steered me backwards into the walk-in pantry. His head lowered again, but just as I thought he was going to continue with his love bite, he instead kissed me, long and hard, then spun me around so I was leaning over the work counter.

'Oh how wrong you are, Stella.' The hem of my skirt was flicked up over my back so swiftly that I barely even felt it, but as I gasped, Nathan leaned down close to my ear.

'How many spanks do you think you should receive for teasing me?' he breathed hotly against my cheek and I quickly realised my mistake. This was Nathan we were talking about; of course he would have no issue with spanking me with my mum just a few metres away.

I could feel the heat of his erection digging into my thigh, and a heated groan rose in my throat as he ground it against me with several jerky jabs of his hips. Even though I could think of a thousand reasons to tell him to stop, I didn't. Instead, I swallowed hard and answered.

'Two, Sir.' I'd normally say a higher number, but I was still vaguely aware of the fact that my parents were just next door.

Nathan groaned, and gently offered me the handle of a wooden spoon to bite down on, which I immediately accepted. 'Good girl. As we're going with just two, I'll go a little harder than usual. Don't make a sound.'

As Nathan raised his hand to perform the first smack he knocked a cake tin off the shelf beside us with his other hand. It was a genius move, because the clatter effectively covered the ringing noise of his hand connecting firmly with my buttock, and the muffled sound of me groaning my thanks. He was speedy with his next strike, too, this time knocking off a baking tray before flicking my skirt back down, chucking the wooden spoon aside, and kissing my gasps away.

The squeak of the kitchen door opening made my eyes fly wide open. A second later, my mum appeared behind Nathan in the doorway to the pantry. 'Is everything all right in here? You haven't dropped the pudding, I hope!'

I couldn't even speak. My legs were rubbery, my arse

was smarting, and my tongue felt thick in my mouth from the lust pulsing around my system.

'All good, Mrs M,' Nathan replied, stealing Kenny's usual nickname for my mother and suddenly turning on the charm and looking completely calm. *Ha!* Quite apparently, all Nathan needed to do to relax himself around my mum was to give me a good hard spanking before interacting with her. 'Stella just knocked a couple of things down. I was helping her pick them up. We'll bring the dessert through now.'

My mum seemed satisfied and, thankfully, returned to the dining room, leaving me to sink into his arms and repeat my earlier question.

'So what does the collaring ceremony involve?'

'In simple terms, it's where you officially offer yourself to me, and I place a collar around your neck, claiming you as mine.' Nathan leaned his head down to watch my reaction, and bless him, he looked genuinely worried about what my reaction might be. 'We'll have it at Club Twist. There's more to it than that, obviously, but we probably need a little more time to discuss it than we have now.'

I nodded, smiling broadly at the thought that Nathan craved me enough that he wanted to make it official in front of all his associates at Club Twist. However you dressed it up, it was a fairly big deal.

Before I could pick up the pudding, Nathan grabbed me and ducked down behind me. He lifted my skirt and caressed my burning bum cheeks, the gentleness of his touch causing goose pimples to rush across my heated skin.

I felt his fingers shifting the lace of my panties and then a deep, erotic groan grumbled from his throat as he examined my heated arse. 'Fuck, Stella. You're wearing my handprint on both your buttocks like a neon sign.'

Craning my neck, I looked over my shoulder and managed to see a blurry reflection of myself in the darkened glass of the kitchen door. Even though the reflection wasn't clear I could see the redness that had bloomed on my bum. Huh. And I'd been worried that he was going to mark my neck. Mind you, at least my mother wouldn't be able to see these beauties.

Nathan rearranged my clothes for me. He stood up, looking visibly flushed, and ran his hands through his hair before adjusting a very large bulge in his trousers. 'I am so fucking hard right now.' Leaning in close, he dragged me against him so our hips clashed and his erection dug into my stomach. 'Dessert. Coffee. Then they go and I get to bury myself inside you.' My eyes boggled at the bluntness of his words and my nostrils flared with the effort of dragging enough air into my lungs to breathe properly. 'Don't even think of inviting everyone to stay for cheese.'

Given the lowness of his tone, I should have taken his final statement as a warning, but Nathan telling me not to offer our dinner guests cheese so that he could have his wicked way with me sounded so random that I immediately snorted out a very inelegant laugh.

'Fuck, Stella!' Nathan gave me an exasperated look and rolled his eyes. 'Why the hell I let you tease me like this is beyond me.'

Maybe it was the adrenalin flowing around my system from his impromptu and arousing spanking, but I was feeling floaty and in great spirits, so I grabbed his shirt collar and tugged his gorgeous mouth down to mine and kissed him hard as a broad grin split my lips. 'Because you love me and want to claim me in some strange ceremony.' With my sing-songy voice it came out like "lurve meee", which I knew would bug the hell out of my already tetchy man.

Considering it had taken Nathan so long to admit his feelings for me, it was really refreshing that we were now at a stage in our relationship where I could joke about it with him like this and feel 100 per cent confident that he really did care about me that much.

'That I do, and it's made me into a right pussy,' he grumbled, stepping away from me and picking up the pot of cream. As I went to reach for the cherry pie he took me completely by surprise by landing another resounding slap on my left buttock. It rang around the room and caused me to yelp loudly. There was no way our guests would have been able to mistake that for anything other than what it was.

'Just as well you love me, too, hmm? We'll continue this later.' Nathan flashed me a wicked wink and headed back into the dining room, humming under his breath.

Bastard. But he was right; I really did love him. I was excited about the idea of the ceremony, too, but more immediately than that, I couldn't wait to see if he would carry out his threat of "continuing this later".

Chapter Five

Rebecca

Waving goodbye to Stella and Nathan, I followed Nicholas down the steps to our car. 'Are you OK, babe? You've gone really pale.' Nicholas sounded worried, and as I turned to him I saw his anxiety reflected in the tightness of his jaw as he quickly bundled me into the car.

'I'm fine. The smell of the coffee that Stella served just made me feel a bit queasy, that's all.'

Thinking about it, I'd been queasy yesterday, too, when Nicholas had made us our usual pot of morning coffee. It was odd. I usually loved coffee. A few moments of silence passed between us as my brain tried to compute a few dates, then I gasped and turned to Nicholas.

'Actually … can we stop at the pharmacy on the way home?'

Before I had even finished speaking, Nicholas had pulled the car into the side of the road and swivelled to face me, looking worried. 'You're feeling that bad? Do you want me to go straight to the doctor's instead?' Bless him. My man didn't half like to panic about my wellbeing.

Swallowing shyly, I shook my head. 'No … I was thinking I should pick up a pregnancy test.'

Nicholas blinked at me several times, his big blue eyes looking almost black in the twilight as he digested my words. 'Really?' he whispered, his voice turning hoarse as obvious excitement lit his features.

'Mmm-hmm.' I didn't want to get his hopes up. We'd had a couple of false alarms since we'd stopped using protection after our wedding, but I'd always got my period before we'd taken a test. Each time Nicholas had looked more heartbroken than me. But today felt … different somehow. I didn't have my diary on me, but I was fairly sure that I should have had my period by now, and if I was pregnant it would certainly explain why my favourite beverage in the whole world was suddenly turning my stomach so violently.

Drawing in a deep breath, Nicholas nodded. He restarted the engine and drove us to the nearest chemist before leaping from the car in his excitement. He was far gentler with me, telling me not to rush and taking my hand to help me from the car almost as if I was made from glass, which caused me to giggle.

Once inside, we surreptitiously searched for the right aisle before coming to a halt by a rack full of condoms, lube, and pregnancy tests. Their choice of product placement was certainly a little bizarre, and just needed a sign to complete it, stating "if you don't use these, you might need this …"

'Which one should we get?' he asked, breaking me from my thoughts. I ran my gaze over the shelves and shrugged, feeling as bemused by the vast array of tests displayed as Nicholas looked.

'I have no idea.' There were some for a couple of pounds, right up to ones for over twenty quid. Jeez. For a twenty-pound note I'd expect the test to sing to me while I did a pee on it.

'Let's get one of each of the top sellers,' Nicholas suddenly decided, grabbing three boxes from the top shelf.

The drive home was short and silent, but draped heavy with anticipation. Once we were inside, I went to the master bedroom and headed to the en-suite with Nicholas fast on my heels. Turning to him, I shook my head. 'Uh-uh.

There's no way I'm letting you watch me pee on these. Regardless of how kinky you might be.'

Nicholas narrowed his eyes and crossed his arms over his chest. 'This has nothing to do with kink.' Licking his lips, he lost the determined look as it morphed into anxiousness. 'I just want to be involved, that's all.'

When he put it like that I could hardly refuse him, could I? Reaching up, I caressed his cheek, then rolled onto my tiptoes to place a gentle kiss on his lips. 'OK, fine. But I still don't want you watching me pee.' We usually shared the bathroom when we were getting ready, and that often involved having a quick wee, but I didn't fancy performing in front of him under intense scrutiny. 'Go and get me one of the plastic cups from that fancy water dispenser in your study.' Seeing his look of confusion, I rolled my eyes. 'I'll pee in that, then we can dip the tests in together and wait for the results.'

Nicholas nodded keenly and dashed off. Sitting down on the side of the bath, I couldn't help but laugh out loud as I heard the door to his study bang, then him clomping up the stairs two at a time in his haste to get back to me.

Looking back to the paper bag in my hand, I chewed on my lower lip nervously. God. Would we finally get the result we'd both been hoping for?

Once Nicholas had returned with a plastic cup I shut him out of the bathroom and awkwardly positioned the cup so I could do my business. I grinned proudly when I managed not to splash any around, which given the tiny cup, was actually quite a feat.

I pulled up my knickers, washed my hands, and took a deep breath. 'OK. You can come in now.'

Nicholas burst through the door and immediately thrust the tests at me, which he had obviously unwrapped while waiting for me. 'All three tests say we need to hold the absorbent tip in the liquid for thirty seconds, no longer.'

Nodding, I took the first test and held it in the liquid

while Nicholas timed me. It was the expensive test, but, disappointingly, it didn't sing for me, or perform any sort of fanfare for the extra cash it had cost us. It also didn't stop the nervous tremble in my fingers.

Following the instructions, I placed the cap on. I laid it on the counter and we repeated the whole process until all three sat there and we were both gazing at them expectantly. My heart was absolutely hammering in my chest, the blood pounding in my ears so hard it made the bathroom sound like we had a booming bass track accompanying us.

'Now we wait for three minutes,' Nicholas said, flapping through the different sets of instructions and looking genuinely flustered. After a minute or so had passed, he huffed out a breath and waggled the papers at me. 'It's so confusing! They all have different symbols for a positive test! One will get a blue cross, one gets two pink lines, and one has a smiley face. How are we supposed to know which is …?'

I stopped his rant by placing a trembling hand on his chest and jerking my chin towards the bathroom counter where our three tests were now displaying a smiley face, two pink lines and a blue cross. I could barely believe my own eyes.

'Oh my God …' Nicholas spluttered, bending closer to inspect them in more detail. 'But it's not been three minutes yet …' he whispered in a shocked tone, glancing at his watch.

My throat was closing up with happy tears, but I just about managed to get some words out. 'It's obviously been long enough because those tests all look pretty definitive to me …'

'We're pregnant?' he croaked, his gaze still pinging between my face and the three pregnancy tests.

The reality of the situation suddenly hit me. 'Y-y-yes

30

'...' I was so overwhelmed that I had to take a second to control myself before I could speak. 'It certainly looks like it.'

Wow. I was really pregnant. Or should I say "we" were pregnant, as Nicholas had worded it.

Letting out a small groan, Nicholas swooped down and encased me in his arms. He pulled me gently against his chest as he placed numerous kisses into my hair.

'God. I never thought I'd ever have a real relationship, let alone be a father. This is amazing, Becky. I love you so much.'

We'd been trying and failing to get pregnant for so long now that this was all quite overwhelming, but I still managed to croakily return his sentiment. 'I love you too, Nicholas.'

His lips descended to mine as he kissed me with such sweet adoration that my tears finally escaped and began to wet my cheeks. 'Just because we did three tests you know this doesn't mean we're having triplets, don't you?' I joked as Nicholas gently wiped away the happy tears that were streaming from my eyes.

'We might be, you never know,' he teased with a wink before carefully lifting me into his arms and carrying me from the bathroom.

Chapter Six

Stella

In the end, we *had* finished our meal with a cheese and a fruit platter, because Mum directly requested it, and so Nathan hadn't been able to say no. I hadn't helped matters by actively encouraging her, but it was just so amusing to watch Nathan's silent strop that I hadn't been able to stop myself.

As I dipped the final wineglass into the washing-up water I smiled, recalling the look on Nathan's face. It had been an absolute picture. Bless him. He hated not being able to control everything in his neat little world, but when my mum came around he lost that control, and that frustrated him no end.

Everyone had left now, but seeing as Nathan had nipped upstairs to check on William I had taken the opportunity to quickly stack the dishwasher and wash the glasses.

The kitchen door squeaked to alert me to his presence and I turned to find him standing in the doorway and staring at me with complete and utter heated focus. His jacket and tie were gone, but he was still dressed in his suit trousers, shirt, and waistcoat.

'I am so hard, Stella. I've been hard on and off ever since you provoked me by touching yourself. I'm desperate to be inside you.'

Well, that was quite a statement, wasn't it?

My breath hitched in my throat as I stared at him greedily. Nathan raised his hands and grabbed the doorframe above his head, stretching out his lean body and almost causing me to drop the glass I was holding. His knuckles turned white, as if gripping the wood was the only thing stopping him from pouncing on me, and suddenly nothing else existed in the world except for my incredible man.

Glancing down, I could indeed see that his words were true, because the front of his grey trousers bulged at the seams. It looked as if I might be getting a second dessert tonight, which was just as well, because I'd been horny all afternoon since my teasing words, too.

I was sure that if I wound Nathan up just enough I'd get my lustiness taken care of very swiftly, so I put on my most innocent expression and fluttered my eyelashes at him. 'You didn't enjoy the cheese course?' I asked huskily, my teasing provoking the exact reaction I was hoping for when I saw his nostrils flare at my cheek.

This was sort of "our thing". He was obviously the dominant one between us, but I would often tread a fine line of teasing and prodding him and trying to provoke a reaction. It was a game we both enjoyed, but for me it took nerves of steel, because his fierce expressions were panty-soakingly good.

'No, Stella, I did not enjoy the cheese course. And don't think I didn't see what you were doing with your mum, encouraging her like that. They stayed later because of you, which meant I have had to wait even longer.' My heart sped up as I watched his gaze darken further, because as much fun as it was playing with him like this, I had to judge when he'd had enough. Nathan's dominant side invariably came out to join the fun and didn't find my games nearly as amusing if I pushed him too far. That was half the enjoyment for me; getting the balance just right so that I teased him but didn't disrespect our Dom/sub bond.

My hands were suddenly trembling as lust zinged around my system and I quickly put the wineglass down before I dropped it. I never quite knew how things would progress when Nathan was as fixated as this. Sometimes he'd initiate a scene and pull out one or more of his toys, but on other occasions he'd literally just pounce on me.

From the way he was now prowling across the kitchen towards me, my money was on the latter. *Oh goody.*

As he got to within two foot of me, he let out a low growl and swooped forward, his arms encasing me. Then his lips sought mine with a hunger that had me gasping and clutching him for support. I loved it when he was like this. His kiss was frantic, stealing my breath and heating my blood to the point where I could barely stay still.

He leaned back, his eyes wild with desire and cheeks flushed as he looked down and assessed my clothing, a chunk of his gorgeous hair flopping over his forehead. The pale pink shirt dress that I was wearing protected me for about two seconds before Nathan gripped at the central join and ripped it open, buttons popping and scattering everywhere as he dragged the material from my arms and threw it to the side.

'Nathan!' My protest was silenced by the heated stare he gave me, which told me in no uncertain terms that he wanted me naked, and he wanted me naked right now. I supposed I couldn't complain too much. He'd lessened his clothes-ripping habit recently, and it was pretty flipping hot to be desired by him to this extent.

'Let's keep you quiet while I get rid of these clothes, shall we?' With those words, Nathan leaned to my left and picked up one of the plums that I'd had on the cheese and fruit platter.

He polished it briefly on his trouser leg, then lifted it to my mouth and dragged it across my lips.

'Open wide then bite down gently.' His command was so low and appealing that it immediately triggered my subservient side and I found myself automatically opening my mouth and holding the soft fruit between my teeth.

I couldn't believe he had just done this, though – gagged me with fruit!

'Don't drop that, and don't dare move otherwise I won't let you come tonight,' Nathan murmured beside my ear, his tone sending a shiver down my spine and leaving me in no doubt that he meant every word he was saying.

He dropped to his haunches, tugging down my leggings and knickers before also throwing them aside. There was none of his usual finesse tonight, and I realised that he hadn't been kidding earlier when he'd said he was desperate.

As much as I tried to stay still, my jaw still shifted around the fruit in my mouth and my teeth broke the skin, coating my tongue with its sweet juice. The plum was so overly ripe that I quickly felt juice dribbling down my chin, too, but there wasn't much I could do about it. I definitely wanted to come tonight, so there was no way in hell that I was going to break his no-moving rule and wipe my mouth.

He stood up, his gaze dropping to the juice trail, and Nathan smiled wickedly at me, his desperation seeming to have calmed somewhat now that he had me well and truly where he wanted me. Reaching around me, he undid my bra with ease, slid it from my body, and placed it on the kitchen counter, leaving me stark naked.

He lifted a hand to brush his thumb from my jaw bone down my neck and into the hollow between my breasts before clicking his tongue in mock disapproval. 'Messy little thing.'

I glanced down to see what he meant and only then realised that the juice from the plum had trickled down my throat and was also coating my breasts with several sticky, purple trails.

Licking his lips, Nathan then wiggled his eyebrows, apparently in his element now. 'Let me clean you up, baby.'

Reaching up, he removed the plum and chucked it in the sink behind us, then dropped his mouth to my lips. He licked them clean with an approving hum before following the sweet trail of juice down to my neck. His hot tongue lashed at my skin, heating me from the inside out, and caused my head to roll back with pleasure as he very thoroughly suckled on my breasts one by one to remove all the traces of juice.

'It tastes almost as good as you,' he murmured against the pebbled skin of my right nipple. Nathan was the only man I'd ever been with who could make me orgasm purely from playing with my breasts, and amazing as I always found this skill, it would seem that he was working his sorcery again, because I could feel the pit of my stomach tightening with a building climax and he hadn't even touched between my legs.

'Nathan … I'm close …'

'Mmm,' he hummed against my skin sending flutters of lust rushing over my body. Then to my dismay, he abruptly stood up. 'Seeing as you made me wait, I think it's your turn for a little frustration.'

Gah! I hated it when he did this! I was about to squawk my complaint when I noticed his wide, cocky stance, and the dark look in his eyes and quickly snapped my mouth closed.

Dominant Nathan was well and truly out to play.

Chapter Seven

Nathan

My girl was seriously pushing my buttons tonight. I'd wanted to fuck her ever since she'd teased me by touching herself as I burped Will, but then she'd gone and made my night by agreeing to the official collaring ceremony, and it had taken all of my control not to fuck her in celebration right there in the kitchen.

I'd had to be the "good boy", though, and behave myself, because her fucking parents were over. Don't get me wrong, they seemed like nice enough people, but I just didn't do family stuff. I had no personal experiences to help me know how I should react, so I always ended up finding these occasions awkward as fuck.

At least her mum seemed to have chilled on the whole wedding topic, which was a relief.

I'd been hoping they would leave after dessert, but Susan had enquired if there was cheese and we'd ended up sitting over yet another course of food. The whole time they were nibbling on their Camembert and crackers all I had been able to focus on were the memories of Stella's arse branded by my handprint. As a result, I'd had a full-on stiffy for over an hour and a half now. Throw in her earlier teasing and I was seriously at my wits' end.

Looking back at my girl, I had to suppress the groan of desire that tried to break free from my throat. She looked so sexy, leaning back on the counter buck naked and waiting with anticipation for my next words. I knew exactly what I wanted us to do, so I wouldn't keep her in suspense any

37

longer.

'Onto your knees, beautiful.' I reached across the small gap between us and tangled a hand through her hair, caressing her soft cheek, then encouraging Stella to lower herself.

The mixture of shock and arousal in her eyes was enough of a turn-on that I felt my cock thicken even further. Christ, I couldn't wait to release it from within my trousers.

Keeping her eyes locked with mine, Stella bit down on her lower lip. She followed my instructions, sinking down onto her knees and siting back on her heels before folding her hands into her lap.

Her ready position.

She was really living up to my nickname for her, too, because she looked stunningly beautiful kneeling there like this. Drawing in a deep breath, I tried to control the flood of emotions that often hit me when I stared at Stella for any length of time. I still couldn't believe I had gotten so lucky.

We were the perfect match, in every aspect of our lives together. She knew me better than anyone ever had, could read me like a book, listened when I needed it, and had wordlessly supported me when all the shit with my father trying to ruin my business had happened.

The fact that we also happened to be smoking hot in the sex department and perfectly compatible as Dom and sub was a rather nice complement to it all.

She loved me taking control almost as much as I loved the act itself, so I flashed her a reassuring wink then sobered my face and allowed my Dom mask to slip into place. I kept my expression neutral, body upright and taut, and widened my legs giving me what Stella always called my "cocksure stance". I felt powerful but, more than that, I felt humbled by the fact that this incredible woman was voluntarily kneeling by my feet.

Christ. I was getting overly sentimental again. That

seemed to happen a lot since William had been born. I was more emotionally open these days, but I wasn't a sap, and I did still have a raging hard-on so it seemed an appropriate time to get the evening back on track.

Keeping my gaze locked with hers, I slowly undid the zip of my trousers and pulled my cock free. It jerked upwards as the cool air hit my skin and I sucked in a deep breath through my nose as I palmed it and squeezed to finally release some of the tension I'd been holding in my body. Fuck! I was so aroused that I could feel it bubbling around my veins as I ran my hand slowly up and down my shaft and stepped closer to my girl.

'You know what to do, baby,' I murmured softly, only just keeping my expression neutral when I saw the thrilled expression on Stella's face as she shuffled towards my thighs. My next breath hissed through my teeth, because Stella wasted no time at all latching on to my dick with that hot little mouth of hers and running her tongue around the top like it was an ice-cream cone full of her favourite flavoured treat.

Holy fuck, she was so goddamn good at this.

That was another reason I was a lucky son of a bitch; Stella loved giving me head. In fact, she didn't seem to be able to get enough of it, and had actually climaxed on more than one occasion just from giving me pleasure. I loved going down on her, too, so I guess we were evenly matched in that department as well.

I needed to maintain my role tonight, though, and so tightened the grip I had in her hair to briefly pause her actions. 'This is a punishment for making me wait earlier. You're not allowed to come until I say so, Stella. If you do I won't allow you a climax for the rest of the week.'

Her eyes widened at my words, but, sensing how serious I was being, she briefly lifted her mouth off me and nodded. 'I understand, Sir.'

'Good girl. I'm close, fuck me with your mouth.'

Her eyes sparkled with delight at my command and she got right back to her task, sucking me back into her hot mouth and hollowing out her cheeks as she worked her tongue up and down my shaft. Her hands joined in, one gripping the base of my cock and working in time with the movement of her lips, and the other dipping between my legs to cup and fondle my balls.

Holy fuck, this felt so incredible that I wanted it to last forever, while also desperately chasing my much-needed release. My hands clenched with the effort of not grabbing her hair, but I knew when she made me come it would be incredible and I didn't want to risk hurting her if I lost control.

She shifted the hand at my balls slightly further back and Stella pressed two fingers against my perineum, beginning to massage the sensitive skin behind my balls in the way she knew I loved. Jesus, it felt like she was inside me, touching the base of my dick, and the sensation had my balls rising and my cock thickening as my orgasm quickly approached.

Stella moaned, apparently sensing my imminent release, and moved her efforts to the top of my dick where she began to suck hard while performing shorter movements with her mouth. Her grip stayed tight, and she hollowed her cheeks again, using her lips to work up and down over the skin around my foreskin until I had to lean forwards and rest one hand on the kitchen counter to steady myself.

She knew this was what I liked when I was about to come. Deep throat didn't do it for me at all. The top of my dick was the most sensitive and when she gave it as much attention as she currently was I knew I wouldn't last much longer.

She twirled her tongue, dragging her lips across my shaft one last time. With a strangled moan, I felt my balls explode as I pressed forwards into her mouth and started to come. Stella wrapped her mouth around me, sucking and swallowing everything I had to give, not stopping with her movements until I was sagging above her, my knees weak from the power of my climax and sweat dripping from my forehead.

I fell to my knees and gathered her into my embrace. Then I leaned back on the kitchen cupboard while I tried to get my wits back.

That had been even better than I'd expected. A lazy grin crawled across my lips as Stella snuggled into my arms. My girl really was utter perfection.

Stella

Even though I hadn't come yet, I was feeling far more relaxed now. Still horny as hell, but a little more relaxed. Pleasuring Nathan always did that to me. I loved it. Loved making him feel good and knowing that it was me who made him lose control.

Shifting below me, Nathan dropped a kiss on the top of my head, then helped me to stand from his lap. His face was still flushed from his climax, but amazingly, one quick glance down showed me that he was still hard. This was often the case with Nathan. It didn't mean he hadn't been satisfied, it was just a show of how insatiable he was. He could come multiple times in a night, and put the stamina of all my previous boyfriends to shame.

He brushed down his waistcoat, then winced as he forced his cock back inside his trousers and zipped them up with difficulty. I noticed the unfairness in our state of dress – I was starkers, but he was still suited and booted – but I didn't really care. Nathan had made it plain he loved my body, and I was secretly hoping that after my recent performance he might even up our orgasm count now and give me the climax I was so desperate for.

He must have seen the needy expression on my face, because he reached up and brushed some hairs from my face with a soft smile. 'Are you in need of some relief, baby?'

'I am … Sir.' I wasn't sure if I should have used his title, as we only used it during scenes, but seeing as it was so soon after finishing I decided to keep with the theme. It seemed to please him, because his eyes twinkled with pleasure and he cupped my jaw and pulled me forwards for a brief kiss.

'Let's go upstairs and sort you out then, shall we?' His words sent a flood of moisture to my core and I actually shuddered with desire as I nodded my head and turned keenly for the door.

The disapproving click of his tongue stopped me in my tracks and I glanced back at him. 'After all this time, you still nod at me?'

The low, growled words made me pause, and one look at his desire-saturated stare instantly reminded me of his dislike of nodding, not to mention his love of trying to keep me in line, so I quickly added the audible response he so liked. 'Sorry, Sir. I meant to say yes please.'

Nathan winked at me, his features instantly softening, and as we dashed towards our bedroom I couldn't help grinning at how bloody perfect we were for each other.

Chapter Eight

Nicholas

My eyes widened as I looked up from the newspaper to see Rebecca pushing open the lounge door and struggling with a pile of cookery books in her arms and her laptop balanced on top. 'Woah! Let me get those for you!' I leaped to my feet, grabbing the books and laptop before Becky could reply, then ushering her towards the sofa.

'You should be resting, sit.'

Instead of doing as I told her, Rebecca shoved a hand on her hip and rolled her eyes at me. 'I'm not ill, Nicholas, I'm pregnant. Honestly, you're worrying over everything.'

I placed the books on the coffee table and sunk into the sofa, but remained quiet. I couldn't really say much to her reply, because it was true. I was worrying over everything, but that was because, as sappy as it sounded, Rebecca was *my everything*, and now she was carrying our baby I was even more inclined to try to take care of her.

We'd known about the baby for quite a few weeks now, but I was still struggling to adjust and probably driving Rebecca nuts at the same time. Remembering that Dr Philips had told me I needed to talk when I was feeling stressed, rather than holding things inside, I decided that maybe now would be a good time. I was getting better at expressing my feelings, but this type of thing always made me feel a little uneasy.

'I … I'm so excited about the baby, and I really want to be involved, but I just feel like a bit of a spare part,' I blurted awkwardly.

Rebecca paused, her irritated expression began to soften as I continued. 'It's inside you, so you already have a close bond with it. I guess that fussing over you and the baby is a way for me to feel more connected to it all.'

Finishing my confession, I looked up to find Rebecca staring at me with the oddest look on her face. It was almost like she was awestruck; her eyes were wide and filled with moisture and her mouth was parted as if she wanted to speak, but couldn't.

Feeling my defences rise a little at her strange expression, I straightened my spine and frowned. 'What's that look for?'

'Nothing, I just feel really guilty for snapping at you now.' Rebecca came to my side. She sat on the sofa and immediately picked up my hand before leaning in and placing a lingering kiss on my lips. 'That was a really sweet thing to say, Nicholas. I'm sorry if I've not been appreciative. Blame it on my hormones, yeah?'

Slipping back on the sofa, I gently tugged Rebecca across so she was sitting in my lap and lying on my chest. Burying my nose in her hair, I took a moment to breathe in her light floral scent.

She started to caress my chest and I felt my tension relaxing away. 'I want you to be involved, too. You've been coming to all the doctor's appointments and stuff so I thought you'd feel included, but I'm sure we can think of other things we can do to help.'

This conversation was just what I had needed, but was also making me feel a bit self-conscious. Was it right for the guy in a relationship to be acting this needy? I was never like this usually, but wham, put a baby in my woman and I suddenly felt the desperate urge to surround her in bubble wrap and seal her inside a glass box. It was fucking ridiculous, but such a strong reaction that I could barely contain it.

Pushing aside my insecurity, I shrugged. 'The way I see it, it's your job to carry the baby and have a healthy pregnancy, but it's my job to ensure you have everything for that healthy pregnancy. That's why I keep fussing.'

Rebecca sniffed, as if feeling a bit emotional all of a sudden, then nodded. 'In which case, you have my permission to fuss away as much as you want,' she agreed softly, before suddenly narrowing her eyes. 'I can't promise I'll always accept it graciously, though. My hormones are making me crazy some days.'

Rolling my lips tight, I nodded, trying to suppress my smile, because she was right about that; there had been several days where I'd almost wanted to don protective armour to withstand her mood swings.

'To be honest, I didn't want to burden you. I know you've got a lot on with your concert schedule at the moment.'

'It wouldn't be a burden, trust me.'

'OK then, well, I'll draw up a list of things we can do together,' Rebecca said with a smile. 'The baby really likes massages and bubble baths, so you know, anytime you feel like arranging them I'm sure Bump would love it.'

Grinning at the playful glint in Rebecca's eye, I narrowed my eyes. 'Oh, *the baby* likes those, does it?'

'Mmm hmm. And milk chocolate ...' she added hopefully before linking her fingers with mine and smiling up at me.

'I'm sure all of those things can be arranged,' I said, rather liking the idea of pampering my girl for the next few months.

After a moment of silence where she simply played with my fingers, Rebecca gave my hand a squeeze that drew my gaze up to hers.

'I have an idea that might make you feel more involved ...' she said speculatively.

Narrowing my eyes at both her tone and the look on her face, I was cautious as I answered. 'OK …'

'You could talk to the baby.'

Blinking several times, I ran her words through my mind again, trying to work out exactly what she meant. 'What, now?'

Rebecca grinned happily at my apparent acceptance of her idea, but I was still unsure. I mean, talking to her was nice, but talking to a tiny bunch of chromosomes buried inside her stomach? That just sounded crazy.

'Yeah. I talk to the bump all the time. Just go for it.'

Looking at her belly then back at her again I frowned. 'Um … what do I say?'

'Anything! Just say hello!' Rebecca shrugged as she settled herself back onto the armrest so her belly was fully exposed to me.

Licking my lips, I placed my hands on her bump and tried to work out what the hell I should say.

'Um … hello …' As soon as I started speaking I felt stupid. I sat back with a huffed breath and looked at Rebecca. 'I feel ridiculous.'

Raising her eyebrows at my pathetic attempt, she thought for a second, then seemed to have an idea because she suddenly leaned over the side of the sofa and grabbed her MP3 player and headphones. 'What about if I don't listen?' she asked, waggling the music player in my face. 'These are sound-cancelling headphones; you know how well they work. I'll put them on and I won't be able to hear a word you say.'

Without waiting for me to agree or not, she popped the headphones on, closed her eyes, and rested back as she started to bob her head in time to whatever she was listening to.

Looking back at her bump, I kept my hands gently moving across her belly as I did my best to put my reluctance aside and try again. 'Hello, Baby. So, I guess I'll be meeting you in a few months. That seems a kind of strange idea …'

Becky had been right, it was easier without her listening in, and once I started, I suddenly couldn't seem to stop. I told the bump about my piano, my love of music, and how I had met Rebecca. I was just about to move on to tell it how amazing she was when Rebecca opened her eyes and grinned at me. She wouldn't be able to hear me, so I carried on, but the rate at which my lips were moving surely gave away the fact that I was in full conversation flow now.

Suddenly, Rebecca ripped the headphones off and propped herself up on her elbows. 'Oh my God, did you feel that? The baby just kicked!'

My eyes widened and I quickly splayed my hands wider on her belly, trying to feel for any movements. 'That's a good thing, right?'

'Yes! It's the first time the baby has done it.' Rebecca joined her hands with mine as we both sat there in silence, feeling her stomach, but there wasn't any more movement. 'It's stopped. Maybe it was because you were talking to it?' she speculated quietly. 'Do you like your daddy's voice little one?' she asked, staring expectantly at her belly. 'Speak again, Nicholas!'

I cleared my throat and leaned a little closer, wondering what the hell I should say this time. 'Hey, Baby. Ummm … so, I forgot to introduce myself last time. I'm your daddy.' Just as I was finishing I felt a jolt under my right hand and Rebecca drew in a thrilled gasp.

'Again, Nicholas!'

Seeing her elated expression, I tried to improvise. 'I … I mean, me and your mummy can't wait to meet you …'

There was another kick and both Rebecca and I gasped and looked at each other. 'Feeling more involved now?' she asked tearfully, and I nodded my reply, feeling a bit too choked up to answer audibly. My baby liked the sound of my voice. It was all the involvement I'd wanted, and so much more.

Chapter Nine

Rebecca

It was now four weeks since Nicholas and I had discovered that we were expecting a baby, and we still hadn't told anyone. It had been murder keeping it from Stella, but she and Nathan had been busy preparing for the move to their new house, so we hadn't seen them as regularly as usual.

We'd waited because we'd wanted to get it officially confirmed by a doctor, and also, because we'd had a couple of failed attempts in the past six months, we had decided to play it safe and wait for our twelve-week scan. That had been yesterday, and as it had turned out, we were probably a little further on than we had expected, with the doctor suggesting that we were probably nearer to the four-and-a-half-month mark. How the bloody hell I hadn't realised I was pregnant sooner was beyond me, but the doctor had told me that it was surprisingly common.

I still couldn't believe I had a little life growing inside of me, a life that Nicholas and I had created together, and I dropped my hand instinctively to the curve of my belly to give a fond rub, even though it was hidden behind my woollen jumper.

Today we had popped around to Nathan and Stella's house and were finally going to break the news. I was excited; she'd been hinting for months that she was hoping for a niece or nephew, and now she was going to get her wish.

'Hi!' Opening the door with her usual smile, Stella looked down at the bottle of champagne that Nicholas was holding and her expression transformed to a grin as she was joined by Nathan. 'Well, this is a nice surprise!' Glancing at her watch, she wiggled her eyebrows. 'It's a little early, but we may as well crack this open. Go on through to the lounge; I'll grab some glasses.'

We followed Nathan to the lounge as she disappeared off in the direction of the kitchen which left me in the daunting company of both the Jackson brothers.

Not that I found them particularly daunting any more, I reflected, watching fondly as Nathan shifted William on his shoulder and patted his back. I'd been terrified of Nicholas's blond-haired brother when I'd first met him, and now look at him, a doting daddy. As if sensing that I was thinking about him, Nathan suddenly looked directly at me with his icy blue stare and my earlier thoughts fell away as his gaze instantly made me tense.

I knew he was intrinsically a nice guy, but wow, he could still be so intimidating. Swallowing hard, I tried to smile back and then awkwardly turned away and sunk into the nearest sofa to escape.

Nicholas began to peel the foil from the bottle as Stella came back in with four champagne flutes. 'We were talking this morning about how good that weekend in Stow was over New Year,' he commented as he smiled down at me and flashed me a wink.

'It really was. We had a great time, too,' Nathan said, as he fixed Stella with a heated stare behind his brother's back. The resulting flush of desire that rose to her cheeks almost made me feel uncomfortable, but it seemed that the bond between the two of them was similar in intensity to what Nicholas and I shared. One look from Nicholas could have me on edge and aroused in under a minute.

Nicholas turned to his brother with a smirk, lips twitching in a half smile. 'I'm sure you did.' Nicholas was clearly referring to the night we babysat for them so that

51

Stella and Nathan could have some uninterrupted time together. It didn't take a genius to work out what they had spent that time doing.

The cork popped from the bottle and Nicholas quickly took a glass from Stella and began to pour, thankfully drawing us away from the previous conversation. From what Stella had told me, she and Nathan were extremely sexual, just as Nicholas and I were, but as much fun as it was to gossip about it with her in private, it wasn't exactly something I wanted to chat about with the brothers in the room.

Nicholas poured three full glasses and one half glass and then set the bottle down.

'Actually, Nicholas, I'm not breastfeeding William any more, so I can have a full glass.' Stella hadn't been drinking a great deal while she'd been breastfeeding, so her assumption that the half glass was for her made sense. Little did she know that it was for me.

As she reached for the bottle to top herself up, Nicholas stopped her and handed the glass to me, causing my friend to look across at me and widen her eyes.

'Rebecca and I have some news …'

Judging from the expectant look now crossing Stella's face she'd already guessed what Nicholas was about to say, but he pulled me close to his side and smiled down at me before speaking anyway. 'We're pregnant. William is going to have a cousin.'

Stella bundled me into a hug, then gave Nicholas a quick, slightly awkward embrace before standing back with a grin. 'Wow, congratulations! I like the way you said "we're pregnant", that's so sweet.'

It *was* kind of sweet, but I laughed and rolled my eyes before poking Nicholas playfully in the ribs. 'We? I don't see you jumping up at five in the morning to throw your guts up, or needing to pee continuously.'

52

'I do get up and hold your hair back when you're throwing up, though,' he added quietly, which was true. I couldn't moan really. Since the day we'd done the test and Nicholas had declared that he "wanted to be involved in every step", he had done exactly that. He attended doctor's appointments with me, had researched the best foods for me and the baby, had taken over the majority of the housework, and, yes, when I was suffering with morning sickness he did indeed hold my hair back and get me drinks of water and ginger tea.

I gave him a reassuring smile and turned back to Stella and Nathan just as Nathan was holding his glass aloft to toast. 'Congratulations!'

We all chinked glasses and took a sip, and I had to smile at the way that Nicholas watched me drink like a hawk. 'Not too much, baby.'

'A few sips won't hurt, Nicholas. Anyway, you barely poured me a thimbleful, so there's no risk of me having too much!'

I could see that this was difficult for him. Nicholas's impulsive side was desperate to assert his control and stop me drinking, but his sensible head also knew that what I said was true so he was trying to hold back. Bless him. He was so much better at suppressing his irrational outbursts now, but I suspected this pregnancy was really going to test him and his need to protect me.

'We would have told you sooner, but couldn't get the scan done until yesterday. My usual consultant was away, and the only person available to do the three-month scan was less senior,' I explained, before giving Nicholas another amused glance.

My man was having none of it, though, and he straightened his shoulders and fixed me with an unrelenting stare, completely unwilling to back down. 'Nicholas was uncomfortable with that, so we waited for Dr Reece to return from her holiday.'

Stella almost spat out her champagne at that and then giggled. 'Let me guess, you only wanted the best doctors for Rebecca?'

Glancing up at my fella, I saw him narrowing his eyes at her question, but she had hit the nail right on the head.

'It's OK, don't look embarrassed. Nathan was the same. I think we had the most expensive private consultant in London at my first scan!' she replied casually. I had suspected Nathan would have been similarly protective. As brothers went, these two had more than just their good looks in common; their demand for perfection in everything was incredibly similar, too.

Now both of our Jackson brothers looked irritated, something which Stella also noticed because she flashed me a glance that seemed to say "oops" and quickly changed the subject. 'So you've already had your three-month scan, then?'

'Yep, the doctor actually thinks we might be closer to four and a half months along.'

Stella's face lit up, then her gaze dropped to my stomach, obviously looking for a bump.

'I have started to show in the last few weeks, but being cold it's been easy to hide it under my baggy jumpers.'

Pulling my top tight made the bump obvious, and Stella made a goofy face as she looked at it.

'I've got some pregnancy books upstairs. Do you want to borrow them?'

'Ooh, yes please. Nicholas has bought us some already, but let's have a look at what you've got.' I took another small sip of my fizz before popping it on the table and following her from the room.

Stella

'This is so exciting, Becky!' I squeaked as we made our way up the stairs.

'I know! It feels like we've been trying for ages, so when we got the tests half of me had expected it to be another false alarm. But nope!'

I pulled the stack of books from the shelf, then stood up and dumped them on the bed before turning back to Rebecca.

Instead of looking at the books she was looking at my necklace with a smile. 'Wow, I never noticed before just how well the jewels in your necklace match your ring. It's like they were made as a set.' Leaning in closer, she examined my collar in greater detail and nodded. 'Now you'll never be able to take it off.'

Ha! If only she knew! Not that I would ever want to remove my collar, but I literally couldn't take it off, because it had been locked by Nathan and the key was currently tucked away in his safe. Not that Becky was aware of that, of course. I'd simply told her that it was my favourite necklace, and given that as the excuse for why I always wore it.

'So, while I have you alone I have to ask you what Nathan was like during your pregnancy, because Nicholas is already driving me nuts!' Rebecca gave me a knowing look and sunk down onto the side of the bed as she began to flick through the first book.

'A little over-protective, is he?' I asked, before a full-on belly laugh escaped my throat as I fondly remembered how stressed Nathan had got himself in his desperation at keeping me "safe".

'God, yes. It's sweet, really, but I just wondered if it was something both brothers did.'

Sitting down beside her, I nodded and gave my best sympathetic smile. 'If Nicholas is even half as bad as Nathan was then you'll have to get used to it. He even tried to cut up my food for me for several weeks in case I choked …'

'Seriously?' Rebecca squeaked, her eyes widening.

'Yep. We had his chef friend Marcus living with us for a while, too, to make sure I was eating balanced meals that were good for me and Will.'

'Oh my God. It seems I'm getting off lightly at the moment!' Rebecca laughed, before a slightly concerned look crossed her face. 'I shouldn't complain. It's lovely that he's so interested in it all. I know some women have to do it all alone.'

'Very true. Our fellas might be a little OTT on the possessive and protective fronts, but it's kinda sweet really. I think we're both pretty lucky, actually.'

'We are,' Rebecca agreed with a nod. 'Maybe we should get back downstairs, though, just in case Nathan is giving Nicholas any more ideas …'

Chapter Ten

Nicholas

Clearing my throat, I glanced at Nathan and decided to spit my question out while I had the chance. 'While the girls are upstairs there's something I wanted to ask you, brother.'

Nathan looked intrigued, folding his arms and nodding. 'Of course, fire away.'

'I was just wondering … well, I mean …' Bloody hell, this was far harder than I'd thought. 'I wanted to ask about Rebecca's pregnancy, and … sex.'

'Good question.' Leaning forwards, Nathan rested his hands onto his knees and gave a slow, solemn nod as if he were about to impart some great secret upon me. 'Yes, sex is indeed how she got pregnant.'

It took a second for his lame attempt at a joke to sink in, especially because his facial expression was so serious, but when it finally clicked I rolled my eyes and hit out at him with a punch to the arm. 'Piss off, Nathan.' My fuckwad brother threw his head back and laughed, and the sound made me pause for a second in surprise. I could probably count on one hand the times I'd heard him laugh when we were growing up. He'd been so grave and intense as a kid – we both had, I suppose – but now, since meeting Stella and having William, he laughed a lot more frequently. It was really good to see, but didn't lessen the fact that he was teasing me now, when I actually wanted his advice.

'You know what I mean.' It was embarrassing enough asking this stuff in the first place, but to have him take the piss as well meant that my cheeks were now burning.

'Sorry, I couldn't resist winding you up. What did you want to know?'

Pulling in a breath, I shrugged self-consciously, not sure I wanted to carry on the conversation any more. 'I've read a load of the pregnancy books and they say we're OK to have sex right the way through the pregnancy, but I can't help worrying that I'll hurt Becky, or the baby. I just wondered how you dealt with it?'

Nodding his head in understanding, he rubbed at his jaw as he considered his answer, thankfully seeming to take it seriously now. 'I had the same concerns, so I spoke to a doctor when Stella was carrying Will. He said the same. Sex is fine.' Nathan paused, then flashed me a filthy grin. 'Even with tackle the size of mine.' I wasn't exactly small in that department, either, and it had been one of the reasons for my concern. Big dicks – it was probably the only thing we had to thank our miserable excuse of a father for, but I let out a relieved breath and joined my brother in a grin.

'Thank God for that, because the pregnancy hormones are making Rebecca really horny and I'm struggling to hold back when she keeps throwing herself at me.'

Laughing again, Nathan nodded. 'Oh yeah, Stella was the same – even more insatiable than usual. Make the most of it!'

Nathan topped up my champagne and stood to refill Stella's glass, too. 'We did stop most of the kink, though. I'm not sure if you and Rebecca do that, but I cut out a lot of the toys.'

'You don't do it any more?' I asked in surprise, only to be granted by another bark of laughter from Nathan and an incredulous glance.

'Of course we do it again now. I just meant during the pregnancy. What do you think I am, a fucking saint? This is me we're talking about, Nicholas. I hardly have a vanilla bone in my body.'

Digesting this, I nodded, knowing that he had always been more into that lifestyle than I had. What I had with Becky was perfect. I mostly had control over the bedroom stuff, and we occasionally used a toy or two, but I suspected we were poles apart from the relationship that Nathan and Stella shared.

As Nathan got to Rebecca's almost empty glass I leaned forwards and put my hand over it. 'I think she has enough in there for now.'

Placing the bottle down, Nathan smirked at me. 'Getting a little overprotective, are you?'

A huge sigh slipped from my lips and I looked across at my brother and nodded. 'I can't help it. I try to control it, but it's overwhelming. It's taken every ounce of my self-control not to empty her glass while they've been out of the room. It's stupid, isn't it?'

'Nah. Sounds fairly reasonable to me.'

'Did you find you were worrying about Stella all the time like this?'

'Brother, I worry about her all the time anyway. Regardless of pregnancy,' Nathan said with an ironic chuckle. 'I'm so pussy-whipped it would be shameful if we weren't so fucking perfect for each other.'

Hearing Nathan's confession was hugely reassuring for me, because he was the only role model I'd ever really had, and although I might not vocalise it frequently, I really looked up to him.

'Actually, I have some news of my own …' Nathan sounded cautious, so I turned in my seat and gave him my full attention.

'You guys aren't having another baby as well, are you?' I joked, but in response to my words Nathan's face seemed to visibly pale and then he drew in several short breaths.

'No.' His reply was adamant, which confused me

slightly, but then he managed to shock me completely with his next words. 'Stella has agreed to a collaring ceremony with me.'

I raised my eyebrows at his remark. As a couple, Nathan and Stella seemed so vanilla these days that I really hadn't seen that as a possibility.

'Congratulations.' His announcement had been such a shock that it was the only thing I could think to say. 'I hadn't realised that side of things was such a big thing for you these days.'

'It's not like I used to be. We don't live as Dom and sub or anything like that, but we still scene regularly so it plays a part in our lives that way.'

'Wow. And you're having a ceremony, huh?'

Nathan drew in a satisfied breath and smiled, looking the proudest I'd seen him since William was born. 'Yep. At Club Twist. We haven't gotten around to arranging dates or anything yet, but I'm really excited about it.'

I was excited for him, too, and about to say as much when he gave me a hopeful glance. 'I was hoping you would accompany me? Be my attendant?'

I'd been to a few collarings before, and knew that the role of attendant was a bit like a best man at a standard wedding, so I immediately nodded.

'It would be my honour,' I replied, holding my hand out for a firm shake as we shared a quiet moment.

My big brother had protected me as much as he could throughout our childhood, and saved me when times had got to their lowest. It was about time he had his happily ever after, too.

Chapter Eleven

Rebecca

'Becky? Have you got a few minutes?' I presumed Nicholas was calling down from his piano room, because he'd been squirreled away up there for the best part of the morning. Lifting my head from the accounts spreadsheet before me, I rubbed my eyes, glad to rest them for a while.

'Yep, hang on, I'll come up.' I needed a break, and I hated doing the accounts for my bookshop so this gave me a perfect excuse.

Once I got to the landing I found Nicholas waiting for me with a broad grin on his face. It had only been about four hours since I'd seen him at breakfast, but I still paused to appreciate the view. He was wearing a white T-shirt and low-slung light blue jeans which clung to his trim waist. He'd obviously showered, too, because his hair was damp and ruffled, and his feet were bare.

Mmm. Very nice.

Since I'd moved in he had stopped wearing his formal suits all the time. He still graced me with a breath-taking appearance in a three-piece every now and then, but he regularly wore jeans around the house these days. I wasn't sure if it was because he'd just started to relax more, or because he'd noticed how I couldn't drag my eyes off him when he was clad in denim. Either way, I wasn't going to complain.

Taking me by surprise, he dropped to his knees. He placed a kiss on my belly and nuzzled it with his nose, which caused a goofy smile to spread on my lips. 'Hello,

61

Bump,' he murmured affectionately. Since the baby had responded so positively to his voice a few weeks ago, Nicholas now spoke to my bump without nearly as much embarrassment, which always made me smile and appreciate how lucky the baby and I were to have him.

Standing up, he grinned at me. 'Hey, baby momma.'

Rolling my eyes, I propped my hands on my hips and tried to give him my best irritated glare. 'Nicholas, please don't call me that.'

'Why not? I can't call you baby any more, can I? Because our baby is in here,' he stated, gently placing a hand on my belly.

Ever since we'd done the pregnancy tests Nicholas had, for some unknown reason, started to tease me with the silly nickname, always said in his terrible version of an American accent. It was seriously starting to wear thin now, but he seemed to think it was hilarious.

'You *can* still call me baby. Or Rebecca, or Becky.'

'OK, baby momma, I'll think about it.'

I was about to argue further, but got completely distracted when he guided me into his piano room and I saw the change of furniture.

The shiny piano was still the same, but instead of the white armchair he used to have there was now a squishy teal chaise-longue along the wall closest to the piano, and a wooden rocking chair topped with cushions in a corner.

'Wow, you've been shopping. When did you have this delivered?' I asked as I immediately went to try out the rocking chair.

Instead of answering my question, he asked one of his own instead. 'Do you like it?'

'I love it!' Rocking back and forth a few times, I grinned across at him and saw Nicholas sharing my excitement. I got up and went across to the chaise-longue. I prodded at the cushions. When I sunk down onto it I found that it was just as squishy and comfortable as it had looked.

'I thought of another way I could be involved in the pregnancy,' he explained, waving a hand towards his piano. 'Music is supposed to be good for the baby's development, so I thought I could share my piano. What do you think?'

The way he seemed to hang on my answer was so sweet that I immediately nodded my head. 'It's such a great idea, Nicholas!'

He let out a relieved breath and smiled. 'During the rest of the pregnancy, you can sometimes lie in here while I play, and I got the rocking chair in case you ever wanted to feed in here once the baby is born.'

Considering he had been a closed-off, almost neurotically withdrawn guy once upon a time, it was amazing just how much of a sweet and considerate man he'd grown into. He always thought of everything and he always, without fail, put my needs first. It seemed that now he was including our unborn child in that caring, protective circle and I loved him so much for it that I felt a sob break in my throat.

The sudden rush of emotion that flew up on me caused tears to instantly spring to my eyes and several more sobs to escape, and I watched as Nicholas's excited expression morphed into panic as he dropped to his knees before me.

'Don't you like that idea? We don't have to do it! We can even get rid of the furniture, if you don't like it.'

I was still too overwhelmed to speak, so instead I reached across and silenced his panic by placing a finger on his lips. I swallowed hard, then drew in a breath and tried to dig up my composure.

'These are happy tears. Sorry, it's my hormones; I can't control them. It's an amazing idea, Nicholas, you're amazing.'

The relief that crossed his face was instant. It was followed by the small shy smile that I absolutely loved, and completed by the appearance of his dimple. 'Shall I play you both something now?'

Both.

God, I loved how it sounded when he said that. Worried that I was going to cry all over him again, I nodded and gave him my biggest smile. 'I'd love that.'

Nicholas encouraged me to get comfy on the chaise, which really wasn't difficult given how soft the cushions were, and produced a blanket to lay across my legs. Jeez. He'd thought of everything. Where had my old dominant Nicholas gone? I wasn't really complaining; I loved this sweeter side to him, and he still mostly ran our bedroom sessions, so to be honest, I now had the very best of both worlds.

Thinking about it, though, he'd been a little sparse with sexual attention since he'd known I was pregnant. He'd been affectionate and cuddly, but my hormones were making me horny as hell and he seemed to think I might snap in half if he so much as touched me between my legs.

Settling back, I looked across at him and found Nicholas watching me, his face still open and showing the utter depth of his feelings for me. Yeah, we were so good together that I knew without doubt we'd work the sex stuff out eventually. He flashed me a wink, then he took his seat at the piano and briefly shook out his wrists and hands. Without fail, he always did this before playing. I'd never asked, but I assumed it was an inbuilt habit of his now, a bit like the way I subconsciously played with my hair when I was wound up.

Rolling off his shoulders, he placed his hands on the keys and briefly shut his eyes. The utter perfection in his posture and the calm that radiated from his entire being was really quite beautiful to watch.

After settling himself for a second he dipped his shoulders slightly and began to play the first few bars of his

64

piece. It was slow, but compelling, and I settled back and closed my eyes as I listened.

I lost myself in the music, which wasn't difficult to do because it was utterly beautiful, and by the time he finished playing I felt drowsy from the lulling nature of the piece. 'That was beautiful, Nicholas. What was it called?'

'*Stargazer*, by Patrick Hawes. I thought it was perfect for the baby.'

He was right, too; it really was.

I think Nicholas must have seen me about to doze off, because the second piece he began playing was a little quicker, still very relaxing and utterly stunning to listen to, but instead of feeling sleepy I rested my hand on my baby bump and turned myself so I could watch him play.

It was an incredibly sexy sight. Not only was Nicholas gorgeous, but the intensity with which he regarded the sheet music was a huge turn-on for me, too. I knew only too well what it felt like to be on the receiving end of one of his deep, desire-filled stares, and I felt my stomach clench with lust as I continued to watch him.

The way his T-shirt pulled over his back and shoulder muscles as he lightly dipped and swayed when he played gave a tantalizing glimpse of the perfection I knew lay underneath, and then there were his hands. They flew across the keys, caressing the music from the beautiful instrument in an almost unbelievably skilled demonstration that had me remembering exactly how talented those fingers were at other activities. I'm fairly sure Nicholas's intention with this music session hadn't been to get me ridiculously horny, but it had, and I suddenly became determined to get him to stop treating me like glass.

As he finished the second piece he paused and looked across at me, his eyes narrowing as his gaze passed across my features. After a second, he raised his eyebrows as if he had read my wanton expression, then he carefully lowered

65

the piano lid, gracefully stood from the stool, and sauntered across the room towards me.

He dropped to his knees beside me, then peeled the blanket back from my body and gently placed both his hands on my bump. Gently massaging me with his fingers, he lowered his head to place a kiss on my tummy, then kept his lips close so that the material of my T-shirt warmed as he spoke. 'That was Beethoven's Romance number 2. It was supposed to relax you both, but judging from the look on your mummy's face, she's after a different kind of romance at the moment.'

I couldn't help but laugh at his silly comment, but boy, was he right. We hadn't had sex since the night we'd done the pregnancy tests, and that was ages ago now. The laugh dried up in my throat when he glanced up at me and I saw how desire-filled his own gaze had become.

Ever so gently, he slid his hands under my T-shirt and lovingly caressed my growing bump, skin on skin. 'I know I've been a little cautious with you since we found out you were expecting, but it's only because I was worried I might hurt you, or the baby.'

We'd had this conversation before, several times, and each time I'd referred him to the stack of pregnancy books beside the bed, but so far nothing had managed to convince him. 'Sex during pregnancy is totally normal, Nicholas, I promise. Look it up on the internet if you're still not convinced.'

The hands massaging my belly began to shift higher, running across my rib cage and then lifting to settle over my bra. I sucked in my breath as he sought out my nipples through the cotton, and then circled the needy nubs with his fingers. I gasped as they instantly hardened under his touch. Since my pregnancy my breasts had grown larger, and my nipples were super-sensitive so his touch felt incredible and a needy groan rose in my throat.

I didn't care where this had come from, or who had persuaded him, but this was starting to look decidedly promising, not to mention feel amazing.

'The other night when we were at Nathan and Stella's I had a private word with my brother. I feel better about it all now.'

Nathan. Of course. Nicholas might not be willing to listen to the advice of a PhD-owning birth specialist, but he idolised his older brother, and so if anyone would have been able to get through to my worried man, it was Nathan.

'So, does this mean …?' I left my sentence hanging, hoping he'd finish it for me, but Nicholas did even better than that and rose up so he could place a long, lingering kiss on my lips.

It would seem the sex drought in our house was finally over.

As his lips moved against mine and he continued to skim his hands over my body, I realised that Nicholas's touch was still gentler than usual, and his movements less demanding. But as he slowly stripped me of my clothing, piece by piece, he proved that he could be just as efficient a lover when he lowered his dominant streak.

Once I was naked and sprawled across the chaise-longue, Nicholas stood and slowly peeled his T-shirt over his head. I'm not sure he had any clue how divinely sexy he looked when he did that, but my mouth was now hanging open and it took all my self-control not to touch myself in excitement. It was like the old Diet Coke adverts where some sinfully handsome man gets wet and removes his top to display the perfect six-pack below. Nicholas had the looks, and the six-pack, and to top it all off his hair always got ruffled in a way that made him look like a complete bad boy.

As he lowered his hands to the top button of his jeans and popped it open, I actually shuddered. Desire seared

67

through my body, leaving me feeling hot, wanton, and desperate for his touch again.

Nicholas saw my reaction, and his casual undressing suddenly became more frantic as he ripped his jeans open and pushed them and his boxers down his legs and stood up. He was fully erect, his cock so tight and needy that it almost looked angry as it bobbed around. I was almost surprised that he bothered to undress fully, because after weeks of abstinence he must have been gagging to get on with it.

As soon as he'd kicked his clothes aside, Nicholas was on the floor beside the chaise again, encasing me with his warmth as he leaned over and met my lips with a groan. I ran my hands over the warm skin of his back, briefly gripped his firm buttocks, then worked my way back up to loop around his shoulders and play with the hair at the nape of his neck.

He trailed his lips from my mouth, down my neck, and finally found my erect nipples. My breasts had already grown by a cup size, and the nipples were frequently achy from the changes in my body, but as Nicholas's hot mouth covered the tip and he gently lapped at it I felt nothing but pure, undiluted pleasure.

I reached down and managed to slip my hand around his shaft. I began a slow drag and pull with my fist which caused Nicholas to let out a moan against my skin that sent a zing of desire straight to my core. He reciprocated, sliding his hand between my legs, exploring my folds and quickly discovering just how ready I was for him.

A sigh of satisfaction passed his lips as he slid a single finger inside me. My back arched at the delicious sensation and I felt my channel clench around his finger as he began a slow thrust. 'You OK, babe?'

Nodding frantically, I licked my lips. 'More than OK.'

'If you feel any discomfort or want to stop just say so at any point, OK?'

I nodded, and as soon as Nicholas saw how desperate I was he began to manoeuvre us both on the chaise so that I was near the end and my bum was right on the edge.

Nicholas, still kneeling on the floor between my spread knees, helped lower me back so I was lying with my back on the chaise, but my legs were bent at the knees and tucked around his waist.

'This is one of the safest positions to use during pregnancy. Lift your hips,' he murmured hurriedly.

Following his instruction, I raised my hips up and he placed a pillow under my lower back before taking hold of his erection and gently brushing it up and down along my slit. Just that simple movement felt absolutely incredible and I whimpered loudly as he chuckled and repeated the action before lining up with my opening.

Instead of thrusting in, Nicholas gradually leaned himself forwards to close the gap between our bodies. This was probably the gentlest he'd ever been, and I couldn't help a small chuckle of my own as I wondered just how much this was fraying his self-control.

Finally, he was fully inside and we both let out appreciative moans as he slowly rolled his hips several times.

It felt so good, and I was so horny and sensitive that I could have probably come from that simple movement alone. Nicholas circled a few more times. Then, supporting the weight of my legs at his waist, he gently began to rock us both back and forth.

'I'll hold your legs, but I want you to touch yourself for me, baby.'

This position was hitting me in all the right spots without much further action being needed, but as he lowered his gaze to where we were joined I circled my clit with a finger and gasped as the gentlest of touches caused my insides to clench with desire.

Considering we often fucked like rough little bunnies, I was actually quite surprised by just how stimulating this slower, softer lovemaking was. It seemed to be having the same effect on Nicholas, judging from the flush now rising on his cheeks and the strained, near-climax look on his face.

He was basically massaging my G-spot with his cock. Instead of the hard thrusts that it usually took to get me to climax this was a very different sensation, but extremely effective, and one that was proving to be overwhelmingly powerful at the same time.

As he sped up just a little with his movements, I felt him begin to swell inside me, and deliberately clenched my muscles so that I'd really feel his next bump against my G-spot. I did, and it sent me tumbling over into the most delicious orgasm as wave upon wave of pleasure washed over me and rendered me speechless and boneless.

Nicholas followed seconds later, pressing forwards and gripping my legs as he ground in three more times and stilled, his release filling me with warmth as he groaned long and hard, and came even harder.

'I love you, Nicholas.'

Still lazily circling his hips, Nicholas looked up, his gaze heavy-lidded and content as he smiled and nodded. 'I love you, too, so much.'

'Thank you for the music ... and the music room sex.' I giggled, unable to help the small joke escaping, but luckily it made Nicholas chuckle, too, and he leaned forwards and kissed me on the lips.

'My aim is to please ... baby momma.' My eyes widened as he teased me with that stupid nickname again. If he hadn't still been buried deep inside me I would probably have kicked him in the balls for deliberately winding me up, but as it was, I settled for tickling him until he begged me to stop and promised not to call me it again.

Chapter Twelve

Stella

Nathan had woken me up bright and early this morning with the promise of "doing something exciting", which in Nathan's language usually translated as "something sexual", but no, instead of leaping at me, he had surprised me by dragging me out of bed, and insisting I get dressed.

By the time I had showered, I could hear voices downstairs and had discovered Nathan chatting to Marion, our occasional nanny, with William in his arms. Picking a nanny had been a nightmare, because as far as Nathan was concerned, no one was good enough for our son. Marion was an old family friend who'd gone to school with my mum, and had all the right child-care qualifications. After meeting her, Nathan had finally agreed that on those occasions when we needed someone to look after Will she would be our choice.

'We'll be back by dinner time at the latest, Marion. All of his food is prepared in the fridge, bottles are in the cooler, his favourite snuggly is here, and you have our numbers if you need anything else, yes?'

Marion flushed under the intensity of Nathan's stare, but managed to nod as she took Will from him and transferred the precious snuggly blanket that our son adored. 'Yes, Mr Jackson. Don't worry, I've got it all covered.'

I suppressed a giggle at how she still called him Mr Jackson, but I couldn't blame her, really. Nathan was still as impenetrable and intense as he'd been since I'd met him. It was only Will and I who got to see his softer side, and his brother and Rebecca to some extent.

The "something exciting" had certainly turned out to be just that. After remaining tight-lipped about where we were going, Nathan had driven us north of London until I'd finally realised that we were heading for the Cotswolds, and guessed that we were off to see the new house.

We were, and it was *in-cred-i-ble*.

A large driveway with planted gardens on both sides approached the soft Cotswold stone frontage, and as we parked by the double garage I immediately felt like I was home. Nathan had made me an intrinsic part of the planning process right from day one, so even though I'd only visited the building site a few times during construction I already knew the layout of the house inside out.

Nathan's designing flair was evident everywhere we went; the exterior looked traditional, but inside, the house had slick, smooth lines and glass walls that somehow still managed to maintain a timeless style. The entire house was automated, too; sensors controlled the lights and heating and Nathan could control just about everything else with voice commands or a quick press of a button on his phone.

He'd created a house that would bow to his commands. It was utterly perfect for my control freak.

As we continued our tour I saw that most of the furniture we'd ordered was already in place, and started to get incredibly excited about the prospect of actually moving in.

'When can we move in?' I asked, barely able to keep the high-pitched excitement from my voice as he led me along the upper hallway and stopped by some large doors.

'Fairly soon, maybe another week or so? As you can see, upstairs is basically all done, and so are the living areas downstairs, so we can move in as soon as the kitchen is finished.'

Flashing me a wink, he took a deep breath. He grinned,

looking like an excited kid in a sweetshop. 'And this –' turning, he pushed the large double doors open with a flourish and stepped back '– is our finished bedroom.'

After briefly pausing with my jaw hanging open, I finally engaged my tongue and managed to speak.

'Wow.' It's the most unimaginative descriptive word out there, but when faced with the sheer beauty of the room before me, it was about the only syllable I was capable of uttering. I'd helped to pick every piece of furniture in here, but it still looked nothing like I had expected.

'Do you like it?' Nathan enquired, a slight note of panic pitching his voice higher than usual. Turning to him, I saw him watching me carefully, and realised that he might be misinterpreting my silence.

'I love it, Nathan, it's amazing!' And it really was. The bedroom was bigger than the whole of my old apartment put together. The left wall was glass, folded open to reveal a balcony with views over the gardens that we'd just explored. A huge four-poster bed dominated the centre of the room, already made up with cream sheets and a soft suede throw across the bottom. Against one wall was the gorgeous antique dresser that we'd found in a shop in Stow. There was an armchair in one corner, and a large chest at the bottom of the bed, but apart from that the room contained no other furniture.

'No wardrobes yet?' I questioned, remembering that we'd looked at some, but never made a final decision. I stepped into the room and ran my hand over the soft sheets on the bed, and couldn't help the hum of appreciation that slipped from my lips.

'Not exactly. This next part is a surprise. Come, I'll show you.'

Turning to Nathan, I found him standing with one hand extended towards me and a sweet soft smile on his face. When I took his hand, he guided me towards a door which I assumed led to the en-suite, but as he opened the door I instead saw a large room with hanging rails on both sides, sets of drawers lining the walls, and another two doors at the opposite side.

'Walk-in wardrobe,' Nathan murmured, coming up close behind me. 'Isn't that what all women want?'

I was being bombarded by so many amazing things today, I could barely comprehend that we were actually going to be living here. It was like a film star's house.

'The en-suite is through there.' Nathan indicated to one of the two doors, then pushed the other open to reveal another bedroom. 'And this is Will's room. It's separate enough from us that we'll have our privacy, but there are inbuilt baby monitors linked directly to our room.'

I bet there were, too. Nathan was even more protective over William than I was.

Before I'd fully had time to digest how beautiful the pale blue nursery was, Nathan was tugging on my hand and pulling me back into our bedroom. 'I have one more thing to show you,' he murmured, leading me straight towards another door on his side of the room. Had he added two en-suites, perhaps? His and hers?

Initially, as the door swung open, it seemed to be a smaller version of the walk-in wardrobe that we'd just seen, and although Nathan owned more suits than any man I'd ever met, it did seem a bit over the top for us to have a wardrobe each.

'I'm not really planning on keeping much in here, but it's a good divider between the bedroom and what's beyond this door,' he explained, pointing to yet another door in front of us.

Admittedly I couldn't remember a great deal about the layout of the top floor, but I was fairly sure there hadn't been any more rooms on the plans I'd seen. Curious, I stepped forwards and pushed down on the handle, but the door wouldn't budge. Nathan joined me at the door and took my right hand in his before stretching my arm up and placing the pad of my index finger into a plastic rectangle mounted on the top of the doorframe. There was a small click, then, to my surprise, the door swung open.

Blinking in surprise at the *Mission: Impossible*-style technology, I peered curiously into the room, expecting to see a safe, or a vault of some kind. Instead, it was just another bedroom. After the touch pad entry, I'd expected something a little more dramatic. This bedroom was again tastefully decorated in pale greys, and was smaller, though still much larger than the bedroom I'd had in my old apartment. It had a bed in the centre, several large chests of drawers up against the walls, and a large wardrobe to one side. I didn't recognise this furniture from the things we'd picked out together.

Stepping inside, I looked around with interest. There wasn't a crib, but was this ready to be another nursery, maybe? Was Nathan planning on us having another baby soon? Just as I was about to ask why we needed so many bedrooms, Nathan came right up behind me and slid his arms around my waist, before hauling me up against his chest and lowering his face into the hair at the side of my neck.

I hummed my approval and angled my neck to give him better access, which Nathan immediately took advantage of by lightly nipping at the skin below my ear.

'This room is completely soundproof,' he said.

Soundproof? Frowning in confusion, I looked around the space again. As I noticed a series of small discreet metal hooks on the walls, the ceiling, and all four bedposts, clarity dawned on me.

Soundproof.

There was only one reason that a man like Nathanial Jackson would want a bedroom from which no sound could

75

escape, and I had a feeling it might involve me, one of his multitude of "special toys", and quite a lot of kinkiness. I had a sneaking suspicion that there probably wouldn't be too many clothes required in here, either.

'That's right Stella. This room is just for you and me.' He stepped around me and brought our faces together, but just when I thought he was going to kiss me, he instead teasingly brushed his lips across mine for a fleeting second then pulled back a couple of inches.

Since he was teasing me, I pulled from his grasp and walked over to the wardrobe, curious to see what it contained.

Perhaps I could do a bit of teasing myself. 'We have a room just for sex? It's a bit *Fifty Shades*, isn't it?' I quipped, so stunned by this new discovery that I wasn't quite sure what else I could say in this particular moment.

'Not at all,' Nathan scoffed, 'I'm not a billionaire, I don't own a helicopter, and the walls in here aren't even red.'

An amused bubble of laughter rose up my throat at his almost sullen tone, and I was about to argue that the wall colour didn't really matter when he winked at me and shrugged. 'Although I will concede on one similarity – there will definitely be "kinky-fuckery" occurring in this room.'

Woah. What could I say to that, apart from *oh my?* My cheeks instantly heated at the look in his eye, so I turned and pulled open the wardrobe as an attempted distraction. The contents weren't much of a distraction – more of a shock, really, because bloody hell, it was full to the brim with naughtiness! My mind boggled at just how much kinky paraphernalia Nathan and I apparently owned. All of my, and Nathan's, favourite playthings were lovingly displayed on a serious of purpose-built hooks and shelves, giving a display that would cause most people to run for the hills screaming.

Not me, though. In fact, I found myself shifting slightly on the spot as a warm rush of arousal settled in my belly.

Just being here with Nathan in this room was enough to get me feeling a bit heated, but gazing at rows of cuffs, floggers, butt-plugs, and nipple clamps (you name it, we had it) was quite simply overwhelming. I even spotted the crop that Nathan had bought for us last New Year's Eve. Hmm. That had been a particularly fun evening.

A second later, I almost jumped out of my shoes when a warm breath tickled the skin beside my ear. Nathan must have moved across the room like a frigging ninja, because I really hadn't heard him approach me at all. Although maybe that was because my ears were currently filled with the rushing of blood from my accelerated pulse. Our brand-new, state of the art house had a sex room. I really couldn't believe it.

'I need this side of our life, Stella ...' he whispered, his voice a mere rumble by my ear, his few words sending a delicious shiver down my spine. I knew he needed this; his Dom side was an integral part of who Nathan was, and truth be told, I needed it, too.

Not everyone would understand our relationship, but for me there really was no comparable feeling to being on my knees for Nathan, either physically or metaphorically. For the short periods of time when I submitted control to him I felt truly free. Free from burdens, free from worry, free from stress, but most importantly, free to experience every ounce of pleasure that this incredible man could bestow upon me.

'I know ... me, too,' I admitted, feeling my cheeks flush with embarrassed heat, which was ridiculous, given all that Nathan and I had shared in our time together.

'That's why we're so good together, baby,' he agreed, placing a kiss on the exposed skin at my neck.

77

'I think an entire room for it might be slight overkill, though,' I remarked, looking around the space again with an amused shake of my head.

'No. We need it. I ... I would never, ever want William to accidentally see you and I when we were doing a scene ...' A grunted breath gave me an indication that Nathan might suddenly be feeling agitated. My suspicion was further supported as his warm palms splayed across my hips and began to rub in fidgety circles. This was far from the delicacy of his usual sensual touch, so I began to rotate in his arms to face him and fully absorb the details of his handsome face.

As I expected, concern was obvious in the crinkled corners of his troubled blue eyes, his tight lips, and the way his blond brows were dipped low. 'I would never want him experiencing what I did as a kid ...'

At first, I thought he was referring to his father's abusive behaviour, and I was about to reassure him once again that he was nothing like his arsehole of a dad, but then I recalled his story about the time he had accidentally seen his father whipping his mother as a preamble to sex.

With a father who regularly punished both him and his brother for the most minor of misdemeanours, Nathan's upbringing had been far from usual, but he'd been an impressionable teenager, and after witnessing his parents' twisted version of a BDSM relationship he'd thought that type of behaviour was the norm. Suddenly all his concerns, and the need for this room, became clear.

'Ahh,' I mumbled, unsure what else to say.

'Yes. "Ahh" indeed,' he replied, his tone still troubled.

'You know that what you and I have together is totally different to your parents, though, right?' Leaning back a little, I slid a hand up to cup his cheek and smiled reassuringly. 'We love each other.'

Nathan nodded, his eyes darkening at my soft

declaration. 'Yes. We do.' He placed a kiss on my forehead and drew in another deep breath as he sighed heavily. 'And everything we do is consensual. I'm … well, I'm not sure it ever was between my parents.'

My stomach twisted uncomfortably at his words. What Nathan and I shared was only this good because we both wanted it, both consented to it, and both enjoyed it. The idea of someone ever being bullied into any kind of physical relationship sickened me to my core.

This situation was at risk of spoiling what had so far been an amazingly special day, so, placing a quick kiss on his lips, I decided to lighten the mood.

'So, it's soundproof in here, eh?' I tried to give Nathan my most salacious smile. It immediately registered, because his expression lost its worry and instantly transformed into something darker and infinitely more tempting.

'Hm-hmm. Check this out.' Stepping back from me slightly, he cleared his throat and spoke. 'Music. Play the Beastie Boys playlist.'

As if the house was obediently following his commands, just like I so often did in the bedroom, the room suddenly filled with the opening guitar riff of the Beastie Boys track, *Sabotage*. As the loud drum beats followed, Nathan wiggled his eyebrows and spoke again. 'Music. Volume up. Level 15.' I winced as the music suddenly became almost ear-splittingly loud, but then Nathan pulled open the bedroom door and waved his hand in the direction of the exit for me to step out. As soon as I was outside, he grinned and pulled the door shut, leaving me alone in the empty dressing room area.

Silence.

My ears were ringing from the sudden quiet. 'Wow.' I couldn't hear a thing. Not a peep. Placing a hand on the door, I smiled as I felt the bass beat vibrating the wood slightly, but other than that there was no indication that the room beyond was filled with loud music.

It really was soundproof.

As my palm lay on the door, it suddenly shifted as Nathan opened it again from the inside, and once more my ears were filled with the deafening strains of the heavy music.

'Music off,' Nathan called, and like a perfectly trained submissive, the room obeyed and we were suddenly enveloped in complete silence.

'That's pretty impressive,' I remarked, flushing slightly as I imagined what the builders must have thought when given the instruction to build a soundproof room just off the master bedroom. Thank goodness I didn't have to see any of the workmen around any more; that would have been so embarrassing. Mind you, I bet Nathan hadn't even blinked an eyelid when he'd given the instruction. My man had no shame at all when it came to his kinky tendencies.

Nathan held out a hand to me, which I immediately took and let him pull me into his arms. 'Most of the house can be voice controlled – lights, heating, music, that sort of thing. Once we've moved in, I'll programme the system to recognise your voice, too.' Cradling me against his strong chest, he kicked the door shut behind us. Slowly and purposefully, he dragged his tongue along my bottom lip, leaving me to melt pathetically in his arms.

'So, as you've just seen demonstrated, in this space no one can hear you scream.' His eyes narrowed as he spoke, giving him a dark, purposeful expression. I couldn't help but let out a nervous giggle which burst up my throat, accompanied by my eyes popping open in amusement at his humour.

'You're seriously attempting to quote *Alien* to me, seconds after I've discovered that you've designed a purpose-built sex room for us?'

'Mmm-hmm,' he murmured, 'I was also thinking that as

William is with Marion today maybe we should test the soundproofing out … you know, just to be on the safe side …'

Oh goodie. I was hot, horny, and being held up by my man, and it seemed that he had every intention of helping me ease the throbbing between my legs.

'Come on then, Nathan, make me scream. I dare you,' I taunted recklessly, giving him my most sassy eyebrow wiggle.

'You dare me?' he repeated my words, his excitement at my challenge obvious in the raised tone to his voice. 'You … Dare … *Me?*' Each word was punctuated with a mild thrust of his rock-hard groin against my stomach, before he took a step back and folded his arms across that lovely broad chest of his. '*Really?*'

As his stance widened into something far more domineering I was reminded that playing games with Nathan was serious, adrenaline-raising stuff. Gulping nervously at the spark of challenge that danced in his eyes, I desperately tried to keep my cool and nodded as casually as I could manage.

'I see. Well then, Stella, that's an offer too good to refuse.'

Chapter Thirteen

Nathan

Seeing as we were in a room filled to the brim with all my favourite sex toys, I think Stella had assumed I was intending to make her scream by selecting one of my favourites and putting it to good use. But no. I'd decided to go in a different direction, and using my very lowest, most seductive voice, I asked my girl to strip naked and bend over the end of the bed. She did it unerringly, of course, like the perfect little sub that she was when we were together like this.

Building the tension for a while always drove her crazy, so I began shifting several toys around, knocking the handle of a flogger on the wooden cupboard and jingling some cuffs so she would be able to hear the noises but not know which I would select. The anticipation was half of what made our scenes together so intense. If I was on top form, then both Stella and I would be practically gagging for it by the time I finally sunk inside her willing body. Not that I'd let that show on my face, of course, although Stella was now well aware of the affect she had upon me.

My lips pulled into a smile as she started to fidget on the bed, a perfect indication that my plan was working superbly. Stepping closer, I used my foot to nudge her ankles wider, and I watched her shoulder muscles tense lightly as she realised that things were about to get started.

Her breathing changed. She was already panting and I'd barely even touched her. That made me feel smug as hell, until I realised my own breathing was heightened, too, and gave an ironic roll of my eyes. Stella was no doubt waiting in anticipation for the slap of a flogger, or the sting of a crop, so I decided to shock her and adopt a completely different strategy today. Skipping all the toys, I dropped to my knees behind her, gripped her arse in my hands, and then hit her core with the lash of my tongue instead.

I tried to always be full of surprises. That was how I liked our sex life to be. It kept things fresh and meant we never took each other for granted.

It certainly seemed to surprise the hell out of Stella today - that was for sure - because I then proceeded to go down on her like a man possessed. This wasn't about punishment, this was just us christening the new house, so I set about eating her out and making her come over and over again, licking and nibbling at her quivering flesh until her legs gave out and she sagged onto the mattress, crying and begging for me to stop.

I did.

Eventually.

'Fuck me, Nathan, I want you inside me ...' Her voice was groggy as she attempted to top me again, and I smiled. Her bid to order me around was sweet, but laughably bad. It didn't stop me from following through and sinking inside her hot little body, though. After all the build-up, it didn't take me long to chase my own climax and after just a few minutes of deep, hard thrusts I felt my balls tighten, shortly followed by my own release shooting from my tingling cock as I yelled out her name and then collapsed forwards onto her damp back.

After we'd both laid there panting for a while, Stella turned her head to the side and grinned up at me lazily. 'Wow. Just wow,' she murmured, her voice scratchy and raw.

My body felt leaden from my powerful climax, but

somehow, I gathered the energy to slide from within her and drag us both onto the bed. As I pulled the sheets around us I smiled smugly. Stella had challenged me to make her scream, and I think I'd done a bloody magnificent job of it. The proof was in her whispered sentence, because it seemed she'd yelled my name so loudly that she was now hoarse.

As we lay together recovering, Stella giggled in my embrace and brought her flushed face up so I could see her amused gaze. 'When you first showed me the door to this room I'd assumed this was going to be another nursery. How very wrong I was!'

A nursery? Absorbing her words, I blinked several times but could dig up none of the humour she was currently feeling. In fact, my chest started to tighten, and my throat felt like it was being gripped in a vice.

Fuck.

Did Stella want more children?

I peeled her from my arms and shot up the bed to rest against the head board, squeezing my eyes shut as panic started to overwhelm me. I loved William to pieces – he had completed our lives in ways I'd never imagined – but seeing Stella in so much pain during her labour with him had nearly finished me off. I seriously didn't think I could go through that again.

'Nathan? Are you OK?'

The squeaky wheeze that came from my throat was probably all the answer Stella needed, because she was up the bed and beside me in less than a second, her fingers flitting over me supportively before finally resting upon my wrists. My hands had clenched into fists, but she gradually eased them open and softly began to massage my palms.

'Let's do a countdown, hmm?' Without waiting for me to answer, Stella started to draw in long, slow breaths through her nose and release them from her mouth. The fact she knew I needed this was just mind-blowing. I'd never expected to be so in tune with another person, but Stella was incredible. She didn't push me on why I was having a minor meltdown, but skipped right to what she knew would help me.

Closing my eyes, I timed my breathing with hers and did my calming countdown from five to zero. Then I did it again, just to be sure.

When I felt marginally more in control, I opened my eyes and found Stella gazing at me in concern. 'Do you want more babies?' I croaked.

She raised her eyebrows in surprise. 'That's not what I said, Nathan. I had just jumped to the wrong conclusion about what this room was going to be.'

It wasn't like a soundproof sex room was a regular feature in many houses, so I couldn't blame her for that, I supposed. 'But do you want more?' I pushed. 'Because I want you to be happy, and I don't want to let you down, but … but I'm not sure I can go through that again … You looked so pale, and there was so much blood …'

Stella hadn't actually let me go down the business end during her labour. Apparently, she was worried that watching the birth might affect my desire for her. She clearly underestimated how much I loved not only her, but sex, if that was what she thought. I'd still seen the blood on the midwife's hands, though, and watched as Stella had yelled in agony. It had quite literally ranked in the top two worst days of my life – the other being the day I'd found Nicholas after his suicide attempt.

'Honestly? I'm not sure I do,' Stella said finally. I watched her face carefully to see if she was just saying what I wanted to hear, but from her full eye contact and unwavering expression it seemed like she was telling the truth. Giving a shrug, she smiled and made a funny face that helped me relax a little. 'I've never been one of those women who craved kids. I was always kind of ambivalent on the subject, really, then William came along. Don't get me wrong, he's incredible, and I couldn't imagine our lives without him in it … but…' She paused and reached up to cup my jaw, smoothing her thumb over the stubble as she smiled softly.

'This will probably sound really selfish, but I really like how our lives are now. We're doing great and he's such a well-behaved baby, but what if we had another one and it was a nightmare and never slept, or ate, and was always ill? We've been so lucky.'

The biggest breath I've ever held rushed from my lungs with such force that my lips actually vibrated together, making the most ridiculous noise in the quiet room. It acted to ease the tension between us because Stella laughed out loud and leaned forwards to place her lips on mine in a reassuring touch.

'Can I assume from that horse impression that you are quite relieved by my statement?'

'I am. I feel the same. I love William so much, but your labour was …' I shuddered as the images flooded my mind again. 'Hard for me.' It was the biggest fucking understatement of my life, because I'd literally felt like I was going to have a complete breakdown in that labour room. 'I felt so out of control.'

'And we both know how much you love control,' Stella quipped, with an amused glance towards our cupboard of toys. I joined her in a smile, then rested my forehead against hers as I tried to get my hammering pulse to calm down.

'We're so great together now, Nathan. If either of us ever changes our mind we'll talk then, but for now let's just appreciate what we have, yeah?'

I appreciated Stella and Will more than she could ever understand, and more than I was capable of articulating in words, so I did what I always did when I wanted her to know how much she meant to me – I told her with my body. Closing my eyes, I nodded and placed a long, slow kiss on her lips as I dragged her body into my lap and held her close. 'Deal.'

Chapter Fourteen

Stella

Since we'd both had a free day today, Rebecca and I had decided on an impromptu shopping trip to look for any baby bargains for her, and so I could get a last few bits and pieces for the new house. Rebecca was just over five months pregnant now and Nicholas had been his usual overprotective self, dragging a reluctant Nathan out to accompany us. Luckily, after we had lingered in several girly shops they had become completely uninspired by the idea of shopping and had left us to it.

The brothers had headed off to have a coffee at our local deli, grumbling about women and shopping and leaving Rebecca and me in shopping heaven looking at baby clothes and household gadgets.

We parked outside the Hampstead house where Nathan and I were living, and as I unloaded our bounty of bags and boxes I ushered Rebecca to the front door and asked her to find the key in my handbag. I wasn't as overprotective as Nicholas might be, but with her bump visibly growing now I still didn't want her carrying all the bags, so while she unlocked I shuttled the shopping to the door.

Carrying the final package up the front steps, I found her holding a roll of paper in her hand as she grinned at me. 'I'm still not convinced that Nicholas is going to like this wallpaper that I picked out for the nursery.'

I had to agree with her. Nicholas had given two instructions regarding the decorating ideas: no yellow, and something calming. Nothing too busy or patterned. Rebecca had abided by the first rule, because apparently yellow had been the colour of Nicholas's boyhood bedroom and the colour still occasionally triggered some unpleasant memories for him.

The pattern stipulation, however, had gone out of the window, and the roll she held featured a Noah's Ark inspired design with cartoon images of practically every animal I could name, all splashed across a vivid background of waves and, of course, a boat.

It definitely couldn't be described as calming, but I was sure Nicholas would come around. Eventually.

'Get a decorator to put it up while Nicholas is out one day,' I suggested with a cheeky grin as I pushed the front door open and began to drag all of our bags into the hall.

Once we'd shoved the door shut we left our bags and headed straight to the lounge so I could see William, and we could check if the brothers were home yet. Marion was great – as nannies go we couldn't have found better – but I still missed my little man desperately when we were apart.

As we entered, I found Marion by the far wall, cradling Will and staring across at me with a strange expression on her face. She almost looked as if she was going to pass out, and her gaze flashed back and forth around the room unsteadily. Blimey. Was she coming down with something?

I rushed across the room in case she actually did fall over and held my hands out for Will.

'Marion? You look really pale. Are you all right?' She blinked at me several times, not saying a word as she handed my boy to me and let out a shaky sob. Barely a second after I'd taken Will in my arms, the door that joined the lounge to the kitchen opened and another middle-aged lady joined us.

Did Marion have a friend over? Was that why she looked so worried?

I was about to reassure her that it wasn't a problem,

when I heard Rebecca gasp behind me. I watched in confusion as an older man also entered the lounge. Unlike the woman, the man I instantly recognised, and I copied Rebecca's horrified gasp, taking in the icily blank eyes of Nathan's father as he stared across at us smugly.

Mr Jackson.

My entire body tensed, recoiling away from him as my muscles clenched with fear and my heart rate increased so violently that I felt dizzy.

God. Forget Marion possibly passing out, with my light head and suddenly weak knees I started to think that *I* was going to fall over.

It was a hell of a lot to take in, but we were closer to the door than he was, so I gripped Will to my chest and was about to spin on my heel when he raised his arm and I heard a metallic click that sent a sickening shudder to my stomach.

Wincing, I replayed the noise in my head and froze. That had sounded just like a gun being cocked. Not that I'd ever encountered a gun in real life, but it was a noise I'd heard frequently enough when binge-watching episodes of *CSI*.

'Don't even think about running,' he threatened in a low, smug tone that made my skin crawl with dread.

Swallowing around a lump of fear in my throat, I turned my attention back towards Mr Jackson and flinched when my suspicions were confirmed. He did have a gun in his hand. Fuck! It was small and black with what looked like a silencer on the end. I was no expert, but it looked real enough to make me freeze on the spot.

The last time I'd seen this vile man was when he'd turned up outside Nicholas and Rebecca's house to taunt his sons. Nicholas had thrown him out, then Nathan had punched him when he'd found out that he'd been screwing with his business. We'd assumed he had just wanted to come back to wind the brothers up again, and had then disappeared to get on with his life, but it would seem we were wrong.

I'd never in a million years thought I'd see him ever again. Yet here he was. Standing in my living room with a gun aimed at my head.

Holy shit, this was insane. It was so surreal it felt like a movie. A really bad movie, where you had a sickening feeling that it wasn't going to be an all-singing-all-dancing happily ever after for the cast.

Closing my eyes for a second, I tried to get a grip on my tumbling thoughts, but it was no good. I was in a room with my precious baby boy, my pregnant best friend, and an insane gunman. There wasn't going to be any rationalising this into something less dramatic than it was.

My eyes flew open as a cackle echoed around the room. Mr Jackson tipped his head back as he laughed, presumably at the gawking look of utter horror on my face, but the sound held absolutely no humour, just a sickening, cold emptiness that made me shudder.

'Why don't you ladies take a seat?' he suggested, jerking the gun towards the sofa and speaking in a tone that left no room for argument.

As much as I wanted to move away from him I found that my legs were frozen to the spot. All I could seem to do was clutch William to my chest and stare at the carpet.

'I said, sit down,' he barked, getting irritated with my refusal, even though I wasn't being deliberately awkward. I literally couldn't persuade my shocked body to move. I couldn't even breathe properly because my lungs were starting to seize up, making a full breath almost impossible, but as he dropped the gun towards William's sleeping face I yelped, jerked from my trance, and twisted away from Mr Jackson to protect my son.

'*Take. A. Fucking. Seat.* Don't make me repeat myself a

91

third time.'

Marion practically fell into the end seat of the white leather sofa behind us, and I felt a tug on my elbow from Rebecca who had taken the other end and was willing me to obey and join them both. Gradually sinking down to sit, I curled myself around William as protectively as I could, and noticed that Rebecca had one of her arms subconsciously curved across her own stomach, too.

She snaked her free hand across my thigh and found mine and we linked our fingers together in support, which I really needed right now to ground me, because my God, this was fucking horrific. It was all so much to take in that I could barely find words to describe how petrified I was.

'You, too, sit the fuck down,' Mr Jackson snapped as he gave the older woman a sharp prod with the gun in the ribs, making me look at her properly for the first time since we'd arrived home.

Who the hell is she? Her face was ashen, and her eyes were red-rimmed and glassy. She definitely didn't appear to be a willing assistant in all this, whoever she was. Whatever the fuck "this" was. He jabbed her again with the nose of the gun and she wailed quietly and turned her teary eyes onto him.

'Don, this is going too far … please, let's go …' Mr Jackson – *Don* – sneered and pulled the gun back as if he were about to strike her across the face with it. She practically crumpled into the armchair as she raised her hands defensively.

'Shut up, you stupid bitch. Apart from persuading the nanny to let us in you've been a fucking waste of space, just like you always were when we were married. Don't fucking move,' he spat, as she adjusted herself on the seat.

They had been married?

So that woman was Nathan's mother?

I could have sworn that Nathan said they'd split up years ago and she'd moved to America. *Fucking hell, this just got a heck of a lot weirder.* Flashing another glance at the women, who was now openly sobbing, I realised that her features did indeed hold some of the brothers' characteristics. *Shit.* I felt like I'd opened my front door and stepped into a fucking incomprehensible nightmare.

The movement of Mr Jackson turning back to us pulled my attention to him as I focused on the real threat in the room. He drew in a loud breath and ran a hand across his hair to smooth it in a move that was chillingly similar to how Nathan flattened his own hair.

Mr Jackson lifted the gun, weighed it in his hand for a second, and then smiled arrogantly, looking ridiculously pleased with himself.

'Isn't this nice? Bit of a family reunion, but without my irritating boys to get in the way and break up our fun.'

The way he had smoothed his hair had been eerily similar to Nathan, but now I had time to really look at him I saw that they both shared the same wide stance and broad build, too, and their eyes were almost the exact shade of icy blue. Nathan had gained his stature and looks from his father, that was for sure.

The similarities were purely physical, though, I was sure of that. Nathan had proved himself to be a good man: loving, considerate, protective and the best father for William that I could ever have hoped for. When we'd first started a relationship, he had worried that he was like his father, and yes, he had inherited some kinky tendencies, but I would place my life on the fact that he was nothing like the monster stood before me.

Mr Jackson took a step to the left and lowered his body so he could stare directly into Becky's eyes. 'You're Nicholas's feisty one, aren't you? I remember your little outburst from the last time we met, my girl. Don't think

93

I've forgotten.'

Rebecca tightened her fingers around mine, but she remained silent. Glancing across at her, I saw her eyes were wide and trained on the gun in his hand. The appearance of the weapon had stunned her into silence, which was hardly surprising. It was scaring the crap out of me, too.

'Not so mouthy today, I see,' Mr Jackson murmured smugly, briefly tracing the barrel of the gun down her jawline before turning his attention back to me.

Last time we'd had an encounter with the hateful man, Rebecca had been the brave one, standing up to him and yelling right in his face, but I'd been a complete state. I'd been so terrified that I'm not sure I'd even made eye contact with him.

My reaction today was almost a complete reversal of that. Instead of feeling petrified and useless, I was furious. How dare he come into my home and threaten my family with a gun? *How fucking dare he?*

My heart was pounding in my chest, and my muscles twitching with the need to do something, *anything*, to get him out of our house. Perhaps I could leap up and get in a lucky punch? Or I could use my legs. I was in the perfect position to kick his knee out from under him. The fact that it wasn't just me in the room stopped me from trying either of these options, because I knew without a doubt that I would never forgive myself if someone else got hurt as a result of my gung-ho actions.

Pulling in several slow, quiet breaths through my nose to calm myself, I raised my chin defiantly and linked my gaze with his. I might not be willing to risk an attack on him, but I would not let this fucker intimidate me for a second time.

'Well, well, that's quite a glare you've got there,' he murmured, his eyes glimmering with amusement that only upped my irritation to near-nuclear levels.

Raising one eyebrow, I stayed quiet but gave him as

much of a death stare as I could manage.

'You were quite the timid little thing, from what I can remember. Quaking in your boots the last time we met. No doubt why Nathan likes you so much. He takes after me, that boy.'

'He's nothing like you!' I spat, unable to hold back a second longer. Mr Jackson looked momentarily shocked by my outburst, then smiled. It wasn't a pleasant smile, though; his lips had pulled tight and thin, giving away the hatred that simmered beneath the surface.

'Tell yourself that if you want, but I bet I know my son better than you do. I bet he likes to control you in the bedroom, doesn't he? Spank you? Flog you until you're perfectly pink and crying out his name?'

'You're sick!' Rebecca exclaimed in disgust. Little did she know exactly how accurate Mr Jackson's description was. I'd let her in on some of the things that Nathan and I did together, bondage and the like, but she was way more vanilla than me, and I'd always known that she wouldn't understand the more extreme side to our relationship.

'So what if he does? At least everything we do is safe and consensual. I submit to him because I respect him, not because he forces me to.' Ignoring the shocked gasp from Rebecca, I felt my nostrils flare as I darted my gaze to the pathetic figure of Mrs Jackson. I sneered as I looked back to a visibly shocked Mr Jackson. 'Can you say the same? Or are you nothing more than a glorified bully?'

He snorted in anger, my words apparently hitting a nerve, and his face reddened with fury. I suspected respect was what he craved, but instead of earning it, he had tried to force it, which would never get the same outcome.

I was about to say as much when Rebecca clamped her fingers so tightly around mine that I felt a crunch of my bones. It made me snap my mouth shut. *Fuck! What the hell am I doing winding him up?* He was clearly unstable, and wielding a gun at not only me, my best friend, and our nanny, but my beautiful boy, too. I needed to shut the hell up. Right now.

'You've got quite a mouth on you now. Come out of your shell since we last met, haven't you?' He gave his hair another slow brush back with his palm. Once again, it made my skin crawl.

This time I was sensible enough to keep my mouth shut, and simply opted to lower my eyes away from his in what I hoped was enough of a submissive gesture to calm him slightly.

After a tense silence, Mr Jackson drew in a deep breath. 'So, this must be my grandson.' My throat constricted with terror as he reached down with his left hand and rubbed his knuckles across William's chubby little cheek.

Letting out a startled gasp, I tried to twist William away from his touch only to have Mr Jackson raise the gun again and point it directly between my eyes. The snout of the gun pressed against my forehead, the coolness of the metal oddly calming against my flushed skin.

'Behave. We wouldn't want him having any *accidents*, would we?' His threat made my blood run cold, and my head spin, but I managed to hold still as he gave Will a more thorough examination. Surely he wasn't wicked enough to hurt a child?

At the touch to his cheek William began to wake, his little eyes opening, then scrunching up as his face crinkled into a frown. It was as if, even in his innocence, he could already sense the danger nearby.

Praying he wouldn't start crying and irritate Mr Jackson, I quickly calmed him with some gentle rocking and, thankfully, he fell back to sleep. Mr Jackson seemed relatively indifferent to William. After grunting out some indistinct words he stood back up and crossed his arms, the gun still gripped ominously in one hand.

'So where are my sons, then?'

For a moment, I couldn't decide which way to answer. If I said they'd be home soon would he leave now? Or was he here for them, not us? Taking a punt on the fact that he wanted Nathan and Nicholas, I gave a casual shrug. 'Out for the day. They won't be back for hours.' This was a complete lie. Nathan had told me they were planning on getting home by two for a late lunch with us, but there was no way I was telling his father that.

'Hmm. Looks like we've got a wait on our hands, then, doesn't it?'

Damn it. That totally backfired.

Beside me, Rebecca shifted on the sofa, moving her hands over her stomach again, as if instinctively trying to protect her baby from the hell that surrounded us.

Mr Jackson turned his attention to her and narrowed his eyes. 'That's the third time I've seen you do that. Why do you keep covering your stomach?'

Oh God. His words made the blood in my veins turn to ice. *Please don't let him work out why.* I felt Rebecca's entire body tense through the cushion of the sofa, as he held a hand out to her.

'Give me your hand.' Rebecca shook her head, but Mr Jackson pointed the gun straight at William with no hesitation whatsoever. 'Don't push me, you know this gun is already cocked. Now, let's try that again, shall we? Give me your fucking hand.'

Retaining his grip on the gun, he accepted Rebecca's unwilling hand and pulled her to her feet. Stepping back, he ran his gaze down her body, and then back up again. She was wearing a tight tunic top and leggings today, which highlighted the bump now showing on her belly.

My heart sunk as his gaze narrowed in to focus on her stomach, before an evil grin spread on his face. *Fuck.* His expression was pure wickedness. He stepped forwards and used the back of his knuckles to stroke her stomach, causing Rebecca to visibly flinch as he touched her.

'Oh, this is just perfect!' He grinned as she wrapped her hands around her midsection with a small, frustrated moan. 'You're pregnant, too?' Before Becky could confirm or deny his words Mr Jackson let out a humourless bark of laughter. 'Fucking hell. Well at least my sons know how to do something right, I suppose.' Spinning away from us, he glared at his wife, or ex-wife, and nodded with apparent glee on his features. 'This will be a double whammy for them. They'll never recover from this …'

His disturbing rant was interrupted by the sound of a key in the front door and I tensed with the realisation that Nathan and Nicholas were home. I couldn't for the life of me decide if I were thrilled or terrified by that fact.

Chapter Fifteen

Stella

As I frantically tried to come up with a plan to warn Nathan and Nicholas of the danger inside the house, Rebecca reacted first.

'Nicholas! Call the police …' she yelled, but her warning was cut short as Mr Jackson spun back around. He jabbed his hand forcefully forwards, punching her right in the stomach.

The sound that came from Rebecca's throat was a mix of agony and pure terror as she was thrown backwards into the seat beside me. She clutched her stomach, her eyes wide and face instantly bleaching of colour. *Holy shit.* He'd hit her really hard.

Knowing she was pregnant, he'd still punched her. This man was even more evil than I'd first thought. If I hadn't been holding William, I would have been on the bastard in a second, regardless of the gun in his hand. As it was, I had to think of my boy, so I cradled him as far away from Mr Jackson as I could and reached out my free arm to protect Rebecca from any further blows he might throw.

'Back off, you fucker!' I yelled, before turning urgently to my friend. 'Becky? Are you OK?' I asked desperately, but she just stared at the door with tears streaming down her face. Turning in the same direction, I watched as the lounge door finally opened.

Nicholas and Nathan obviously hadn't heard our yelling because they were chatting happily as they appeared in the room. It took them a moment to clock what was going on and they paused. Well, Nathan paused. Nicholas took one look at his father standing over a sobbing Rebecca and leaped into action, flinging himself across the room with a roar in a desperate attempt to get to his wife.

I don't think he had even seen the gun, but the next second Mr Jackson swung around and smashed his fist into the side of Nicholas's head, using the weapon's handle like a club to his skull.

Rebecca's scream seemed to chill the temperature of the entire room. The vicious blow had an instant impact on Nicholas, sending him staggering sideways. He touched his bleeding temple and looked at his crimson-soaked fingers in shock, before making a disorientated attempt to grab his father again. He missed completely, teetering on his feet and crashing down sideways onto the coffee table in a heap.

The glass and metal gave way under his weight as Nicholas writhed around and groaned his frustration. The sound of the glass smashing woke Will and he let out a loud cry in my arms. Bouncing him on my leg, I quickly tried to calm him so that he wouldn't draw Mr Jackson's anger.

Holy fuck. This is insane!

Trying desperately to soothe Will, I swung my glance to Nathan and saw his face so tight with fury that it looked as though his temples might explode at any second. His teeth were bared as he advanced on his father, his fists clenched with whitened knuckles, and his eyes bulging. I'd never seen him so full of anger.

'Stop right there, Nathanial,' Mr Jackson warned in an ominously low tone. 'On your knees, over there next to your brother.' Spittle flew from his mouth as he yelled at his son, his face contorting into an ugly mask of hatred.

Nathan hesitated for just a split second, which was apparently too long for Mr Jackson, because he flicked the gun towards a vacant armchair beside him and fired a warning round into the back cushion. The muffled noise made me, Marion, and Rebecca scream as Nathan and Nicholas both lost even more of the colour from their cheeks.

So the gun was definitely real. The shot had barely even finished discharging before he had swivelled the weapon back to point at William and me. Once again, I tried to hunker my body around Will to protect him. When I turned my head, my gaze connected with Nathan's and I watched as one single tear slid from his eye. He dashed it away before his father could notice, but looked utterly defeated, and the sight sent shivers of fear skating across my skin.

'I'm not fucking around, son. The next bullet won't be aimed into an armchair. Get on your fucking knees.'

There was no pause this time. Flashing me a pained, apologetic look, Nathan moved beside the sprawled body of his brother and dropped to his knees.

The sight of him looking his usual slick self in one of his stylish three-piece suits, kneeling in broken glass next to his blood-covered brother, was so incongruent that it seemed to finally bring home to me exactly how serious the situation really was.

Fuck. I really couldn't see a way out of this.

'Stay down there, Nick, hands behind your head, or I'll hit your pregnant wife even harder next time.'

At his father's cruel words Nicholas howled his frustration and thumped the ground in anger, before throwing his hands up behind his head as requested. Rebecca let out another cry, beginning to sob even harder.

Nathan grunted something inaudible, but thankfully both brothers were just about in control enough to stay down and not enrage their father further.

Once everyone around him was still and silent, Mr Jackson threw his head back and let out a triumphant yell before pulling in a deep breath and glaring down at his sons. 'I am in control! Understand? I'll always control

101

you!'

Nathan made a snorting noise in his throat and spat at his father's feet, an action that infuriated Mr Jackson. Without any words of warning he advanced on Nathan and kicked him in the stomach with enough force to make me scream and clutch Will to my chest as Nathan reeled forwards onto his hands with a low grunt. His father kicked him like you would a penalty in a football match, which must have really hurt, even to someone with abs as solid as Nathan's, but there was no evidence of pain in his blank expression as he looked up.

To my utter disbelief, Nathan straightened himself out almost immediately. His hair was a mess, falling over his brow, but he calmly brushed the broken glass from his palms, smoothed his hair back, and stared resolutely up at his father in some sort of silent challenge. Mr Jackson might be in charge of this situation, but it was clear Nathan would never let his father control him again.

'Still the fucking tough guy, eh? You always were numb to the pain, you fucking freak.'

I saw pain briefly flicker in Nathan's eyes at the insult and felt my heart crumble for my man. Nathan might be strong physically, but that tiny glimmer of pain had shown me exactly how emotionally vulnerable he was in front of his father. Thankfully, Mr Jackson seemed so absorbed in the moment that he was unaware of just how much he could hurt his son with words.

William began to get fidgety in my arms, as if sensing the tension around him, and I rocked him, praying that he would fall asleep again and not disturb this lunatic to the point where he might try to shut him up.

What a situation ...

Marion started muttering softly beside me. I probably wouldn't have heard her words if she hadn't been sitting right next to me, but it almost seemed like she was praying.

'Praise the lord,' she repeated. 'Thank goodness.' The words were mixed with an occasional utterance of what sounded like the name "Kenny".

Kenny? I was fairly sure there wasn't a deity named Kenny, so I had no idea what the hell was she was on about. Maybe the stress of this situation had caused her to have some sort of breakdown. It wouldn't be surprising. I felt really fucking close to the edge myself.

As I was about to dismiss her words as the rantings of someone who believed she was about to die, something occurred to me. *Kenny*. Kenny was supposed to be joining us all for lunch today. My gaze flashed to the lounge door, which was slightly ajar, and I saw a brief flash of Kenny's bearded face in the dim light of the hallway before it disappeared again.

Glancing at Mr Jackson, I noticed that he was too focused on Nathan and Nicholas to see Kenny, and I quickly gave Marion's hand a squeeze to try and quieten her down so she didn't alert Mr Jackson to our visitor.

God, out of all the saviours I would have hoped for, Kenny was hardly top of my list. He was my best friend and an all-round lovely guy, but bravery was hardly a strong point for him. I hoped he would have the sense to backtrack to the garden and call the police so we might have a vague hope of getting out of here unharmed.

Straining my hearing, I listened for any distant sirens that might indicate that Kenny had placed a call to the emergency services. Instead, there was a sudden loud banging noise from the closed door behind Mr Jackson. The door that led to the kitchen.

'What the fuck was that? Is someone else here?' Mr Jackson demanded, glancing around the room as we all sat in stunned silence looking just as confused as he was. There was another banging noise, this time louder, and I winced as I wondered what the hell Kenny was playing at. He must

103

have used the other door to go around the back way to the kitchen, but what was he planning on doing next? Did he even know that Mr Jackson had a gun?

I was weighing up the idea of shouting a warning to Kenny, but snapped my mouth closed again as Mr Jackson delved a hand inside his jacket and pulled a second gun from a shoulder holster.

The situation had been fucked up enough with just one gun, but now there were two. Where the fuck was he getting these things from? One gun remained trained on me, and he pointed the other in the direction of the kitchen as he cautiously edged towards the door to explore. Slowly walking past his wife, he holstered the gun that had been aimed at me. He reached for the door handle, and it was at that point that everything seemed to start happening in slow motion.

Mr Jackson had just tugged the door open a fraction and was advancing forwards when he suddenly seemed to stumble and stagger sideways. There was a soft "pop" as the gun went off, then he tumbled forwards into the dining table. A sickening crack echoed around the room as his head hit the corner of the heavy wooden table top before he collapsed in a heap on the floor with a grunt.

All of us sat in stunned silence for a millisecond, before Nathan suddenly shot into action. He leaped from his knees and dived towards his father to kick the gun from his hand. Then he quickly unsheathed the other from his holster and slid it away.

Kneeling above him so he couldn't move, Nathan then checked for a pulse, which seemed to take forever. As he searched the skin of his father's neck with his fingers, the room remained cloaked in tense silence. None of us moved or spoke until Nathan looked across at me, licked his lips, and slowly shook his head.

Mr Jackson was dead.

Holy crap, this is crazy.

As I was trying to digest this turn of events, Kenny popped his head out from behind the kitchen door. He walked into the room, holding a large knife in one hand and a pan in the other. His face was as pale as Nathan's, but I saw him let out a huge breath when he noticed Mr Jackson motionless on the floor.

'The police are on their way, and an ambulance, too,' Kenny murmured as he dumped the knife and pan down. He winced as he limped to a chair and rubbed at his upper thigh. Following his movement, I saw a red stain was blooming on the denim of his jeans and blood coated his hand.

'Kenny? Have you been shot?' I squeaked, pulling Will tighter in my arms and pushing myself to standing.

'Um. Yeah. I think so,' he replied distantly as he started to apply pressure to the wound. 'It only caught the side of my leg, though, so I should be fine,' he added, which was surprisingly brave for Kenny, though I guessed the shock hadn't hit him yet.

I wanted to help so many people at once that I barely knew where to start. My maternal instincts kicking in, I took Will to the cot we had in the lounge for his afternoon naps and laid him down before rushing back to the group of people who meant the most to me in the whole world.

I didn't know who to go to first. Rebecca was pregnant and had been punched in the stomach, Kenny was bleeding from a gunshot wound, Nicholas was covered in cuts from crashing into the coffee table glass, Marion was a sobbing wreck, and Mrs Jackson was rocking back and forth, looking catatonic from shock.

William, my man and I seemed to be the only ones who were unscathed, and I sent a prayer of thanks to whoever might be listening.

Nathan might be physically fine, but he still looked a

shadow of his usual self as he stood over his father's body. He dug his hands into his hair before tugging harshly on the tablecloth and draping it over his father's corpse. Pausing for a second, he stared down at the body at his feet with wild eyes and then spun towards me. He covered the distance in just a few strides and dragged me into his arms.

'Fuck. Are you OK, Stella?'

Burying my face in his chest, I inhaled his scent, hoping the gorgeous smell might help me calm down. 'I am ... I think. That was pretty fucking crazy.'

We held each other close, forgetting everything else for just a few seconds. Nathan dropped his face into my hair as he clung to me and breathed raggedly by my ear for several moments, as if only just holding himself together.

Behind me, William started crying, but as I went to pull myself from Nathan's embrace Marion struggled to her feet and drew in a deep breath. 'Let me see to him. I need something to distract my mind.'

I nodded my agreement, then assessed the room. Looking to Rebecca, I saw that she was still on the sofa, clutching her stomach, with tears running down her cheeks. Nicholas knelt before her, rubbing her shoulders as if trying to get some warmth back into her system. He was speaking softly to her, but she looked so shocked that his words didn't really seem to be getting through.

'I feel wet. Am I wet?' she asked.

Nicholas shook his head and lifted a hand to wipe gently at the tears on Rebecca's face. 'It's just your tears. It's OK now, baby. Lie down and rest, it's OK.'

Rebecca didn't lie down immediately. Instead she began to shake her head, more tears falling as she took one of Nicholas's hands. 'I'm so sorry,' she murmured as she followed his suggestion and made herself comfortable in the space that Marion had left.

As Rebecca shifted herself, several things seemed to

happen at once. Firstly, Nicholas's entire body tensed, then he shook his head over and over as he whispered under his breath, 'No ... fuck .... No ... Becky ...' At the same time, I focused my attention on the seat she had been occupying and my stomach dropped.

The white leather sofa was stained crimson, as was the crotch of her leggings.

'Noooooooo!' The noise Nicholas let out was the most agonising sound I think I'd ever heard. It caused goose pimples to flood my skin as terror once again flooded my system.

'Call an ambulance,' he muttered hoarsely towards Nathan. He frantically stroked Rebecca's hair and trailed one hand across her body, as if trying to work out what had happened. 'It's OK, baby, it's going to be OK.'

I didn't know if he was talking to Rebecca or their unborn child but quite clearly from the amount of blood, everything was not OK.

I couldn't breathe properly, but thankfully Nathan was calmer than me and immediately grabbed his mobile and dialled 999.

'I already called an ambulance,' Kenny intervened, but Nathan simply shook his head and held the phone up.

'I'll tell them to fucking hurry up, then.' After tersely reeling off his name and the address he drew in a breath and flashed an agonised glance at Rebecca. 'Yes, hello, there's been a disturbance at this address. The police are already on their way, but I have an update for you. My sister-in-law is pregnant, but she's bleeding ... There's a lot of blood.' Turning to me, he covered the mouthpiece and frowned. 'Did my father really hit her like he said? Or is this from the stress?' he asked, sounding completely horrified.

Swallowing a huge lump in my throat I nodded. 'He hit her in the stomach. Punched her. It looked quite hard, like he meant to really hurt her.'

107

He scrunched his face up with anger, blood rushing to his cheeks as he cast a disgusted glance at the sheet-covered body of his father. 'Fuck!' He raised his free hand to his hair, digging in the strands so aggressively that I flinched at the ripping sound.

Returning to the call, he closed his eyes, squeezing them tight shut. 'She was hit in the stomach. Yes. We need the ambulance immediately.' He listened for a second and nodded. 'How quickly can you be here?' There was a pause, then Nathan let out a relieved breath. 'OK, thanks. I'll leave the front door open for you.'

Once he'd hung up, he pocketed his phone and crouched beside Rebecca, lowering his tone to a soft whisper. 'There's an ambulance just around the corner, Rebecca. Not long now, OK?'

Rebecca didn't respond, and I could see that Nicholas was fast losing his control as tears streamed down his cheeks, too. 'Becky, baby,' he choked. 'Can you hear me?'

'Yes,' Rebecca finally replied in a tone that was so quiet my heart just about died for her. 'I'm so sorry, Nicholas,' she murmured, leaning forwards and wrapping her arms around his neck and burying her head into his shoulder.

'Stop saying that, this is not your fault. We just want to make sure you're OK.' As Nicholas shifted himself closer to Rebecca, I heard the first faint strains of a siren in the air and sent out a silent prayer of thanks that there had been an ambulance so close by.

Nathan gave me a slightly unsteady look. I thought for a second he was going to pass out, but then he tugged at one of his shirt cuffs and almost fell forwards as he peppered my face with kisses. 'God, I love you so much, Stella.' His declaration was whispered, but urgent, and I think the shock of the situation was having a similar effect on him as it was on me, making him appreciate how lucky the two of us – and Will – had been.

'I'm going to go and flag the ambulance down.' He dropped another kiss on my forehead then jogged away towards the front door. I turned back to the carnage of our living room and hurried across to Kenny to check on him.

The paramedics were amazing, so calm and in control, regardless of the obvious distress that Rebecca and Nicholas were in. As they set about working on Rebecca and Kenny, Nathan went over to Marion and took Will from her arms, holding him close and closing his eyes in relief as he cradled him to his chest and breathed in his scent.

He scanned the chaos of the room in utter confusion before bringing his attention back to me. 'What the fuck happened here, Stella?'

Shrugging helplessly, I blew out a long breath. 'I have no idea, we only got here about fifteen minutes before you. Marion was here with Will, then I saw another woman … your mother, I assume … and then your father appeared with the gun.'

Beside me Marion let out a loud sob. 'Mr Jackson, I'm so sorry, I had no idea. They were at the front door saying they were coming to meet you for lunch, and the woman was so chatty that I started to talk to her and then he … he pulled a gun on me and forced me back inside the house!' Marion only just managed to get her words out before bursting into tears again.

'Marion, it's OK. It's not your fault, please try and calm down.' Nathan wasn't the most sensitive of men, but his attempt at soothing her distress was rather sweet, really. Placing a reassuring hand on her shoulder, I carried on from where she had paused.

'Rebecca and I got home and as we came in the lounge we found Marion here with your parents. You father had the gun, and ordered us to all sit down. Just before you

109

came in, he had spotted Rebecca's bump … She was standing up, and called a warning to you and Nicholas, but …' Sickening images of the bastard hitting her swum in my mind so vividly that I could barely say it. 'He … he … punched her in the stomach.' Nathan cursed low under his breath and closed his eyes as I finished. 'That was basically when you arrived.'

Glancing again at the sheet-covered body on our lounge floor, I shuddered. The man might have been an abusive arsehole, but he was still Nathan's father, and so I felt I should say something. The problem was, I had no idea *what* to say. 'Nathan, I … I know you and your dad had a strange relationship, but I'm really sorr …' I didn't get to finish, because Nathan turned to me and shook his head decisively.

'No. Don't. He held a gun at your head, and William's. That piece of shit was no father of mine, and he deserves no sympathy for what has happened.' Nathan ran a hand through his hair, just like his father had, and frowned. 'I still don't understand how he fell over, though.'

'If he hadn't tripped, I would have stopped him. I couldn't let him hurt you boys any more.' The voice that spoke was timid, and as I glanced around Nathan I saw it belonged to Mrs Jackson. I think we'd both been so caught up in the moment that neither of us had seen her move, but she now stood beside Nathan, gazing up at him with red-rimmed eyes and holding our steel letter opener in her hand.

'This was on the table beside my chair,' she explained in an oddly detached tone as she twirled the blade in her hand. 'I was just about to go for him with it when he fell. I suppose fate must have intervened.'

'Jesus, Mum!' Nathan grabbed the paper opener and flung it onto the dresser before casting a glance at the paramedics, who thankfully seemed too busy to overhear her words.

Mrs Jackson's eyes filled with moisture and her

110

expression crumpled. 'I can't remember the last time you called me Mum ... even as a child you hardly ever did.'

For the briefest instant, Nathan's face visibly paled. Then his well-practised defensive mask fell back in place, leaving him looking almost expressionless. 'Can you blame me?' he hissed, before taking a small step away from his mother.

'No, I suppose not. I'm weak, I always have been, and I know you must hate me for not stopping him when you were younger ... But you're still my boys. I couldn't stand to watch him abuse you for one more second. I'm glad he tripped.'

Jeez. Talk about emotional. A solid lump had formed in my throat that seemed almost impossible to swallow, and judging from the tension in Nathan's face, he was experiencing something quite similar himself.

Mrs Jackson gave a limp shrug. She glanced sadly at her husband's body, shrouded in the sheet. 'I didn't want him to die ... but if it stops him hurting my family again then maybe it's better this way.'

After she spoke, she wrapped her arms around her stomach and turned away. She walked to an armchair and slumped into it as if utterly drained.

'I don't get it. How could he fall? There's nothing to trip on. Do you think ...' I paused, trying to be careful about how I worded my next sentence. 'I mean, he was just in front of your mum's armchair. Do you think she deliberately tripped him?'

'If she had, surely she would just have admitted it?' Nathan chewed on his lower lip, his brows still lowered with confusion. Suddenly, he gave me a look. 'Let's check the nanny cams.'

Of course! Nathan was so protective over William that when we'd taken the step of getting Marion he had insisted on installing various hidden cameras around the house to keep an eye on her behaviour. There were two in this room alone. Marion hadn't ever put a foot wrong, but Nathan had insisted the cameras stay, "just in case". They might finally be about to come in useful.

I dashed after him to the study and watched as he tapped away on the keyboard and brought up the footage from the first camera. I felt sick to my stomach as I watched Mr Jackson waving the gun around in our faces, but the viewpoint didn't show anything different to what I'd witnessed myself: he was walking cautiously to the kitchen, and fell. The one good thing was that the images clearly showed Nicholas and Nathan far away from him, so at least the police couldn't suspect any foul play on their part.

'I still don't see what happened to him. Maybe he just lost his footing somehow,' I murmured, lowering myself to perch on the desk beside Nathan.

'Me neither. Let's try the other camera. It faces the room from the kitchen end.' Nathan whizzed through the footage from the second camera. He played it at normal speed as we watched Mr Jackson spin his face in the direction of the camera when he heard the banging noise. This time, he was walking towards the camera, and as he reached the kitchen door I watched what happened and gasped loudly. Mrs Jackson was in the foreground of the image, and as I looked closely I could see she was gripping the letter opener. Something had tripped him, but it definitely wasn't her.

'Oh my God. Did you see that?' I squawked, gripping Nathan's arm.

'No, what?'

'Rewind, I'll show you.'

Nathan played the scene again and I leaned over him to pause the footage while Mr Jackson was still standing. I pointed at the carpet on the screen. There on the floor was a small, round rattle; it was one of William's favourites. Nathan pressed play again and we watched as Mr Jackson stood on the rattle. It sent him flying and the small toy skittered under the armchair.

It had been an accident, after all.

Nathan watched the scene with a grim look on his face, his eyes narrowed and jaw tense as he nodded. Standing up, he dug both hands into his hair and let out a low breath.

He was clearly struggling with all of this, and who could blame him? This was a seriously large quantity of information to process. Not only had his father returned, hurt Rebecca, and threatened Will, his nanny, and me with a gun, but his mother – the woman who had allowed his childhood abuse to go undetected for years – had just laid some exceptionally heavy emotional baggage on him. My brain was struggling to comprehend it all, so God only knows how Nathan was feeling.

I wanted to offer my support, but Nathan wasn't the most emotionally open of men when he was stressed, so I wasn't sure he'd want it at the moment. Deciding to risk it, I carefully stepped in front of him and slid my arms around his waist. To my surprise, he immediately caged me with his embrace, his grip almost tight enough to affect my breathing. 'What a day,' I whispered softly, at a loss for anything more useful to say.

Burying his head in my neck, he drew in several deep breaths then let out a heavy sigh. 'After all those years where I begged my mother to help Nicholas … I … can't believe she was going to stab my dad. I could see the intent in her eyes, I really think she was going to do it.' He leaned back and looked into my eyes, his gaze wide and unsure. 'She was finally going to step up and protect us.'

From what Nathan had told me about the abuse he'd suffered at his father's hands, it hadn't just been Nicholas who had needed saving. His mother's intervention was about 16 years late in my view, but then I suppose none of us could ever really understand what it must have been like

113

for her, living with a man like Don Jackson.

Nathan swooped down and placed a long, lingering kiss on my lips, but unlike his usual advances, there was nothing sexual in this kiss. It was a possessive, drugging kiss, but one that spoke more of relief and love than lust. It was just what I needed, giving me contact and reassurance, but instead of continuing it, I focused on what was most important right now. My best friends. 'Let's get back out there and check on Rebecca and Kenny.'

'And speak to the police. They must be here by now,' Nathan added grimly.

Chapter Sixteen

Nicholas

As the paramedics lifted Rebecca onto the trolley I saw her leggings on the floor. They had been cut away during her examination and now lay there as a blood-soaked reminder of this hellish afternoon. The sight made me sick to my core, and I had to hurriedly turn away as a dry heave ripped from my stomach. Swallowing down the acidic bile that had risen in my throat, I wiped at my mouth and turned back to Rebecca, hoping she couldn't see how fucked up I currently was.

Fuck. I couldn't believe this was all happening.

Rubbing my hands over my face, I tried to calm myself down, but only ended up getting more and more worked up as I thought about what so much blood loss would mean for both Rebecca and our baby. She had to be OK. I couldn't go on without Becky. Pulling in a ragged breath, I realised I was crying, tears streaming down my cheeks and dripping from my jaw. My whole body shook as I watched the woman I loved being covered in a blanket and tended to by the medics.

'Nicholas. You need to pull yourself together, brother.' Nathan's deep, low tone sounded beside me, but it was his hand landing on my shoulder that finally pulled me away from my panic and drew my gaze to his.

'I know this is all really fucked up, but this is when Rebecca is going to need you to be the strong one. Get a grip of yourself, for Becky.'

Blinking several times, I tried to absorb some of the

115

composure that Nathan was radiating. He was right. Rebecca was remarkably calm now, talking to the paramedics and asking all the questions that I had been thinking. I should be dealing with all of this for Rebecca, taking away some of the pressure that she was no doubt feeling, not standing here sobbing like an idiot. Glancing at Nathan again, I gave him a sharp nod. I hastily wiped away my tears and went to Becky's side now that the paramedics had moved out of the way. Taking her hand in mine, I gave it a firm squeeze and began to rub circles on her palm to help soothe her as she was wheeled from the room.

We'd left Nathan to deal with the police and were now in a small private room within the Royal London Hospital. Any number of doctors and nurses flitted around Becky, including Karen, our amazing private midwife, who had rushed across London to be here after I'd called her.

The air was full of the beeps of machines, the clattering of instruments being shifted around trays, and an almost non-stop clamour of urgent conversation as the specialists discussed God knows what.

The small space in the room felt too full for me, too busy. All I wanted was to be alone with Becky, but I knew everyone needed to be there.

The worry about Rebecca had relieved me of my usual pickiness over specific doctors, because the three we'd had today had all been different levels of seniority and were all fantastic. I didn't care who treated her any more; I just wanted to make sure she was going to be OK.

I felt so useless it was almost unbearable. The only things keeping me grounded were the feel of Rebecca's fingers gripping at mine, and Nathan's parting words to me as we'd left the house. 'Be strong, Nicholas, for Rebecca. *For your family*. I know you can do it, brother.'

So I was.

For my family.

Finally, the majority of people in the room cleared, leaving just Becky, me, and the head sonographer – the ultrasound specialist – who was still running the probe over Becky's stomach and looking intently at the ever-changing images on the small screen before him.

'I've lost it, haven't I?' Becky finally croaked. The sight of her sad expression and red eyes was unbearable to me and I felt the enormity of her words settle directly over my heart like a crushing weight.

'Actually … no.' The sonographer turned to us with a smile and I think my mouth dropped open.

No? 'But there was so much blood …' I murmured, thrilled by his words, but not able to allow myself to believe them.

'There was.' He continued, addressing Becky directly. 'You sustained a tear in your placenta, presumably from the blow you received, which is the cause of the blood loss, but it's very small and definitely nothing to worry about.'

'Do I need to do anything differently while it heals?' Rebecca asked, practical as ever, when I was still struggling to comprehend the fact that the baby was OK.

'Just take it easy. I'd advise no sex for the next four to six weeks, and we'll get you scanned more regularly just to keep an eye on it, but other than that, you'll be fine.'

I hadn't realised my expression was so sceptical till he gave me a reassuring nod. 'Honestly, three of us have checked this, and we're all specialists in our field. The tear is tiny. Blood spreads and often looks worse than it is. I'm sure today has been incredibly stressful for you, but at least there's a light at the end of the tunnel, eh?' His attempt at lightening the mood fell on deaf ears, because both Rebecca and I just sat there, still gawking at him in shock. Clearing his throat, he looked back to the screen and nodded. 'I can see you're both still worried, but I can assure you, Rebecca, that both you, and your babies are OK.'

Relief seemed to fill my lungs faster than the air could escape and I almost felt as if I was going to burst from the enormity of his words. Not only was Becky OK, but, miraculously, our baby had also survived. 'Did you hear that, Becky? You're both OK, you and the baby.'

Rebecca stared at me for a second, blinked several times, and looked at the sonographer in confusion. *'Babies?'*

It was only when my girl repeated the sonographer's words that they sunk in. *You and your babies are OK.* Babies. Plural. I whipped my head around to look at the monitor so quickly that I think I nearly gave myself whiplash.

'Babies?' I demanded, leaping to my feet and unable to keep my voice at a low volume.

'Yes, did you not know?' He replied with a smile, moving the sonar probe over Rebecca's belly again and then pointing at the grainy image on the screen. 'You're having twins. We might have missed it at your first few scans because they can sometimes line up and trick us, but there are definitely two heartbeats. Look.'

I couldn't see anything other than some swirly grey and black blobs, but I nodded my head anyway as I tried to comprehend this incredible piece of news. I was going to be a dad to not one baby, but two.

'These are some legs here … and these bits here are arms. Look, she's got her hand up by her face as if she's waving.'

'She? We're having a girl?'

Nodding, the sonographer peered closer to the screen. 'It's still quite difficult to tell for sure, but I'd say I'm 80 per cent positive that this one in front is a girl.'

As he looked up at me the smile on his face suddenly faded. 'Oops. Did you not want to know the sexes?' He appeared panicked and apologetic as he winced. 'I'm so sorry, I just assumed that you knew ...' Seeing his worried expression I quickly shook my head in reassurance.

'No, it's fine. To be honest, I'm just so relieved they're both OK. Can you see what the other one is?'

He bent close to the screen and manoeuvred the wand some more before shaking his head. 'Not really, they're lying one in front of the other at the moment.' He flicked through some paperwork and nodded. 'But the notes from the previous scan say they thought it might have been a boy, so I'd say the chances are that you are having one of each. We'll probably be able to confirm for sure at your next scan.'

One of each. A girl and a boy.

Looking at the sonographer with the most serious expression I could muster, I frowned and then prepared to try to lighten the mood a little. 'Are you sure there aren't three in there? Because we did three pregnancy tests and they were all positive ...'

'Nicholas!' Becky exclaimed in embarrassment, just as I burst out laughing and held my hands up in surrender.

'I was kidding!'

The sonographer laughed along with us, then left us alone for a moment, giving me the perfect opportunity to lean down and kiss Rebecca. She let out a small chuckle. 'Twins, eh? Looks like we've got double trouble coming our way.'

Absorbing the sight of her beautiful smile, I let out a breath of relief and cupped her face. 'It's so good to see you smiling again, baby. God, I was so worried about you.'

'Well it would seem I'm OK, but I'm still worried about *you*,' she chastised softly. 'You need to go and get these cuts seen to.' Rebecca ran her finger gently over my torn shirt and I looked down with a grimace at the blood-soaked material. In truth, I was quite shredded up, but in the panic over Becky and the pregnancy I had barely felt any pain.

When we'd arrived at the hospital some junior nurse had seen the blood on my shirt and attempted to take me away for treatment. I'd nearly ended up punching him in the face in my desperation to stay with Rebecca. Luckily, after I'd growled at him he'd backed off and no one had dared come near me after that.

'There's a couple of deep ones, but they aren't serious. Honestly, they look worse than they are,' I said, glancing down at my side and wincing. Seeing the firm look Rebecca was now firing at me I smiled, glad to have her back on her usual form and trying to keep me in line. Holding up my hands in surrender, I stood up. 'OK, OK, I'll go and get them taken care of now. But I'm coming straight back afterwards.'

Chapter Seventeen

Nathan

As there had been a death in our house I'd expected the police interviews to take far longer than they had. But once I showed them the CCTV footage which clearly showed my father slipping of his own accord, the detective in charge said that though they'd have to carry out a thorough forensic examination, it looked to be a fairly cut-and-dried case. He didn't seem to be particularly shocked when I explained that the man threatening us with a gun was my father, but I guess in his line of work he'd probably seen it all before, and worse.

Thankfully, after a quick phone call, Stella's parents had driven across and taken William for the night so we could try to sort things out with the police. We were all taken to the local station for questioning, but mercifully the interviews weren't as gruelling as I'd imagined. They seemed more like a formality.

I was second to be processed, and as I walked back out to the reception area I found Stella and my mother waiting for me. My spine tensed at the sight of my mother still here. Given where they were sitting, I'd have to walk right past her to get out, so a brief interaction couldn't really be avoided.

They both stood up as I came nearer, but Mum immediately moved to my side, which caused me to recoil and bump into a doorframe. 'My darling boy,' she whispered, before lifting a shaking hand and trying to cup my cheek. I was so stunned by her perseverance that she succeeded, but only for a split second before I flinched away from her touch and sidestepped towards Stella. *Jesus.* I was shifting so much it was as though I was doing some terribly uncoordinated dance.

'You must hate me,' my mother said. 'I understand, I hate myself, too. I just wanted to explain a little, if I may?'

Drawing in a calming breath, I did a quick countdown in my head, took Stella's hand for support, and nodded sharply at my mother.

'Thank you. I just wanted you to know that when you were younger I tried to leave him, Nathan, I really did. The bags were packed and everything was set for me to take you boys with me ... but he found out and beat me so badly that I ended up in hospital.' She wiped away an errant tear and sniffed loudly. 'When I was released from hospital I came home and found you had been beaten black and blue. He told me next time I tried to leave he'd kill you both.'

Her words were so horrifying that I felt an icy sensation slithering through my veins as I tried to take it all in. If what she said was true, then this was a side to my childhood that I had no recollection of at all. I remembered the beatings, of course I did, but they varied in severity and I often had bruises from them, so what she was saying could be right. However, I'd had no idea that my mother had been blackmailed into staying with my father. She'd always seemed so distant with us, so cold, as if she hadn't really wanted Nicholas and me.

'But you never cared ...' My voice was so scratchy that I had to pause to clear my throat. As I did, Stella gave my fingers a supportive squeeze. 'Whenever me or Nicholas were hurt you never even helped to clean us up, or soothe us.'

'I wasn't allowed to! Nathan, you have to believe me. I wanted to, I did. More than you'll ever know. But he had rules for me, and I knew he'd hurt you more if I broke them. He wanted you to hate me, and respect him.' A sob tore up her throat, and I suddenly had the oddest urge to hug her. This woman might be my mother, but she was a virtual stranger to me. Still, there was a strange, clawing sensation in my gut as I witnessed her obvious distress, and eventually I found myself giving her shoulder a brief, reassuring touch before shoving my free hand into my trouser pocket again.

All these years I'd hated her, and she had been just as trapped as Nicholas and me. If only we'd known, we could all have tried to escape together – not that our father had ever really left us alone for long, but still. Fuck, this shed so much light on the earlier years of my life that it was a hell of a lot to take in.

'You remember the day Nicholas tried to take his own life and you drove him to the hospital?' My mother paused and looked me straight in the eye, which felt beyond strange seeing as neither of us had been allowed to make eye contact when I was a kid. 'I've never felt such relief in my entire life as the moment I knew Nicholas was OK. The truth was out and my boys were finally free of him. I know it must have been tough getting over that day, and bringing Nicholas up on your own, but you've done such a wonderful job, Nathan.'

God. My throat was so tight that I actually felt as if I was going to burst out crying like a small child might. 'You went to prison ...'

'I deserved to. Just because he had me emotionally trapped didn't make me any less guilty of letting him hurt you for all that time.' She lowered her gaze and latched her hands together, wringing them in distress.

Fuck. This was so much to try to get my head around. Just as I was trying to think which question to ask first, a female officer appeared behind us.

'Mrs Jackson, if we could have you for your interview

now, please.'

My mother gave me another long look and I felt the need to say something, anything. 'Will you be all right getting home?'

Nodding, she smiled at me. Her expression was still filled with so much sadness that it almost crippled me. 'Thank you, but I'll be fine. I only live around the corner. You two get going.'

That was news to me. 'You live in London now? I thought you moved to America?'

'I was living in the States, but not any more. I have a small place in Highgate.' Maybe she could see my confusion because she smiled softly again. 'Nicholas mustn't have told you ... I came to the UK after your car accident last year. I was hoping to try and explain ... maybe build some bridges, but he wouldn't let me visit you. I understood why, but it still hurt. After that, I decided to relocate back here to be closer to you both.' Turning to Stella, my mum pulled in a deep breath. 'Take care of my boy for me, won't you?'

Stella's taut, emotion-filled expression surely matched mine, and as my mother turned to walk away, Stella flicked an uncertain glance at me and then looked back at my mum.

'Maybe we could all get a coffee sometime?' Stella asked cautiously, looking from me to my mother hopefully, and obviously deciding that it might finally be time to put the past behind us.

My mother stayed quiet, leaving the decision to me, and as I thought back over all that she must have also endured I found myself feeling uncharacteristic sympathy towards her.

'Fine by me,' I replied gruffly, not sure what the hell had gotten into me. Whatever it was, my mum looked thrilled and her eyes filled with tears again.

'I would love that, Stella ... Nathan, thank you.'

124

I thought that she was about to break down and cry, but my mother dug up some inner reserve of strength, gave us both a teary smile, and turned to follow the officer.

Watching her walk away, I drew in several breaths and did another calming countdown. Stella stayed quiet by my side and simply offered me the support of her close contact.

She must have been counting with me, because as I reached zero, Stella reached up and placed a brief kiss on my lips. Her eyes showed she was clearly worried she'd overstepped the mark.

'I hope that was OK for me to do?'

'It was fine. After what my mother told us just now I'm starting to see things in a different light, and I have a lot of questions. You did what I hadn't been brave enough to do. Thank you.'

I was still going to get my security team to perform a background check on my mother, just to be on the safe side, but if what she had said was true then the least we could do was meet for a coffee.

'I'll admit I kinda hated her at first for what she'd put you through, but I agree, after hearing her side of things I've changed my mind ... She just seemed so lost,' Stella murmured as she relaxed against me and let out a relieved breath.

'Let's head to the hospital and check on Rebecca and Kenny.' I took Stella's hand and pulled her from the police station, still feeling as if my brain had been put through a spin dryer of emotion.

Chapter Eighteen

Stella

Nicholas and I had left a happy and healthy Rebecca to get some rest ten minutes ago, and had finally navigated the maze of hospital corridors to find the accident and emergency ward where Kenny had been taken.

Drawing in a deep breath, I pushed back the curtain to see Kenny sitting on a hospital bed as a male nurse tended to his thigh. The left leg of his jeans had been cut away from just below his groin, exposing his leg, and I winced as I saw the amount of blood coating his skin. Going by his animated expression and dramatic arm-flapping it seemed he was OK, though, and I immediately relaxed. Kenny appeared to be replaying the events of this afternoon and using the situation to get a little bit of attention from the nurse, which was about right for my favourite drama queen.

Once his leg had been stitched, the nurse cleaned it up and pulled the curtain back around the cubicle, leaving us together.

I immediately stepped up to the bedside, running my gaze over him to reassure myself that he was definitely all right. 'Oh Kenny, I'm so glad you're OK!' I pulled him into a hug and gave him a slightly extended squeeze as the events of the day finally caught up with me and started to sink in.

'How's Rebecca?' he asked, once I had released him from my vice-like cuddle.

'She's being kept in for observation, but she's OK, thank goodness, and so are the babies.'

'Babies?' Kenny repeated, his face twisting with confusion and causing me to grin.

'Yes, Nicholas just told me and Nathan that they're having twins. Isn't that great?'

'Wow. Twins, eh? Bet that was a surprise! Well, tell them I'm always happy to babysit.'

Nathan stepped up beside me and wrapped a protective arm around my waist before clearing his throat. 'You were very brave today, Kenny. Thank you. You quite possibly saved all of our lives.'

Kenny puffed his chest out proudly, and his cheeks flushed as he accepted the compliment from Nathan. It would seem from that blush that he still had a little bit of a crush on my man. Not that I could blame him, really. With his chiselled good looks and striking figure, Nathan had more than his fair share of admirers. It made it all the sweeter that he was all mine.

I saw Kenny pull in a breath as if he were going to speak. Then he hesitated as he looked at Nathan. 'Nathan, I'm … well, you know, I'm sorry how everything turned out.' He obviously had the same thoughts as me about today's events. Mr Jackson might have been a vicious bully who had emotionally abused his sons for years, but he had still been Nathan's father, and now he was dead, it felt right to say something on the matter.

Beside me I felt Nathan tense, and let out a slow breath, almost as if he were doing a quick, calming countdown. Then he nodded briskly and dismissed Kenny's words. 'Thank you, but I'm fine. He was like a stranger to me. He threatened my family; he doesn't deserve our sympathy.'

An awkward tension hung in the air for several moments. Sensing a need to change the subject, I looked at the line of stiches on Kenny's exposed thigh. They were tight and neat, but even though it had been cleaned, the skin was bruised and discoloured. 'So, is it going to scar, then?'

'I bloody well hope so!' Kenny exclaimed with a scoffed laugh. 'It's not every day you get shot, is it? I at least want to be able to show it off!'

Beside me, Nathan gave a disbelieving snort. As I glanced up at him, I saw him rolling his eyes.

'I think Tom will be seriously impressed with it,' Kenny added proudly.

Just then, the man in question burst in through the privacy curtain. He got momentarily tangled in its folds before throwing the blue material back and darting his gaze around the room. Tom looked far less calm and controlled than when we'd last met him, and after giving Nathan and me a cursory nod of acknowledgement he rushed to Kenny's side.

'Kenny, I got here as quickly as I could. My God, are you OK?'

If I'd ever needed confirmation that Tom really was serious about Kenny, I got it right at that moment, because the poor guy looked absolutely frantic with worry.

'I'm all right, T, honestly, don't worry.' I raised my brow at Kenny's significantly played down reply. Maybe Tom's calmer nature was helping Kenny wind in his overtly dramatic side.

Tom's hands were shaking slightly as he gently laid a palm just below Kenny's bullet wound. 'I can't believe you've been shot.' His voice was quiet and hollow, as if he was imagining what the outcome might have been if the bullet had been a foot higher.

It was something I'd considered briefly, too, but I needed to focus of the positives. He *was* OK, so, with a shudder, I pushed the unpleasant thoughts away and tried to give my bestie a bit of a boost in front of his beau.

'Kenny was amazing. He saved us all,' I murmured, giving Kenny's hand a squeeze. Tom looked at me with wide eyes, but, my words were completely true. If Kenny hadn't made the noise in the kitchen and distracted Mr Jackson, then who knows how the afternoon might have turned out. That thought gave me another shudder, which Nathan picked up on this time, because he slid his grip from my back and instead gave my hand a reassuring squeeze as he looked down at me in concern. Giving him the brightest smile I could manage, I squeezed his hand back then focused on the boys again.

'Jesus, Ken ...' Tom wheezed, seemingly overwhelmed. 'Can you walk?'

Kenny gave a shrug. 'I dunno. I've not tried yet. The doctor said he was coming back later to assess the muscle damage and talk about physio options.'

Tom nodded then gave us all a determined look. 'Well, you can't stay on your own. You're moving in with me while you recover, no arguments.'

From the thrilled expression on Kenny's face, he hadn't been about to argue at all, and I had to supress a smirk at just how excited he looked at the prospect of being pampered by Tom for a while.

'In fact ...' Tom flashed Nathan and me a slightly embarrassed glance, as if he wished we weren't in the room, before taking hold of Kenny's hand and looking him directly in the eye. 'Move in with me full time. I ... I love you, Kenny, and I have the space ... what do you say?'

Instead of saying anything, Kenny emitted the strangest noise I think I'd ever heard him make. It was like a high-pitched squeal mixed with a breathy wheeze, all wrapped up in a slightly wet sob. 'Oh my gosh, I love you, too, Tom! I'd love to live with you!'

Gasping at how exciting this all was, I was just about to dive on them both and offer my congratulations, but I felt Nathan give my hand a tug, and looked up at him. He, too, was smiling at the sweet scene that had just unfolded, but flashed me a wink and jerked his head towards the door. 'Come on, let's give them some privacy. We need to rest, too. This has been a really stressful day all round.'

That was a serious understatement if I'd ever heard one, but he was right about needing a rest. I felt so drained from today's rollercoaster of emotions that I was amazed I was still standing up, and so, after offering brief congratulations to a thrilled-looking Tom and an overwhelmed but gleeful Kenny, we headed off, glad to escape the neon-lit corridors of the hospital.

Chapter Nineteen

Stella

We walked back out to the carpark in silence, but my mind wasn't quiet; thoughts of today's events were churning around in my brain, over and over again. The shock of seeing Mr Jackson once more, him hitting Rebecca, the sight of her blood on the snow-white sofa, the gun, Mr Jackson dying on the carpet … A huge shudder ran through me and I tucked my arms tightly around myself to try to get some warmth back in my chilled body.

While we'd been in the hospital we'd had a call to say the crime scene had been released and we were free to go home, but after everything that had happened, I really didn't want to.

It was all too much. So much so, that when we arrived at Nathan's car I didn't get in. Instead, I reached out and grabbed his arm as he opened my door for me. 'I … I don't really want to go home tonight.'

Moonlight illuminated his features, and I saw Nathan's face soften, his brows creasing deeply in the middle as sadness filled his expression. Nodding, he drew in a deep breath and instantly circled me in the warmth of his arms. 'I completely understand. I kinda feel the same way.' Glancing at his watch, he sighed. 'It's too late to head to the new house, but seeing as your mum has William for the night, why don't you and I just check into a hotel?'

All my tension seemed to dissolve as I nodded keenly. 'God, that sounds amazing.'

Nathan smiled at my enthusiasm and leaned down to

place a soft kiss on my lips. 'In the morning, we can head over to the house and grab some clothes, then get Will from your parents and head to the new place if it's ready.'

Thank goodness our current house was a temporary rental until we moved to the place in the Cotswolds, because after all that had happened today I honestly couldn't see myself ever wanting to go back in there. 'That sounds perfect. Thank you, Nathan.'

Nathan, being Nathan, didn't take us to any old hotel, oh no. Nope, there certainly wouldn't be any budget accommodation looming in my near future, because after just 15 minutes he was pulling into a car park outside The Dorchester on Park Lane.

I mean, seriously? The Dorchester? Until today, the only time I'd ever been on Park Lane was when I'd played Monopoly as a kid.

As he reversed into a space, I gawked at the line of cars opposite us; there was a fire red Lamborghini, a sleek black Ferrari, a stunning vintage Rolls Royce, a Bentley ... *My god, it's like a supercar showroom!*

'Shall we?' Nathan's amused tone broke me from my trance and I quickly reeled my tongue in and turned to him in astonishment.

'There's a much cheaper hotel just down the road,' I squeaked, panicking that my rumpled clothes really weren't anywhere near smart enough for a swanky place like this. I'd been attacked by a gun-wielding maniac, spent hours with the police, then plodded around the hospital. I hardly looked fresh.

Nathan made a dismissive raspberry sound in reply to my suggestion and raised an eyebrow. 'I don't think so.'

He was so set in his ways that I suppose the chances of me persuading him to lower his hotel expectations were fairly minimal, but perhaps I could grab a change of clothes from somewhere. The problem was, the only shops we'd passed around here were really fancy-looking ones. Joining him beside the car, I desperately looked around us for inspiration, but all I could see was the greenery of Hyde Park and two large, red double-decker buses making their way along the road.

'Is there anywhere around here where I could buy some clothes? I feel really scruffy,' I said, eyeing the fancy hotel behind Nathan. 'I've been wearing these all day, and after being in the police station and the hospital I feel really dirty.'

Nathan's nostrils flared slightly, as if he was also getting a flashback of our day, and he nodded briskly, before talking my hand and tugging me back towards the car.

'Wolfe and Badger isn't too far. I think you'd like their clothes. We can drive.'

'Wait! We're in central London on a Saturday night. Parking will be a nightmare; let's grab a cab.'

Nathan dipped his eyebrows at my suggestion, and a giggle bubbled up my throat as I had a sudden recollection of the first time I'd taken him on the London Underground. My man and his compulsive need for cleanliness did *not* do public transport; a fact that I had somehow forgotten in our time together.

To my surprise, Nathan conceded, and a few moments later, we were climbing into one of London's famous black cabs. Just like he had on the train that time, Nathan sat himself down with the ultimate care, resting his hands on his knees and looking extremely uncomfortable with our transport even though the interior was spotless and smelt far better than some cabs I'd travelled in.

As soon as we climbed out after our short trip, Nathan breathed a sigh of relief. He dug into his trouser pocket before pulling out a small bottle of hand sanitizer. Offering a squirt to me, he then proceeded to give his hands a very thorough clean while I desperately attempted to suppress my amused smile.

'Do you have one of those in every pair of trousers you own?' I joked, but my attempt at humour fell flat, because Nathan merely looked at the bottle, and nodded in complete seriousness, obviously not hearing the humour in my tone at all.

'Pretty much.' Pocketing the sanitizer again, he took my hand and dragged me towards the shop. He cast a sulky look over his shoulder at me. 'And we can walk back. I'm not going in another cab.' The disgusted curl to his lip had me stifling another laugh as I rolled my eyes at his funny traits and followed him inside.

***

Nathan had been right; I did like the clothes in here. They had everything from on-trend dresses and heels to casual jeans, and seemingly catered for all budgets. Once I'd picked out an outfit, I paid for it and asked the lady serving me if she'd mind me keeping the clothes on. I used the mirror in the changing room to apply some minimal make-up, and then emerged dressed in smart black jeans, a pale pink top, and my own jacket, feeling much happier with the prospect of going inside a fancy hotel.

I grabbed a set of underwear for the morning, too, and Nathan picked out a change of clothes for himself, but chose to remain in his suit for the time being. Typically, even after the stress of the day, he still looked immaculate, with barely a hair out of place. I have no idea how he did it, but I'd love to know his secret.

Once we had made the 15-minute walk back to the hotel, Nathan grinned at me as a uniformed doorman immediately stepped forwards to open the door for us with a flourish before giving a small bow.

'After you, madam,' Nathan murmured in amusement,

waving a hand before him and grinning when my eyes boggled as I stepped in and got my first look at the sumptuous foyer.

Blimey. It was so fancy that I practically tripped over my own feet as I struggled to take in the beauty of the décor around me. With the polished marble floors, pillars, soft, leaf-green sofas and exotic palms lining the reception area, I almost felt as if I was in an exotic jungle hotel somewhere.

Unlike me, Nathan seemed completely at ease with the luxury surrounding us and merely buttoned his suit jacket, smoothed his already perfect hair, and took my hand as we approached the reception desk.

The smartly dressed gentleman behind the counter also gave a small bow of his head and smiled at us. 'Good evening, welcome to The Dorchester. Do you have a reservation, Sir?'

Nathan gave his shirt cuffs a brief tug and then shook his head. 'I'm afraid not. We've had a … *situation* at our house and need a room for the night.'

A situation. That was certainly a polite way of describing the hell we'd gone through today.

'Of course, Sir. Have you stayed with us before? You look familiar.'

Nathan smiled and adopted his customary wide-legged stance which screamed cool, calm composure. 'Not for a while, but I do book you for my business acquaintances when they're travelling in from out of town. I was hoping one of the suites might be available. Perhaps the Eisenhower?'

'An excellent choice, Sir! Let me check for you.' The man had raised his eyebrows with apparent pleasure at Nathan's request, and from his thrilled expression I could only assume that the suite Nathan had requested was probably quite expensive. Why we couldn't just get a normal double room was beyond me, but I knew it was pointless saying anything.

After a few brief clicks on the computer before him, the man looked up. 'You're in luck, it's available.'

After giving over his card details for the deposit, Nathan and I accepted our key and made our way towards the lifts.

'Eisenhower, huh? Have they named all the rooms after someone famous?'

Pressing the button for our floor, Nathan shook his head and slid a hand into his pocket. 'Nope, the suite I've requested was actually used by Eisenhower when he served as Commander-in-Chief of the Allied Forces.'

Woah. That's certainly some history!

The lift stopped. After just a few steps, Nathan had used our key card and was pushing open the door to a huge, light suite. Stepping in, I felt my mouth hang open as I looked around. *Jeez, this is seriously flashy.*

'Apparently, he planned the Normandy invasion from within this very room. People like Winston Churchill met him in here for meetings, too. It's not the most expensive suite in the hotel. In fact, this is probably low to mid-range compared to some of their more expensive rooms, but I like the view and sense of history in here.'

I knew he was still speaking, but I was so gobsmacked by the room that I could hardly take in his words. Or should that be rooms, because there was a sitting area, dining area, and bedroom in here. This was what Nathan classed as "low to mid-range"? I couldn't understand how this could be bettered, so I'd love to see some of the more expensive rooms.

With its wooden panelling, mid-yellow walls, beautifully carved wooden furniture and high, airy ceilings it was the fanciest place I'd ever stepped foot in, let alone stayed for the night.

I padded across the thick cream carpet and ran my

fingertips across the cool wood of the sumptuous four-poster bed, then made my way to the window to look at the view Nathan had mentioned. Pulling back the curtain, I gasped, immediately seeing why he liked it; the entire window was dominated by its setting just across from Hyde Park, with trees and open grassland all that I could see. We even had a balcony, but this wasn't like the small balconies you got at some hotels; this was big enough for a full set of outdoor furniture and several lusciously healthy plants.

Turning back around to face Nathan, I shook my head. 'This place is incredible.'

Nathan smiled, nodding. Then he shucked off his jacket and began to undo his shirt buttons as he walked towards me. Usually, this sight would fill me with lust, but I could see from the tired droop to his eyelids that the long day was starting to take its toll on him. It was on me, too; I was so physically and emotionally drained that sex was the last thing on my mind right now.

'I don't know about you,' he said, 'but I'm exhausted. I propose that we fuck up our sleep schedule and have a nap now, followed by a massage in the spa and then a light dinner later on. What do you think?'

Considering all that we'd been through today, I think we deserved a little pampering, so it sounded pretty damn ideal to me. 'I think it sounds perfect. I'm so tired and that bed looks incredibly inviting.'

I took off my new outfit, hanging it carefully in one of the huge wardrobes, and turned to find Nathan stripped and climbing into the bed. I didn't hesitate in following, immediately going to him and letting him pull me into his arms so we could snuggle below the thick covers. It wasn't often that we went to bed together and didn't do something intimate first, but after he'd placed a brief kiss on my lips I felt my eyelids drooping with exhaustion. Nathan chuckled, tucking me into his body and flicking off the light.

137

After a much-needed nap, we took a brief shower, still with no sexy stuff occurring, which was decidedly out of character for Nathan, and spoke volumes about how screwed up the day had left him. We snacked on the complimentary pastries and fruit that had been left in the room then made our way down to the spa. Once we were changed into our dressing gowns, I met Nathan back in the reception area and took a second to appreciate how gorgeous he looked in his fluffy robe. The white material made his skin appear golden, and with his blond hair, gleaming blue eyes, and trace of stubble he looked like some handsome sex god, or perhaps even a striking Norseman.

Dragging my gaze away from him, I looked around at the empty space. The lights were dimmed, the changing room had been empty except for me, and I couldn't see or hear any other people around. 'Is the spa even open? It's gone nine o'clock now.'

Adjusting the tie on his robe, Nathan shook his head. 'Technically, no. But I explained that today had been particularly stressful and they were happy to oblige us with a massage.'

This hotel really was something special. 'Really? Just like that?'

'Well, it's true that the staff here are supremely accommodating, but it helped that I also booked and paid for the Terrace Suite for our anniversary later this year.'

I raised my eyebrows, firstly at the fact that he had remembered an anniversary I wasn't aware of, but also his mention of booking us another night here.

'The Terrace Suite?' I croaked, confused.

'Yep. It has its own Jacuzzi, and the bathroom is linked to the terrace so you can enjoy a view over London while you relax in the tub. It's incredible.'

138

A sudden, unexpected bout of jealousy flew at me from nowhere and my back stiffened as I wondered how exactly Nathan knew this fact. It had been a while since I'd had cause to think about the other women he'd been with in the past, and the strength of my feelings shocked me slightly. Had he brought a different woman here in the past and enjoyed the Jacuzzi with a view?

I knew I was being irrational and struggled to control my face so I didn't give myself away, but it would seem that my attempt failed miserably because Nathan cocked his head and watched me for a moment before a satisfied smile tugged at the corners of his mouth. 'I don't have personal experience of it, Stella, so you have no reason to feel envious. When I originally set up my business account here the hotel gave me a tour and I remember thinking how stunning that particular feature was. I thought it would appeal to you.'

Oh. That's actually very thoughtful of him. But still, how the hell can he always read my mind like this?

Stepping forward, Nathan took hold of the tie around my dressing gown and tugged me towards him so our hips rubbed together. 'But you know how much I love it when you get jealous over me, babe …' he growled, dropping a hard, almost bruising kiss on my mouth before soothing it with a quick lick.

Biting my lower lip, I realised I could *feel* how much he loved it, too, as his arousal pressed forwards from under the cosy confines of his plush dressing gown. It was amazing how easily he'd calmed my worry, because now, instead of jealousy, an altogether different emotion was running around my system – red-hot lust.

'Anyway, it's the most expensive suite they have. Well, bar the two-bedroomed suite, but we'll get a babysitter for the night so I didn't think we'd need that.'

My mind swirled with desire, but at his words it went

back to his mention of our anniversary and I panicked slightly, wondering what date was he thinking about. It was usually women who were good at dates and relationship milestones, but I had no clue. I mean it wasn't like we were married, so we had no wedding anniversary to celebrate. The date we met? When we signed our D/s contracts? Or maybe the day he had given me my new commitment ring?

'So ... what date do you count as our anniversary, then?' I asked as casually as possible, hoping that he couldn't read my mind on this topic as well as he had before.

Nathan blinked twice and gave a tiny, shy smile. 'Well, I was thinking it could be our first anniversary.'

Confused, I frowned up at him, my brain too exhausted to try to keep up.

Seeing my expression, he took my hand between his. 'Do you remember how I mentioned making us official by having a collaring ceremony at Club Twist?'

I raised my free hand and touched my necklace fondly, but I felt the same stirrings of nervousness that I'd had the last time he'd mentioned this subject. 'I do ... so would it be like our own Dom/sub version of a wedding service?'

He gave a small shrug. 'In a way, yes. But there won't be cake, and I wouldn't invite your mother if I were you.' The twinkle in his eye and his sudden dry humour helped my nerves subside and I giggled, my shoulders relaxing.

'I've booked and paid upfront for the suite so we can stay here afterwards,' he went on. 'We just need to confirm a date with them. It wouldn't really be our anniversary, I know, but certainly it will be a date to celebrate in years to come.'

Wow. This would make quite a place to spend the night after my collaring. I didn't really like that title, though; it didn't quite seem to encompass all that Nathan and I were together, so perhaps I'd refer to it as my "nearly-but-not-quite-a-wedding" night.

Before we could discuss it any further, the door opened and we were joined by our two masseurs, who, much to my amusement, were both young, handsome guys. It was only amusing because Nathan looked them both up and down and visibly bristled beside me before making a show of grabbing my hand as if claiming me.

'Mrs Jackson, we're in Treatment Room 1. This way, please,' said the younger of the two staff. I immediately knew that I wouldn't be following him, because Nathan's hand tightened on mine with almost bone-crushing force.

Glancing up, I saw a vein in Nathan's temple throbbing with his pulse, and his eyes were bulging. He looked like he might actually have an aneurism from the stress, so I gently enquired if there were any rooms with two beds.

'Of course. We have a joint therapy room.'

Thank God for that.

Considering I'd had my own bout of the green-eyed monster a few minutes ago, I couldn't really say anything, but it did give me a warm feeling in my belly to know that Nathan was just as possessive over me as I was over him.

Chapter Twenty

Rebecca

Blinking awake again, I looked around drowsily and took in the unfamiliar room I was in. White walls, clock, a table over the foot of the bed, a jug of water ... As my eyes landed on the medical chart I remembered where I was, and more specifically, *why* I was here, and I moved my hands instinctively to protect my bump.

God. Today has certainly been eventful. Rolling my eyes at the huge understatement, I drew in a deep breath and tried to calm my pulse. I was OK, and so were the babies.

Glancing to my right, I saw Nicholas asleep in the chair next to my bed and couldn't help the smile that jumped to my lips. I loved him so much.

He looked so uncomfortable with his tall, broad frame cramped into the tiny armchair. One leg was bent at the knee and had fallen to the side and the other was stretched out before him. His arms were squashed inside the armrests and placed awkwardly across his chest, and his head had lolled forwards so that his neck must surely be painfully contorted. Or it certainly would be if he stayed like that for much longer.

Bless him; I should wake him so he could change position, but he looked exhausted. He'd been my absolute rock today. Knowing how explosive his emotions could be when placed under any sort of stress, I'd expected him to completely lose it, or have some kind of breakdown, but after a brief few minutes of panic he'd pulled himself together and held strong the whole time I'd needed him.

As if sensing my gaze on him, Nicholas began to stir, his eyelids fluttering. He let out a grumble and hauled himself into a more upright sitting position. Yawning, he stretched his arms, then reached up and rubbed at his neck with a grimace before looking across at me. Seeing my gaze, his own pain was seemingly forgotten as he jumped up and came to my side.

'Hey, beautiful, you're awake. How are you feeling?'

I briefly assessed my body, and nodded. 'Pretty good, all things considered,' I said with a shrug, before confessing that I was actually a little uncomfortable. 'My arse is going numb in this position, but I'm too scared to move in case it makes me bleed again.' It was stupid, because the doctors had reassured me that the tiny rip had clotted over really well, but I still felt anxious about it.

Nicholas's face softened with concern as he nodded and leaned down to brush a kiss across my lips. 'I'm sure you'll be fine to move, but let me see if I can find someone to ask.'

Nicholas

I didn't like leaving Rebecca's side, not even for a second. Just then, I heard the unmistakeable South African accent of Karen our midwife, shortly before I saw her red-blonde hair and grinning face as she strode past our room, joking with whoever she was speaking to. Perfect timing or what? She was the ideal person to ask.

I dashed into the corridor to grab her. I pulled the door shut and saw Karen standing at the nurses' station, laughing with one of the doctors. I might not be much of a people person, but there was no denying our midwife's likability; Karen oozed approachability in a way that made you instantly trust her implicitly.

Judging by the fact that she was wearing her coat and had a large bag slung over her shoulder, she was heading home for the night, so I approached, and waited for a lull in their conversation before politely coughing to make myself known.

'Karen, could I just have a quick word?'

'Hi, Nicholas! I was just going to pop in on you two again before I went home. What can I do for you?'

Thankfully, the doctor bid us goodnight and left us alone, so I got straight to the point. 'Rebecca's not very comfortable, but she's a little worried about moving too much in case she bleeds again.'

Karen's face softened in understanding and she nodded. 'She'll be fine to move, as long as she doesn't try doing any cartwheels. Let me come and help get you both settled for the night.'

I couldn't help the irritable grumble that rose in my throat at her words. I wished *we* could get settled for the

144

night, I was so desperate to hold Rebecca in my arms, but I could barely even hug her properly because she was in the bed surrounded by machines.

Karen cocked her head and assessed me for a second, which I didn't like one little bit. 'Getting impatient for a cuddle, are you?' She smiled.

How the hell had she read me so easily? No one could do that, except perhaps Rebecca and Nathan. Seeing as she'd hit the nail on the head, I nodded reluctantly.

'Aww, Nicholas! You put on this stern front, but you're actually a big ol' softie, aren't you?' She was teasing me, I knew that, but I frowned anyway until Karen rolled her eyes, and gave me a light punch on the arm before stepping back towards Rebecca's private room. 'Come on. I'll help Rebecca get comfortable and then you can hop in bed with her. I won't tell the nurses,' she whispered as she flashed me a wink and opened the door.

Grabbing her arm in surprise, I lowered my voice so Becky wouldn't hear. 'Really? Won't I hurt her?'

Karen grinned at me again, presumably amused at what a fucking softie I was, but then shook her head. 'As long as you don't lie on top of her, you'll be fine to have a little cuddle.' Her demeanour lightened further as she addressed Becky. 'Hi, Becky! I'm so glad everything's settled down now. And twins, eh? That was a bit of a surprise, wasn't it?' Karen chuckled, placing her hands on her hips and grinning at both Rebecca and me in turn. 'Can't believe I didn't spot that at your last scan. One of them must have been hiding!'

She moved to the side of the bed, picked up a spare pillow, and nodded her head. 'So, your lovely young man says you're uncomfortable. You're fine to move, just take it easy when you do. Shall we try lying on your side?'

Rebecca smiled with relief, nodding her head enthusiastically as Karen pulled the blankets back to expose

Rebecca's bare legs. I tensed slightly, feeling my irrational jealousy rising to the surface as I saw all the pale skin being revealed, and had to ram my hands in my pockets to stop myself snatching the blanket and pulling it back over her. Rolling my eyes, I remained fixed to the spot and let Karen do her job. I would always dislike anyone seeing my girl half-dressed, even if it was our midwife, but at least now I knew my reaction was irrational, I supposed.

'On my side with a pillow between my knees and one under the bump has been the most comfortable for sleeping recently,' Rebecca informed her as she shifted gingerly with Karen's gentle guidance. I was itching to help out, but too unsure of what I should do. I seemed to feel like that a lot at the moment.

Once my girl was on her side with the pillows in place, Karen turned and flashed me a wink. 'You can hop in now, Nicholas. I hope you enjoy your spooning,' she added with a wink before bidding us goodnight and leaving.

I approached the bed and leaned down close to Becky's head and gently brushed some hairs back from her brow. A tightness constricted my chest as she smiled up at me. Her expression was so open, seeming to shine with how she felt about me. God, I loved her so much. I still couldn't believe I'd found her.

'Do you need anything, baby?' I asked softly, my voice tight with emotion as I found myself unable to resist the temptation of cupping her cheek. Her eyes fluttered shut and she nuzzled into my hand with a soft humming sound that made the tautness in my chest constrict even more.

'Just you, wrapped around me,' she replied softly, turning her face to place a kiss on my palm.

Well, OK. I might have been feeling a bit unsure of what I could do to help recently, but snuggling was certainly within my areas of expertise. A smile pulled at my lips at my last thought. Snuggling had never been something I'd entertained before Rebecca. Women had literally never stayed in my bed long enough for any sort of affectionate behaviour to occur. Sex had been nothing more than a release for me, and as I thought about it now I realised just how unsatisfactory those encounters had been.

I bent down to place a quick kiss on her brow and walked to the opposite side of the bed, kicking off my shoes as I went. As we were in a hospital, I decided to keep my clothes on. I carefully climbed into the bed and shifted myself across until I was spooned around Becky's warmth as closely as I could get.

Inhaling the scent of her hair, I closed my eyes with a smile and looped an arm over her so I could link our fingers on top of her bump. Rebecca let out a contented sigh and wiggled her bum backwards to get more contact with me, which predictably sent a twitch straight to my cock and made her giggle.

'Cool it, stud. No sex for six weeks, remember?'

Boy, did I. I knew she was only teasing me, but there was no way I'd have been attempting to initiate sex after today's events, regardless of the doctor's orders. Seeing Rebecca bleeding like that had been the singular most terrifying experience of my life, and I fully intended to treat her like she was made of glass for the foreseeable future. I'd wrap her in bubble wrap for the remainder of the pregnancy if she'd let me. Unfortunately, I knew only too well that my feisty woman would be having none of that.

'Don't wiggle then, you little temptress.' Predictably she wriggled again, just because she could, and we both shared a chuckle as I carefully pulled her closer. God, it felt so good to have her in my arms once more.

'After everything that has happened today, this is exactly what I need,' Rebecca whispered, giving my hand a squeeze.

It was exactly what I needed, too. 'I love you so much,

147

Rebecca,' I blurted, unable to hold the words in for a second longer. Instead of the usual emotional response they got, Rebecca giggled in my arms, which surprised me.

'You beat me to it, Nicholas, because I was just about to say the very same thing,' she murmured softly, the humour leaving her voice as she pulled in a deep breath. 'I love you, too. You've been incredible today, thank you. I wouldn't have got through it all without you being so calm.'

She was right, I *had* been remarkably calm today, which had surprised the hell out of me, too. As we lay there quietly I felt her relax in my arms as she began to drift towards sleep, and I finally let a few much-needed tears escape as I cradled Rebecca close and appreciated just how bloody lucky we were.

Chapter Twenty-One

Nathan

Stepping out of the joint therapy room forty minutes later, I stretched after my massage. I looked down at Stella and saw her drowsy expression and flushed cheeks. 'Did you enjoy that?'

She almost looked boneless as she leaned against a wall and nodded languidly at me. 'Oh my God, yes. That massage was *in-cred-i-ble*. Out of this world good. I feel so relaxed.'

My massage had also been executed proficiently, but I had barely been able to unwind, because I'd been constantly aware that just three feet away from me there had been another male with his hands on Stella. The fact that she had obviously enjoyed it made me relax slightly, and I drew in a deep breath, hoping it had distracted her mind away from today's events.

My therapist handed us some samples of the lavender oil to take away with us, then picked up two towels with a smile. 'The manager mentioned that you requested access to the sauna and Jacuzzi as well. I'm afraid with no staff on duty I can't let you into the Jacuzzi for safety reasons, but the saunas run on 15-minute cycles, so the manager told us that if we set one up for you before we go he would come and shut everything down fully afterwards.'

Nodding, I accepted my towel. 'That would be fine, thank you.'

'The doors to the spa are only accessible with staff key cards at this time of night, so you'll be on your own. Just

149

shut the doors behind you when you leave.' After pressing several buttons on a console to activate the sauna he bid us goodnight and we were left alone. Finally. Both of those guys had been far too handsome, and way too hands-on for my liking.

'I can't believe they left us to have the run of this place!' Stella exclaimed excitedly.

Cocking an eyebrow, I shrugged. 'It's only for 15 minutes or so. Besides, they have my credit card details upstairs; I'm sure that's enough of a reassurance for them.'

The sauna soon heated up, and knowing that we only had 15 minutes, we quickly shed our towels and entered. The scent of warm pine and lavender immediately enveloped us and as I closed the door I turned to see Stella standing with her eyes closed, inhaling the fragrant air with a small smile.

The sound of the door closing seemed to wake her from her trance, because she turned and caught me red-handed in running my gaze down her underwear-clad body. She was wearing a pale blue lace bra and matching blue French knickers and looked hot enough to rival the temperature of the air around us.

From her shocked look, I don't think she'd been expecting to see lust on my face, not after everything that had happened today, but fuck it. I might be struggling slightly to absorb everything that had gone on, but I knew one thing that would distract me.

Her body.

Or more precisely, losing myself in Stella's soft, warm skin then burying myself inside her.

Tomorrow, I would sit down and sort through the myriad of fucked-up-ness that had occurred today, but right now I was turning to my tried and tested coping strategy – sex.

With Rebecca and Kenny in the hospital, it almost felt

wrong to have the deep heat of desire coursing through my veins, but then again, perhaps that was exactly why I was feeling this way. We'd all survived. Stella, Will, and I were all OK, and I was so bloody grateful for that fact and feeling decidedly appreciative of how lucky we were.

In a fucked-up way, it had been quite a life-affirming day, and really, what better way to end it than reconnecting physically with a nice hard fuck?

I reached out and looped a fingertip under the shoulder strap of her bra, giving it a light ping before crossing my arms over my chest. 'Take it off,' I murmured, my voice low and gravelly from the lust affecting my system.

Even though there was a clear sign beside her stating that swimsuits must be worn at all times, my girl obeyed the demand immediately and I grinned at her and flashed a wink.

As she removed her bra and knickers, I quickly stepped out of my boxers, folded them, and placed them on one of the pine benches. I would usually watch her strip teases avidly, but we only had 15 minutes, so there was no time to waste.

Once I was naked, I crossed my arms again, enjoying the sensation of the hot air around my erect cock. I watched in slack-jawed appreciation as Stella went one step further and adopted her ready position for me; hands linked, and eyes averted.

A groan rose up my tight throat at the sight before me and my dick lurched in excitement. 'You are so fucking sexy, Stella.'

She was perfect. *My* perfect.

I very rarely asked her to lower her gaze any more, but as I watched her I grinned smugly, realising *why* her eyes were lowered. Her gaze was directly aimed at my lower half, and from the looks of it, she was pointedly staring at my erection.

151

'God, you really are magnificent … *Sir*.' The final word seemed to be added as an afterthought, almost as if she had meant to think the sentence in her head and had realised that she'd accidentally said it out loud. Not that I was going to complain; she could compliment me on my "magnificent" tackle any day of the week.

'Eyes up, sweetheart,' I said softly, drawing her stare up to meet my gaze. Swallowing hard, I decided to get something off my chest that had been weighing really fucking hard all afternoon. 'I don't like admitting weakness, Stella, you know that, but … but I was so fucking scared today when I saw that gun pointed at you and Will.'

I hadn't even felt fear like that as a kid when my father had been beating me until I bled. 'I've never been so terrified in my life.' After my quiet declaration, I closed my eyes and did a calming countdown, going from five to zero and feeling the warm, scented air around us relax me again.

'I need to be inside you,' I murmured. 'I need to feel us, and to know we're really OK.'

Opening my eyes again, I saw the complete understanding on Stella's face. Without saying anything further she stepped into my open arms and tilted her head back to offer her lips to me.

I was many things, but a gentle lover was not something that would often spring to mind when I thought about my character traits. Tonight, though, that was exactly what I tried to be. I wanted Stella to feel how much I loved her, and how much she meant to me, and just how bloody glad I was that we'd all made it out alive today.

I did my best attempt at treasuring her, keeping my touches lighter than usual, so they were mere caresses, and exploring our connection by touching and cherishing every single part of her as my fingertips trailed across her skin.

My kiss was as gentle as I could manage, still deep, but

152

tasting, and exploring, coaxing her to melt against me, which she soon did, so I shifted us both to the slatted wooden benches that lined the sauna.

After laying down towels to soften the wood for her, I kissed Stella again. This time, I guided her to lie backwards as I followed her down and blanketed her with my hard nakedness. My cock felt scorching hot as it pressed against her warm skin, and a hiss escaped my lips as I rubbed it against her belly, my hips moving of their own accord, desperate for the contact.

My hands were so familiar with her body by now, but today, after the fear of death had loomed over us all, I was appreciating just how lucky I was and felt like I was exploring her for the first time again. Stella seemed to be sharing the same mind-set, because she was greedily running her fingers across the bumps and ridges of my abs, trailing through my happy trail, gripping at my biceps, and circling my tight nipples until I cursed. It seemed like she couldn't get enough of me, either.

I'm not sure I'd ever worshipped her so thoroughly, which was quite a statement, seeing as I prided myself on knowing every single sweet spot on her body. I wanted to be the best and most attentive lover she had ever had, and I thought I'd always done that. But tonight – tonight everything felt brand-new and priceless. It was like our first time all over again.

Stella began to writhe around below me, the small noises she made driving me insane with lust, so I shifted and slid a hand between her legs, smiling smugly when I felt just how wet she was for me. Imagining all the things I'd like to do to her delicious pussy, I sighed, irritatingly aware of our time constraints.

'I'd love to taste you right now, and spend an age with my face buried between your thighs, but I'm aware of the time and I don't really fancy the manager getting an eyeful of you spread naked before him.' With the way I felt about her, I knew I'd probably burst a blood vessel from stress if another man saw my girl naked.

Moving so I was sitting upright on the bench and leaning back against the wall, I then helped Stella up to straddle me, her knees falling on either side of my thighs and cushioned by the thick towels.

With a happy sigh, my girl lowered herself down, using one hand between us to position the thick head of my cock with her opening and gripping my shoulder for balance with the other. God, she felt so good.

I placed my hands on her hips, but didn't grip, even though I was desperate to exert my usual control and pull her down onto me hard and fast. This was about cherishing, I had to keep reminding myself of that, but it felt important somehow. Instead, I busied my needy hands by massaging her skin, making goose pimples of desire flood the parts I touched.

Stella stared me in the eyes as she edged the first inch of me inside her damp entrance, and I watched with pleasure as her eyes became heavy-lidded and she bit down on her lower lip, struggling for control. I must have had a similar expression my face, because the urge to jerk upwards was almost overpowering.

I loved that she was just as affected by this as I was. It reassured me that no matter how fucked up I was, I still had Stella. She got me like no one ever had. If I believed in pansy shit like soul mates, then I'd say that perhaps she was mine.

The slide of her channel taking another inch of me caused her to gasp as I felt her muscles stretching around me, a sensation so fucking amazing that I let out a strangled moan. It seemed to vibrate right through me to where we were joined.

Bracing herself on my shoulders, Stella began to let her

legs relax. She edged them sideways so she dropped down the rest of my length in one go, causing us both to inhale sharply then bark out curses, mine being the loudest.

'Fuck, Stella!' Finally, I gave in and gripped her tighter, feeling like I might break the skin at her hips as I threw my head back from the pleasure shooting through my cock.

'Yes. Tighter,' she murmured, and I knew that the slight tinge of pain from my increased grip was welcomed by my girl. She liked a dash of pain with her sex; it heightened her arousal. Her lusty response to it always heightened mine as well, so it was a win-win situation, really.

Biting on her lower lip, Stella circled herself down and ground even deeper onto my throbbing cock. It felt fucking amazing, but even with the overwhelming sensations I couldn't drag my gaze away from where she was biting on her lip. The tender flesh was already reddening, and that irritated the fuck out of me.

'Lip, Stella.' My ground-out words were enough, because she immediately freed it, looking chastised.

'Sorry, Sir, blame it on the heat of the moment?' I could only assume she wasn't just referring to the heat in the sauna around us, because this was some seriously hot sex happening right now.

Nodding my acceptance of her excuse, I leaned forwards and captured her lip in between my own, gently sucking and soothing it with my tongue before pressing inside her mouth and kissing her hard and deep.

Stella started to shift, as if she were about to up the pace, but once again the emotions of today came rushing up on me. I held her still, tugging her firmly down so my throbbing shaft was buried deep inside her, feeling like it was going to burn us both from the inside out.

Leaning forwards, I pressed my forehead against hers and brought one hand up to slide into the hair by her temple. 'I love you, Stella, so fucking much.' I didn't say

155

those words nearly as much as she deserved, so I decided to blurt them out now while they were at the forefront of my mind.

We were both panting, our breath mingling in the tiny space between us, although I was so turned on that my breathing sounded more like I was hyperventilating. Stella was barely moving, clutching me close and seeming to want to absorb us.

Just us.

Joined together.

After several moments, she brought her hands up to cup my face. I watched her eyes closing as we shared the tender moment, but they soon opened again as I spoke.

'You and Will … you mean everything to me.' My voice was low, because emotional declarations like this still weren't easy for me. In fact, it was almost so quiet that she might struggle to hear it, but I hoped that even if that were the case, then perhaps my eyes would show the depth of my feelings for her.

'I'm so sorry you had to go through that today.' Pressing my lips to hers again, she sucked in a breath and squeezed her eyes shut tight, but not before one single tear slid free. 'I love you too, Nathan. I can't ever imagine being without you.'

'Never …' I wanted to say more, to tell her that would never happen, not if I had anything to say about it, but my throat closed up.

Sliding my hands across the slick skin of her neck, I clutched her to me and nodded instead, my throat still too tight to return the sentiment as I desperately struggled to hold my emotions in check. I could have lost her. Stella and Will … They both could have been gone today, in the blink of an eye. It was a thought so horrific and unbearable that goose bumps immediately rose on my skin, and I had to take a moment to compose myself before I forced my mind to focus on the positives again.

We were safe and we were together. Literally. I was buried so deep within her that we'd struggle to get much more together than this.

Finally, I felt able to speak. 'You don't need to imagine that, because that will never fucking happen,' I stated with such absolute certainly that Stella gave me a little squeeze.

After my heated declaration, I decided that we'd done enough talking for now and used my grip on her hips to set Stella circling on my shaft again. Practically purring her contentment, she kissed me and followed my lead.

Pure pleasure pinged around my system, focusing in my balls as her tight channel clenched around me again and again as she moved. Stella moaned, long and low, catapulting my arousal and causing my skin to almost sizzle in every spot where we were connected.

The rhythm we set was slower than usual, but seemed to suit us both perfectly today. I would usually take over at this point and use rougher thrusts and movements than this, but seeing as I was set on showing Stella just what she meant to me, I didn't. In fact, I let her completely lead the pace, giving just the occasional upward thrust when the pressure in my balls got too much.

Our gaze stayed connected the whole time, then Stella began to move with more purpose. With our faces close and our breath mixing, it was one of the most intimate experiences we'd shared for a long time, but probably what we'd both needed tonight to help calm us. I had certainly needed it, and it was working a treat because all my stresses and worries felt a million miles away, as all I could focus on was the utter contentment I felt when I had this woman in my arms.

Utter contentment mixed with red-hot lust.

This was probably the exact definition of "lovemaking", if there was indeed one, because that was exactly what we were doing – creating a physical impression of the love that we shared and reaffirming it to each other after the stresses of the day. If it hadn't felt so fucking good I might have been a bit embarrassed by the sappiness of that thought.

As Stella continued to move on top of me, I started to add in more upward thrusts knowing that she'd need attention on either her clit or her G-spot to help her tip over into climax.

I'm fairly sure my expression was the most open it had been in a long time, my face no doubt declaring every feeling I had for this incredible woman, even if my lips were currently silent.

Stella's channel tightened around my cock in a sure-fire signal that she was getting near to climax. Sensing her imminent release, I began to jerk my hips upwards, grunting at the pleasure that exploded in my cock as I did so. Fuck, I was so close. Our bodies were slick against each other, but I still managed perfect hits to her clit and G-spot with every thrust, and suddenly I could feel her tipping over the edge of pleasure and falling apart in my arms.

The skin below my fingers tensed, and heat flooded Stella's face as her orgasm reared up on her and caused her to scream her enjoyment. It felt pretty bloody good for me, too, because in her climax Stella's body clamped around my cock like a fist and I knew I wouldn't last long.

Cursing loudly, I gripped her hips and thrust upwards three more times before burying my head in her neck and clamping my teeth down on the skin to hide my yell as I began to release inside her.

My climax went on and on, draining me and yet somehow exhilarating me at the same time.

We clung together as we came down from our high, my cock still twitching away inside her with aftershocks of my orgasm, and Stella's pussy grasping at my shaft in response, as if they were high-fiving each other in celebration of a breath-taking performance.

Opening my eyes, I leaned back and smiled down at my girl when I saw just how content she looked. She was so sated that her eyes had begun to droop. 'I'm so comfy I could fall asleep right here,' she murmured as I caged her against me with my arms to make sure she didn't fall. Being buried deep inside her and surrounded by the warmth of not only her body, but the sauna, too, felt so ideal that I wasn't in a great rush to move, either.

Moving would mean going back to face real life again, and I was happy to block that out for another few minutes, so I let my lips explore, licking, kissing, and sucking at her neck as I gently caressed the soft skin of her back.

Finally, I knew we had to leave, otherwise we'd risk being caught by the manager in our intimate position. 'Let's get you to bed, hmm?' I murmured beside her ear, bringing Stella back from the brink of slumber as she blinked up at me sleepily.

As we were retying our dressing gowns, the door to the spa opened and the smartly dressed hotel manager from earlier breezed in to check on us.

Talk about good timing! A minute earlier and he'd have found me buried to the hilt inside Stella. Rearranging my features into an expression that gave away nothing of my earlier lust, I thanked him and gave him a generous tip for opening the spa out of hours for us. Then I took Stella's hand to lead her back to our room.

After that steamy exchange, and the draining exhaustion from today's harrowing events, we were both so tired that we fell straight into bed. Stella sighed with happiness when I tucked her into our four-poster bed and pulled her against my chest. Seconds later, I felt the welcome heaviness of sleep blanketing me.

Chapter Twenty-Two

Stella

The following morning, I felt refreshed and amazingly well rested considering all that had happened the day before. Nathan's plan to have the massage had been brilliant, and between that and the unusually gentle lovemaking afterwards I'd fallen into such a deep sleep that I hadn't even shifted position during the night.

Nathan was still curled around my back when I woke, and I smiled at just how tightly he was holding me. It was like he couldn't get me close enough, even in his sleep, but as I listened to his regular breathing I could tell he was already awake, and so snuggled back into his firm embrace and heard him hum his approval. 'Morning.'

'Morning, sweetheart.' Nathan nuzzled his lips into my neck and kissed me, and I felt a slight ache there as I tilted to give him better access. Recalling the power of his climax last night and the way he'd bitten my neck to quieten his yell, I suspected I had yet another love bite.

'As much as I'd like to stay here all day with you in my arms, we need to check out soon.'

Blinking in surprise, I glanced at the clock on the bedside table and saw that it was gone half-past ten in the morning. 'Half-ten?' I squeaked in shock, amazed I'd slept so long.

'Yep. We must have needed it. Come on, babe, let's jump in the shower.'

After the shower, Nathan made some calls to see if the

Cotswold house was ready to move into, and I phoned Becky to check in on her. I managed to get through to speak directly to her, and relaxed when she told me that the doctors were really pleased with her morning test results, and she should be released later today.

Now Nathan and I were back in his car and heading to the Hampstead house to get some clothes, but with every mile we covered I felt my good spirits dropping. We were heading back to the "crime scene", and as we pulled up outside the place we had called home for nearly a year I felt the same dread as last night settle in my stomach. I really didn't want to go inside. I knew the police had cleared out and the cleaning team had reassured us that all traces of yesterday's events had been removed, but even so … I'd gone through a hell of an experience in there, and it was still sitting heavily on my nerves.

Beside me, Nathan was his usual gruff self, staring up at the house with a look of grim determination on his face. He'd been quiet during the drive, and I knew this must all be just as hard for him, if not harder, so I dragged up my reserves of bravery and offered to accompany him inside.

'I'll come in with you …'

He shook his head, and his eyes remained locked on the door to the house. 'No, I'll be fine.'

He was saying no, but I could see the tension in his jaw so I pulled in a breath for bravery and jumped out of the car. 'Come on, we'll be quicker if we both go in.'

Once he'd locked the car, Nathan joined me at the steps. 'OK, how about I make some calls to removal companies about getting the rest of our stuff packed and moved next week, and you nip upstairs and pack some cases for us to last a few days? Get whatever you want for you and Will and just pack me a couple of casual outfits and about three suits.'

I raised an eyebrow as I tried to supress an amused

smirk.

'What?'

'I'm just surprised that you're letting me touch your precious suits, that's all.' It was hardly the time for joking around, but I couldn't resist one little dig to ease some of the tension. 'I mean, what if I fold them?' Folding his precious suits and putting creases where creases didn't belong would be a nightmare for Nathan.

His eyes narrowed at my joke, but even after all of our recent stress I saw a twinkle of humour reflected in his gaze, so my distraction technique seemed to be working.

'You wouldn't dare …'

'I might, if it causes that look on your face.'

Before I had time to tease him further, Nathan swooped down and captured me in his embrace, kissing me soundly on the lips and stopping any further comment. 'Three suits, *hung* in a suit bag. No folding, or else I'll redden your arse so much you won't be able to sit down for days.'

Hmm. It might be worth ruining one of his prized suits just to get that "punishment".

Once I'd made it through the front door and up the stairs I found that being back inside the house wasn't so bad. The upstairs rooms all held really fond memories for me, and this was the place we'd brought William home to after he was born, so I focused on those thoughts instead of recalling yesterday's traumatic events.

It didn't take me long to shove some clothes in a couple of bags. I packed the most for William, because he was obviously the messiest, and then I pulled out a few pairs of jeans for Nathan and me, some tops, a couple of jumpers each, and, of course, his three suits.

Hung.

Not folded.

I might not have packed many clothes, but by the time

162

I'd gathered together everything William would need at the new house I had quite a pile of stuff accumulated at the bottom of the stairs.

I trotted down with the last load, then paused and listened for the sound of Nathan talking on the phone, wondering if he was still speaking to removal companies. The house seemed silent, but I was certain he wouldn't have gone outside without me. After checking the downstairs study and kitchen and finding them empty, I nervously eyed the door to the lounge and felt a wave of queasiness settle in my stomach again.

It was stupid, because I knew the body would be gone, and the room cleared, but I felt really scared about going inside.

Edging forwards, I placed a hand on the wood. 'Nathan?' He didn't reply, but I could definitely hear movement inside, so I pushed open the door and peered around it into the room. My stomach might have been feeling queasy before, but it absolutely fell when I took in the sight before me.

Nathan stood to the side of the room, furiously scrubbing at the wall with a sponge from the kitchen. His suit jacket had been thrown carelessly over a dining chair, and his shirt sleeves were rolled up so haphazardly that he hardly looked anything like my usually pristine man. Add to that his reddened cheeks, crazy hair, bulging eyes, and low muttering and he seemed practically set to explode.

What the heck was going on?

He was still rubbing on the wall almost viciously, and when I glanced down I saw that he had a small bowl of soapy water to his side. This peculiar sight was enough to get me over my fear of the room, so I quickly entered and ran to his side.

'Nathan? What's going on? What are you doing?'
'Blood.'

163

There had been a special clean-up team in here last night, and I could see no trace of what had occurred yesterday, so I had no clue what he was talking about, but I reached down to try to stop his agitated rubbing. As soon as I touched his forearm he abruptly stopped and stood up, looking around the room and avoiding my worried gaze.

'They missed a bit. There was a spot of blood on the wall. *His* blood.' Nathan glared at the carpet, and I turned, realising exactly where we were waiting – right beside the dining table where his father had hit his head and died. Jesus. The carpet was clean now, but Mr Jackson had been lying just a foot away from here. *Shit.*

'Needed it clean.' Nathan was still staring at the carpet as if considering moving his scrubbing there next. He chewed viciously on his lower lip and didn't seem to be able to form full sentences at the moment. I was fairly sure he was having a meltdown of some kind, because he was clearly distressed, but I had absolutely no idea what to do.

His face had turned almost puce now, the veins in his neck were pulsing, and his eyes were unblinking. Before I could say any vaguely supportive words he dropped the sponge, threw his head back, and let out an almighty roar that was so loud it made the glasses in the minibar shake.

Fuck.

Lowering his head, he glanced at his hand with distaste as if the blood had somehow gone through the sponge into his skin. Then he looked up at me with such a tortured expression on his face that it nearly broke me.

The reality of his father's death had obviously just sunk in, and he was clearly struggling with it, but I had no idea what to say to comfort him. His father had been a vile human being, and I certainly didn't feel particularly sad that he was gone.

He pulled in a deep breath and shook his head again, sending his hair flopping messily over his forehead. Then he closed his eyes, seeming utterly lost, before taking a step back so he was leaning against the wall. He held his wet hand out to the side of him as if disgusted by it, which given his handwashing compulsion was a high possibility, and then tipped his head back.

In this position, I couldn't see his eyes, but his chest began rapidly rising and falling as he seemed to be gripped by some sort of panic attack, and I knew I needed to act quickly to help him.

I dropped my handbag and ran to the kitchen, searching the counters and grabbing the first tea towel I could find. Having doused it with water and some liquid soap, I sprinted back to Nathan. I then gently took his clenched hand into mine. Opening out his fingers, I saw that his skin was completely clean, but perhaps if I washed it anyway he would feel better. Cleansed, perhaps.

I quickly wiped the palm and fingers before cleaning the joints of his knuckles and doing my best to get around his nails, too. It wasn't as thorough a job as my obsessive-compulsive man would have done, but for now it would have to do.

He watched me silently the entire time, then raised his head, his eyes meeting mine and catching me in his intense gaze. And just when I thought he'd calmed down, Nathan managed to shock me further.

He started to cry.

My big, strong, tough guy was crying. He took two huge, ragged breaths, which I thought were sighs, but were actually sobs, and then the tears began. Floods of them. Within seconds, his face was soaked as his entire body shook with the intensity of his wracking sobs. Seconds later, his legs gave way and he slid down the wall until he was sitting on the floor with his hands buried in his hair and tears running down his cheeks, looking completely and utterly defeated.

Holy shit. I'd thought he'd been dealing with this all pretty well up until our arrival back here, but clearly, he had just been bottling everything up. Knowing Nathan, he'd probably been holding himself together for my sake, but as far as I could tell, his internal pressure valve had just exploded.

'Stella … need you,' he whispered, breaking me from my panicked thoughts. It had all happened so quickly that I could barely keep up, but somehow his words registered in my shocked brain and prompted me to try to help him. The only thing I could think of was with some physical contact.

I dropped down onto the floor. Lifting one leg over him, I carefully lowered myself so I was straddling his lap. Leaning into his chest, I wrapped my arms around his stiff shoulders and did my best attempt at blanketing him with my body, even though I could feel his muscles were like granite below me.

After I'd been holding him for a few minutes I gradually felt his breathing settle and his muscles begin to relax. 'Do you want to talk about it?'

'No.' He practically snarled the word, his emotions rearing to the surface again so quickly that it made my muscles tense up. 'I want to get out of here.'

Relaxing slightly, I nodded. That I could do. I stood up and offered my hands to help him up but Nathan ignored me and pushed himself to standing before averting his eyes, huffing out an irritated breath and stalking from the room.

Shit. His detached behaviour was starting to really worry me now. I knew he must be feeling embarrassed because of his tears, and no doubt confused about his feelings towards his father, but the fact he was pushing me away was a real concern.

Nathan had done this once before, back when we'd first got together and his feelings for me had become too much for him to handle. He'd distanced himself from me and tried to walk away from us. He'd come around in the end, though, and we were so much stronger now than we had been back then, so surely he wouldn't do something similar a second time?

My man had a volatile relationship with his emotions, I knew that very well, but all I could do was hope that instead of pushing me away this time, he might turn to me for support. He had said he needed me earlier, which was a good start.

Suspecting that his aloofness was just a knee-jerk reaction to his tears I didn't try to push anything on him just yet. Instead, I stood back to give him space and prayed that, given a little time, he'd let me get close enough to help him recover.

I followed him from the room, feeling sick with nerves. We silently grabbed the bags from the hall and left the house, the slam of the front door ringing in the quiet of the morning around us and making me wince.

Chapter Twenty-Three

Stella

'Is everything all right, love?' My mum sounded worried as she answered the phone to me, and well she might. Things were not all right in the slightest. Nathan had refused to say a single word to me since his tears and was now holed up in the car while I stood on the pavement, making the call. Seeing his tight posture and blank expression, I chewed on my lower lip, trying to press down the panic that was threatening to engulf me.

'Honestly? No. Yesterday was hellish, and Nathan's really struggling with it all.' Which was a huge understatement, but about the best I could say without completely freaking out. I gave my mum a brief rundown of the situation and she offered to have Will for another night and drive him up to the new house the following lunchtime.

Closing my eyes in relief, I pulled in a shaky breath. I cast another glance at Nathan, who was now staring at his clenched fists. 'Mum, that would be amazing, but only if you're sure?'

'I love having him, Stella, and it sounds like you need to give Nathan your attention right now. The poor boy must be beside himself after his father's death.' Mum and Dad knew Nathan wasn't really in contact with his parents, but they weren't aware of his history, or the fact that his dad had been abusive. Now was hardly the time to go into those details, so I just nodded and thanked her again.

'It's no trouble,' she assured me. 'Besides, we want to see your new house now it's furnished, so this way we can do both.'

I couldn't exactly see Nathan wanting to run a guided tour tomorrow, but I kept quiet about that and accepted her kind offer. 'OK, thanks so much, Mum.'

'It's not a problem at all, sweetheart. You two must be feeling quite shocked by everything that's happened.'

You could say that again. Staring at the blue sky above, I tried to block the myriad of grisly images that threatened to invade my brain again.

'We don't want to intrude,' she went on, 'but your father and I are happy to stay for a few days next week, too, if you like, just until Marion decides if she's coming back or not.'

'OK, let me talk to Nathan and I'll let you know.' Glancing at the car again, I saw Nathan clenching and unclenching his fists and decided I needed to get him home as soon as possible. 'I've got to go, Mum. I'll see you tomorrow.'

To my amazement, Nathan let me drive, silently moving to the passenger seat and belting himself in, which was just another show of how screwed up he must be feeling. With the tension inside the car, it felt like the journey to the new house took hours, but in reality, it was just over forty minutes from South Hampstead.

That was one of the reasons Nathan and I had chosen the location; we had all the benefits of living in the gorgeous countryside of the Cotswolds, but were within easy reach of London if we needed it.

Arriving here for the first time since the house was completed should have been an exciting moment, but Nathan had remained quiet and withdrawn in car and I was starting to worry that I wasn't going to be able to drag him out of it. He could be so stubborn when he wanted, but he was an immensely proud man, and I had a feeling that his emotional breakdown in front of me would be laying heavy on his mind. We might be together, and stronger than ever, but Nathan was fiercely defensive where it came to his outward appearance. He didn't tolerate weakness in himself, at all. It was a trait that had no doubt been engrained into him by his father when he was younger, I realised bitterly.

As soon as I stopped the car, Nathan jumped out, grabbed a couple of the bags, and made his way to the front door without waiting for me. Watching him go, I ran a hand though my hair, not sure how to deal with the silent treatment that I was getting.

When I walked through the front door, I saw that the house looked much as it had when we'd last visited, but now the builders' dust was gone and it looked and smelt spotlessly clean. I was keen to go and explore the newly finished kitchen, but that could wait. Right now, I had one priority, and he was currently stalking around the hallway with his shoulders hunched and a tight expression on his face.

I drew in a deep breath and watched him for several seconds before deciding to try something he normally wouldn't tolerate, but just might need today.

I was going to try to top him.

Right now, he was so closed off that I couldn't see any other way of getting him to loosen up. Of course, it might fail miserably, and cause him to pull away from me even more, but I was lost for any other ideas to try.

Holding my back as straight as I could, I strode towards him and took hold of one of his hands before turning for the staircase.

'Come with me.' I nearly added "please", as I usually would, but managed to leave it off at the last minute so my words were more of a demand than a request. I needed him to follow me, otherwise this plan would nosedive before it even got started.

170

At my words, and the slight tug on his hand, Nathan raised his gaze and made eye contact with me for almost the first time since his breakdown at our old house, but he remained rigidly in place. It was like tugging on a dead weight. 'Now, Nathan, don't make me repeat myself,' I added, my tone as firm as I could make it. He continued to stare at me almost blankly for another few seconds, then, to my surprise, he gave one small nod and took a step to follow me.

Holy crap, it's working! I was sorely tempted to tell him off for nodding and not answering me audibly, but I sensed that might cause him to withdraw again, so I stowed my cheek away for later.

Walking with purpose, I led him up the stairs, through the master bedroom and straight into the bathroom, glad that I had accurately recalled the room layout and not ended up getting lost.

My heart was pounding by the time I let go of his hand, but I calmly set about turning on the bath taps. Then I turned back to him and jerked my chin towards him.

'Take your clothes off,' I requested, wishing that my voice held half the volume and demand that his usually did in situations like this. Just one word from Dominant Nathan could have my knees trembling and panties soaked.

At my words, he frowned, seeming to finally catch up on my whole "topping from the bottom" thing. As his jaw tensed he very slowly shook his head.

Shit.

He's saying no.

What did I do now? Swallowing hard, I tried to imagine what he would do if the roles were reversed. After a second, I was still convinced that this was the way to go right now, so I crossed my arms over my chest, just as he would, and raised an eyebrow in my best impression of him. 'Nathan, earlier you said you needed me. Well, you have me, all of

171

me, and right now I want to take care of you like you always do for me.' I licked my lips and pushed my luck by trying one more command. 'Now take your clothes off.' My tone this time was far stronger, and hopefully just what he needed to kick him into action.

My man stood motionless for a second longer, his eyes fixed to mine, as he appeared to battle with my request. As he stood frozen to the spot I'd almost convinced myself that he was going to say no again. Then, finally, he blinked, and the corner of his mouth gave just the tiniest of twitches.

Was he about to comply?

His gaze remained locked with mine, and then finally he took hold of the knot in his tie and gripped it, his lips curling with that tiny smile again. My pulse jumped at the sight – it looked like I might have won the battle. He might still be stressed, but at least he seemed to be finding my pathetic attempt at controlling him amusing. Well, good. Amused was better than withdrawn and silent.

Without breaking eye contact, Nathan pulled his tie free and looped it over the towel rail, then popped the first button at his collar open. Slowly, button by button, he began to undo his shirt, until it was loose and hanging open at the front, then he slid it from his broad shoulders before carefully folding it and placing it on the sink unit. I watched avidly the entire time; his firm muscles rippled with his movements, actually making my mouth salivate with the need to touch and taste him. His socks followed, then his trousers, each item folded to perfection and added to the pile, and I found myself fidgeting on the spot and really struggling with the role reversal of this scene.

How he kept such a cool front when I was undressing in front of him I had no idea, because the temptation to rip my clothes off and leap on him was almost overwhelming.

Once he was just in his boxers he held his hands out to

the side and quirked an eyebrow. 'Shall I dance for you now?'

As tempting as it was to laugh, I didn't. Instead, I shook my head slowly and unfolded my arms before placing my hands on my hips. 'I said take your clothes off. That means all of them.'

His eyes widened briefly in surprise, then, to my amazement, he obliged me by bending down and removing his boxers, which were also folded and piled on the counter.

Wow. Submissive Nathan really was quite a sight to behold.

I had no intention of making this a sexual scene, I wanted to reassure him, comfort him, and support him, but the sight of his erect cock bobbing free did at least reassure me that I was on the right track with my actions, no matter how strange they felt.

Swallowing hard, I dragged my eyes up from his arousal and jerked a thumb towards the nearly full bathtub as I began to take off my own clothes. 'In you get.'

In my haste, my undressing wasn't quite as organised as his. There was no folding; instead, I bundled all my clothes into a ball and popped them in the wash bin before turning back towards the bath and coming to a halt.

Instead of relaxing back in the water as I had expected, Nathan sat in the centre of the tub with his arms wrapped around his knees, staring at me expectantly as if waiting for me to tell him what to do next.

Was this what I looked like when I submitted to him? Passive? Eager to please? Trusting? I supposed it must be. I wouldn't want to switch roles like this often – it just didn't feel quite right to me – but it was actually very interesting to see this all from the opposite perspective for a change.

I couldn't quite decide what to do first. Should I climb in behind him and encourage him to lay back on me and talk? Or snuggle into his chest in front of him?

173

In the end, I did neither. The bath was bigger than usual tubs, almost oval in shape, with two Jacuzzi-styles seats moulded into the plastic at the back, but I decided to take advantage of the space and sit facing him.

Before I tried to get him to talk, I wanted him to relax, and I knew that feeling really, really clean would do that for him. It was part of his obsessive-compulsive behaviour, but if it worked I didn't care.

Sex would probably relax him, too, but seeing as he'd had a pretty major breakdown earlier I thought it was most important to try to get him to talk to me, and sex with Nathan might be many things, but conducive to conversation it wasn't. In fact, I was usually too exhausted to even slur a sentence after he'd had his wicked way with me.

Without speaking, I climbed into the bath and set about arranging him how I wanted. I peeled his hands apart and placed them in the water by his sides, then encouraged him to sit cross-legged opposite me, all of which he complied with. Then I simply began taking care of my man. I squirted shower gel into my hands and soaped up his arms, shoulders, neck and chest until every body part above the water was covered in lather. Once I was happy with the bubbles covering him, I used a soft sponge to collect handfuls of water and rinse him off by squeezing it over his body.

His hands were next. I took my time cleaning them to his exacting standards, getting in all the creases of skin and using the file next to the bath to clean under the nails, too.

It was a little trickier to clean his legs, as they were under the water, but I gave it my best attempt and used the sponge to help me as I worked my way from his hips all the way to his toes.

When I'd finished, I wordlessly held the sponge out to him, hoping he might take it and reciprocate, as it would

174

focus his mind on something other than troublesome thoughts. He did, but not before raising his eyebrows and giving me a tiny glimpse of a wicked smile.

'I think you missed a bit.' His gaze dropped to the water lapping by his groin and then rose to mine again, his pupils dilated with arousal.

My cheeks flamed, but he was right; I had deliberately avoided that area. As tempting as he was – and believe me, Nathan naked, aroused, and wet was always a test of my self-restraint – I was determined to keep this non-sexual.

For now, anyway.

If we talked and addressed today's issues, then maybe later we could progress things in that direction to further aid our relaxation. But not yet. As much as he'd like to believe it, not everything could be solved by sex.

'I know. But this isn't about sex,' I murmured softly.

Nathan's nostrils flared slightly as he drew in a deep breath of understanding, but then he took the sponge from me and began to return the favour of washing me. He started with my arms and shoulders, then moved down to my breasts. Instead of avoiding them, he deliberately paid extra attention to them, the bastard. I didn't allow my groans of arousal to escape, even though my beaded nipples would have made it obvious that his attention was very much enjoyed.

Instead of leaning around me to do my back, Nathan actually shifted me around so I was facing away from him, and began to run the soapy sponge across the backs of my shoulders.

My eyes had just closed from the relaxing sensations running across my skin, and it was at this point that he suddenly decided to talk.

'I … I'm sorry for my meltdown earlier.' I heard him let out a sigh, as if his first words had been a relief to get out. 'I shouldn't have snapped at you, but I was really struggling

175

with my emotions. It felt like a pressure valve had exploded inside me.'

I gave him time to see if he was going to continue, and when he remained silent I nodded. 'I'd say that is a perfectly normal response to yesterday's events.' I didn't try to turn and face him; I suspected that Nathan found it easier to express himself when the pressure of eye contact had been removed, but I did reach under the water and give one of his thighs a supportive rub.

It was as if my contact reassured him enough to continue, because he blurted out a question so hurriedly it was almost as if he needed to expel the words from inside him. 'I feel so confused, Stella. Do you think my father ever loved me?'

God. What a question. Especially given what I knew about his childhood, and the relationship between his mother and father. I genuinely wasn't sure Mr Jackson had ever been capable of love, but I had a feeling that wasn't what Nathan needed to hear, though, so I desperately attempted to put together a tactful response.

'I'm sure he cared in his own way, Nathan. I just think that maybe his thoughts and ideas were a little different to how we think and act.'

Under the water, his hands settled on my hips and began to knead and massage the skin as if he needed the movement to calm himself. 'Maybe. I thought I'd resolved how I felt about him years ago ... But now he's gone ... I feel like all the memories have come flooding back. After everything he did to Nicholas and me ... I ... I shouldn't feel sad. *I can't.*' I felt the warmth of his forehead on my back as he dropped it forwards and took several deep breaths. 'But I almost do. I feel ... I'm not sure, but it's close to sadness and I hate that. He made my childhood hell, threatened you and Will, and hurt Rebecca ... He doesn't deserve my sadness.'

I truly didn't know what to say. Losing your abusive father must be one hell of a weird thing to go through; the mixture of grief and relief so difficult to analyse and cope with. 'I was thinking about it in the car on the way up here, and I think I worked out why I'm so messed up over it.'

I remained silent, hoping he'd choose to share with me, but not about to push him into it. 'I always thought that maybe one day Dad would come to his senses and see that what he'd done to us as kids was wrong, but he never did.'

And now he never could.

Suddenly, I realised exactly what Nathan must be feeling, a complete loss of any tiny thread of remaining hope, but before I could offer him support he voiced exactly what was going through my mind. 'Now he's actually dead it puts to rest the final hope I had that he might one day turn out to be the dad I'd always wanted.'

My eyes closed as pain for Nathan swept through my system. After all these years, all the time that had passed, he had still hoped that one day his abuser would turn into the thing he'd always wanted – a real dad. His dad. God, that was just so heartbreaking that my eyes stung and I felt a hot tear escape my eye and trickle down my face.

'I hated you seeing me cry, Stella. I hate being weak, but my head felt monumentally fucked up. I think things are clearer now.' Nathan snaked his arms around me and encouraged me to lean back into him, which I did. He enveloped me in the warmth of his body, and I raised my hands to hold his forearms in support.

Clearing my thick throat, I swallowed and let my head fall onto his chest. 'Crying is a natural way to vent emotion, Nathan. It's not a weakness, and neither is asking for help.'

Nathan didn't give an immediate reply to that, so I stayed quiet, too, slipping my hand down his strong forearm and smiling as he made the first move and linked his fingers with mine.

177

An idea sprung to my mind, but I really wasn't sure how open to it Nathan would be. He was so different to when we'd first met – more relaxed, better at expressing his feelings instead of just clamming up – but this might still be a step too far for him. It was worth a shot, though.

'Rebecca has mentioned that Nicholas sees a therapist sometimes, to help with his emotional issues … She said it's been really useful.' Instead of ploughing straight on and suggesting he could try it, too, I left the sentence dangling to see how Nathan reacted.

When he didn't immediately tense up or dismiss the idea, I decided to push my luck a little.

'Maybe you could try a session with him? He would be able to help you balance out all these difficult feelings.'

Nathan gave a grunt below me, which sounded neither positive nor negative, so I gave his hand a supportive squeeze which seemed to prompt him into talking. 'Yeah, Nicholas has told me about him. Dr Philips.'

A loud sigh blew across my shoulder and Nathan rested his head sideways so he could press his lips into my hair.

'I thought Nicholas was weak when he first told me he was seeing him, but it really seems to have helped. I suppose talking to someone completely detached from the situation might be useful. Would you …?' There was a long pause, then Nathan spoke again, his voice so quiet I could barely hear it. 'Would you come with me?'

At his words, I felt almost overwhelmed with relief and happiness. He wasn't shutting me out; in fact, he was doing the complete opposite and actively inviting me to be a part of his recovery. This man was my everything, but maybe I was his everything, too.

'Of course.' Nathan gripped me tighter and I snuggled back into his embrace.

The man wrapped around me might be a million miles away from the no-strings Dominant I'd initially got

178

together with, but he was most certainly the man I had fallen head over heels in love with.

Chapter Twenty-Four

Nathan

Tonight had certainly been ... enlightening. When I'd first realised that Stella had been trying to take control of me, I'd nearly baulked and shut her out. Visions of my father forcing me to my knees had filled my mind, and my age-old mantra of *no one can control me, I am in ultimate control* had immediately fought for space in my mind.

But this wasn't my father, this was Stella, and as I'd looked into her firm but supportive eyes I'd realised that she wasn't trying to control *me*, she was trying to take control of the situation. An already fucked-up situation that I'd let get wildly out of hand by failing to regulate my emotions. Once again, my girl had managed to read me perfectly and respond in the exact way I'd needed. It fucking blew my mind that we were so attuned to each other, but we were. She was incredible; able to see inside my head almost better than I could.

My mind felt clearer after talking it over, and although I didn't feel indifferent to my father's death as I suspected Nicholas might, I did understand why I'd had the strange collapse of my composure when it had sunk in that he was dead.

He was never going to be the dad I'd always hoped for, but I wouldn't let that hold me back. I would make it my life's mission to be everything he never was. An amazing father to William and the best partner for Stella that I could.

Jesus. I'm turning into a right sap. Rolling my eyes, I adjusted Stella in my arms and decided I'd had enough of the mushy crap for now. It was time for me to get our balance back on track; I wanted to be in control again. Needed to. And as much as I had needed her intervention earlier, I felt the inherent need to discuss it and make it clear that I didn't plan on letting it happen again.

'Come on, the water's getting cool. Let's get out.'

I helped Stella stand up, then followed her from the tub and grabbed a fluffy towel to wrap around her body. Draping it around her shoulders, I retained my hold on the ends and used the towel to pull her closer as I gave her an amused glance. 'You never fail to surprise me, Stella.'

From her look of confusion, Stella didn't have a clue what I was referring to, so I placed a brief kiss on the tip of her nose and explained. 'Topping me like that, I hadn't expected it.'

Her cheeks flushed in that way I loved, and she briefly bit down on her lower lip. 'Oh, that …' She paused, darting her gaze to mine as if worried that she'd overstepped my boundaries. 'It only worked because you let me get away with it.'

That was one way of looking at it, I supposed. 'Maybe.'

Stella pouted briefly. 'I wasn't very good at it, though, was I?'

'On the contrary, it was surprisingly hot,' I admitted, enjoying the way Stella's eyes widened at my confession, but it was no word of a lie. Her little show before bath time where she'd demanded I remove my clothes had made me hard as granite within seconds.

I wasn't a switch, though, of that I was certain. Giving momentary control to Stella was one thing, but the need for control was too deeply engrained within me for me to ever really enjoy submitting to someone.

The last person to truly control me had been my father. But the day I carried a half-dead Nicholas out of that house, I had vowed I would never let anyone control me ever again. I didn't want to bring another downer on our evening, so I kept my thoughts to myself, instead simply letting her know where I stood. 'Not that we'll be doing it again anytime soon, though.'

Her shoulders visibly relaxed and my girl flashed me an adorable smile as her cheeks flushed. 'Thank God for that. I don't mind taking the lead when I'm at work, but with you …' She gave a shrug. 'It's different … I like how we are. It's perfect.'

And it really was. We were like two jigsaw pieces; my need for control fitted completely with Stella's need to submit.

I placed a quick kiss on her lips. We then began to dry ourselves off and headed to the bedroom. As usual, we both remained naked as we climbed under the covers before snuggling closer.

Stella and I still had the same high sex drives we'd had when we met. Often, we would make love before sleeping. Occasionally, we'd indulge in some form of kinky play, and on other days I'd simply lay a deep, passionate kiss on her that had her writhing in my arms, horny and aroused, and I'd whisper in her ear that I'd wake her up later by slipping inside her. I loved that game, but it was incredibly draining because it took all of my self-control to not take her immediately. I usually managed to last an hour or so, and wake her up sleepy and disorientated before following up on my promise.

We hardly ever went to sleep without something sexual occurring, but tonight, after everything that had happened, it didn't feel quite right. Just holding Stella felt perfect. She surrounded me with her arms, gently stroking my hair, as if she, too, just needed to feel me close. Sex could wait until the morning. In some ways, this was even more intimate, and I smiled contentedly as I held her tightly to me and drifted off in our new bed for the first time.

Chapter Twenty-Five

Stella

Nathan was sound asleep when I woke up. He was normally the early riser out of the two of us, but after yesterday's stresses I suspected he needed the rest, so I carefully slipped from the bed, miraculously managing not to wake him.

After a shower, I spent twenty minutes wandering around the house again with a mile-wide grin stretching on my face. I could hardly believe that this place was now my home. *Our* home. It was incredible.

Nathan's designs were simply stunning. The house was somehow open and airy while still feeling cosy and homely. William would adore all the corridors to run around when he got a little older; not to mention the outside spaces, too.

I grinned like a fool as I explored the new kitchen, opening drawers and cupboards and finding them to be stocked with food and filled with all the utensils we could ever need. Next, I set to work figuring out how to operate the new coffee maker, and after one failed attempt where I'd ended up with a mug of frothed milk, I was now sitting by the breakfast bar with an amazing cup of strong Columbian coffee, reading the news on my iPad.

A rustle of fabric alerted me to Nathan's arrival as he strode into the kitchen and paused by the windows. The news suddenly lost its interest when I looked across and saw that he was wearing my favourite navy blue suit. Well, the trousers and waistcoat, at least. He was jacketless, but wearing a pale blue shirt and a tie, which was, as always, knotted to perfection.

He looked mighty fine, and I was glad I'd had a shower and put on some make-up so I didn't feel like a complete dog when compared to his breath-taking perfection.

I had to suppress a smile at his smartness. We had nowhere to go today, our main plan being spending the day getting settled in the new house, but he was still dressed as if going to the office. He really was funny about his suits. Not that I was complaining, because he looked super-hot in that waistcoat. He slid his hands into his trouser pockets and cocked his head as he stood there watching me. 'Good morning. You got up without me.'

His tone seemed to say more than his words implied. Sensing he wanted something, I shut down my iPad and gave him my full attention. 'Morning. You looked peaceful so I left you to sleep. Everything OK?' I asked carefully, not quite able to decipher the strange look on his face.

'It is,' he replied, his tone dropping to match his expression. With the deep, gravelly inflection in those two words it almost sounded like the voice he used when he was slipping into Dom mode, but it was barely eight-thirty in the morning, and I couldn't for the life of me think what would have triggered that. I must be reading him wrongly.

'After my … slip … yesterday, I feel the need to …' He paused and rubbed his chin thoughtfully for a few seconds. 'Let's just say I'm feeling an urge to reassert my usual self.' He reached behind him and seemed to fiddle with something in his back pocket.

His slip?

Was he referring to letting me take control yesterday? He'd admitted that had been a monumental moment for him. Or maybe he was referring to when he'd cried, because it wasn't something I'd ever seen Nathan do before. Both were things he probably disliked showing me,

184

because he would call them weaknesses, but I wouldn't. I wouldn't refer to them as a slip, either. We all needed to vent every now and then with a good old cry, and as for me topping him, I'd simply done what was necessary to get him talking.

As I processed his words, I was about to say something reassuring when my mouth dropped open and stayed open. Nathan had rendered me speechless by smoothly producing our suede flogger and his favourite crop from behind his back, which he now carefully placed on the kitchen counter between us.

Holy fuck.

'Strip, and assume your ready position,' he requested crisply, before adjusting his stance just enough to make it wide, cocksure, and sexy as hell.

Ok-ay … So perhaps I hadn't been reading him wrong earlier. Dominant Nathan was indeed in the room.

Out of shock, I hesitated for a few seconds, which was apparently a few seconds too long for Nathan, because he narrowed his eyes and folded his arms across his chest. 'I hope you aren't going to make me repeat myself, Stella, because you know how much I dislike that.'

This was all really frigging surprising, but God, I loved it when he was like this. Jumping up, without any further delay I peeled my T-shirt over my head and dropped it on the floor in my hurry.

Nathan pointedly glared at my discarded clothing then turned his stare upon me. 'You're messing up our new house, gorgeous. Fold it up.'

A shudder of pure lust slithered through my body. I couldn't explain why I got so turned on when he took control like this, but by God I did. The fact that nowadays he added his fond endearments like "baby" or "gorgeous" only added to my desire, because there really was no greater feeling than knowing how much he desired me, and my submission.

I scooped up the T-shirt, carefully folded it, and placed it on the counter, smiling to myself as I saw Nathan give an approving nod. 'Jeans next, please.' He'd only spoken a handful of words to me and already moisture flooded between my legs.

When we'd first got together, Nathan had been unsure of me and our connection, and he'd frequently dropped back to his Dominant comfort zone for reassurance. He was still intense and controlling nowadays, but I wasn't treated to these impressive displays nearly as much as I'd like.

Thinking about it, it was probably why I was such a tease to him, because I knew my cheeky side both amused him and triggered his inherent need to try to control and tame me.

My initial shock had faded now, and I was starting to get into the swing of things, so I took my time with my jeans. I kept my gaze firmly connected with his as I popped the top button and oh so slowly pulled the zip down. My effort didn't go unnoticed, because I saw his pupils dilate, and a light flush break on his cheeks. It was all the encouragement I needed, so I then made a show of slightly turning away from him as I slid them down my legs, knowing that it would give him a prime view of my lace-clad arse.

I never wore plain cotton knickers any more. Nathan had made sure of that by purchasing me an entire new set of underwear when we'd moved in together, but his most recent obsession were the French-style lace knickers, and I happened to be wearing a particularly nice black pair today.

When I turned back and began to carefully fold my jeans, I saw that even though he hadn't moved a muscle, Nathan's cheeks definitely had a full flush to them now, and his eyes were lowered as he checked out my underwear. 'Very nice, Stella.' He unfolded his arms and held up one hand, pointed his finger up into the air and made a spinning motion, seemingly indicating that he wanted me to rotate on the spot.

Checking out the goods, was he? It was just a shame that I was barefoot because I could have made this a whole lot sexier if I'd been wearing a pair of my killer high heels. Still, I'd make the best of it. Trying to imagine what would look the sexiest, I pulled my spine straight, thrust my chest out, placed one hand on my hip and the other by my side and very slowly turned on the spot for him.

'Once more,' he growled, clearly affected by my little show. So, with a pleased smile, I began to repeat my twirl. This time I only made it halfway around before he grabbed hold of my arse with one hand and splayed his other over my stomach to drag me back flush against his warm body.

Within seconds, he had released my bra catch and it fell from my body as his hands roughly cupped my needy breasts. His head dropped into the crook of my neck and as he sought my nipples and began to tease them with his fingers, then I felt his rapid breathing fan across my neck and the solid heat of his erection digging into my back. It would seem my strip tease had had an instant impact.

And this was all before breakfast.

'So sexy, Stella.' The hand on my arse gave a hard squeeze, causing me to roll onto my tiptoes as a gasp left my lips. Then Nathan was kissing my neck almost frantically. He lowered both of his hands to my bottom, and as he massaged the flesh he spoke just below my ear.

'This isn't about punishment, Stella. You are perfect, you've done nothing wrong. This is simply to slake a desire in me.' Just like any good Dom should, Nathan would always, always, make sure I understood exactly what our scenes would involve, and why they were taking place. He wouldn't dream of spanking me, or flogging me, without first explaining why.

187

He dropped to his haunches to remove my knickers, placed a hot, open-mouthed kiss on the base of my spine, then stood up. Turning me to face him, he made a show of folding them and slipping them into his trouser pocket with a grin which was so filthy it made me flush.

He lifted me up by my hips and sat me on the edge of the kitchen counter, then nudged his way in between my thighs until we were chest to chest. He lowered his head to mine as he kissed me and I twined my legs around his waist and dragged him as close as I could get him.

Nathan was such a good kisser that I was moaning into his mouth within seconds, and squirming on the cool marble top, trying to find some relief from my pounding arousal. Lifting his head, Nathan gave me an intense look then glanced down between the two of us. 'It would appear you are messing up our lovely new house again.'

Glancing down, I felt my cheeks heat as I saw the obvious evidence of my desire glistening on the marble work surface between my legs. *Oops.*

'Let me clean it up.' I seriously thought that Nathan was about to get out a cloth and the anti-bac spray and perform an impromptu spring clean, but no. A second later, he dropped to his knees and buried his face between my spread thighs.

Crikey. I rolled my eyes shut as Nathan rather thoroughly set about cleaning me up, ignoring the mess on the counter and instead licking and sucking at my clit and saturated folds until I was almost on the brink of an orgasm.

He stood again and grinned at me, his lips glistening with my arousal. Then he winked. 'If I had stayed down there much longer I'd have lost track of my main focus.' He gave the crop and flogger a glance then looked back to me as his eyes darkened with pure wickedness. 'So, I have selected these two options. Are they agreeable to you?'

Looking at the crop and the flogger, I felt my core

clench in anticipation and nodded, before quickly vocalising my consent. 'Definitely, Sir.'

Nathan gave an approving growl against my heated neck and helped me to stand from the counter, squeezing my bum again, hard enough to elicit another gasp from me. I might well have fingerprint-shaped bruises there tomorrow if he kept on doing that. As if reading my mind, he licked my earlobe and spoke again.

'Do you want to be marked, or not? Neither answer is right nor wrong; this is simply your choice.'

I would always pretend to grumble when he gave me a love bite, but we both knew that I actually loved wearing his mark. The fact that he craved me enough to claim me as his was a huge turn-on for me. After yesterday, where he'd felt weak and out of control, I suspected that I knew exactly what his preference would be today.

'Marks, Sir. Claim me.'

His hands tightened on my hips and the groan from behind me was the most erotic thing I'd ever heard. I tipped my head back onto his shoulder, already dizzy with lust.

'Mine.' He nuzzled my neck again as his lips kissed below my ear and his teeth locked on to the skin. It was enough to arouse me further and have me wriggling in his arms, but not enough to break the skin, and would leave a mark for no more a few minutes.

Nathan kissed me into a frenzy, then gently urged me forwards so my feet were still on the floor but my upper body was now splayed across the cold marble. I sucked in a gasp as the iciness peaked my nipples into tiny pebbles, but then relaxed as his hands began to caress and calm me. Once my muscles had liquefied, Nathan swapped to the crop and used the small leather tab to continue his warm-up routine. Small, gentle flicks of his hand brought the leather tab into contact with my skin with just enough power that it warmed and aroused me, but didn't hurt. Not a centimetre of my arse was left untouched, and by the time I felt one of his hands caress me again, I was completely relaxed on the counter and spaced out with longing.

'I'm going to go harder, now, and leave some marks on this gorgeous arse. What's your colour?'

I was so horny and floaty that I could barely get my mouth to cooperate and speak, but finally I did, even if my two words came out as a slurred whisper. 'Green, Sir.'

The first swat to my bum was familiar to me, and I smiled lazily as I recognised the soft feel of my favourite suede flogger. He used it several more times on me and I found myself humming my approval. Even if used with power, it didn't really hurt, the softness of the material limiting its impact to a tingling warmth. Nathan loved how pink it made my skin, though, which was no doubt why he was using it now.

'Good girl. This next part will be a little different to anything we've done before, so use your colours if you need to, OK?'

Different? Rather than being worried, I found myself curious and excited. I trusted Nathan implicitly, so didn't bother to enquire how it would be different. Instead, I just gave him the consent he was checking for. 'OK, Sir.'

I heard him putting down the flogger beside me, then there was a small swishing noise of the air being disturbed, followed by a sharp, stinging sensation across my arse.

He was right, it was different, and hurt way more than the flogger had. A ragged gasp tore up my throat, followed by a burning sensation on my buttocks that was unlike anything I'd experienced before. It felt like I'd been hit with a ruler. What the hell had he used?

'This crop has a longer shaft than most. With the shorter models the leather tab is best used, but with this one it can almost be used as a cane.' OK, so that was why it had hurt more. Nathan had never caned me before, so this was definitely new.

'Are you OK, Stella?' I gripped at the counter, but as he began to caress my smarting skin with an almost silken touch my core flooded with moisture. The sensation was actually quite incredible. The pain and pleasure mix created a euphoric high in my system. My blood was pounding, not with fear or pain, but need. I needed it again.

'Yes, Sir. Again, please.'

Nathan was still caressing me with his hands, then he leaned down to place a heated kiss on my shoulder blade. 'Good girl.' I felt the leather tab of the crop trace down my spine and I raised my arse instinctively towards the touch, causing him to let out a satisfied moan.

'Six strikes in total, I think. So, five more to go.' There was barely a second of delay after his words, then my arse received its second blow. The same drugging rush of feelings swept over me, and I arched my back as I found myself automatically counting and thanking him as I usually would during a scene. 'Two. Thank you, Sir.'

My gurgled words were apparently exactly what Nathan had wanted to hear because he swore and massaged my arse again with a groan. 'Jesus, Stella, you are so fucking perfect.'

Strikes three to six remained at the same level of power, but Nathan did swap sides halfway through. When he was finished, he laid himself over the top of me, blanketing me with his warmth and littering my skin with kisses.

I felt completely boneless; that had been incredible. Shifting himself to the side, he ran his right hand down my spine, over my heated buttocks, through my arse crack and down to my soaked folds.

'Fuck. So wet.' He immediately began to circle at my clitoris with his fingers, and after the last few minutes the sensitivity was almost too much for me to cope with and I whimpered softly. Nathan obviously knew exactly how

191

turned on I was, because he skipped any soft introductions and moved his hand with almost ruthless speed against my needy bud.

Gasping loudly, I curled my hands around the edge of the counter, feeling my orgasm already teetering on the edge as his fingers skilfully circled me then suddenly pinched.

Hard.

Really hard.

How he managed to get a grip when I was so wet I have no idea, but he did, then immediately followed it up with a twist to my flesh that sent me spiralling into an orgasm so powerful that I yelled out and flailed on the counter as my muscles went into delicious orgasmic spasms. My mind felt floaty, my body was like a liquid being rolling across waves of bliss, and through it all there was Nathan, grounding me to the pleasure that consumed me.

After that performance, it was very clear that Nathan was indeed back in control. But God, how I loved it.

He continued to gently tease me with his fingers, working me down from my orgasm and seemingly content to just pleasure me today. There was no way I was having that, though. I wanted him to get his release, too, and as I lay there sated and relaxed I suddenly thought of a different way that he could really claim me.

My heart sped up again at the idea, because it slightly scared me, but I knew Nathan would probably love it, and it would tick off yet another thing we'd never done together.

Swallowing my slight fear, I reached down and took hold of his wrist, gently guiding it from my slick folds until it rested higher, over the crack of my arse. Nathan and I had done some play with butt plugs and his fingers, but we'd still never had anal sex. At the start of our relationship I'd said I wasn't keen, and like the true gent he was, he'd never once returned to the subject.

The thing was, now we were so strong together, and the sex between us was so incredible, I'd started to get curious. The things he did with the plugs had felt amazing, and even if I decided I didn't want to do it regularly, I was keen to try it at least once.

Nathan used his finger to gently caress me there and I relaxed against his careful touch. Keeping hold of his wrist, I pressed his hand more firmly against my arse to make my point clear as I whispered my next words. 'I want you inside me. Here.'

Nathan's touch stilled, and the next second he pulled his hand from my grip and moved it away completely.

The hands that landed on my shoulders a second later felt urgent in their pressure, but as he helped me sit up he treated me as if I was made of glass. 'That's one of your hard limits, Stella,' he growled, his eyes searching my face as if trying to see right inside my brain.

Of course. Nathan and his rules and contracts.

'I know. It was, at the start, but ... those contracts don't represent us now, Nathan. We've changed so much.' I swallowed, wondering how I could possibly explain how deeply I trusted him, and how much I wanted to try this. 'I'm curious. I know you'd make it good for me, and I ... I want to try it.' He said nothing, and I wondered if I had misread his interest in this area of sex, and frowned. 'Unless you don't want to, of course.'

In reply to my worry, Nathan made a dismissive noise which was almost like a dry laugh, then smothered any further words by crushing his lips down onto mine. 'I want to. Believe me. Let's go upstairs.'

Chapter Twenty-Six

Stella

As Nathan lifted me from the counter top, I took a moment to look between us with amusement. I was completely naked, wobbly-legged, and flushed from my recent climax, but Nathan was still suited, booted and immaculate.

Apart from the large bulge straining at the front of his trousers that was, which looked so desperate it must surely be painful.

'Come,' he murmured, taking my hand. He had a determined look on his face as he led me from the kitchen and up the stairs to our bedroom. From his purposeful strides, I got the distinct feeling that he was almost tempted to run, bless him, but his all-important self-control must have won out, because we walked, albeit rather quickly.

When we entered our room, Nathan spun me into his arms and kissed me again until I was dizzy, then left me standing in the centre of the room as he disappeared into the en-suite. I looked around the room, marvelling again at just how beautiful it was, and caught a glimpse of my reflection in the huge mirror.

My hair was wild, my cheeks pink, and my eyes dilated – all in all, I had the look of a thoroughly sated woman. Turning slightly to the side, I looked at my arse and gasped. *Oh my God ...* I was now the proud owner of some seriously red lines across my buttocks. Six lines were equally spaced down the soft flesh of my arse, mirrored perfectly with three on each cheek.

Now I understood why he had swapped sides halfway

through; he'd wanted to spread the pattern so it was equal.

I was exploring them with my fingers to see how painful they were when Nathan joined me again. He chucked a couple of tubes and a box onto the bed and immediately moved to my side.

'Are they too sore?' he asked in concern, placing a hand on my arm and hunkering his shoulders down to meet my gaze with his worry-filled blue eyes.

'No, they aren't too bad.' I brushed off his concern with a smile and saw his shoulders relax. 'I quite like the feeling, actually,' I admitted. Which sounded stupid as I said it, but was totally true. I liked the fact that he had given me these marks. 'They're very equally spread,' I observed, looking in the mirror again as Nathan dropped to his haunches and gave my arse a heated stare.

As if unable to simply look and not touch, he raised a hand and ran his fingers gently over my bottom. His palm felt cool on my heated skin and I wriggled it closer, causing him to laugh and trace the closest line with a gentle finger. 'Of course. You know I like things neat and tidy.'

Ha! Isn't that the truth! I just hadn't realised that his OCD tendencies would spread quite this far.

'They look so sexy,' he murmured. 'No, actually, *you* look so fucking sexy,' he amended, before giving my arse another gentle massage that had my eyes fluttering shut with pleasure. Then he stood up to kiss me. Taking his time, he ran his tongue along the seam of my lips, nibbled at the corner of my mouth, and pressed his tongue inside, meeting mine with warm, rolling movements and gentle explorations.

As his lips moved softly against mine, I got the feeling that we were moving away from our scene for this next bit. No more Sir and sub; we were just Nathan and Stella exploring each other on another, new level, and so I took the opportunity to reach up and start undoing his waistcoat.

195

He didn't stop me, or give me a different instruction, so I relaxed into it and continued with his tie, then moved to his shirt buttons as he joined in and quickly shucked his trousers, socks, and boxers.

With a smirk, I noticed that the clothes didn't get folded this time, but Nathan didn't seem to be bothered about "messing up the new house" as he dropped them unceremoniously by our feet. Not that I passed comment; I was way too engrossed in the moment to speak.

My legs were still a little jellified from the kitchen action, so I was immensely grateful when Nathan steered us towards the bed and guided me down onto my back. His lips barely left mine as he continued to kiss me, and we skated our hands over each other's skin as we continuously caressed and aroused one another further.

Finally, Nathan sat up and helped me over onto my hands and knees. He must have felt the way my body tensed slightly with nerves, because he spent a good while longer relaxing me by kissing my back, running his hands across my skin, and gently playing with my nipples and clit until I was pressing back against him, desperate for more.

The first warning I got that he might be losing the battle with his self-control was when I felt the tip of his cock brush against my inner thigh then bump against my moist folds. He held me close, his hands wrapped around me, as he curled over the top of me to speak just below my ear. 'Are you definitely sure about this, sweetheart?'

There was no hesitation in my reply. 'Yes. I've never done it before, but with you I want to. I want you to be my first.'

I'd thought my words would please him, which I think they did, judging by how his grip increased on my hips, but apparently, I'd riled him, too. 'And your last,' he added, his voice gruff and holding a touch of warning to it, even though I hadn't meant to tease him with my remark at all.

I wanted to roll my eyes at his needless worry, but I didn't. 'Of course my last, Nathan. You're it for me, you know that.'

'Hmm. Good. I like the sound of that. A lot.' I was rewarded with a kiss to the back of my shoulder blades, then Nathan reached beside us and grabbed the things he'd thrown down earlier. As I glanced across I saw they were a tube of lube, a box of condoms, a wrapped baby wipe, and a tub of arnica gel.

He was prepared, wasn't he?

'Condoms?' I enquired, unable to keep the surprise from my voice, because Nathan had always been keen to go bare when we were together.

'Yes. For what I have planned this is better. But if you enjoy what we do today and want to try this again, then I will definitely be going bareback and coming when I'm buried deep inside your arse.'

His deep, possessive tone went straight through me and caused my clit to pulse several times with excitement as my whole body shivered with desire.

'But as this is your first time,' he went on, 'I want you to get maximum enjoyment out of it, so a condom is better, more hygienic. Trust me.'

I did. I trusted him with my life, so I nodded and didn't mention it any further. 'OK.'

He quickly donned a condom, then I felt a cool sensation in between my buttocks as he squirted some lube there. His left hand was still on my back, massaging and trailing across the skin, keeping me relaxed, but with his other hand he used a finger to gently circle my rear entrance a few times before beginning to press in.

I shuddered with desire, the feeling so arousing that I closed my eyes and pressed back against him in a silent demand for more. He groaned approvingly as I angled my hips backwards to allow his finger to slip past the tight ring

197

of muscles then move inside me until it was in to the knuckle.

There was another strained noise from Nathan, then I felt the tip of his cock at my front entrance, eagerly pushing inside in a long, gentle thrust so that both my holes were full.

My skin peppered with goose pimples, but flooded with heat at the same time. The feeling of the condom was strange, but apart from that it was all good. We'd gone as far as this before with his fingers or butt plugs, and I hung my head forwards as Nathan began to move his finger and slowly thrust his hips.

'Mmmm.' It felt good. Really good. And it got even better a second later when he used his free hand to move around and circle my clitoris.

I noticed when he upped the finger in my rear to two because he scissored his fingers a little and the stretch was noticeable, but not painful. I was so carried away in the moment and my heightening emotions, I barely even reacted. Instead, I arched my back and moaned, feeling wanton and sexual and utterly free.

I didn't care if some people would consider this dirty or taboo. I was with the man I loved, and I fucking loved the things he did to me.

Just as I thought I might come from the overwhelming sensations building within me, Nathan eased himself out of both my entrances. He briefly wiped his hand on the baby wipe, then I heard the squirt of more lube being applied. With one hand still circling my clit, he pressed the slippery tip of his sheathed cock against my tight ring of muscles. Regardless of how aroused I was, I instinctively tensed.

'Just try to relax, baby,' Nathan whispered, his voice soft and full of love. This might hurt a little, but I knew he would make it good for me.

From what I had read, the first part was the trickiest,

because of the muscles there, so I took in a deep breath. As I released it, I began to press myself backwards onto his shaft.

My entrance stretched and I jumped a bit as my muscles suddenly relaxed. With only a slight sting, his tip pressed inside me, causing a surge of delicious sensation to spiral through my body. I felt heady from the pleasure, and nearly laughed from the relief as I realised that it had hardly hurt at all. Obviously, all the play with his fingers and butt plugs over our time together had prepared me.

'Fuck, Stella. You are so fucking sexy.' I couldn't help but grin at how gritty Nathan's voice was. I'd place money on the fact that he was watching his cock press into my arse right this second, but I didn't feel embarrassed, I felt empowered. He was massively turned on and struggling for control, and it was all because of me.

Nathan didn't rush me; instead, he used small, shallow thrusts of his hips to gradually work his length inside me bit by bit. The feeling was different, but with his fingers still massaging my clit I was focusing more on the pleasure than any discomfort. Feeling more confident because of the slipperiness of the lube, I began to gently rock in time to his movements, pressing back against his thrusts and moaning at how good it felt.

'Are you OK, baby?' he whispered, his hip movements still gentle, as he continuously massaged my hip, coaxing me to relax.

'I am. It feels ... tight, but ... but it's good ...really good ...' I panted, making Nathan hum appreciatively and stroke my back again.

'I'll add more lube to help,' he offered, and after another squirt of cool gel he gripped my hip with one hand and ground himself forwards again, this time with just a little more pressure. 'God. I'm all the way in. You feel amazing, Stella.'

As he spoke, I realised I could now feel his belly on my bum cheeks and let out a breath in astonishment. *Holy shit.* He was completely inside me. And I knew from first-hand experience just how well-endowed Nathan was, so this was really some feat.

'Now you're mine in every way ...' he murmured, his tone almost awestruck, which surprised me. I'd expected him to be possessive or domineering, but he really sounded quite affected by the moment.

Which made two of us, because this surely was as intimate as a man and woman could get together.

Slowly but surely, Nathan began to build his pace up, and I was surprised to find that even though the sensations were entirely different to when he hit my G-spot during sex, I was still quickly moving towards a climax. My breathing was erratic, skin hot, and head almost dizzy from the desire coursing around my system.

Nathan thrust into me with vigour, our bodies slapping together as our control began to fade, but suddenly, he dragged his cock from within me, tore the condom off, and thrust inside my pussy with so much force that I fell forwards onto my elbows. He didn't stop, though; he merely adjusted to the new position, following me and curling himself around me as he continued to thrust with abandon and grip at my breasts with a low growl.

The change of position was unexpected, but as he thrust in to the hilt and hit my G-spot with utter perfection I couldn't say I was complaining. Nathan dropped his right hand to my clit again and sped up his circling, the fingers now beginning to rub in just the spot that always made me explode, and as he continued with a hard, stabbing rhythm of his hips I felt my orgasm rear up on me.

There were no pre-orgasmic quivers this time. My climax hit me like a truck and was so powerful that it literally took my breath away. I didn't even have enough oxygen in my lungs to scream his name, because I was struggling with the crippling pleasure searing my entire body from the inside out. My lungs felt paralysed, I gripped at the duvet in desperation, and my muscles all seemed to give in and collapse at the same moment, which happened to be the exact second that Nathan came with a fierce roar as I felt his release scorching inside me.

He followed my trembling body down to the mattress, thrusting out his climax with a few more jerking jabs of his hips before swearing under his breath. Then he collapsed to the side of me and dragged me into his arms so I was cradled against him, my back to his front.

Holy fuck.

My heart was pounding, my arse cheeks still smarted from his crop earlier, my back passage felt twitchy and used, and my pussy was convulsing with the aftershocks of my out-of-body orgasm.

Nathan was panting heavily against my shoulder, and I was still struggling to draw in a full breath. That had been sex like I'd never known before. One thing stuck slightly in my mind, though, and I decided to voice it now while I was facing away from him and didn't have the intensity of eye contact to add to my embarrassment.

'Why didn't you want to come inside me?'

'I did come inside you,' he stated with satisfaction. When he'd rolled to the side and pulled me down with him, most of his cock had slipped from inside me, but the tip and first inch or so was still in my channel, and I felt him give a lazy thrust now, some of his come leaking out and wetting my thighs as if to prove his point.

'You know that's not what I meant. You didn't come in my …' Even though I'd just done it, I still couldn't bring myself to say the word.

'Arse? Is that the word you're searching for, beautiful?' he teased, with obvious amusement in his voice.

201

'Yeah.' This was mortifying enough without him teasing me, too. 'Why was that?'

The bed shifted as Nathan pulled out of me and moved himself so he was leaning up on one elbow, rolling me so I was on my back gazing up at him and couldn't avoid his eyes. His cheeks were flushed, but his eyes were blazing. He looked so happy that I almost told him not to bother answering my question.

'It was your first time back there, and I wanted to make sure you enjoyed the experience and had good memories of it.' He licked his lips and smiled down at me sweetly. 'Not everyone reacts in the same manner, so I couldn't be sure that I could make you come that way, but I know for sure that I can make you come when I fuck you normally, so I decided we could do a bit of both. Start with the new, and then move back to the tried and tested so you got a climax, too.'

When he put it that way it was rather sweet of him. It also explained why he had wanted the condom on, because going from the back hole to the front wouldn't be the most hygienic of acts.

He leaned in close to place a kiss on my lips then grinned smugly. 'For the record, from the way you reacted to me just now I'm almost 100 per cent certain that I can make you come from anal penetration, too, so next time, I won't bother with the rubber. If there is a next time,' he added quickly, flashing me a wink before sobering his face. 'So, how did you find it?'

Blinking, I licked my lips and tried to assess my feelings. It had all been pretty surprising, in a good way. The build-up swum in my mind; that incredible session in the kitchen. My arse certainly hadn't forgotten about Nathan's use of the crop, that was for sure, but I'd loved it. Then we'd moved to the bedroom for round two. He'd been so thoughtful, making sure I was comfortable and relaxed the entire time. I'd come harder than I had in a long time, too, which was never a bad thing.

'It was ... amazing.' I caught Nathan's eye and saw from his expression that he wanted, or perhaps needed, more reassurance from me, so I gave a self-conscious shrug as my cheeks bloomed with heat. 'I'd been worried that it would hurt, but you did everything perfectly, Nathan. You made it really special for me. Thank you.'

Nathan seemed to let out a relieved breath, then placed a kiss on my lips. 'Plus, you came so hard you ripped our new sheets,' he commented lightly, before brushing some stray hairs from my face.

What? Bolting upright, I looked down at the crumpled bed sheets. To my horror, he was right. There was a gaping hole where my hands had been. I didn't even know I had that kind of strength within me.

'Oops ...'

'Oops indeed,' Nathan murmured in amusement as he rolled onto his back and tucked my body in by his side.

As I lay there for a few more minutes to get my breath back I suddenly found myself giggling. The first little bubble of laughter rippled up my throat, followed by another, and another. It must be the adrenaline from what we'd just done escaping my body, I supposed, but whatever it was, I found that once I'd started I just couldn't stop.

'What?' Nathan sounded perplexed. He sat himself up and stared down at me.

'Well, I was thinking that we only moved in here last night and not only have I just ripped a set of brand-new sheets, we've already christened the bedroom *and* the kitchen with sex.'

Nathan watched me giggling for a second more then joined me, his handsome face creasing at the corners of his eyes as he laughed along with me. He gave the side of my hip a tickle. 'Don't forget your arse. That just got christened, too.' His cheeky remark had me gasping, then laughing with embarrassment again, before he offered me his hand and pulled me from the bed.

'Come on, let's shower. I want to get some arnica on those marks to make sure you don't bruise.'

Accepting his hand, I allowed him to lead me into the huge walk-in shower. This side of him never failed to amuse me; he liked – no, he *loved* marking me with a nice circular hickey, a reddened hand print, or a crop mark, but would be absolutely beside himself if he left other associated bruising on my skin. He was so contradictory on this area, and he knew it, and I found myself shaking my head in amusement.

I didn't comment. Instead, I let him sweep me into his arms under the hot spray of the water and kiss my laughter away.

Chapter Twenty-Seven

Nathan

After that unexpected turn to the morning's events I was feeling fucking fabulous, but there was still one thing playing on my mind. My brother. Even though we were grown men now, I'd always looked out for him. Always. The last few days had been stressful enough for me, but he'd had it so much worse; he'd had all the shit to deal with regarding the sudden return of our parents, and in addition to that, he had Rebecca still in hospital. I could hardly imagine how he was feeling, but I needed to make sure he was OK.

'I'd like to pop back to the hospital today and check on Nicholas.'

Stella finished the last bite of her sandwich and nodded. 'Of course.'

'I was thinking we could save your parents a trip and drive down to St Albans. I'll drop you off so you can see William and your folks, then I'll head on to the hospital from there.'

Stella's parents had offered to come and stay with us for a few days to look after Will while we dealt with the fallout of this nightmare week, but as much as I liked them, and was grateful for their support, I really wanted to avoid having them over to stay.

Parental meet-ups were something I was only just getting acclimatised to, and I generally managed a few hours with the Marsdens before I got twitchy, wondering when Mrs Marsden was going to corner me and give me another talk about marriage. If they were staying here, I'd be on alert 24 fucking hours a day, which was not a thought I relished.

As if reading my thoughts, Stella smiled. 'On the way back, you can get me and Will, and then the three of us can spend our first night here all together as a family.'

My family. Swallowing around a sudden lump in my throat, I nodded. 'Sounds good.'

As I had suspected, Nicholas hadn't wanted to leave Rebecca's side, and I didn't want to talk about our parents in front of Rebecca, so I'd had to wait until an opportunity arose. Luckily, that hadn't taken too long, because a specialist came in wanting to do a private assessment and had ushered both Nicholas and me out of the room.

'Quick coffee?' I'd asked hopefully, sighing in relief when Nicholas nodded his agreement.

Once we had located the cafeteria and both had a cup of coffee we found a table and sat in silence for a second or two. As siblings went, Nicholas and I were close, but with our background and all the issues surrounding our upbringing, emotional outpourings were still relatively few and far between.

Nicholas took a sip of his coffee, grimaced, and pushed the polystyrene cup away. Seeing his reaction, I didn't even bother to taste mine, because I was even more of a coffee snob than my brother, if that was possible. So I simply moved the cup aside and focused my attention on him.

Pulling in a deep breath, I decided to get straight down to business. 'So, how are you feeling about everything now?'

Running a hand through his hair, Nicholas let out a long breath and made eye contact with me. 'Well, Rebecca and the babies are definitely OK, so I guess I'm all right.'

I tugged at my shirt sleeves in agitation and rephrased

my question. 'I actually meant about seeing our parents again ... and ... what happened to Father ...'

Nicholas's nostrils flared as he drew in an angry breath and shook his head adamantly. 'He put me, *us –*' he reinforced this correction by rapidly waving his hand between the two of us before leaning closer and dropping his voice to a whisper '– through years of hell with his abuse. Then, to top it off, he nearly killed my babies, Nathan.' Sitting back, he folded his arms, appearing calmer now. He briefly closed his eyes. 'All I feel is relief for his death. I'm glad he's gone, and I don't even feel guilty for saying that.'

Wow. When did my little brother get so kick-arse and strong? Jesus, he's dealing with Dad's death better than I am. I almost laughed at how the tables had turned, but instead I did something I hardly ever did; I decided to reveal a weakness to him. I had always tried to be the stronger older brother, a good role model for him, and someone he could look up to, but today I really needed to share this with him. Stella had been amazing at listening yesterday, but nobody except for Nicholas could ever really understand how I was feeling, because they hadn't been there when we were growing up.

They hadn't experienced Dad and all his ugliness first hand.

'I had a bit of a meltdown,' I admitted, averting my eyes out of embarrassment.

Nicholas immediately stood and came around my side of the table. He slipped into the seat beside me and placed a reassuring hand on my shoulder. 'Are you OK?'

His concern affected me far more than it should have, and, to my horror, I felt a brief burn of unshed tears at the back of my eyes. Blinking several times, I got a grip on myself and nodded. I might be feeling a bit fucked up by all of this, but I would not cry again.

Nicholas understood the screwed-up relationship I'd had with Dad better than anyone else, and while he had felt nothing but hatred for our father growing up, he knew that on some level I'd idolised Dad for a while. I'd been in awe of the power and control he'd been able to exert, I'd believed his beatings were to make me better, and for a short time, perhaps, I'd even wanted to be like him.

The very thought of that now made me sick to my stomach.

'I am. Stella was incredible. She knew exactly what to do to help me.'

There was a moment's pause, then I finally made eye contact with him again.

'You know he got exactly what he deserved, don't you?' Nicholas asked quietly, his calm seeping across the gap between us. It was infinitely reassuring for me.

'I do now, yes. Yesterday I … I was upset.' I saw Nicholas's jaw tense at my admission, so quickly set him straight. 'Even after all these years, I'd held a shard of hope that he might suddenly see the errors of his ways and apologise.'

Closing his eyes in understanding, Nicholas nodded. 'Be the dad we'd always wanted?' he said hoarsely.

'Yes. It's stupid, because nothing could ever have made up for how he treated us, but now he's gone I have to just accept him for what he was; a vile excuse for a man and the worst possible example of a father.'

'When I was a kid and the beatings first started, I used to hope he'd change too,' Nicholas admitted quietly, before a frown creased his brows. 'But I gave up that hope a very long time ago.'

We sat in silence for a second, both lost in memories, no doubt, before Nicholas broke the peace and spoke. 'It's up to us to put it all right, Nathan. We need to do the complete opposite of what he did to us – be the best fathers we possibly can. You're doing such a good job with Will, you're going to have to help me out when the twins come along.'

I could see the excitement in his eyes, even if it was accompanied by a touch of nerves, and I nodded, smiling as I did so. 'Of course, brother. I'm always here for you.'

Flicking at the faded table surface, Nicholas bit on his lip. He was unable to meet my gaze. 'So, uh, did you speak to Mum at all?'

That was a whole other pot of confusion, wasn't it? But, somehow, I was hopeful that in the future we might be able to build some bridges. I didn't have any gilded visons of us becoming a perfect family – too much had passed between us for that – but perhaps we could be on speaking terms and make up for some of the hurt.

'I did.' I wondered where to start, when Nicholas beat me to it.

'Was she working with Dad, or what? Because everything was utter chaos, but I remember seeing her clutching a knife in her hand and it really looked like it was him she was going for.'

My eyes fluttered shut as I recalled how she'd said she couldn't let him hurt us any more, and a strange pain circled my heart as I slowly told Nicholas all that had occurred, from Father blackmailing her to stay with him, right up to Stella's invitation for us all to meet for coffee.

Turning my head sideways, I saw that Nicholas's face had drained of colour. 'All that time we thought she didn't care about us, but he was basically forcing her to stay with him?'

I nodded, not keen to think about Dad for a second longer than I needed to.

'Beating her just as he did us?' Nicholas slammed his

hand down on the table then dug it through his hair. 'Fuck!' He seemed to be having a similar reaction to that news as I had. If only we'd known, we could have worked as a team and got out of there.

'She used to sneak me chocolate biscuits,' he said. 'On a Sunday after lights out she'd open the door and put an envelope on the dresser, then leave without saying a word.'

A strange chill of remembrance skittered across my skin. God, the envelopes. Until he mentioned it, I'd forgotten about them. 'I got them, too. Bourbon biscuits,' I replied, my voice suddenly thick and raspy.

Now we knew that Dad had banned her from overly interacting with us, things were becoming clearer. She hadn't been all bad.

Nicholas smiled sadly. 'And I remember we got waffles on a Friday morning for breakfast because Dad always had to be at the base so was never home.'

Waffles with maple syrup. It was all coming back to me. Mum never spoke much as she served them, but she always smiled as me and Nicholas had tucked in with gusto.

Fuck. Closing my eyes, I started to feel quite overwhelmed by the flood of memories. Somehow, in the fog of time the few good memories had been lost among the torrent of bad. But now we'd started discussing them they seemed to be flooding back.

'Do you remember the comic books?' I asked, smiling genuinely for the first time in our conversation. 'Dad banned them from the house, but once a month Mum would sneak two in for us to share.'

It continued like this for several minutes, both of us picking out the good things we could remember and sharing some smiles until Nicholas's phone interrupted us with a beep. He glanced at the screen, then pocketed the phone and looked across at me. 'It's Rebecca. They've finished the examination and she asked me to take her back a

210

sandwich.'

We both stood a little awkwardly after our deluge of sentimental talk, but then Nicholas laughed and gave me a half-hug, patting me on the back firmly before standing back. 'Enough of this soppy shit. I need to feed my woman or she'll get cranky.'

Grinning at how under the thumb he was – how under the thumb we both were these days – I gave him a hearty pat on the shoulder, feeling a million times lighter after our talk.

'Thanks for the chat, Nicholas, I needed it.'

'Any time, bro, you know that.' I was about to turn away when Nicholas touched my arm to stop me. 'Let me know when you're having coffee with Mum, and I'll … I'll come, too.'

Drawing in a deep breath, I nodded, immensely thankful that I wouldn't have to meet her alone. Then I strode from the hospital, keen to head back to Stella and my boy.

Chapter Twenty-Eight

Nicholas

My eyes were fixed to the restaurant door. I stared at it obsessively as I waited for our mother to enter. As yet another stranger came in and moved to a vacant table, I drew in a calming breath to try to relax. I even thought about doing one of Nathan's patented calming countdowns, but it was no good. My stomach was still churning, and I could feel my heart rate accelerating by the second.

'OK, brother?' Nathan asked beside me, pulling my gaze away from the door.

'Yeah …' Shaking out the nervous energy in my system, I turned to Nathan and saw him sitting passively, but watching me with concern. 'I just … Seeing her still brings a real mix of emotions, you know?'

Today would be our third meet-up with our mum since all the shit had happened with Dad, three months ago. After an initially tense coffee where we'd all tried to come to terms with what had occurred, Nathan and I had agreed that we'd meet with her once a month in an attempt at rebuilding some bridges. It was tough going. Reliving my horrific childhood was probably one of the hardest things I'd ever done in my life, but we were getting there, slowly but surely.

Nathan's nostrils flared as he also took a deep breath, but he nodded. 'I do, I totally understand.' Running a hand through his blond hair he then drummed his fingers on the table several times, giving a small indication that he was feeling just as agitated as I was, even if his expression didn't show it. 'Whenever you have doubts, just remember that my best security guy checked her out. Everything she has told us is true. Her claims about being abused and hospitalised by Dad were real. He did hit her, on more than one occasion. It's all on record.'

At first, Nathan had been very cautious about Mum's reappearance into our lives, but she'd been checked out by his security team so thoroughly now that she could probably get clearance to work in Buckingham Palace.

We shared a moment of quiet, presumably both caught up in the tumble of emotions that always came with thoughts of our father.

'I know. I can't believe we didn't realise,' I added quietly, my voice filled with the regret of what could have been. All three of us could have escaped and been free of him, and our lives could have been so different.

'There's no point dwelling on it, Nicholas. We've been dealt our cards; now we need to make the best of them,' Nathan murmured, correctly interpreting my broody expression. And he was right. After years of thinking the worst of her and then finding out it had all been wrong, these meetings with Mum were a small step in the right direction.

Nodding, I sipped my coffee, the warmth of the beverage going some way towards calming me. 'I'm slightly regretting my decision to leave Rebecca at home, though. She makes me feel so much calmer,' I admitted quietly, embarrassed by my confession, but able to voice it because I suspected that Nathan felt a similar bond with Stella.

Closing his eyes for a second, Nathan nodded. 'Yeah.' He went silent, but from the way he suddenly tugged on his shirt cuffs I knew he had more to say. Expressing our feelings still wasn't exactly our finest skill, but we were improving. 'I ... I'm the same with Stella. Independently, we're both strong, but when we're together I feel almost invincible.' Blowing out a breath, as if the emotional statement had been too much for him, he then turned and nodded at me. 'You were right in your reasoning, though. Rebecca's so far along in the pregnancy now that she doesn't need any undue stress.'

Both Rebecca and Stella had attended the previous two meet-ups, and it had been good to have some female back-up to take the pressure off Nathan and me, but also to make Mum feel more at ease. Today we'd decided to come alone, because Rebecca was just four weeks from her due date, and even though our last two meetings had been calm enough, the topics of conversation were wrought with emotion and I knew that Rebecca was like a sponge to my stress. When I felt it, she felt it, and so, wanting to try to keep her shielded from any undue worry, I had asked her to stay at home with Stella today.

Just then, my mother entered the restaurant. Timidly, she ran her gaze over the diners, looking for us. It seemed from her expression that she still got as nervous about these meet-ups as Nathan and I did.

'Ready?' Nathan asked, and in response I nodded and raised a hand so mother could see where we were sitting.

We both stood as she approached, and had to go through the awkward moment where she went to hug us, only to stop when she saw our unresponsive body language. I wanted to tell her it wasn't just her, that Nathan and I were almost incapable of physical contact with anyone since Dad had banned it during childhood. But that seemed like rubbing salt in the wound, so instead I tried to give a half-handshake, half-hug, which caused her to smile at me with a look of hope on her face.

I nodded and stepped back. *Jeez*. This initial first few minutes never got easier. Thankfully, once Mum had a cup of tea in front of her and we all relaxed a little, the conversation started to flow relatively easily, jumping between topics like my work, Mum's job at a shelter for abused women, and Nathan's company.

'I heard back from the police this morning,' Nathan announced, and the air between the three of us filled with tension. 'The official inquest into father's accident has been completed. A verdict of accidental death was given, and the case has been closed.'

Closed. Perhaps we could now put that horrific day behind us and all begin to move on. Just as I was thinking that, Mum made a small, sniffling noise and I looked across to see that her eyes were wet with moisture.

Surely she wasn't crying for that fucker, was she?

'I know I've said it before, but I'm so sorry that I didn't stop him coming to your house that day.' Mum had already explained what had happened, but as she had been forcefully coerced into tricking Marion I could understand why she felt guilty. Apparently, Dad had tracked her down to her apartment in London. He'd forced his way in and told her that he was going to kill Nathan and me, but that he wanted her there, too. He'd already picked up the guns from an old army friend, and he'd told her she had to go with him, or die. He'd made her hold one of the unloaded pistols, then taken the gun back and dragged her to Nathan's house.

'I'm just so glad you all got out, and that Rebecca and the babies are OK,' she sniffled, drying her eyes on a napkin.

Nathan and I suspected that Dad had planned to kill all of us, Mum included, and use the gun that she had touched to make it look like she had murdered her own sons before committing suicide. Luckily, we'd never have to find out.

'Mum, you don't have to apologise about that again. We know what he was like. I know he forced you. We saw it on the CCTV from your flats.' We'd seen him smash her

215

phone and slap her around the face so she fell to her knees, too; it had all been caught on the camera feed. Then he'd dragged her from her house at gunpoint. It could all have been staged, of course, but from the terror in her eyes Nathan and I had decided that it wasn't.

After that, we shifted the conversation to Rebecca's impending birth and the tension between us all dissipated.

Really, the support was … nice. Not that we were going to rush things. We weren't suddenly going to be a solid family unit, and I'm not sure we ever would, but at least we were in contact again, and airing the past was turning out to be incredibly cathartic for all of us.

Chapter Twenty-Nine

Rebecca

'So how do you think Jean is dealing with the boys without us there?' I asked, chewing on a nail as I tried to imagine poor Mrs Jackson dealing with a meet-up with the brothers on their own. They were gorgeous, and the perfect men for Stella and me, but they were hardly the most sociably comfortable. To be honest, I had visions of the three of them sitting there in uncomfortable silence until one broke and made an excuse to leave.

'I think she'll be OK. She's been getting more confident each time, and I think they're genuinely enjoying getting to know her again.' Stella pulled out the coffee grinder and shrugged. 'They've all been through a lot of hurt, and meeting is going to be hard on them all at first, but I think in the long run it will help them all heal. I know Nathan struggled with all the returning memories. I'm sure Nicholas has too?'

'Yes and no. He's been so focused on the babies that he seems to have coped really well with their dad's death. I haven't seen any anger, or hurt or ... well, anything, really. I'm hoping he's not keeping it bottled up inside, but I genuinely think he's OK with it all.'

'Nathan was really angry at first, so we went to see Dr Philips to talk it all over, and he was amazing, I can see why Nicholas uses him.' Stella commented, as she pulled out a bag of coffee beans.

'Nicholas mentioned that Nathan had asked for his number. We spoke to Dr Philips about it all, too, and he said for a victim like Nicholas, the death of the abuser can be like the opening of a pressure valve. It can go either way; intense relief that they can finally move on, or extreme sadness and anger that they will never get the justice, payback, or apology they wanted. It sounds like maybe Nathan is the latter. I think Nicholas is a prime example of the first, though; he's just so relieved that we're all OK, not to mention excited about the babies, and that seems to have helped him move on from it all.'

There were a few minutes of silence as Stella got some mugs out and set the kettle boiling, then she glanced over her shoulder with a smile.

'Anyway, enough of that depressing stuff. How are you feeling? Your bump looks almost ready to burst now!'

She wasn't kidding, either. I looked and felt the size of an oil tanker. I actually couldn't remember the last time I'd seen my toes. Nicholas had to help me get my underwear and trousers on every day now, too, because my bump was so enormous that I couldn't bend over properly. 'I am so over this pregnancy,' I moaned, giving the bump an affectionate rub. 'The discomfort in my ribs is incredible. I feel like I can't even take a full breath.'

'I bet. I had that enough when it was just Will inside me, and he was a small baby. I can't imagine how you must be feeling with twins camped out in there.'

'I almost feel ready to grab a crowbar and get them out!' I giggled. 'But no, in all seriousness, apart from feeling the size of a whale, I can't complain. I've had no morning sickness since month five, I'm not as tired as I was, my skin looks incredible, and my boobs are the biggest they've ever been.'

'That sounds pretty good going to me,' Stella agreed with a smile. She handed me my cup of ginger tea then turned back to prepare her coffee.

Something had been niggling at the back of my mind

since the incident with Mr Jackson, but I'd been so worried about the babies and our recovery that I hadn't had time to give it much thought. Now I knew we were all OK, and had some time alone with Stella while the brothers were with their mother, I decided to follow it up.

'I've been meaning to ask you something …'

'Oh yeah? Ask away,' Stella murmured, distracted by her task of making coffee.

'OK … well, I was just curious … When all that stuff happened with Mr Jackson, he made a comment about Nathan liking to hit you in the bedroom, and I'd expected you to deny it … But, well … you didn't.'

There was a clatter as Stella dropped the spoonful of coffee beans that she had been loading into the grinder. She spun around looking bright red and so uncomfortable that I immediately regretted asking.

'Sorry … it's none of my business. I shouldn't have asked. I knew you guys weren't exactly vanilla, but I was just intrigued …'

Drawing in a deep breath, Stella shook her head. 'Don't be silly, you're my best friend. Of course you can ask.' She bent down and started to collect the scattered coffee beans, which she dumped in the bin before giving me a cautious glance.

'So, which bit had you curious?'

I had started this conversation, but now I was the one blushing as red as a tomato. 'Well, Nicholas and I do certain stuff, too, as you know, but it's mostly just using toys or, you know … objects.'

Stella raised an eyebrow in amusement. 'I'm sorry, Becks, but you're going to have to be more specific there.'

With a groan, I rubbed at my flaming cheeks, not wanting to elaborate but knowing I had to. 'Like vibrators, or nipple clamps. He's used a flogger a few times, too, but that's it. I … I was just surprised when you said you submitted to Nathan. I mean, I know that's how you met, but after he asked my advice on mainstreaming I thought you guys were more regular now?'

Stella's eyes shot open wide and she held up a hand. 'Woah! Time out! Nathan asked your advice on mainstreaming? When?'

'Gosh, it was ages ago now. Back when you and I first met at that dinner party at Nathan's old apartment.'

Stella smiled goofily and blushed. 'Wow. I'm actually quite touched that he went to that much trouble to try and adapt for me.'

'It was rather sweet,' I agreed with a fond smile, leaving out the part where Nathan had terrified me with the drilling intensity of his pale blue stare.

'I would really like to be having this conversation after a few glasses of wine, but seeing as you're preggers and it's only ten-thirty in the morning I guess super-strong coffee will have to do.' Stella took a sip of her coffee and chewed on her lower lip. 'But in answer to your question, yes, we do still do that stuff. Not full time, but occasionally if we're both in the right mood we'll do a scene and I'll submit to him.'

I was lost already. 'A scene?'

'Yeah, Nathan likes to be in control in the bedroom, and I really like the release that handing over power to him gives me. So sometimes we play in those roles. He'll be the dominant and I'll be his sub. It's all with full consent, and fulfils a need that we both have. It's one of the reasons we're so well suited, I think.'

Wow. Just wow.

I enjoyed Nicholas's more demanding side, so perhaps I had more of a submissive inclination than I'd realised. We'd never explored it much further than using a few toys and him taking the lead, though.

'Do you have to kneel for him?'

Stella paled slightly and shook her head. 'No. Nathan doesn't like that … Their father … he used to make them kneel for him when he was beating them.'

That was a new nugget of information. I'd known Mr Jackson used to beat them both with his belt, but I hadn't known about the kneeling part.

'I call him Sir. But only when we're doing a scene.'

As she spoke, I remembered the one occasion when Nicholas had taken me to his spare room to show me his darker side. He'd instructed me to call him Sir or Master, and I'd had to wear a gag when I forgot. I'd been terrified at first, and hadn't been keen on the gag, but the rest of the time in there had been remarkably erotic.

'And you like all of that?' I asked in a curious whisper.

The flush on Stella's cheeks was all the answer I needed, but she nodded her confirmation, too. 'I do.' She tipped her head to one side and assessed me through narrowed eyes. 'With all these questions, I'm starting to wonder if you're a little curious to try it yourself, Becky …'

The mouthful of ginger tea that I had just sipped practically flew from my mouth in shock as I clutched one hand over my lips and the other over my belly. 'I'm pregnant!'

'So? I was super-horny during pregnancy. We might have tamed things down a bit while I was carrying Will, but we certainly didn't stop having sex.'

I was really regretting ever starting this stupid conversation now. 'I am, and we are, but just not any kinky stuff. Nicholas is being very loving and gentle with me. It's … sweet.' If somewhat frustrating on occasion. 'I guess after Mr Jackson said that you must let Nathan hit you in the bedroom I wondered if it was that straightforward? You said you guys do more extreme stuff … what does it involve?'

'He doesn't beat me, if that's what you're asking. It's

more …' Stella shrugged awkwardly. 'More erotic than that. Nathan is very good at building anticipation. He uses floggers or his palm to do just that … It involves a certain degree of pain, but as that mixes with pleasure and arousal it's really quite amazing … It's pleasure like I've never experienced before, indescribably good.'

Wow. OK, then.

Stella started to gather her things up, then gave me an apologetic look. 'I'm sorry to rush off, but I'm meeting Nathan and the traffic will be a nightmare this time so I need to go. We're popping in to see Kenny. I can't believe he actually moved in with Tom; it's so exciting!'

My concerns for Stella were laid to rest, but my inquisitiveness was well and truly piqued, and strangely, I was feeling quite horny. I'd have to pounce on Nicholas when he got back. Well, perhaps not pounce, roll might be more appropriate, but I'd definitely be initiating some loving later today. Perhaps after the birth, when things had settled down again, Nicholas and I could even do some experimentation of our own. We did still have his box of toys in the house somewhere. We hadn't used them in ages, but maybe it was time for them to make a reappearance.

Chapter Thirty

Nicholas

All in all, the coffee meet with Mum had gone well. There'd been a few strained pauses, but mostly it had been relatively pleasant, and I think it was helping Mum too, because she had definitely seemed surer of herself this time.

As I arrived home and slid my key in the lock, I realised I was whistling to myself. I really was in a good mood recently. Rolling my eyes at how drastically my life had changed, I shook my head and grinned. It was about to change even more dramatically in the next month once the twins arrived.

I was distracted from my thoughts as my phone buzzed in my pocket. Pulling it out, I saw Rebecca's number on the display and frowned as I stepped into the hall. As I pulled the message up, I came to a halt. It contained just four words: *I'm in the bedroom.*

The bedroom? It was barely gone lunchtime. Was something wrong? Was she ill? Immediately, I charged for the stairs, fear slicing through me as I bounded up them two at a time. I threw open the door so fiercely that it bounced off the wall and rebounded back into my arm.

'Becky? Are you all ri …? *Holy fuck …*' My question dissolved at the sight before me, morphing into a heated curse as my mouth fell open and my cock instantly hardened.

Rebecca was sitting on the bed. No, not sitting, kneeling … Rebecca was kneeling on the bed completely naked, her gorgeous hair trailing down over her shoulders and breasts and just tickling the top of her beautiful bump.

She looked almost submissive with her head slightly lowered and her hands splayed on her thighs, and fuck me, she looked so glorious I couldn't drag my eyes away.

'I'm horny, Nicholas.'

A startled laugh stuck in my throat as I struggled to get a grip on my spiralling arousal and the mix of emotions that came with it.

'Becky, fuck, you look incredible.' And she did. I loved her pregnancy body, and I mean really fucking loved it. She was beautiful like this; her bump that contained our precious babies, her rounded hips that I found myself having to touch every time she was close, not to mention her breasts which were even larger and more perfect than ever.

'We shouldn't, though... the babies,' I choked out, wanting nothing else at that precise moment than to bury myself inside her, but not able to fully rid my mind of the image of her bleeding after my father's attack. The small rupture to her placenta was healed now, according to our most recent scan, but still ...

Finally, Rebecca raised her eyes and nodded. 'I was worried about that, too, but we've waited longer than the doctors recommended, and the last two scans have been fine.' As if sensing that I might need more persuasion, which I did, she pushed her hair back from her face and grinned at me. 'You were there when Karen said sex was fine again.' She knew how much I respected our midwife's opinion, and it was true; Karen had been adamant that we were good to go again.

It was certainly tempting, seeing as my cock was as stiff as a board and Becky looked well and truly irresistible kneeling there like that.

Rebecca stared at me imploringly. Seeing my continued hesitation, she slowly trailed her hand down her thigh and slipped it under her bump and between her legs. A groan rose in my throat, and I shifted on the spot as I watched my girl pleasure herself with heavy-lidded eyes. God, it had been so long since I'd been inside her. Too long …

'I had to get Stella to help me take off my leggings and knickers, which was pretty mortifying. Please don't say that all my preparations are going to be a waste?'

Stella had helped undress her? My eyebrows rose, and as an amused grin stretched on my lips, I gave in and practically threw my jacket from my shoulders.

I undressed in probably the quickest time I'd ever managed. Gone was my usual control. All I could think about was reconnecting with Rebecca.

'Well if you're feeling horny, it's my job to sort you out, isn't it?' I conceded with a smile as I climbed onto the bed and knelt before her. I slid a hand to the nape of her neck and gently tilted her towards me so our lips met in a slow kiss.

'We're going to do this my way, though. No gymnastics.'

'Yes, Sir,' she murmured against my lips, causing my cock to jolt with arousal at her surprise phrase. Sir? Where the hell had that come from? But there was no denying I liked the sound of it. My old dominant side leaped to the surface in glee and my cock gave another lurch which Becky noticed and giggled at.

We explored with eager hands, skimming over skin and arousing each other in the ways that only we knew, and when I could hear Becky panting with need, I threw myself to my back on the bed and gave my stomach a pat. 'Climb on board, baby, I want you to make yourself come.'

Rebecca raised her eyebrows at me as if surprised by me handing over control, but really, given the size of her bump, this was about the only position that I could see being feasible.

225

As I helped her to move and straddle me, I grinned at just how keen she looked. Keen and so fucking beautiful it made my chest hurt. I might not suggest this position a great deal, but it certainly had its benefits, one of them being the fact that I had easy access to her gorgeous breasts, which I immediately began to caress again.

'Nice and easy, baby,' I murmured as she took my cock in her hand and rubbed me back and forth against her molten core. Christ, she was so wet. A groan clawed its way from my chest, and I had to leave her breasts and grip at her hips to hold back the urge to jerk upwards into her.

Slowly, Rebecca positioned me at her entrance and began to sink down on me, inch by inch. Fuck. She felt so good. Hot, wet, and tighter than ever, and I could feel my cock twitching away inside her as if screaming at me to move. I wouldn't, though. If I got to come, too, then that would be a nice benefit, but after everything we'd been through with this pregnancy this was about her needs, her pleasure.

Instinctively, I moved my hands to caress her bump and I couldn't help the grin that stretched my lips as her hands found mine and we linked our fingers for a few moments. Our babies were in there. It still fucking amazed me.

She sunk down until I was completely buried inside her and our bodies were as tight together as they could get. Both of us paused in that position, absorbing the feeling and moaning, making noises so innately sexual that they could have been straight from the sound reel of a porn film.

Then she met my gaze, licked her lips, and began to move. Gazing up at her as she rode me for her pleasure was probably one of the most erotic sights I've ever seen; her expression was full of love and lust, her breasts swayed with her gentle movement, and her hair dropped down to curtain us in our own private bubble.

I loved her so fucking much. 'God, you are so beautiful.' The words were in my head, and seemed to fall from my lips accidentally, but Rebecca absorbed them with a soft, shy smile as she ground down on me again and growled as my cock hit her G-spot.

This might be predominantly about her pleasure, but hearing her make those sounds while her body clutched at my cock made my hands twitchy, and I slid one around to grip her buttock while my other hand dipped below her bump and found her clitoris.

She practically purred when I began to circle the slick nub. 'Ahhh ... Yes. Just like that.'

As I continued to play with her clit, I angled my hips slightly so that my shaft would rub against her G-spot every time she dropped down onto me, a move which clearly worked, because she gasped, and the next second she began speeding up her moves, moving one hand to her breast and fondling it as her head fell backwards.

'Eyes, Becky, let me see them.' I couldn't help the demand in my tone as the words fell from my tongue, but I needed to see her beautiful eyes. I always needed that intimate contact. Immediately, my girl brought her head forwards and smiled at me as her hips kept up the "up, down, grind" rhythm that she had settled into, and I could see from her dilated pupils that she was getting close.

I was, too. Her channel clenched around me so perfectly that it was taking everything I had to hold back my release.

'Oh God, Nicholas, I'm close,' she murmured, her cheeks flushing as she slammed her hands down onto my chest and clawed at the skin in a move so fucking erotic that I felt my balls tighten and lift.

'Come for me, baby ...' I ground out through clenched teeth as I desperately tried to cling to the swirling sensation at the base of my cock that signalled my imminent climax.

I would *not* come before she did.

227

Leaning forwards, she nodded and really ground herself down onto my cock, so much so that my hand at her clit struggled to move. Instead, I pinched at the tender nub, and her channel gripped me like a vice as she exploded around me.

'Nicholas!'

As she cried out my name, her body started to shake above me, the muscles of her core convulsing around me as she rode out her orgasm until I had no choice but to follow her lead. Allowing myself one upward thrust, I buried my length within her, gripped her hips to hold her still, and felt my release fire from within my balls like an electric shock shooting straight through my cock. It was so fucking good, and so powerful it was almost painful. If this was pain, then I'd take it from her every single day for the rest of my life.

'You OK, baby?' I asked, hoping it hadn't caused her or the babies any discomfort.

'OK? Are you kidding me? Holy fuck, Nicholas, that was incredible,' Becky panted above me, her face flushed from her orgasm and eyes twinkling with happiness. It was pretty much the perfect view, as far as I could see.

Returning her grin, I placed my hands on her bump again and gave a gentle rub. 'Don't listen to that foul language. That's just your baby momma forgetting herself.'

Raising an eyebrow at my use of the teasing nickname that I knew she hated, Rebecca linked her fingers with mine and gave a squeeze before rubbing the bump herself. 'Yes, well, "baby momma" only uses that language for two reasons. One, when your daddy is being an arse, or two, when he's being very, very naughty with mummy.'

'Being an "arse"?' I repeated, trying to sound outraged, but failing miserably.

'Mmm-hmm. Luckily, you've carried out your daddy duties to an exemplary level and I feel so sated and relaxed that I can't even be bothered to argue with you. You can help me in the shower, though, and then make me pancakes.'

From the twinkle in her eye, I could tell Rebecca was enjoying this banter, too. As she pulled me towards the shower, I started whistling to myself again, deciding that my day really couldn't get much better.

Chapter Thirty-One

Nathan

I wouldn't usually have tagged along when Stella was meeting up with Kenny, because I knew they had a close bond, and now I'd got over my jealousy about it, I tried to respect it and let them do their own thing when they met up.

I *was* tagging along today, though, because when Stella had mentioned Tom's address my jaw had nearly hit the floor. He lived in one of the new apartments in Battersea which had been designed and built by an architectural firm that I considered my closest rival in London.

It was a project I had admired from the start, but my pride had stopped me from ever going to see the finished buildings, in case it looked like I had a case of professional envy. I didn't, since my company was doing very nicely indeed, and I hadn't even put in a bid for the Battersea work, but still, I hadn't visited.

Now I had the perfect excuse, because we were coming across to see our friends.

The site from the outside was impressive; it was a conversion of an old industrial building, but as we walked towards the entrance I could immediately see that, rather than knock down the existing structure, they had managed to keep its integrity, and simply bring it up to date by adding glass walls, exposed brickwork and some modern metalwork. It worked rather well, but what I really wanted to see was the inside.

Almost as soon as Stella had pressed the intercom Kenny's excited voice answered, followed by a buzzing as the security door clicked open.

We wound our way through the brightly lit corridors and came to their door as it was flung open by Kenny, who then pulled Stella, Will, and me into a huge hug.

'Hi guys! Welcome!'

My arms remained rigidly by my sides and I clenched my teeth as he wobbled us all about gleefully and chuckled something about a "group hug". This was one of the reasons I tended to avoid Stella's regular meet-ups with Kenny, because over-the-top gestures of physical contact still made me feel uncomfortable, regardless of who was delivering them. Unless it was Stella, of course. Then the rules were reversed and I liked as much contact as possible. Preferably intimate, and deep.

Pulling my thoughts from the gutter, I persuaded a tight smile to my lips as Kenny released us and gave me a hearty pat on the shoulder, as if trying to offset his hug by being overly manly with me.

He really was the king of bodily contact. I flinched at yet more touchy-feely actions and clenched my jaw, but I stood my ground and managed not to brush him off, which was progress for me.

He picked up William and swung him around, causing my boy to gurgle with joy, and I couldn't stop my smile becoming just a little more genuine. He might be a little over-physical, but Kenny was an amazing friend to Stella, and a great "uncle" to Will, so I really shouldn't complain.

Once Kenny had finished his display, he handed Will back to me, and Tom stepped forwards and extended his hand to me with a smile. Balancing my boy on my hip, I shook Tom's hand. He was far more reserved than Kenny, which was easier for me to deal with, but also perhaps one of the reasons they worked so well together as a couple. He gave Stella a quick hug then stepped back, took hold of Kenny's hand, and waved us inside. 'Come on in!'

As I had expected, the apartment was stunning. We entered straight into a large open-plan lounge area, and just within this space I could see three different types of walls: glass, warm wood panelling, and exposed brick. It managed to maintain an industrial feel while still being modern to the extreme.

From this initial glance, I could tell the development had been designed and built to an incredibly high standard, and I felt excitement settle in my belly at the prospect of seeing more.

Nicholas might be able to lose himself in his music, but for me, architecture was my thing. More specifically, good architecture was what did it for me.

We took off our coats and shoes and moved further into the living space just as Will started to fidget in my arms.

'Would you like a look around?' Tom enquired casually, seemingly unaware of just how eager I was.

'Absolutely,' I replied, my voice sounding high-pitched from my excitement. I cleared my throat, slightly irritated that I'd let my enthusiasm be so bloody obvious. I sounded like a little kid on helium.

Beside me, Stella flashed me a reassuring smile and gave my free hand a squeeze, as if understanding my expression perfectly. It always seemed like she could see through me, which, given that she knew me better than anyone ever had, she no doubt could. I still hated losing control over my emotions, though, even if it was just in front of our friends. Stella was always telling me it was OK to loosen up now, but after so many years of guarding my inner feelings from everyone around me – my parents, the bullies at school, my teachers, my submissives – I still found it incredibly difficult to do so.

I could be described as a work in progress. Luckily for me, Stella seemed to have the patience of a saint.

Will started to get more upset in my arms, and Stella

glanced at her watch. 'He probably needs his snack. Are you hungry, bubs?' she cooed. She grabbed a pot of yoghurt from the baby bag and held out her arms for him. Spying the food, William smiled and went into his mum's arms with a gurgle of excitement that wasn't too far away from the noise I'd made just a few minutes ago.

'I know Nathan is dying to look around, so you guys go ahead. I'll feed the little man and then have a tour later.'

'I'll stay with you, Stella,' Kenny said. 'T's the expert on this place, aren't you, babe?'

Tom smiled shyly, but then nodded and looked at me with an excitement that almost seemed to match my own. 'I bought this place when they were first designing them, so I had a little bit of a say on the layout. I still have the blueprints and initial drawings if you'd like to see them?'

Now he was talking my language. 'Like to? I'd bloody love to see them.'

Stella

Grinning at how in his element Nathan appeared at the mention of the word "blueprint", I blew him a kiss as he stepped away. Immediately, he became engrossed in a discussion about the internal structure of the apartment with Tom. Bless him, my man did love buildings.

Sitting on one of the black leather sofas, I opened the pot of yoghurt and gave Will a spoonful. As he was munching away, I glanced around the space before nodding to myself. This place really was perfect for Kenny and his overly tidy habits: smooth lines, minimalist décor, and spotlessly clean, but with several rugs scattered around and collections of personal photographs on the walls it still had a homely, cosy feel.

I knew Nathan was mainly here because he wanted to look at the internal design, but I had a different agenda – I wanted to get the latest gossip, so as soon as Tom had led Nathan away on their tour, I grabbed my chance.

'You look like the cat that got the cream, Ken,' I declared with a grin, which Kenny quickly matched. It had been obvious how happy he and Tom were as soon as we walked in. Both were relaxed, with genuine smiles on their faces, and they had held hands as soon as the hugs were finished, but I still wanted to hear the details from the horse's mouth. 'How's it all going?'

Kenny glanced over his shoulder to check the others were out of sight then flapped his hands excitedly before leaping from his sofa and coming across to sit next to me. 'God, Stella, it's amazing, *he's* amazing!' I smiled fondly at my friend's happiness, fairly sure I'd used almost those exact sentiments to describe Nathan and me when we'd first

234

got together. 'I never knew I could be this happy!'

I'd never seen him look this content, either; his eyes were twinkling and his complexion was rosy with health. Living with Tom was obviously good for him. Great, now I was almost crying. Feeling my throat close up with emotion, I sniffed back an errant tear and grinned at Kenny. 'So you haven't driven him nuts with your need for tidiness, then?'

Tweaking his beard, Kenny shook his head with a smug smile. 'Nope, if he'd been messy it might have ruined everything but we seem to be perfectly matched on that scale, thank goodness.' Knowing how particular Kenny had always been when I'd lived with him, I could well believe it.

What was it about me that attracted clean freaks into my life? First, I'd had Kenny and his love of a neat and tidy house, and now Nathan, who liked things spotless, but was particularly obsessed with hygiene and clean hands. Maybe I'd been a dirty slapper in a previous life and these men had been sent to show me the right path.

'We just get on so well, Stel!' Kenny grasped his cheeks as if they hurt from smiling so much, which seeing as he couldn't seem to stop, they probably did. He sighed happily. 'I know we've not even been together a year, but it's the best relationship I've ever had. It's what I've always wanted, you know?'

Nodding jerkily, I blinked away even more tears and reached across with my free hand to give his a squeeze. 'I'm so happy for you, Kenny, I truly am.'

I'd known Kenny a long time now, and his generous nature had often led to him being targeted by the wrong kind of guys. Users who said all the right things for a week or so, then upped and left without so much as a goodbye.

With his good looks, he'd never had any trouble getting guys interested, and as a result of his love for sex and his

235

lack of willpower he'd had a string of one-night stands and failed relationships, but he'd never found the one. Not until now, anyway.

'I love him so much, Stella. He seems to know me better than I know myself sometimes.' That was a sentiment I was also familiar with, because Nathan knew me so well it was like he could see right into my soul sometimes.

'And the sex is incredible,' Kenny finished softly, hugging a pillow to his chest and smiling dreamily. Kenny usually didn't hold back on the details of his encounters, but with William in my arms today I was glad he spared me the in-depth analysis and went for the broad summary.

'So, are there wedding bells in the air yet?' I asked as a joke to lighten the air, but to my surprise, Kenny blushed, and fidgeted on his seat.

'Actually, it's funny you should say that …'

'Oh my God!' I shrieked, my eyes flying open wide. 'I was kidding! Are you serious? You guys are getting married?' I squeaked, my voice high, but luckily muted by the hand that I'd slapped over my own mouth.

'Well no, not yet, but the other day I met Tom's oldest mate, Brent, and afterwards, on the way home, T said that Brent would be his best man when we got married.' Chewing on his lower lip, Kenny leaned in close and gave me an intent stare.

'He actually said those exact words – "when we get married."' Kenny nodded gleefully then shrugged. 'Then he got a bit embarrassed afterwards and we haven't mentioned it again, but that's a good sign, right?'

Nodding my head, I smiled so broadly that my cheeks started to hurt. 'I think that sounds like a very good sign, Ken. He wouldn't have said it if it hadn't been on his mind.'

Drawing in a huge breath, Kenny flopped back on the sofa again. He grinned like a loon. 'That's what I thought!'

He ran a hand through his hair and gently nudged me in the ribs. 'I hope you can rock a tuxedo, because you'll have to be my best man – well, best "woman", I suppose – when the time comes.'

I raised my eyebrows and yet again my eyes filled with moisture. 'It would be my honour,' I whispered, before quickly dashing the tears away with the back of my hand and distracting myself by feeding Will another spoonful of yoghurt. 'God, Kenny, that's three times you've almost made me cry today!'

'Sorry, babes!' He giggled, pulling me into a side hug so I could still feed Will, but also rest my head briefly on his shoulder.

'Talking of best men,' I started hesitantly, drawing Kenny's interest. 'My collaring with Nathan is next month …' Kenny knew all about the ceremony after I'd blurted it out in a panicked phone call to him a few months ago, but I'd never got around to asking him to be my assistant. 'I can't have bridesmaids, or best men, but I was really hoping you'd come with me as my assistant beforehand to keep me from freaking out?'

Wiggling his eyebrows, he grinned from ear to ear. 'It would be my absolute pleasure, Stel. The date's already in my diary.' Giving me another squeeze, he let out an amused chuckle. 'Check us out, both settling down! Who'd have ever thought it, eh?'

Who'd have thought it indeed? Especially given Nathan's history, but it was really happening. He was mine, and he seemed intent on it remaining that way.

Just then, I heard the sound of Nathan and Tom making their way back towards the lounge, still engaged in what sounded like a serious technical conversation. It seemed the two of them had certainly hit it off.

'Sometimes I feel so lucky to have found him that I still can't believe it's real. I have to pinch myself,' Kenny whispered as they re-entered the lounge, looking relaxed and content. Nathan's gaze was still skimming all around the room, and I could tell from the slight bounce in his step that he was in a really good mood.

As they approached, Kenny stood up and moved to the free sofa so he and Tom could sit together. Tom looked from me to Kenny with a playful, narrow-eyed look. 'My ears are burning. Have you been talking about me?'

Kenny faked shock, clutching his chest in the overly dramatic way that only he could pull off. 'Of course not!'

Raising an eyebrow, Tom took Kenny's hand and looked at me for an answer, so I giggled and shrugged guiltily. 'Maybe just a little, but it was all good, Tom, don't worry.'

'Glad to hear it.' He wrapped an arm around Kenny's shoulder. The two of them exchanged a satisfied smile and my heart gave a little squeeze at just how good they looked together. It seemed that my friend had finally found his happily ever after, too.

'Get used to it with these two, Tom. I'm always the focus of their conversation when I'm out of earshot,' Nathan murmured, flashing me a wink.

'That's because you're just so fascinating to talk about, my dear,' I teased, waggling my eyebrows at him, which caused Kenny to stifle his spluttered laugh.

When I thought about it, my words were totally true. Nathanial Jackson might be the love of my life and the father of my child, but he was the most complex, multifaceted man I'd ever met. He could be dominant, gentle, troubled, and carefree all within the space of just a few hours. It made him utterly fascinating to me and was why I loved him with all my heart.

Chapter Thirty-Two

Rebecca

The babies were being awkward this morning; whatever position I lay in wasn't good enough for them. My ribs were killing me and they had been wriggling away and kicking me since before five a.m., when I had given up on sleeping and moved me and my gigantic bump downstairs.

Nicholas had dragged himself out of bed to keep me company and was sitting on the sofa beside me reading the news on his iPad. He looked lovely, with a serious case of bed head, a night's worth of stubble, and still wearing his blue pyjama bottoms and a white T-shirt. I might be almost through my nine months of pregnancy, and about as large as a mountain, but I could still appreciate how lovely he looked when he was relaxed and ruffled like this.

The twins chose that moment to initiate another round of kicking and I sighed and rubbed at my belly. I already felt like a beached whale, but now I was a beached whale with a football match going on in her belly. Marvellous.

As a lovely addition to the twins fighting in my stomach, I'd also had a return of my Braxton Hicks contractions – only a few in the last hour, so it wasn't too bad really, but they were adding to my discomfort. Finally giving up on my idea of a restful morning, I sighed and chucked my Kindle aside. 'I can't get comfortable today. I think I'll have a walk round for a bit. Maybe make a cup of tea.'

No sooner were the words were out of my mouth then Nicholas was on his feet and holding his hands out to help me up. A month or so ago he'd have been trying to make me stay put while he made the tea for me, but luckily, after a few firm reminders that I could still do things myself, he'd managed to cut back on some of his coddling, and we now had a nice balance going.

Considering I was the size of a beach ball, I did accept his offer of assistance, and let him pull me gently to my feet. As I steadied myself on his forearm, I felt the most peculiar popping sensation between my legs, followed by a sudden warming wetness.

Uh oh.

I still had just over two weeks to go until my due date, so surely that wasn't what I thought it was? Wincing, I tried to press my legs together as another gush of liquid escaped and soaked into my leggings. I sighed heavily. 'The tea might have to wait.'

'Why? Are you feeling OK?' Nicholas asked, frowning at me in concern.

Knowing how overprotective my man could get, I didn't want to freak him out, but there really was no gentle way of putting this. 'My waters just broke. I think maybe the babies might be coming.'

I'd expected him to freak out, melt down or go into panic mode, but my husband did none of those. Instead, he looked slightly wide-eyed, then nodded calmly.

'OK. Hospital it is, then. Do I have time to change out of my pyjamas or shall we just go now?'

I had no idea, but I didn't feel like the twins were about to make an imminent arrival so I shrugged. 'I'm fine. Change, and I'll text Karen.'

Nicholas dashed off upstairs and I waddled my way to the hall and slid down onto the stool by the coat rack just as another contraction hit. I'd thought they were Braxton Hicks earlier, but I guess maybe these were the real deal.

I pulled up the number to Karen and fired off a message. I got an almost immediate response telling me she'd meet us at the hospital, which helped relax me somewhat. 'Can you grab me some clean underwear and another pair of my yoga pants, too, please!' I called up to Nicholas. I might be about to go into labour, but the feeling of being soaked between my legs was horrible. That immediately made me think about other horrible sensations I would be having between my legs shortly, but I quickly pushed them away, deciding not to think about the pain until it actually kicked in.

Breathing in the way I'd been instructed by Karen, I had just got through the worst of my current contraction when Nicholas came jogging back down the stairs in jeans, boots, and the same T-shirt as earlier.

'Just as well we packed the hospital bag early, eh?' he said, waggling the holdall at me, then holding out his spare arm to help me up. 'Right, let's go, baby momma.'

'Nicholas!' I gasped, wanting to hit him for using that bloody stupid nickname, but at that moment another contraction started and so instead I grabbed his arm and almost dragged him out of the front door.

Nicholas

Holy fucking shit. Rebecca's in labour! I'd read in so many of the pregnancy books how important it was for the dad to stay relaxed when the labour started, but fuck me if it wasn't literally taking every shred of my self-control to remain calm.

Calm on the outside at least. Inside my head, I was a complete mess. It felt like a tornado was whipping up to top speed and throwing my entire life into an absolute mess of panic.

So many questions were fighting for space in my brain that I could barely think straight as I led Rebecca out to the car and got her safely belted in. Would we make it to the hospital in time? Was it a problem that she was going into labour early? Would she be OK? Would the babies be OK? Would I know what the hell to do to help her? Would I be a good dad …?

And breathe.

I needed to calm the fuck down, so I focused on the task of driving to distract me. *Ignition, gear, throttle, pull away.*

Thankfully as it was Saturday and still early, the drive through London wasn't bad at all, and in just ten minutes we had arrived at the hospital, where Rebecca was taken inside in a wheelchair.

All I can say is thank fuck for Karen. Over the next God knows how many hours she was bloody incredible: calm, cheerful, and so totally in control that she really put me to shame. I checked my hands on several occasions throughout the day, and each time found them trembling, presumably from the adrenaline rushing around my system, but there wasn't even a hint of a tremor in Karen's cool demeanour.

Becky was amazing, too. Dealing with the pain and intrusive check-ups without a complaint, and still managing to smile even as the day wore on and she surely must have been feeling completely exhausted.

I'd just got back from a rushed trip to the toilet when the hold she had on my hand began to tighten. As I looked down I saw her face had paled and she was showing signs of tension around her eyes. 'Are you OK, Becky?' I whispered.

Instead of an answering smile, this time all I got was a tight-lipped, 'Mmm-hmm.'

She was clearly struggling, and that made me feel so useless, not to mention helpless. A second later, she threw her head back and yelled, her face contorting with pain and her brow soaked with sweat.

Fuck, this is unbearable.

Nathan had tried to prepare me for this moment, warned me that I would feel like I was losing control over everything, but nothing, nothing could have prepared me for this. My skin went clammy and cold, and my heart was absolutely attempting to beat its way out of my chest. God only knows how Rebecca was feeling.

Karen popped her head up from her latest check-up and she grinned at us both. 'Looks like twin number one will be making an appearance any second now, Rebecca. You're doing so brilliantly. Keep up that breathing until I tell you to push.'

Oh God. It was really happening. Suddenly, I couldn't breathe properly and I started to wheeze aloud.

In one of our "pre-birth" coffee meet-ups Nathan had also told me about his breathing techniques, and how he had needed them during Stella's labour to stop him from freaking out. He'd called them his calming countdowns. I wasn't sure if I was too far gone in my panic for it to work,

243

but as Becky crushed my fingers and yelled out again I decided to give it a try.

Five, four, three, two, one ...

Chapter Thirty-Three

Stella

The house was calm and peaceful this morning; William was still asleep after his morning feed, I had done the bits of consultancy work I needed to, and Nathan was down in his office finishing off the final paperwork for a deal he was completing.

I was feeling decidedly horny, too. I don't know if it was just that I had more spare time while I was still on maternity leave, or if it was the time in my cycle, but I'd been craving Nathan even more than usual over these last few days.

When I wandered down to his office, I found the door slightly open. So I put on my best sultry expression, positioned myself leaning against the doorframe in what I hoped was a sexy stance, and used a finger to push the door open.

As the door swung wide I saw Nathan wasn't in his usual position in the chair behind his desk, but was instead sitting propped against the front of it while talking on the phone. His gaze immediately sought mine, a chunk of blond hair falling over his brow as he ran his eyes briefly over my body. His expression shifted towards desire before he joined his gaze with mine and raised an eyebrow in amusement.

Hmm. His long legs were crossed at the ankle, navy trousers sinfully snug in all the right places, and the grey shirt he had on made his blue eyes appear even lighter than usual. He looked almost good enough to eat. Perhaps that's how I could start things off. He might not order me to kneel for him when we were in a scene, but he certainly never complained when I dropped to my knees for him and slid his zip down.

'See you soon. Bye.' Nathan hung up the phone, placed it on the desk, and folded his arms as he continued to stare at me. 'Well, I have to say that's a very promising expression on your face, Stella, but I'm afraid you're going to have to save that idea for later.'

Eh? Nathan was turning down sex? In what universe did that ever happen? Even if he was busy, he never, ever turned down the chance of a quickie, so this was decidedly strange.

My attempt at a sultry expression quickly morphed into confused disappointment as I straightened from the doorframe and crossed my arms defensively.

Nathan laughed at my pout, stalking across the room and hunkering down before me so that our eyes were level. 'You know I'd love to, baby, but we have somewhere to be.'

When I'd looked this morning, my diary had been free for the entire week, so I had no clue what he was talking about. 'Where?'

'I just spoke to Nicholas. Rebecca went into labour, and they think the twins are due any moment now.'

'Oh my God! Why didn't you just say that?' I squawked, trying to work out my dates, and realising that she was at least two weeks early.

'I was enjoying the sultry look on your face,' Nathan replied with a wicked grin. 'Anyway, I just called Marion and she's on her way to watch Will for us so we can head to London. Apparently, Rebecca is doing really well, but I think Nicholas would quite like some support.'

'Let's get ready, then we can leave as soon as Marion gets here.'

Chapter Thirty-Four

Rebecca

I knew there were two small faces gazing up at me, but my eyes were so full with tears that all I could see were blurry pink blobs. The tears had started as soon as the first baby had arrived, and now I literally couldn't seem to stop them. I think they were happy tears, or possibly tears of relief because the pressure on my ribs had finally been released, but whatever the cause, they flowed endlessly.

'Right, everyone is cleaned up, so I'll give you four a bit of time alone,' Karen announced, before quietly leaving the room.

I wanted to thank her again for everything she'd done during the birth because she had been utterly incredible, but I was so drained and emotional that the words wouldn't form. Hopefully I'd manage to get a grip on myself soon, then I could say it when she next came in. I suspected Nicholas was crying, too, because I had heard several quiet sniffles next to me. Not that he'd want me to know, I'm sure.

Nicholas gave a louder sniff and then, after fiddling with a box of tissues, he began to wipe at my eyes for me. Gradually, as he cleared my vision, I started to get control of my tears. Then, finally, I could see my man leaning over me with his super-shy smile. The one he reserved just for me.

'I'm so proud of you, Becky,' he said gruffly, before dropping his gaze and looking down into my arms. Following his gaze, I sucked in a breath when I finally got a proper look at our babies. They were so perfect!

Expertly wrapped in white blankets by Karen, they looked like little matching dolls, both with chubby pink cheeks, a spattering of dark hair, and dark eyelashes fanning on their cheeks as they slept.

'Would you like to hold them?' I asked softly, still slightly shocked that we had twins. Obviously, I'd known I was carrying them for the majority of the pregnancy, but seeing them both here really brought it home to me.

We had two babies. Two.

'I'd love to ... I'm a bit scared I might hurt them,' he confessed quietly.

'Tell me about it! They're so tiny,' I joked, not that they had felt tiny when they were coming out. 'Just make sure you support the back of the head, and I don't think you can go far wrong.'

'I can't imagine how any parent could ever hurt their child.' Nicholas murmured the words so softly that I wasn't sure he'd meant to voice them out loud. But I heard it, and my heart just about broke for him and the childhood he'd endured.

With ultimate care, Nicholas picked up the twin closest to him, scooping them into his arms and cradling the back of the head before gently rocking his arms and gazing down with utter awe.

'So now they're here, do you want to stick with the names we planned?' he asked.

Considering it for a second, I nodded. 'I still think they're good choices. What about you?'

'Yeah, Benjamin and Holly. Except maybe we can shorten his to Ben? They look too small for long, formal names.'

'I like that idea,' I whispered as I watched Nicholas linking his little finger through the tiny fingers of our baby. He shook his head in amazement and grinned at me, his eyes shining with moisture again. 'Her fingers are so small … or maybe his fingers?' Suddenly frowning, he looked at me in concern. 'Is it just me, or can you not tell the difference between them either yet?'

I had no clue which was which. Both were wrapped up tight so that only their faces showed, and they were so new that their skin was pink and wrinkly, giving no indication at all of which was Holly and which was Ben.

I giggled, then gently pulled the swaddling open so I could see which twin I had. 'Well, judging from the anatomy I can see this is definitely Ben,' I observed with a giggle. 'Hey baby,' I cooed, wrapping him back up and pulling him higher in my arms to snuggle him.

'Holly,' Nicholas murmured, seemingly lost in his own world as he gazed at his baby girl, then gasped as she briefly blinked her eyes open. 'Hi there, I'm your daddy.'

I was so exhausted and emotional that his softly spoken words were all it took to make me sniffle again, but thankfully I was distracted from a full breakdown by a quiet knock at the door.

'You OK for visitors?' Nicholas asked, still gently rocking Holly in his embrace.

After taking a deep breath and wiping away a lone tear, I smiled and nodded to Nicholas, who carefully carried Holly to the door. He pulled it open to reveal two huge helium balloons bobbing away – one blue and one pink – and glimpses of a very excited-looking Stella behind them.

'Oh my gosh, he's so tiny!' she squeaked, dragging Nathan into the room and looking at the baby in Nicholas's arms while grinning broadly.

They quickly tied the balloons to the leg of a table then approached the bed.

'Actually, this is Holly,' Nicholas announced proudly.

'And this is Benjamin, but I think we'll shorten it to Ben,' I added as Stella bent down to give me a hug.

'Holly and Ben! Such perfect names. Hello, Ben!' Stella cooed, leaning closer and looking decidedly close to tears as she smiled at my little boy. We'd kept the names secret, but Nathan and Stella had known about the sexes of the babies since we'd found out.

'Congratulations, you two. Or should I say you four?' Nathan murmured dryly, not looking entirely comfortable with the little people in the room, but apparently doing his best to stay calm.

'Thanks, Nathan, your advice did me proud.' Nicholas said, supporting Holly in one hand and shaking Nathan's hand with the other.

'Would you like a cuddle?' I asked, laughing as Stella held her hands out in delight and gently took Ben from me.

'They're so small,' Stella crooned, looking towards Nathan with a grin. 'I'd almost forgotten that William was ever this tiny!'

'Stella will be wanting more if you're not careful, Nathan,' Nicholas joked. Nathan paled at his words, looking distinctly panicked for a second until Stella moved to his side and leaned up to place a kiss on his cheek.

'Actually, I don't. We're more than happy as we are.' Lifting onto her tiptoes she then whispered something by his ear, or perhaps just kissed him there, but whatever she did or said it seemed to soothe Nathan, as he stared down at her intently, nodded once and visibly relaxed.

'No more babies on the horizon, but I will hold one,' he said, relenting and moving to Nicholas's side. 'If you trust me to,' he added, actually looking unsure, which was quite a novelty where Nathanial Jackson was concerned. Usually he was cool, calm, and in control of everything.

In response, Nicholas laughed and held Holly carefully towards Nathan. 'I trust you with my life, brother, and theirs,' he stated, meaning every word. Nathan might be quite shuttered, but after getting to know him I knew

250

without doubt that Nicholas's sentiments were true. Nathan would do anything for his brother, and I was fairly sure that bond would extend to me and our twins, too.

As the brothers shared a meaningful glance I looked at Stella and found her also watching them with an affectionate smile on her face. Then she looked back to Ben in her arms and grinned.

When I'd first met Nicholas and he'd told me he wanted to "fuck me over his grand piano" I'd never for the life of me thought that one day I'd be married to him and have his babies.

But we were, and we did, and I couldn't be happier about it.

Life certainly worked in mysterious ways, that was for sure.

Chapter Thirty-Five

Stella

Nathan slid back into the car and looked across at me as if considering something. 'While we're in London, I thought it might be a good opportunity to pop to Club Twist and finalise a few details for this weekend. Sound OK?'

This weekend.

Our collaring.

Nerves settled in my belly as they always did when I thought about it, but then I touched the necklace around my throat and felt my flutters settle. There was nothing to be nervous about; it was simply going to be a special day where Nathan and I formalised our bond.

In front of a full club of people. But still, as long as I could push that part to the back of my mind I could convince myself that it wouldn't be much different from our usual trips to Club Twist.

'Stella?' As Nathan spoke I realised I hadn't answered his question and smiled at him.

'Sorry, yes, that sounds fine.'

'You looked miles away, everything OK?'

Giving his thigh a reassuring rub, I nodded. 'Yeah, I was just imagining how full the club will be on Saturday and … Well, I get a bit nervous if I let myself dwell on it.'

'Try not to worry, sweetheart. The only people who matter are you and me; that's what it's all about.'

It was basically what I'd told myself, too; still, it was very nice to hear Nathan reflect my sentiments.

It was still relatively early when we got to the Club, so although it was technically open, there weren't many customers around yet, just a few people at the bar, some staff I recognised, and us.

It reminded me of the very first time I'd come here. I'd arrived at opening time that night, too, and the club had been completely empty apart from David Halton behind the bar, who, coincidentally, was also serving tonight. About an hour after entering I'd been introduced to Nathan as a potential no-strings Dom for me, and I'd been utterly terrified of him, thinking that it would never work between us.

What a difference some time can make! Just look at us now. Bringing up a child together, happy, strong, and about to make our relationship official to all the members of the club. I was grinning from ear to ear by the time we reached the bar. Nathan gave me a quizzical look and I shrugged and explained. 'I was just thinking about the night we first met here.'

Nathan's eyes darkened, and he slid a hand around my waist, pulling me tight against his body. 'I knew instantly that you were special,' he murmured, which, given his difficulty with expressing emotions, was actually a pretty big statement for him. 'I was too emotionally withdrawn to realise why, but I was so drawn to you, beyond just physically, I mean, that I could sense meeting you was going to change my life somehow.'

Wow. His first emotion-laden statement just got totally trumped by that second one. Holy crap, Nathan's on fire tonight.

I didn't try to compete with his lovely declarations. Instead, I rolled up onto my tiptoes and laid a kiss on his lips. Usually when we were in the club I would adopt my submissive role and wouldn't dream of doing something as

253

forward as this, but the place was practically empty, and he'd just made me so happy with his words that I couldn't hold back.

It seemed Nathan couldn't, either, because as soon as my lips brushed his, the hold he had on me increased and his mouth crushed down on mine as his tongue joined in the fun.

I slid my hands around his waist, gripping at his belt for support as my legs started to feel wobbly, but just as things were starting to get really interesting we were interrupted by an amused voice to our left.

'Don't let me interrupt you, but if you plan on carrying on, feel free to take it to the stage. I'm sure everyone would love to get a good look.'

I broke apart from Nathan and turned to see David behind the bar with his tattooed arms folded and a broad grin on his face. My face flushed, and an embarrassed giggle rose up my throat.

'Fuck off, David,' Nathan growled in warning to him, causing David to back off while laughing heartily. I liked David a lot. He was a funny guy and had always been lovely to me whenever I'd been in the club, but Nathan didn't seem to tolerate his touchy-feely behaviour very well. Glancing down at me, Nathan softened his expression, then took a step back, looking reluctant. He raised a hand to smooth his hair and tug his shirt sleeves down, then let out a slow breath as if trying to get control of himself again.

'So, I just want to go and confirm a few details with David. You'll be OK here?'

'Of course. I'll get a glass of wine and check my emails on my phone.'

As if by magic, David had a glass of red poured and set before me within seconds. After flashing me a wink, he led Nathan out of the bar towards the office.

I took a sip of my wine and hummed my approval, then

pulled out my phone to start checking my work emails. I'd had a peaceful few minutes and got through a decent handful of emails when a deep voice at my shoulder made me jump in my seat.

'You can still change your mind, you know.'

Spinning on my stool so quickly that I very nearly fell off the bloody thing, I came face to face with Dominic, another of the owners of Club Twist, and a guy who seriously gave me the creeps. I say I came "face to face", but seeing as he was gargantuan and standing, and I was on a stool it was more like "face to chest", really.

'I could, but I don't want to.' I attempted my most disinterested expression, which was difficult when I felt as uncomfortable as I did now.

'Hmm.' Dominic stood a little straighter, fixing me with a stare that was almost as penetrating as Nathan's. He pursed his lips. 'Shame.'

Letting out a sigh that hopefully sounded bored, I was about to slip from the stool and move away from him, when he reached out a hand and placed it on my forearm.

'I could show you such a good time,' he murmured, but instead of appealing to me his words revolted me.

'Get off me,' I grated as I tried to shake him away, but he held on. Looking down at his hand, I drew in an irritated breath at his cheek and reached down to prise his fingers off me.

My hand was just grappling with his when I heard a crash behind me.

'What the fuck is going on here?' The hairs on the back of my neck stood up at the furious tone in my man's voice, because of course Nathan would pick that exact bloody moment to reappear, wouldn't he? Rolling my eyes at the unlucky timing, I continued my mission, finally manging to free myself from Dominic's unwanted touch and then sliding from the stool to create some distance between us.

'I was just offering her an alternative, that's all. I was only playing, Nathan, chill out.' Dominic seemed to be totally relaxed about the encounter, but as I turned to Nathan I saw the complete opposite; his eyes were budging, his nostrils flared, and a vein in his neck throbbed like it was about to explode.

I was fairly sure that Dominic hadn't been "just playing", but with Nathan looking homicidal I decided not to point that out and stayed silent.

Nathan covered the gap between us in three huge strides before he leaned right up into Dominic's face, his entire frame bristling with anger. 'Don't ever lay your hands on her again, understand?'

'She touched me, too. Practically held my hand,' Dominic replied cockily, and I could no longer stay silent.

'No, I bloody well didn't! I was peeling your hand off my arm because you wouldn't move it.'

At this point, the tension in the air was thick with impending violence, both Nathan and Dominic refusing to back down from their face-off. Somebody was going to snap, and I had a feeling it would be Nathan, because I was a very sensitive subject for my possessive man. David had obviously picked up on the possibility of a fight, too, because he stepped in between Nathan and Dominic and placed his hands on their chests.

It was just as well that David clearly worked out, because I wouldn't fancy the chances of many guys standing between Nathan and Dominic. Using his substantial muscles to push them apart, David glared at them both in turn. 'Enough, the pair of you. Dominic, no one likes your stupid games. Fuck off, would you?'

Dominic finally stepped back and brushed down the front of his shirt before fixing Nathan with a smug smile. 'See you Saturday,' he drawled as he sauntered away.

A breath of relief flew from my lungs, but Nathan didn't

calm down quite as quickly as I did. 'I do not want that fucker here on Saturday,' he ground in David's direction, before stepping to my side and taking a tight hold of my hand.

David brushed his wild hair back and tucked his hands into the pockets of his jeans. 'Nathan, you know he's one of the only ones senior enough to oversee certain parts of the collaring ceremony. He was just being a dick like usual tonight. You know how he likes to wind people up. I'll speak to him, OK?'

Nathan dragged in a harsh breath, then cursed. 'Fuck. He'd better be on his best behaviour, David, because I swear to God if he touches Stella again I won't hold back my punches.'

David calmly crossed his arms and nodded. 'Understood.' Giving us another glance, he went back behind the bar and busied himself down the other end, cleaning some glasses. It made quite an incongruous image; a big, tattooed guy in a leather waistcoat polishing delicate wineglasses.

I quickly turned back to Nathan and placed a hand on his arm, hoping to soothe him. 'Nathan, I know that looked bad, but he was just being stupid. And for the record, I really was pulling his hand away, OK?'

My statement was met with silence, Nathan simply stood watching me with a brooding expression on his face before he extended a hand to me. 'Let's go.'

Glancing at my full glass of wine, I frowned, and looked back to him. 'Where are we going?' I'd thought that now Dominic had gone we might stay to finish the drink before leaving.

'Home. I want you in my bedroom.'

My eyes widened slightly at his words, because there was only one room in our new house that Nathan ever referred to as his bedroom, and that was the playroom, the

257

room where he was master and commander.

As much as I liked our scenes in that room, I wasn't entirely sure that it was such a great idea right now, because he was so obviously wound up. Mind you, it would be at least a half an hour's drive home, so that would give him plenty of time to cool off. Maybe we could talk in the car.

When I didn't reply, he nodded his head once and gave a pointed look at his still outstretched hand. I trusted him implicitly, and I knew Nathan would never hurt me, no matter how highly strung he was feeling, so I took his hand and allowed him to pull me from the club.

Once we hit the fresh air outside, Nathan strode towards his car before opening the door for me and then pausing and cupping my cheek. 'This isn't about punishment, Stella, if that's what you're thinking. I trust you completely. I know you didn't touch him out of choice.'

Leaning into his touch, I sighed happily. I knew he trusted me, but I was still incredibly glad to hear those words. When I looked at his face, I could still see a faint red tinge in his cheeks from his earlier anger.

'This is about me.' Clearing his throat, he averted his eyes and swallowed hard. 'Sometimes when things like that happen I … I just need to reassure myself that you're really mine.'

How someone could be so dominant and yet so vulnerable at the same time was still a mystery to me, but my heart just about melted at his softly whispered confession. My strong, dominant man could reduce me to an emotional puddle with just a few words, and once again, he had. My throat clogged up with emotion and rendered me speechless, so I tightened my arms around him in reassurance and clung to him for dear life, trying to express how much he meant to me.

When I finally felt able to speak, I leaned back and placed a brief, chaste kiss on his lips. 'Nathan, you don't need to question that. Ever. I'm yours. Always.'

He swept his eyes across my face. He must have seen the utter conviction behind my words, as his body gradually began to relax below my hands. Letting out a long breath, he lifted one hand and gently traced the edge of my lips with the tip of his index finger, causing a delicious shudder to run through my body.

'Mine.'

Knowing he'd want me to acknowledge his statement, I smiled and nodded my agreement, then felt the stirring of his groin against my stomach as he pulled me against him and began to harden. A chuckle was about to rise in my throat at how mercurial he could be, flipping from irritation inside the club to lust just a few seconds later, but the darkening of his expression dried the laughter.

'Did you just nod at me, Stella?' Nathan murmured in a low, warning tone that seemed to vibrate right through my body. I knew him well enough by now to know he was faking his incredulity, but his growled words still caused my senses to ignite as I watched his eyes clear of their earlier uncertainty and fill with his more common determination and dominance.

The Dominic disaster of a few minutes ago seemed like distant history now, as things seemed to be taking a much more promising turn. Deciding to up the stakes a little, I further pushed his buttons by repeating my nod then biting down on my lower lip as I waited nervously for his response. His eyes briefly widened in surprise at my deliberate taunt, but they narrowed to slivers of gleaming blue as a wicked half-smile curved his lips.

'Get in the car, baby, I need to get you home. Right now.' He lowered his head towards mine and placed an open-mouthed kiss on my lips, then sucked my bottom lip out from between my teeth before nipping at it and running the tip of his nose along my jawline to my ear. He guided

259

me into my seat, then jogged around the front of the car and quickly slid into his seat.

'I may have said this wasn't about punishment, Stella, but you know that deliberate provocation like lip-biting will always have consequences, yes?'

That was what I'd been hoping for. My throat was so dry from lust that I struggled to speak, but finally, after several swallows, I managed to squeeze out two simple words. 'Yes, Sir.'

Inhaling sharply at my choice of title, he made a low, growling noise at the back of his throat and started the ignition.

He leaned across the car to grip my thigh and kissed my jaw. 'Tell me again,' he demanded breathily against the lobe of my ear, and I immediately knew what he was referring to. 'I'm yours, Nathan.'

Pulling in a calm breath, he seemed to take a few seconds to absorb my words. Then he opened his eyes, winked at me and began to pull out of the carpark. 'Think of the drive home as a method of delayed gratification.'

Oh God. With the lust-drenched look he had just thrown at me I had a feeling that the next forty minutes were going to be hell.

Nathan

Desire was now burning around my system, but every time I allowed my mind to flick back to visions of Dominic touching Stella, my fiery lust bubbled into a completely different type of heat. Sizzling anger. Dominic was a dick towards practically everyone, but I'd always had a particularly tense relationship with him, which I could only assume was a testosterone battle that neither of us was willing to lose. Club Twist had a few other senior Doms as members, and none had a good relationship with Dominic, a fact that further supported my speculation.

Once we arrived home, we both went to check on William and Marion. Thankfully, she had agreed to resume working with us, and even though we were now further from her house in North London, a pay rise and a private bedroom in our new property had easily persuaded her to remain our nanny.

William was already fast asleep, and Marion decided to head back home as we didn't need her again until the following weekend.

As soon as she had left, I turned to Stella and continued exactly where I had left off in the car park of Club Twist. Practically pouncing on her, I buried my lips into the crook of her neck, then ran hot kisses across her skin. This had an almost instant impact as her legs seemed to turn to jelly and she clutched at me to stay upright, my name falling from her lips in a gasp.

That was a particularly pleasing response, but I wanted her screaming my name, not gasping it, and I had plans on exactly how I could accomplish that. For what I had in mind we were in the wrong room, though, as soundproofing

261

would be required.

Nodding sharply, I released my hold on Stella's waist. As her wobbly legs began to buckle I bent down to scoop her into my arms before striding purposefully towards the stairs.

'Need you. Right now.' That was perhaps a little more emotionally open than I would usually aim for in a scene, but fuck it, it was true so I might as well goddamn well say it.

Pausing outside the soundproof room, I smiled down at Stella as she reached up her finger to open it using the fingerprint scanner. She hadn't needed prompting, which told me just how keen she was to get things started, too. Delayed gratification was all very well, but fuck me if I wasn't desperate to get what I wanted now.

Once we'd entered the bedroom, I pushed the door shut behind us and placed Stella gently down on the end of the bed. I quickly walked to the sound panel and switched on the baby monitors so we'd know if Will needed us, then turned back to look at my girl.

Her gaze was fixed on me, eyes bright with excitement and cheeks flushed in anticipation. 'So, now that you have me here, Sir, what will you do with me?'

I couldn't help but grin at her cheek. She loved to wind me up, but luckily, I loved it as much as she did. As tempting as it was to spank her for her teasing words, I didn't want to risk any possible marks being left for next weekend. There was a possibility that people might see her skin at the ceremony, because her chosen dress was sleeveless and did show some leg.

So that meant no spanking, crop work or flogging today. I could work with that, though; our wardrobe was stuffed with things designed for our particular taste in fun, so there were plenty of other things I could do.

'I'd like you to undress me, please.' I mostly did this myself, and I saw Stella's eyes light with excitement at the opportunity as she jumped up and dashed towards me.

She began to pop open the buttons of my shirt, but seeing how frantic she was, I decided to slow things down a bit, even if I was feeling just as desperate as her. After all, she was in need of a punishment for her earlier lip-biting, and I happened to know that delaying and denying her pleasure was one of her pet hates.

She loved spanking, flogging, and my use of the crop, so, as enjoyable as they were for me to perform, I knew that they weren't any form of punishment for her. This, though, would work a treat.

'Slow down.'

At my growled words, Stella paused, looking confused by my command. Presumably she had assumed I was gagging for it as much as she was. Of course, I was, but part of being a Dom meant always keeping her on her toes, and it was clear from her surprise that I had just done that.

I redid the buttons, then hung my arms by my sides. 'Start again, and do it properly this time,' I murmured in a deadly soft tone, only just managing to hold back my smirk at her shocked, stuttering cough.

'Sorry, Sir,' she whispered, her voice so soft and sexy that I would have forgiven any misdemeanour.

With my cock now doing its best impression of a tent pole, I tried to maintain my poise as she raised her hands and began again, this time taking a steadying breath and slowing down. After a second, Stella got into the swing of things, gently trailing her fingers across the front of my shirt as a way of delaying the next button. Then *pop*, she'd flick it open and repeat her mini-massage.

I might be the master of anticipation, but she was certainly the mistress of a good tease.

Once my shirt was undone, I watched as she eyed my

chest greedily then slid her hands inside the material before splaying them across my ribs. My self-control was good, but I couldn't help the hiss of pleasure that escaped when she ran her hands up my chest and briefly toyed with my nipples before moving to my shoulders. She slipped the shirt from my body and quickly folded it.

'Trousers next,' I muttered gruffly, hoping like hell that she wouldn't take as bloody long to remove these as she had my shirt. I couldn't say anything, though, because I had been the one to tell her to go slowly. Sometimes I really was my own worst enemy.

Thankfully, Stella seemed to tune in to my thoughts, because although she didn't rush, she certainly wasn't as long-winded as before. Before she unzipped me, she briefly cupped the bulge at my groin, my cock feeling like it was going to explode from the pleasure of her touch and my eyes briefly fluttering shut. Then she began to push the zip down, which was a tricky task given my current arousal, before she finally gripped the waistband of both my trousers and boxers and made a show of slowly lowering them down my legs.

I'd removed my shoes and socks when we'd got in – it was my house habit – so now I stood before her completely naked, and from her flushed cheeks and the twinkle in her eye my girl liked the view.

A lot.

'Let's even things up a little, shall we?' I murmured as I began to undress her, starting with her jeans because I couldn't wait to see what lace beauties were hidden below. Deep plum-coloured knickers entered my view as I dragged her jeans down and I smiled my appreciation at the sexy colour choice.

Now to see if she was wearing a matching bra. I stood up, lightly gripping the hem of her top, and jerked my chin upwards to indicate she lift her arms. Stella responded immediately to my sign language and I couldn't resist dropping a brief kiss on her lips before removing her top.

'Gorgeous.' The word slipped from my lips as I took in the matching bra and Stella's figure with curves in all the right places. She really was perfect.

After the drive home, the break while we checked on William, and Stella's teasing removal of my clothes, my famed control was finally starting to fray at the edges, and I feared that I would rip her delicate underwear from her body as soon as my fingers so much as touched the soft lace.

Seeing as it was one of my favourite sets and tearing them would be sacrilege, I stepped back, leaving the job to her. 'Take them off, please.' Folding my arms across my chest, I widened my stance to watch, not caring that I was naked. I was well aware that my cock was swinging away between my legs now, and quite apparently so was Stella. As she reached around behind herself to undo her bra, then slid off her panties, I saw her eyes dip briefly to my manhood and jump back up again as she bit down hard on her lower lip and let out a soft, aroused moan.

Fuck me, the noises she made were sent to test me, because that had been so hot it sent a jolt of pure lust shooting to my already stiff dick.

'Lip, Stella,' I growled.

Her gaze flashed to mine guiltily before she released the lip and gave me a repentant smile. 'Sorry, Sir.'

Nodding at her apology, I leaned forwards and ran my tongue along her lip, a move which elicited another breathy moan from her. The sound had my balls screaming at me with the need to release. 'Lie down on the bed, face up, arms and legs spread.' My voice sounded strangled, so before she could see how much I was battling with my control I turned towards the wardrobe to select the items I needed.

'Yes, Sir.'

I pulled out the softest leather cuffs we owned and quickly set about cuffing her to the four posts of the bed so she was open for my eyes alone. She made such a stunning sight lying there like this. Her blonde hair was cascading across the pillows, her skin was flushed pink with excitement, and between her legs I could see just how aroused she was.

I wanted to bury myself in her heat so desperately that my cock actually ached for it. But first I needed to deal with her earlier lip biting. 'As I don't wish to risk you having any bruises for next weekend I'm going to use a different technique for your punishment today.'

Stella whimpered, but it was a noise so low and full of arousal that I couldn't help but groan in response.

'Why are you being punished, Stella?' I asked softly as I climbed on the bed and bent to lick at one breast. She loved a little pain with her sex, and one of her most favourite acts was for me to bite her nipples, which was exactly what I did next to indicate that her reply was taking too long. I sucked the bullet-hard tip into my mouth and bit down. Hard. Stella arched her back and a breathy gasp left her lips as her eyes fluttered shut. 'Because I bit my lip again, Sir.'

'Yes, you did. Multiple times. So, as payback I shall bring you to the brink of orgasm multiple times, too, but not allow you to come.'

The noise Stella made was almost that of a petulant teenager, so I lifted up onto my elbows and looked her in the eyes. 'Do you have a problem with that, gorgeous?'

It was obvious from the lusty, desperate expression on her face that she did have a problem with it, but like a true pro she blinked, shook her head, and delivered the correct answer. 'No Sir.'

'If you're a good girl I may allow you to come later,' I

murmured, a second before I lowered my head to her opposite breast and began my torture.

Stella and I were so in tune with each other that I could bring her to climax extremely quickly, especially when she was as aroused as she was today, so it didn't take me long to draw her to the peak of her pleasure before removing all contact and denying her the final touch that would send her over. She briefly flinched against her restraints, but after a warning tut from me she immediately stilled, and I smiled when I heard her taking several deep breaths.

It was like her very own version of a calming countdown.

As soon as her body had relaxed and pulled away from her climax, I repeated my moves, licking, sucking, and using my fingers to quickly raise her arousal to almost bursting level before stopping again.

And again.

And again.

After the fourth time, Stella was covered in a sheen of perspiration and threw her head back into the pillow as she tugged at her cuffs.

'Sir, please … I'm begging. Please …'

I didn't give in because she begged, although that did sound rather lovely falling from her tongue, but I couldn't take any more either, so I manoeuvred myself over her and teasingly rubbed the tip of my cock up and down her soaking entrance several times.

'You may come at any point now,' I murmured as I jerked my hips forwards and buried myself inside her in one hard, deep thrust.

As soon as I felt the deliciously tight heat of her pussy clamp around me I knew that this was going to be fast and furious. With my hands planted on either side of her head, my hips seemed to move of their own accord as I took my

267

pleasure. Stella was with me every step of the way. She might have been tied down, but her hips were gyrating against mine, meeting every one of my hard, deep thrusts with an upward tilt of her own so that I went in to the hilt on each move.

It was as if she knew how much I needed this, how much I wanted to claim her back as mine after that fucker Dominic had touched her.

Fucking Dominic. Touching what was mine. Subconsciously, I dropped my lips to her neck and began to suck, and even though she must have felt what I was doing, Stella didn't try to stop me. In fact, she angled her head to give me better access as if knowing how much this small gesture would reassure me. I knew the love bite would leave her with a mark, but this was one I didn't mind her displaying next weekend.

As I sucked her skin harder, Stella let out a pleasured whimper and began to climax below me, her body clenching around my cock as her channel greedily pulled me deeper. It was all I needed, and as I lifted my lips from her skin I thrust in deep and hard, then felt my own release fill her insides.

As we came down from the incredible session I leaned up and examined her neck where my mark was now prominently visible. I leaned down to gently soothe it with several licks and couldn't help but smile.

Mine.

Chapter Thirty-Six

Nathan

The day of the collaring was finally here. I had been looking forward to this for so long that I could barely wait to get started. But wait I must. There were traditions to adhere to, rules to meet, and rushing it wouldn't be the done thing at all.

The only slight disappointment about the day was that Nicholas wasn't able to be here with me. It was my fault, really, for planning the collaring around the same time as their due date, but I hadn't expected Rebecca to go into labour two weeks early. He'd been all set to come down and act as my support guy, but now he'd opted to stay at home with Rebecca and the twins, because they were still learning to cope with two babies, which I could completely understand.

'So, are you ready, Nathan?' The smooth baritone voice broke me from my thoughts and I turned to watch as Oliver Wolfe strode across the room towards me.

Oliver, part-owner of Club Twist, a friend, and above all else, my former trainer. This was the man who had taught me how to control my anger and become a respected Dominant. He was probably the most revered member of the club, too, which wasn't bad going considering he was only 41.

'Oliver,' I greeted him simply, and even though I didn't call him Sir any more, I did give a respectful bow of my head. 'I couldn't be more ready,' I replied, to which Oliver gave an amused smile.

He was one of those men who just oozed confidence. Mind you, with his mother being Spanish he had taken on her olive skin, characteristic dark hair, and dark eyes, and gained his broad, tall frame from his father so he was certainly attractive to women. I suppose he had no reason not to feel confident. He wore suits with ease, drew the gaze of people wherever he went, walked like he owned the very ground beneath his feet, but somehow managed to do all this without being overtly arrogant.

'Nice suit,' he remarked, that same smile lingering as he took in the sharp cut of my navy tailored three-piece.

'Thank you. As is yours,' I replied, admiring the classic styling of his dark charcoal-grey suit. It was undoubtedly from the same tailor as mine, because as well as training me to be a Dominant, Oliver had guided me on becoming a man, too, including how to dress, where to shop, and even teaching me about the best foods and wines.

'Anderson and Sheppard?' I asked, naming my tailor.

'Of course, they are the best.'

Even though he was only 11 years older than me, Oliver had been a major role model for me when I was in my late teens and early twenties – certainly a better man to look up to than my father – and I'd tried to copy his immaculate dress sense, perfect posture, and sure strides to such an extent that I'd almost idolised him.

I'd like to think I'd mostly been successful. The one area I'd failed in was to copy his consistent aura of calm. Oliver never lost his cool – not that I'd ever witnessed anyway – which was something I still occasionally struggled with.

Moreover, he was probably the only man to ever make me quake in my boots. He'd made me do a hell of a lot more than just tremble, back when he'd trained me to be a Dominant, but the past was no doubt best left where it was.

'Thank you so much for agreeing to be my attendant.' Oliver had agreed to take over after Nicholas pulled out, so

270

I thanked him warmly with a handshake, wincing as he nearly dislocated my shoulder. *Jeez.* I prided myself on a firm shake, but that one was knuckle-crunching.

As my attendant, his role today was much like that of a best man at a wedding, except instead of doing a comical speech, Oliver would be expected to make a statement about my suitability as a good Dominant for Stella.

'It's my absolute pleasure,' he replied in his lilting accent. He'd lived in England since the age of six, but his voice still retained just a hint of his Spanish roots. It was almost upper class, but somehow filled with so much more darkness that it still sent a small shiver through me now. He was the very epitome of what a dominant should be; calm, self-aware, controlled – not to mention having the highest moral standards of anyone I'd ever met. He was famed for being supremely strict, but always, always abiding by the rules. It probably helped that he was also wickedly inventive with his use of toys.

When Oliver had initially taken me on as a trainee I'd been an arrogant little fucker, rejecting his help because he was a male, and stating stubbornly that I could never learn anything about sex from him because he'd never be able to turn me on.

In response, he'd calmly nodded, tied me to a St Andrew's cross, and proceeded to use light flicks of his flogger to stimulate and arouse me until my dick had been like a flagpole and I'd begged him over and over to make me come.

Only once I'd apologised for being a "stubborn little shite" did he use his flogger again to flick at my balls until I shot my load all over the training room floor. He'd made me clean up the mess afterwards, too.

I twisted my lips wryly at the memory. Even though Oliver had been teaching me a lesson, that encounter was the closest we'd ever come to something sexual occurring

271

between just the two of us, because all our future sessions had also included a female sub.

I'd been so mortified at how easily I'd succumbed that I hadn't been able to look him in the eye for weeks, choosing to favour the averted gaze that my father had always demanded. It had been effective, though, and from that day, instead of questioning his authority I'd started to see him as a figure that I could learn from. I thought I'd done fairly well; I might not command Oliver's level of respect within the club, but I was certainly up there, and that was all down to his effective training.

Oliver's firm treatment had been just what I'd needed back then. I'd been full of anger towards my father, and my mother to some respect, and if I hadn't received the correct guidance and been forced to dig up my reserves of respect for others I may well have ended up as a very different individual to the man I was today. I owed him everything.

Distracting myself from thoughts of the past, I looked around the club at the rows of seating which had been added to the dancefloor. With the old theatre stage and curtains still in situ, it made quite a dramatic venue.

As the room began to fill around us and people took their seats, Oliver guided me to our spot near the back.

It was nearly time to officially claim Stella as mine, and I could not fucking wait.

Stella

Peering through the thick velvet curtain, I felt my stomach drop to my ankles as I saw how many people were now seated in the club, and a small squeak rose in my throat. *Jeez, there must be at least a hundred people out there!*

'Shh! Someone might see you!' Natalia whispered, dragging me back and grinning at my no doubt terrified expression.

Natalia was one of the bar staff at the club. She was lovely, but incredibly shy, and had volunteered to keep me company before the ceremony started because Kenny was running late due to car trouble. I was so grateful to have her with me, because the nerves were seriously starting to settle in. Kenny had just texted to say he was only a few minutes away, which was a relief, but the more support I had around me, the better.

It would have been nice to have Rebecca with me too, but that was never going to happen, because a) she'd just given birth to twins, and b) even if she wasn't busy with baby duties, I was fairly sure she'd freak out if she saw what went on inside the walls of Club Twist.

Natalia might be shy, but she had proven to be well versed on the scene and had been so helpful since I'd arrived an hour ago, helping me get my hair pinned up and applying some light make-up for me before giving me a rundown of what to expect. Nathan had gone through it all with me, too, in great detail, but it was always nice to have a woman's view on things.

I peeked out of the curtain again, and my chest tightened with fear as I ran my gaze over the gathered people. 'The club is so full!' I squeaked nervously, just a second before I

273

let out a muffled shriek as Kenny leaped in front of me with a grin, scaring the life out of me.

'You're not supposed to out here!' he chided me, shoving me back behind the curtain before pulling me into a warm, aftershave-scented embrace. 'Sorry I'm late, babes. Bloody car broke down.'

'You're here now. That's all that matters.' I returned his hug, then stepped back and tried to calm myself down by shaking out my trembling hands and giving Kenny a worried look. 'I was just looking at how full it is out there.'

'Of course it's full! There hasn't been a collaring here for ages, apparently, so I'm sure everyone with an invitation has turned up,' Natalia informed us with a shy smile, shaking hands with Kenny.

'Great, no pressure, then …' I mumbled miserably.

'Don't look so worried, Stella! It's going to be amazing,' Kenny announced with a confident nod. Taking my hand, he pulled me away from the club. 'Which is your dressing room?' I pointed to our designated room – it was, in fact, one of the club's rentable rooms, with a classroom theme – and allowed him and Natalia to lead me inside.

He grabbed the clothes bag from the back of the door and grinned at Natalia, then flashed me a wink. 'Time to get you in your dress!'

It didn't take long to get ready, because I was wearing a tunic-style dress which zipped all the way up the back. Its design might be simple, as was expected at these events from what I'd been told, but the fine weave of pearlescent stitching that covered its surface made it almost sparkle under the lights. I loved it, and even better, Nathan loved it, too, and had helped me to choose it, so it was even more special.

'Gorgeous, babe,' Kenny stated, giving his beard a stroke as he stepped back and cast his analytical gaze over me. 'Even if Nathan has been up to his naughty love bite tricks again,' he added with a smirk before gently touching my neck where I knew there were still the remains of my most recent hickey. I could have covered it with make-up, but I'd chosen not to, I had a feeling Nathan would like it there for all to see.

'The dress is lovely, and you look stunning, Stella,' Natalia agreed softly, clutching at her cheeks as she gazed dreamily at my dress. 'Nathan is so lucky to have found you.'

I felt pretty lucky to have found him, too, but I was feeling so nervous that I wasn't sure I could actually speak.

She sighed. 'I wish I could find someone, but I'm so shy that it makes it really difficult.'

Clearing my throat, I tried to regain some of my usual calm, but still couldn't manage it, so Kenny intervened for me. 'Are you a sub, too?' he asked, appearing to have no qualms whatsoever about just blurting it out in front of someone he'd only just met.

Natalia's cheeks flushed, but she nodded. 'Yeah, but I want a relationship, too. I need to really trust the guy before I can submit to him, and it's hard to find a Dom who's in it for the long haul these days.' Licking her lips, she shrugged. 'I'd thought taking this bar job might help boost my confidence, and it has, but I'm still no good at talking to guys I like. I seem to either clam up, or talk absolute rubbish!' She looked between me and Kenny with a small smile. 'Anyway, enough about me! Can you remember your lines, Stella?'

Pulling in a breath, I quickly ran my pre-planned lines through my head twice, then nodded.

'Excellent.' Just then, we heard the chime of a bell from within the main room of the club and Kenny clapped his hands with glee.

'It's time! That's the signal for you to go in!' He pulled me into a brief hug before stepping back and making some

275

final touch-ups to my hair. 'Just remember, if you get nervous, stand tall, stick your gorgeous tits out, and pretend you're the queen of the whole fucking world!' Kenny advised with a wiggle of his eyebrows. 'Or if that fails, imagine them all naked.'

Natalia giggled at Kenny's words, then did a mock curtsey to me and waved me towards the door with a grin. 'Good luck, not that you'll need it!'

It was silly getting myself so worked up. At the end of the day, this was just about me giving myself to Nathan, and there was nothing scary in that. Natalia was right, I wouldn't need luck, but as I pulled back the velvet curtain and saw at least twenty sets of critical eyes swivel my way I suddenly wasn't so sure.

Chapter Thirty-Seven

Nathan

Once everyone was seated, I heard the chime of a small bell ring out within the club to indicate that we were ready to start. I'd attended a few collarings over the years, and they'd all varied to some degree, but I was fairly sure that today's would be the simplest and least formal that most of the gathered crowd had ever witnessed. Smirking, I crossed my arms as I anticipated the reaction of some of the more senior Doms within the room. They'd no doubt mock the way I'd chosen to carry out the collaring, but hey, I'd always liked to stand out from the crowd, so why change the habit of a lifetime now?

I watched from the shadows in the back corner as Stella appeared from a small doorway behind a heavy velvet curtain and began her walk down the central aisle. Her back was straight and confident, and her steps were sure. All in all, she was perhaps the least submissive sub I'd ever watched walk towards her collaring, and a smile tugged at my lips at the thought. Usually the girls appeared timid, meek even, but not my Stella.

Even in her simple outfit she took my breath away. The plain cream tunic-style dress she wore was quite common in ceremonies like these, with a broad, wide neckline that would allow her new collar to be seen by all as I placed it around her neck in just a few minutes' time.

The thought made my heart rate accelerate as a rush of blood flooded towards my groin. She was mine, and now everyone here would know it.

277

Trying to distract myself from my growing erection, I continued to take in the details of her preparation. Her hair was pinned up, again to allow full access to her neck, and apart from her current collar she wore no other jewellery or accessories at all. I raised one of my eyebrows as I noticed the mark on her neck from my most recent love bite, and I couldn't help but smile. Perhaps everyone could already tell she was mine.

As she reached the front of the room, Stella stopped by the table and bowed her head slightly, as I'd advised her to do, but still she had her shoulders pulled back confidently. My chest puffed with pride as I watched her. My girl, so brave, even though she must surely be feeling nervous.

Now that things were about to get started properly, Dominic stepped towards her and used the key I'd given him to undo the necklace she wore. I felt my hackles rise and clenched my teeth. I disliked the man immensely, but at Club Twist the only people with enough authority to oversee the ceremonies were Oliver and Dominic, and seeing as Oliver was accompanying me as my attendant, that only left Dominic to be in charge.

The musclebound sadist was the last person I wanted putting his paws on my Stella after what had occurred last Saturday, but unfortunately, I'd had very little choice. David had assured me that he'd spoken to Dominic, but watching as he leered down at my girl and seemed to take longer than necessary to unclasp her necklace, I felt my temper snap. *Motherfucker.*

I went to charge forwards to rip his hands away from her, but paused when a strong hand landed on my forearm and pulled me backwards. 'Calm, Nathan.'

Oliver's tone left absolutely no room for manoeuvre and was so soaked with authority that I very nearly regressed back to my initial training and replied with, 'Yes, Sir.' Instead, I drew in a breath, did a calming countdown in my head, and nodded at him briskly. Since Nicholas couldn't be here, it was nice to have him with me to watch my back.

Once Dominic had removed the collar, he placed it on the table and stood back as a second bell chimed around the darkened space to indicate that Stella was now free to be formally claimed by me.

'It's time. Let's go and get your girl,' Oliver murmured, giving my shoulder a firm squeeze before stepping out and leading me towards the front of the room.

I was now almost within touching distance of Stella, but Oliver had to speak before I could move towards her. The whole time he was making his statement about my accomplishments as a Dominant, I couldn't take my eyes off my girl. She had her hands still linked before her, but her eyes were firmly locked on mine, a small hint of a smile twitching at the corner of her lips. Oliver rounded off his speech by stating my ability to be a competent master, then he stood back, taking his place beside Dominic, so that I could finally step up to Stella.

Her face relaxed as soon as I was close and I couldn't help but flash her a brief wink of reassurance.

'Avert your eyes and kneel before your new master!' someone called from the crowd. Stella's eyes widened in concern, as if she had done something wrong, and I quickly reached out and took one of her hands before she could follow their order and fall to her knees.

'No.'

My word cut through the room like the snap of a well-handled whip, promptly quieting the crowd until you could have heard a pin drop.

Turning to the gathered guests, I ran my hardest stare across them, and felt a smug satisfaction when I saw several of them quake away from my glare. 'Quite simply, Stella will not kneel before me or avert her eyes, because I do not wish her to.' I let my words sink in for a moment, then

279

passed my gaze around the room again, seeing a mixture of shocked faces, curious ones, and even a derisive sneer from one or two, but I held my resolve.

'What I have in Stella is a beautiful, independent, strong woman who willingly gives me her submission when I request it. She *would* kneel, if I asked her to, but for me, the joy of dominance is that I have the power and control whatever position she is in. That is the most powerful feeling in the world.'

To my surprise, I heard several hums of agreement from within the crowd, and as I briefly flicked my gaze across it again, I noticed multiple nods.

'As for averting her eyes, as so many of you wish your partners to do, why would I forgo myself the beauty of her eyes? Stella's gaze is a gift that I not only expect, but treasure.'

Once my speech was done, I turned my attention back to Stella and found her gazing up at me with eyes that were bright with unshed tears, my words apparently having just as much impact on her as they were on me.

Clearing his throat, Dominic stepped forwards. 'So, no pillow for kneeling, then …' He chuckled as he picked up the small cushion and tossed it aside.

'No. No pillow,' I confirmed dryly.

I turned back to Stella. We shared a lingering look and I gave a small nod to indicate that she could now say her memorised line. She swallowed and then spoke. 'It is my desire to be yours for life. Will you take me and guide me, Sir?'

Fuck yes, was the answer that flew to my mind, but thankfully, I collected my wits and replied with my correct line. 'I accept your offer, and promise to care for you, protect you, and guide you to the best of my ability on our forward journey through life.'

God. I actually felt a bit choked. But there was no

fucking way I could cry in front of all these people. Drawing in a deep breath, I turned away from the gathered guests and accepted the long black box that Oliver was now holding out to me. I flicked open the lid, and gently removed the new collar I'd had had made for Stella from the box. This was something else that would no doubt draw comment from my peers, because it wasn't a leather strip or metal collar like some made their subs wear. It was a platinum necklace, just like the last one had been, but this one had small diamonds encrusted throughout its design so it sparkled delicately as the light hit it.

'Will you accept this collar as a symbol of my ownership and our joint connection?'

Stella's breath briefly caught as she looked at the new chain in my hand, but then she nodded and re-established our eye contact. 'I will wear it proudly for all of my days, Sir.'

Letting out a breath I hadn't realised I'd been holding, I nodded then linked the necklace around her neck and locked it in place before pocketing the key. 'You now belong to me, as I belong to you.'

Another line many would disagree with. Traditionally I should have said "You now belong to me" and left it at that, but what Stella and I shared went way beyond any ideas of ownership. We were a team, and as such, connected. I belonged to her just as much as she did to me.

'Come closer.' Using one finger under the necklace, I tugged gently to pull her towards me, something Stella was obviously eager to do, because she shot into my arms, burying her head into the crook of my neck and wrapping her arms around me as she let out a shaky breath.

I leaned back to place a thumb on her chin and tilted her head back and made eye contact. 'You know that nothing in our lifestyle is quite as significant as this.' I couldn't help but trail my fingers to the new collar at her neck and gently

281

stroke it. 'Thank you for today; you've made me the happiest man alive. I love you, Stella.'

As she went to return the sentiment, I placed a kiss on her lips, stealing her breath and sealing our new bond. As soon as our lips touched, something potent sparked between us and our kiss quickly deepened. I pressed my tongue into her mouth and captured the gasp that she made, much to the joy of the spectators, because we were suddenly deafened by whooping and hollering for more.

It might not have been a traditional collaring ceremony, but it seemed that everyone watching was just as thrilled by the outcome as I was.

Chapter Thirty-Eight

Stella

The nerves I'd experienced earlier had now dissipated, and the rush of adrenaline had converted to a lovely, warm, humming sensation running through my system. I felt energised, excited, and incredibly loved up.

Kenny had stayed for a congratulatory drink, but had to leave to get back to Tom, so I had stuck to Nathan's side as he led me around various people to introduce me. Some I had recognised from the club already, but others were totally new to me. We were technically still in our roles, so I remained relatively quiet, happy just to hold Nathan's hand and soak up how proud he sounded as he announced to everyone how lucky he was to have me.

As I observed what was going on around us I noticed someone watching us from across the room. When I made eye contact with him he nodded at me, slid from his stool, and began to make a beeline for us. He was the man who had accompanied Nathan down the aisle. I'd never met him before, but from their interactions it was clear they knew each other well. As I watched him confidently cutting through the crowd, I realised he actually had a similar air to him as Nathan. He was dark-haired, not blond like Nathan, but everything else matched; his posture oozed confidence, his gaze was coolly assessing, and his swagger just a little too sure. All in all, he very nearly came across as arrogant, but not quite; there was something rather reserved about him, too. He was tall and broad, but his features couldn't quite be described as classically handsome. His eyes were too penetrating, his jaw a bit too square, and his nose had a slight kink in it as if he'd broken it at some point.

He was definitely good-looking, though. There was something undeniably attractive about him, and as he got closer and I saw his olive-toned skin I had to wonder if he were perhaps from the Mediterranean somewhere. His impeccably fitting three-piece suit didn't harm the overall visual, either. In fact, judging from the quality of the material it wouldn't surprise me if he used the same tailor as Nathan.

As he reached our side, Nathan's grip tightened on my hand, then he extended his free hand to shake the outstretched hand of the man. The stranger was taller than I'd first thought, and for some reason he made me feel nervous, even though he hadn't spoken one word to me yet. Yet another similarity with Nathan, then, because I distinctly remember nearly wetting myself with fear when I'd first laid eyes on him at this very same bar.

Nathan took a step towards him and inclined his head respectfully. 'I'd hoped to introduce the two of you before the ceremony, but there wasn't time. Stella, this is Oliver.'

Smiling nervously, I nodded and tried to appear just as calm and composed as the two men now surrounding me. 'Hi, Oliver, nice to meet you.'

'Nice to meet you, *Sir*,' Oliver corrected me, as he casually slipped one hand into the pocket of his trousers and continued to stare down at me with those steely eyes of his.

Sir?

What? Maybe I needed to rewind my last thoughts about him not being an arrogant arse, because the only person I called Sir was the man currently holding my hand, and the man who was surely going to flip his lid at Oliver for his cheek towards me. Before my eyebrows could leap up at Oliver's cockiness, though, I felt Nathan give the smallest squeeze on my hand, as if urging me to comply.

Flicking a brief glance to Nathan, I found his eyes steadily focused on Oliver, and his expression neutral, but the muscle twitching in his jaw gave the impression that he was still urging me to follow the instruction. It wouldn't be particularly difficult to do, since Oliver's demeanour screamed authority, but it seemed strange to me, because Nathan was the only one I ever called Sir.

I couldn't imagine why he would want me to use the title with someone else, but it seemed that he did. Swallowing my issues, and desperately hoping I hadn't read the situation wrong, I returned my gaze to Oliver and gave a respectful tilt of my head. 'My apologies, *Sir*. It's a pleasure to meet you.'

Oliver briefly curled his lips into a pleased smile as he nodded, and Nathan simultaneously gave my hand a squeeze of thanks. This was all very bizarre. Who the heck was this guy?

'The pleasure is all mine. I must apologise for not meeting you sooner, Stella. Knowing Nathan as well as I do, I was keen to meet the woman who had finally tamed him, but you two don't seem to come down here quite as much any more.'

'No. Like I told you, Oliver, Stella and I are far more mainstream nowadays.'

'Hence the no-kneeling rule during the ceremony, eh?' he asked with a slight smirk that caused Nathan to let out a small sigh. Appearing far more relaxed now he'd had his dig, Oliver turned on the charm and smiled at me. 'I'm sure you've learned to ignore his moods, Stella? He always was an irritable bastard, and I see not much has changed where that's concerned.' He winked amiably at Nathan. 'How you run your relationship is no business of mine, Nathan. Whatever you're doing seems to be working wonders for both of you,' he said, before surprising the hell out of me by taking my hand, lifting it to his lips, and placing a brief kiss on the back of my knuckles.

Arrogant arse one second, to a charming gent the next. I could hardly keep up. 'You are stunning, just as Nathan has told me, and you performed your part in the ceremony to perfection.' His words were pleasantly complimentary, and seemed totally genuine, but caused me to tense, as I waited for Nathan to fly forwards and attempt to kill Oliver for daring to touch me.

But he didn't.

To my complete surprise, my usually hot-headed dominant just stood there, giving a small, proud smile when he and Oliver shared a look.

Who exactly was this man? Nathan was treating him like a king. My man would normally gouge out the eyes of anyone trying to make me call them Sir, let alone someone kissing my hand, so it all seemed completely surreal.

'I promise to make time for a proper catch-up later, but I have one or two things I need to discuss with David before the evening shift gets busy.' With another nod to us both, Oliver turned and walked away, leaving Nathan and I alone so I could finally ask the question spinning around my brain.

'Who the hell is he?' As I turned to Nathan, I found him looking down at me with a narrow-eyed look of disapproval and realised I'd blurted my question rather rudely. I grimaced apologetically.

'His name is Oliver Wolfe. He's one of the owners of this place.'

OK, so that obviously made him relatively important, but surely not high enough to be raised onto a pedestal and treated like royalty as Nathan just had. After all, Dominic also had a share in the club, and Nathan hated him.

With an intent look, Nathan licked his lips and lowered his voice as he moved himself closer to me. 'The reason it was polite for you to call him, Sir, is because he was also my trainer. To show respect for him is an extension of the respect that you and I share.'

My expression folded into a frown of complete confusion. 'Trainer? When you studied architecture?'

Giving a small, dry laugh, Nathan shook his head. His eyes darkened with a wicked twinkle. 'No. He trained me to be a dominant, Stella.'

What? Wow. Blinking several times, I tried to digest this news. I'd always assumed that Nathan had learned the ropes through practicing over the years. I hadn't expected him to have had official training. Glancing around me, I started to see this place in a different light. Did the club act as some kind of school of submission and dominance during the weekdays? Were there classrooms hidden away somewhere behind the scenes?

'How do you do that, exactly?' I asked, fascinated by this new information I was learning about Nathan, and keen to extract as much detail from him as possible.

'There are various methods, but seeing as I had issues with my temper, Oliver used the most direct course. He made me his submissive.'

He did what? I boggled at the images now flooding my mind. Strong-willed Nathan as a sub? I just couldn't picture it.

At all.

Ever.

In any universe.

'What …? You … you were his sub?' Even saying the words sounded ridiculous, because Nathan was a Dominant through and through. Even when we weren't actively in our roles of Dom and sub, he found it difficult not to take the lead in things.

Nodding slowly, Nathan continued to stare at me, apparently enjoying my shock. 'Indeed. For a short while.'

287

This was actually quite shocking news, but I supposed it made sense, really, Nathan seemed to be a rather skilled Dom; he knew exactly how much I could take, and when to stop, and those things could only be learned if you had once been on the receiving end of things.

Did this mean that Oliver and Nathan had … done things together? Sexual things? God. I should probably have been jealous, or irked, and if it had been a woman we were discussing then I definitely would have been, but with Oliver being the subject, I wasn't. The idea of the two of them doing stuff to each other was making me feel hot under the collar and, well, really bloody horny.

'Does that mean that you and he …?' My tongue felt fat and useless in my mouth from the shock, and I saw the amused look on Nathan's face.

'Do you really want to know the answer to that question, my love?' Nathan whispered hotly against my ear before leaning back with a smirk, clearly loving my open-mouthed reaction.

Flashing another glance to the tall, broad frame of Oliver across the room, I licked my lips and felt a shiver run up my spine. Did I want to know? I'm not sure I did. The images currently in my mind were so erotic that I might actually find myself disappointed if Nathan told me they had just sat in a classroom with a textbook for a while.

'Eyes on me,' Nathan commanded, snapping my attention back to him. I found him staring down at me with a look of mild irritation on his face. 'I would prefer you to aim your lustful glances at me,' he growled, but I could see a playful glint in his eyes. 'And before you ask, no, we're not having a threesome with him.'

Nathan's eyes darkened as my cheeks flushed at his words. I'd never wanted a threesome before, but if it meant I got to see Nathan and Oliver naked together then maybe I could make an exception. The idea of that much masculinity getting it on right in front of me, and possibly even *with* me, was almost too much for my brain to handle.

'I can see that look in your eyes Stella, and the answer is no. You're mine now. No one else gets to touch you.'

Sensing that now might not be the time to tell him that I didn't have to join in as long as I could watch him and Oliver touching each other, I simply nodded and smiled at his reaction.

'There's no "look in my eyes", Nathan,' I corrected him with a smile. 'You know you're the only one for me. I was just intrigued by the idea of the two of you training together.' Which was the complete truth. As much as Oliver might interest me, Nathan was all the man I'd ever want or need.

He assessed me for a few seconds and relaxed his shoulders, nodding and sliding a hand around my waist. 'Good.' He dropped a kiss on my temple, then began to lead me towards the bar. He seemed to have finally accepted that I really was only interested in sharing my life with him.

Chapter Thirty-Nine

Nathan

David slid the drink towards me across the bar, cast a glance at Stella, and smiled at us. I knew that smile; it was the most charming in his repertoire, which meant he wanted something. Mind you, it seemed to me that David always wanted something. Usually, he would blather on in my ear while I desperately tried to get away and avoid any of his overly touchy-feely behaviour. Stella seemed to like him, though, so maybe I was just being oversensitive.

'So, we've had several requests for you and your lovely new sub to do a scene, Nathan. What do you say?'

There it was. I knew he wanted something, but what a request it was. And my answer was no. I shook my head slowly and firmly. Beside me, I felt Stella tense up. As if reading our minds, David leaned forwards onto his elbows and continued. 'It doesn't have to be anything too full on. How about a demo with your flogger? Those were always really popular with the crowd. What do you say? It is the usual custom after the ceremony that the Dom and their newly collared sub do a scene together.'

Annoyingly, that part was true. Every ceremony I'd attended here had involved a show of some kind by the newly joined couple. Not that we had to, of course; I'd already broken enough traditions today, it wouldn't matter if we abstained. To my surprise, the idea of being on stage with Stella did quite appeal to me. No way was anyone else getting to see my girl naked, though. They could stare at my cock all day for all I cared, but not my girl. Her body was for my eyes only, so if we did do something it would need to be with Stella mostly clothed.

Scoffing out a laugh at my wayward thoughts, I shook my head again. I might be keen, but I had my doubts that Stella would be. With this in mind, I glanced down at her and was taken aback by the look in her eye. Her expression appeared to be one of mild interest. She didn't look thrilled, exactly, but she wasn't abjectly horrified, either, which was interesting.

David turned away to serve a customer, giving us privacy to talk, and so I leaned down closer to her ear. 'Are you tempted?' I whispered, feeling my groin give a twitch at the mere possibility that she might be. I knew from previous experiences that Stella got quite turned on from having sex or fooling around when we were at risk of getting caught, so perhaps the idea of people watching us *was* appealing to her.

Seeing her continued hesitation, I reeled in my own excitement and gave her arm a reassuring rub. 'It's fine, we don't have to do anything, Stella. Just having the ceremony today means the world to me.'

Stella shared a long look with me, then dropped her gaze, took a long gulp of her vodka and Coke and looked back at me. 'Not on the main stage,' she whispered. Her words were so soft I barely believed I had heard them correctly. 'Perhaps on that side stage, the smaller, darker one?' she suggested. 'David mentioned the flogger … maybe you could use it for pleasure, like you sometimes do?'

Holy fuck, is she actually saying the words I think she is? My heart rate was off the charts and my brain practically malfunctioning at the thought of spreading her out before me on the stage and flogging her beautiful arse until it was rosy red and she was writhing around in ecstasy.

291

'But nothing which shows off my stretch marks,' she added hastily, which made me roll my eyes and shake my head. I knew she was paranoid about the sides of her belly since giving birth to Will, but she really didn't need to be. She was beautiful.

'You don't have any stretch marks, Stella.'

Huffing out a breath, she crossed her arms over her chest. 'It's either no stomach showing, or nothing. That's the offer, take it or leave it.'

Raising my eyebrows at her impetuous tone, I shook my head slowly and disapprovingly. 'I'll overlook the fact that you seem to be attempting to order me around while we are here and in our roles, Stella. But only this one time.' As I spoke, I gave her my best firm look, the one that always had her quivering in her boots within seconds, and soaking between her legs. She might find me a little overwhelming at times, but my girl also loved that firmer side of me.

Good job, really, seeing as it was engrained within who I was.

As usual, the look worked like a treat, and hey presto, a second later I watched Stella's face crumple into an apologetic mask as she bit down on her lower lip, nodded her head sincerely, and gazed up at me with wide eyes.

I leaned forwards till our foreheads were touching, then gently nipped at her lower lip in warning. 'I'll add biting your lip and nodding your head to your list of misdemeanours, Stella. Perhaps you would rather this be a punishment demonstration than a pleasure one?' I asked her quietly. I was deliberately teasing her, but it was so rare that I got to let my Dom side out in public these days that I might as well take full advantage of it now.

A gasp filled the air between us, then Stella leaned back, her eyes an arousing mixture of lust and wariness. 'I'm sorry, Sir.' Her apology was quivery and breathy and sent a jolt of lust straight to my cock. Was it wrong that I totally got off on her slight fear? Probably, but from the way her cheeks were flushing I knew she was aroused, too, and loving this little bit of power play just as much as I was. Breathing in the light scent of her perfume, I took a second to share the moment with her, then took a step back, my mind already planning what I could do to her next.

'So, the side stage, hmm?'

Stella swallowed loudly and drew in a deep breath. 'Only if you'd like to, Sir?' she murmured, suddenly melding herself into the perfect little sub with her well-worded reply, and making my dick as hard as granite in the process. Christ, she was so perfect.

'Hmmm. Yes, I think I would. No nudity though. My rule on that still stands; no one sees you naked except for me. Perhaps just a little flogging demo to liven things up.'

I gave David a subtle nod to let him know we were accepting his offer. I then placed my drink down and guided Stella to the side stage. Pausing beside a wide, sloped bench I assessed its height and decided it would be perfect for a flogging scene.

I left her there for a moment and walked back to the bar to grab my own flogger from my bag. I'd packed it this morning, just in case. What can I say? I'm an optimistic guy.

As I made my way back, I realised a small crowd was gathering in the shadows. People had made their way over here when they saw that a show was about to start, but there would be no words of guidance, or commentary for them tonight. No, this wasn't a training exercise; this was about us existing in our own little bubble and doing what we wanted to do.

I briefly passed my gaze around the room and saw Oliver was also watching us with apparent interest from his

293

usual spot on the other end of the bar. Like me, he had always been a very sexual man, but recently there had been rumours in the club that he was now celibate, because he wouldn't sleep with any of the customers any more. I didn't believe it for a second, though. The Oliver I knew loved sex far too much to ever give up on it, so I suspected he was simply being professional at work and getting his fix somewhere outside the walls of Club Twist. As I turned my gaze away from him and looked down at Stella, an idea began to form in my mind.

It was crazy, because I had serious jealousy issues where it came to Stella, but from somewhere the idea sprung to my mind to ask Oliver to join us on stage. I'd seen the curiosity in her eyes earlier when we'd been speaking to him, so perhaps it would be a fitting tribute for the day. My old Master and my new sub both on the stage together. I had a feeling my girl would enjoy it, too.

It had been a long, long time since I'd shared a scene with Oliver Wolfe. Back in the days after I'd completed my training we'd regularly done scenes together when tutoring others, but regardless of what Stella might have been envisioning in her mind, Oliver and I had never slept together. We'd shared threesomes on several occasions, but we were both heterosexual, hot-blooded males through and through, and while we might have been naked together on multiple occasions, our focus was always on the female who was with us. It was just what made us tick, I suppose.

Yes. Perhaps this could be fun. It would probably be the closest thing to a threesome that I'd ever allow Stella to experience, and the fact that I trusted Oliver implicitly made it seem slightly easier to contemplate.

Deciding to ease her into it by starting on my own, I took her hand and helped her to climb up onto the bench and lie down on her stomach. The bench had a chin rest so I could still see Stella's face, but it meant her head was now at about my hip level and her arms were draped up next to her shoulders.

I prided myself on building anticipation in a scene. I wasn't one for delayed gratification as such, but a few minutes well spent at the start could earn all parties a nice boost in the arousal stakes, and was worth the toll it took on my self-control. Stella had often told me that I was the master of a good build-up so I was obviously doing something right.

Tonight wasn't just about Stella and me, though. We had an audience. I might not be doing this for their benefit, but they would still no doubt appreciate it if I drew the scene out to its full potential. Standing directly in her line of sight, I caught her wide gaze and watched as she licked her lips nervously. I fucking loved how brave she was. The trust between us was incredible, I'd always used safe words in the past, but I'd never felt a complete bond with someone like I did with Stella.

Keeping our eyes locked, I removed my suit jacket, folded it, and hung it over a rail to my left. I loosened my tie, then popped my shirt cuffs open and set about rolling up my sleeves so they sat in meticulous rolls just below my elbows. No slap-dash scrunching of material here; no, this was all about perfect attention to detail. Stella watched every second of my preparation in rapt fascination, her eyes widening even further and her mouth hanging slightly parted as she drew in ragged breaths.

I loved the fact that she was so affected already and I hadn't even laid a finger on her.

God, I was fucking good.

'Tell me your safe words, please.' Stella knew her words, but it was safe practice to always make sure of them, so to set a good example to the clubgoers, I opted to briefly cover the formality before we began.

'Green for good, yellow if I want to discuss something,

and red for stop.'

I thrust my hands into the pockets of my trousers and stood there, prepped, ready, and so aroused that the fly of my trousers was straining forwards, not that I gave a flying fuck if anyone noticed it. 'And your colour now is?'

'Green, Sir.'

'Good girl.' After praising her, I just stared at Stella, not speaking a single word, but tilting my head to one side as if planning what I should do to her. Soon, the anticipation and waiting would get the better of one of us, but I decided to hold my ground and see which of us gave in the sooner.

After about 45 seconds of still, silent, intense eye contact, she huffed out a shallow breath and her tongue darted out again, moistening her bottom lip. Then she briefly chewed on the plumpest part in the centre.

My self-control could be pretty flawless when I really wanted it to be, so I'd expected her to break first, but what I hadn't expected was for her to do it with goddamn lip-chewing. To be honest, I sometimes wondered if she did it on purpose to taunt me, because I knew she liked the punishments I doled out. I wasn't sure, but one thing was certain – just because we were in Club Twist in front of an audience didn't mean I'd let her get away with it.

Narrowing my eyes, I focused my gaze in on the movement and wondered what the best punishment would be. Looking again to where she was rolling her teeth back and forth across her lips, I scowled. Perhaps I should put her mouth to better use; I'd rather like her lips wrapped around my throbbing cock right about now, and it would certainly stop her chewing her bloody lip.

As tempting as that thought was, I decided that I didn't want to blow my load so early on in the scene, so I opted for keeping it simple. Nodding my head, I finally removed my hands from my trouser pockets and briefly rubbed them together.

A good ol' spanking would do nicely, and with the theatrics and noise of the action it was always a crowd pleaser. Stella got a thrill from them, even if I was doing it for punishment, and I certainly enjoyed the sting that it brought to my palm.

Lowering to her eye level, I kept my face as blank as possible, to really kick her heartrate up a few gears, and raised a hand, brushing my thumb across her trapped lip. 'As you have yet again gone against my wishes, we will start tonight's proceedings with a spanking. Tell me what you have done wrong, so that you can learn from it in the future.' My words were more for the crowd's benefit than hers, because Stella knew full well what she'd done to irk me, but it added a nice touch to the scene, and again gave a good indication of safe practice. A submissive should never be punished just for the sake of it; there should always be a reason, and that must be clear and understood by both the Dom and the sub.

I stood up to my full height again and watched as Stella cleared her throat several times before managing to speak. 'I bit my lip, Sir.'

'And?' My retort was instant, and my tone sharp, so I softened it with a wink that only Stella would be able to see. It was brief, but would be enough to reassure her that my harder demeanour was just part of the scene. She might willingly give me her submission when I demanded it, but Stella was well aware how tightly wrapped around her finger she had me in day-to-day life.

Crossing my arms across my chest, I stared down at her, waiting for her reply. 'And I nodded at you, Sir, when I know you prefer an audible reply.'

Pulling in a deep breath I nodded in satisfaction. 'You also forgot your place earlier, and spoke in an incorrect tone,' I reminded her briskly. 'I will spank you ten times for each misdemeanour, making thirty in total.'

297

Stella's cheeks flushed with desire, and her pupils dilated as she absorbed my words. 'Yes, Sir.'

I moved to her side and placed a hand on the nape of her neck. Then I made a show of moving down her body to her hips, dragging my hand as I went so that it ran down the zip of the dress and disappeared between her legs. There was a murmur in the crowd as I paused there, my hand suddenly able to feel the heat coming from Stella's body. Briefly pressing my hand against her crotch, I let out a soft moan at just how wet the material was. Fuck. The urge to roll her over and take her there and then was so overwhelming that I had to force myself to pause and do a calming countdown in my head.

As I counted from five to zero, I massaged my fingers against her sensitive core, but like a true pro Stella managed to remain relatively still. As a reward, when I reached zero, I gave a small pinch to her clit which had her bucking from the bench with a breathy yelp and caused me to smile smugly. Perhaps she wasn't quite as in control as I'd thought.

Immediately removing my fingers, I then pressed down on her lower back to calm her thrashing, and clicked my tongue. 'Punishment first, then pleasure, Stella. Remember?'

I just about heard an impatient grumble under her breath, before she answered me just in time to save herself from an additional punishment. 'Yes, Sir ... sorry.'

Taking my time, I explored her bare legs, running my fingers around her ankles and calves and enjoying the way the skin pebbled into goose pimples below my touch. Finally, when I had calmed myself enough to continue without fucking her senseless, I ran both hands from her knees up to her gorgeous bottom and tapped the cheeks. 'Lift to your knees.'

Stella obliged immediately, lifting her pelvis so I

could carefully fold her dress up around her middle, then adjusting her position so she was crouched on her elbows and knees.

Submissive, wiling and waiting.

Fucking lovely.

Her fabulous arse was now on display, but thankfully she was wearing the lacy French knickers I had given her for today to hide some of her modesty. They were white, which gave a nice "inexperienced sub" vibe to the proceedings, and showed the lower part of her buttocks, but they weren't entirely see-through so just about satisfied my jealous streak.

I could see her arousal dampening the material between her legs, and smirked proudly as I gave her arse another quick caress before pulling my hand back and landing the first sharp smack to one cheek.

Stella gasped and her buttocks tensed, but as a beautiful red bloomed on her arse cheek, she remembered to count her punishment. 'One. Thank you, Sir.'

She continued to be the perfect sub, counting every spank and thanking me each time in a breathy voice which grew higher and needier with each passing second. I shared the blows between her cheeks until both were a gorgeous shade of red, my palms were tingling, and my cock was throbbing in time with my raised pulse.

Once I reached thirty, I walked back to the head of the bench and dropped down onto my haunches so that our faces were level. Cupping her chin, I moved in close enough that our noses were touching and briefly rubbed the tip of mine against hers in a reassuring gesture. Her breath was coming in short, hard pants now, but her eyes were still bright and wide and her cheeks were beautifully flushed, clearly displaying her extreme arousal.

'OK so far, gorgeous?'

Her lips curled into a shy smile at my compliment and

she nodded. 'Yes, Sir.' The response was immediate, and absolutely fucking perfect.

I nodded once and placed a brief kiss on her forehead. Then, taking the flogger in my right hand, I began to use it to warm the skin of her calves and thighs with a series of gentle, flicking strokes. I didn't want to appear completely soft, though, so on the occasions that she writhed around too much, or moaned a touch too loudly, I gave the flicks of my wrist more power so she got a little stinger thrown in the mix every now and then.

Having placed the flogger down on her back, I then rearranged her position on the bench so she was once again lying down on her stomach. This time, though, I took advantage of the stirrups at the bottom of the bench, placing her legs into each one so that her legs were spread.

Standing back, I hummed my approval of the new position. It meant she could lie comfortably, but still gave me access if I wished to get to her inner thighs with the flogger. Which I did. Looking again at the lace between her legs, I briefly found myself breaking one of my own rules and chomping down on my lower lip to try to subdue my lust. Her legs were now wide enough that if she were naked the crowd behind me would have a spectacular view of her pussy. Not that I would ever allow that to happen.

During this brief pause in proceedings, I took the opportunity to look across at Oliver again to see if he was still watching. As I had suspected, he was, and so, with a reverent lowering of my head, I decided to follow through on my earlier idea and gestured to the stage in invitation.

He quirked an eyebrow at me in surprise and briefly rubbed his chin as he considered my offer. Then, after a moment's further pause, he nodded once, stood up, followed my example of removing his jacket, and strode towards me exuding his usual confidence.

I might be heterosexual through and through, but I could

300

see why Stella had been intrigued by him. He oozed confidence.

I picked up my flogger and retrieved a second one from the rack behind me – a rather lovely soft suede one. I handed it to Oliver with another respectful tilt of my head, causing a small murmur to run through the crowd as he weighed it in his hand.

It was rare for me to perform, but even more of a treat to get to see Oliver Wolfe in action, even if this was going to be a fairly tame scene.

Once he'd tucked the flogger under one arm, he rolled up his shirt sleeves, taking his time the way I had, so that the material sat in a neat fold just below his elbows. Apart from our hair colour, we could almost be twins: suit trousers, smart shoes, sleeves rolled up, ties knotted to perfection, and floggers in hand.

'Nathan …' Stella's quiet squeak brought my attention down to her face, but Oliver stepped to her side and landed a swift, snapping flick of the flogger to her right buttock.

'You are in front of an audience. Remember the correct title for your Master,' he reminded her quietly, his tone more coaxing than chastising.

'Yes … Sir. Sorry,' she mumbled, still looking up at me with imploring eyes, even though she was repeatedly flicking her gaze between Oliver and me.

Wanting to check that she was all right, I dropped to my haunches and gently soothed some wayward hairs from her face. 'OK, my sweet girl?'

'I am … Sir. But … I … I don't want him to join in, not sexually, I mean. I meant what I said earlier, I only want you.'

Mine. My eyes fluttered shut at just how perfect her words were, but then I quickly opened them to reassure her. 'No one gets to touch you skin on skin except for me. I would, however, like Oliver to join in and show you his

301

skills with the flogger. He has quite a talent for it. You'd like it, I'm sure.'

And that was a fact I knew from first-hand experience.

'OK. If you're sure, Sir?'

I really loved the fact that she was checking with me. It was exactly what a properly trained sub would do, except perhaps their phrasing would have been slightly slicker, something along the lines of, "If it pleases you, Sir."

Nodding slowly, I stood up and gave her hair a gentle caress. 'I'm sure.' Oliver came to my side and ran the tails of the flogger across Stella's back. Even through the material of her dress she must have felt it, because she shivered slightly, which caused Oliver to smile and meet my gaze.

'Gorgeous. Sensitive, isn't she?' he observed, repeating the movement and receiving the same response from Stella, who was now audibly panting from arousal.

'Exceptionally,' I agreed proudly, amazed that I wasn't feeling my usual stabbing jealousy. It almost felt … *nice* … to share this experience with Oliver. Perhaps it was because of my history with him, or maybe I just knew him well enough to know that he would treat this scene professionally, and not use it as an opportunity to ogle my woman.

I gently lowered the zip on Stella's dress and folded the material out to the sides. Because of the loose design, I could expose a large portion of her lower and mid back.

My left eye gave an impatient twitch when I realised there was no bra strap visible. The little minx had gone braless? *Fuck.* That knowledge sent such a huge jolt of lust to my cock that I almost felt breathless for a second or two.

'I presume that as she has received her punishment you would now like to proceed with a pleasurable flogging?'

Oliver's words helped to ground me, and with a nod, I ran the strands of my flogger through my fingertips as I tried to calm my throbbing arousal. My goddamn groin just wouldn't calm the fuck down at the moment. No doubt my lack of self-control hadn't gone unnoticed by Oliver, but at least I was holding myself back and doing my best to ignore the bulge tenting the front of my trousers.

Swallowing hard, I moved to Stella's left-hand side while Oliver took her right, then, working in tandem, we began to land alternate flicks of our floggers onto her flawless skin.

Starting at the soles of her feet, we spent the next 15 minutes working a teasing trail up her calves, thighs, buttocks, ribs, arms and back until no piece of exposed skin had been ignored.

Initially, Stella had writhed around, moaning her enjoyment, but gradually her body went limp until she simply lay there accepting the pleasure. It was quite possible that she had actually entered subspace now.

I moved in front of her and bent down again to check that she was OK. My suspicions were further supported by the blissed-out expression on her face, which told me everything I needed to know.

'It would appear your girl is rather enjoying herself,' Oliver remarked, nodding approvingly at Stella's dazed expression.

'What colour are you?' I asked her, my voice thick from arousal, and knowing that the question was needless.

'Definitely green, Sir. It's so good. Thank you.' Smiling up at me, she reached out and gripped my thighs, taking me by surprise as she moved one of her hands to cup my erection. 'Let me make it good for you too, Sir …'

Oliver smirked at the moan I let out and moved back towards Stella's legs. 'Do I have your permission to put her out of her misery?'

My body tensed slightly as a spike of possessiveness

303

swept through me. Did I want him to make her come? Would I allow it? It would certainly be a big step for me. Fucking monumental, really.

While I was still debating it, Oliver tilted his head and looked down to where Stella was now attempting to undo the zip of my trousers. 'You have a beautiful woman clawing at your trousers, Nathan. Why not let her take care of you, while I take care of her?'

I hadn't been intending to make this a particularly sexual scene – it was going to be a flogging, and possibly an orgasm for Stella – but as I looked down again and saw the desperation on my girl's face I gave in to the arousal that had been flowing through me all night. I nodded at her to continue before briefly flicking my gaze to Oliver and giving him permission.

'Make her come, but only use the flogger. No touching.'

With an amused grin, Oliver nodded his agreement. He stepped between Stella's legs where he began to flick lightly with the strands of the flogger. I didn't have time to feel jealous of what he might be seeing, because Stella's response was immediate as she gasped, and desperately tugged my zip down and practically gobbled me into her hot mouth.

My head fell back and a pained groan rose up my throat as I fought against my arousal, clinging to a shred of control in an effort not to come in less than one second.

Holy fuck, that felt so good. She was noisier than usual, slurping and licking at me frantically, while also mewling her own pleasure as Oliver continued with the flogger between her legs.

I could tell when Stella got close because she gave up twirling her tongue around my cock and instead she sucked as much of my length into her mouth as she could, uncontrollably sucking and jerking her hand around my base at the same time so that I bumped repeatedly against

304

the back of her throat.

'Come,' Oliver suddenly demanded, the force of his tone and the harder flick of the flogger enough to send both Stella and myself tumbling over into our climaxes as my cock jerked wildly in her mouth and muffled the cries she made as her own orgasm swept through her body.

I wanted to collapse to the floor after the power of my release, but knowing we had an audience, I somehow managed to remain standing. Stella seemed even more of a pro than me, managing to swallow down my release, then work me down with soft licks of her tongue as Oliver carefully folded her dress back in place to cover her lower half.

Once I was tucked back in my trousers, I looked to Oliver and nodded my head in thanks. Returning my gesture, he opened a door behind him and indicated to the darkened recovery room with a sweep of his arm. 'Good scene. I'll catch up with you both later once you've had some time alone.'

I scooped Stella's relaxed body up into my arms and carried her into the adjoining room. I thanked Oliver as he shut the door behind us, leaving me alone with my girl.

This was one of many small chill-out rooms that Club Twist had. They were specifically designed to give customers time to recover after performing a scene. Some Doms had a particular aftercare routine they would carry out with their subs, either physically or emotionally. We didn't have a set routine, but I always liked to discuss how Stella had found the scene, and I liked to keep her close as she came down from her adrenaline rush. This feeling was mirrored by Stella, because she always wanted to be held while she recovered from the highs of the pleasure.

Today's scene must have been a powerful one for Stella, because her breathing took a little longer than usual to calm. Not that I could blame her, because it had been extremely intense. What with the added sensations of having a crowd watching us, and Oliver taking part, it had been really fucking intense for me, too, and I also needed the chill-out time.

Closing my eyes, I rested my head back on the sofa and stroked her hair, enjoying the warm sensation of having her in my arms.

Once Stella's breaths were steady again, along with my own, I gently tilted her head back with my thumb and smiled when I saw the blissed-out expression on her face.

'So, how did you find that?' I asked softly, fairly sure from her expression that she had enjoyed it as much as I had.

She blinked several times, as if trying to come back from her happy place, then finally licked her lips and grinned. 'It was incredible.' Shifting her position on my lap, she sat up so our faces were aligned. 'It felt way more intense than usual, but I'm not sure if that's because of the crowd, the excitement of today, or the addition of an extra person.'

She'd summed it up perfectly, and I supposed there was no definite answer to her pondering. 'I suspect it was a combination of all three of those factors,' I murmured, 'but I agree, it was definitely more intense than usual.'

Stella reached up and cupped my jaw, her eyes suddenly looking a little uncertain. 'I … I think you asked Oliver to join in because you thought I wanted him to?'

Nodding, I brushed some hair back from her face. 'I did.'

'But you still enjoyed it, didn't you?'

Ah, now I saw the root of her concern, and I relaxed as a smile curled my lips. 'Oh yes, very much.'

Stella's body loosened in my arms in relief and she bobbed her head up to place a quick kiss on my lips. 'Thank you. It was different having him there, too, different in a good way, but I'm not looking to extend that exploration any further, if that's OK?'

Thank fuck for that, because there was no way I'd let another man touch her, let alone fuck her. 'That is not a question up for debate. You're mine, Stella. Today was an exception to the rule.' My voice came out a little harsher than I had intended, but I saw Stella smile at my jealous tone. It was just as well she liked my possessive streak.

'He's probably the only person I would have allowed to join us. I trust Oliver with my life,' I stated, meaning every single word. 'As well as being my closest acquaintance, he can keep his feelings controlled during a scene, so he doesn't become too emotionally involved. It's one of the reasons he's exceptionally good at what he does.'

'Wow. Sounds kinda detached. Does he even enjoy it?'

'Of course. He wouldn't do it if he didn't.' I decided not to tell Stella that, usually, if two out of three parties involved achieved climax then it was good manners to ensure the third party also did, unless their orgasm was being deliberately withheld for some reason. Really, we should have also ensured his climax as part of the scene, but I hadn't been able to bring myself to ask Stella to do it, as the sight of her pleasuring another man would kill me. So poor Oliver had gone without. I knew he wouldn't mind, though, and luckily, he was well aware of my possessive streak so no doubt understood the reasons.

However, telling Stella that might make her uncomfortable next time we saw Oliver, so I kept quiet. Instead, I let her know about another courtesy we should extend to him. 'It would be polite to thank him for the scene if we see him again before we leave.'

'OK, I can do that.' Nodding, she smiled up at me, then suddenly opened her eyes wide. 'Oh, I nearly forgot! I have something for you!'

Stella shifted from my lap. She picked up her small

clutch bag and opened it before digging inside and giving me a quizzical look.

She pulled out a small blue box and clicked it open to reveal a ring. 'Last new year you said you'd wear any commitment ring I chose for you ...' she murmured, still sounding apprehensive. 'I've been working with a local designer, and this is what we've come up with. It's platinum, with a band of titanium through the centre. Do you like it?'

I picked the ring up, feeling a peculiar sensation settle in my chest. It wasn't discomfort, though; it was actually very pleasant. The idea that Stella wanted to lay claim to me seemed to be warming me from the inside out.

With its dual tones of grey, it was incredibly masculine, and exactly the type of ring I would have picked myself. Turning it in my fingers, I saw a small inscription inside and brought it closer so I could read it. *Yours, always. S x*

Damn right. Grasping the ring in a clenched fist, I dug my free hand into her hair and dragged her lips to mine for a fierce kiss, our teeth briefly clashing before I managed to press my tongue inside to meet hers.

After several seconds, we drew apart, panting and flushed, and Stella smiled shyly. 'I take it from that reaction that you like it?'

'I *really* like it,' I replied gruffly, feeling quite choked by yet another emotional event occurring today.

'I only picked it up yesterday, but I wasn't sure if you'd want to wear it here in front of your associates, so I thought I'd wait until after the ceremony to give it to you.'

'I'll never take it off.'

She looked thrilled by my words and her cheeks flushed a deeper shade of red. Stella gently peeled my hand open, one finger at a time. She took the ring and carefully placed it on the ring finger of my left hand.

Grinning at me, she placed a quick kiss on my palm and

wiggled her eyebrows. 'Now everyone will know you're taken.'

I laughed, because her words mirrored the sentiment I'd expressed when I'd given her the promise ring she was wearing.

'You can't escape me now,' she joked, leaning in for a kiss, but I merely rolled my eyes, because I knew with 100 per cent certainty that I would never, ever want to leave her.

Stella

I'd just taken part in a live sex show.

I still couldn't believe it. I'd had a threesome with Nathan and his old trainer. How frigging bizarre was that? Not to mention the fact that we'd done it in front of an audience.

And I'd loved every second of it.

Gripping his hand as he led me through the club towards the bar, I grinned as I recalled some of the highlights of the scene. It had all been pretty amazing, but Nathan and Oliver towering over me in their fitted waistcoats with their sleeves rolled up and ties still on was possibly one of the hottest things I'd ever witnessed.

At one point, I'd seriously thought that Nathan was going to suggest they both took me at the same time, and however interesting that might be in terms of new experiences, I certainly hadn't wanted to try it for my first time on a stage in front of an audience! As it was, things had worked out perfectly. I'd shared the experience intimately with Nathan, but still had the thrill of another man making me come, something I'd never expected him to allow in a million years. Nathan had been right about Oliver's flogging technique, though, because it had been highly effective in bringing me to orgasm.

Speak of the devil ... Just as we reached the end of the bar and retook our seats, Oliver appeared from a bar door with David, and after a brief conversation, he came towards where we were seated.

My cheeks started to heat with embarrassment at the prospect of speaking to him again. Less than an hour ago, he'd been standing between my legs, getting up close and personal with my lace knickers as he made me climax.

Before we'd even had a chance to say a word, David placed a silver bucket on the bar containing a bottle of champagne. Then he produced two gleaming champagne flutes before disappearing again with a wink.

'A small gift to congratulate you on your collaring,' Oliver said, giving a nod of his head as he smiled at us both.

'That's very generous of you, Oliver, thank you.' Nathan picked up the bottle and began to undo the foil wrapping and so I took the opportunity to address the elephant in the room.

'Sir … I just wanted to say thank you for joining us in the scene earlier.'

Oliver's smile broadened and he shook his head. 'Thank you for the lovely etiquette, but there are no thanks required, honestly. I'm glad it made for an enjoyable scene on such a special day.'

Now we were talking about it, even if indirectly, I felt less embarrassed and returned his smile. He seemed more relaxed now, and far less daunting than I'd first thought.

My appraisal of Nathan's former trainer was abruptly halted as the champagne cork flew out with a large pop and almost made me slip from my seat in shock.

Nathan leaned over the bar to snag another champagne flute and began to pour. 'You must join us for a glass, Oliver.'

He dragged over a stool and sat. 'It would be my pleasure.' Having accepted the glass, Oliver raised it in a toast. 'To the happy couple.'

For a second, it almost felt as if we'd just got married, but then I remembered the venue, the collar around my neck, and the public flogging I'd received and I couldn't help but grin.

Nathan saw my expression and matched it with a happy

smile of his own which made my heart melt. He looked so relaxed and content; so happy to have me as his.

We really were so good together; our relationship had evolved from the casual Dom/sub weekly meeting to this all-encompassing bond that we now had. It was incredible, really. He was more than just my Dom, my lover, or my partner. He was my everything.

Today might not have been a wedding, but it had been perfect for us, and as I thought back over not only today, but our entire time together, I knew I wouldn't have changed a single thing.

Epilogue

Oliver

Glancing across the bar towards Nathan and Stella, I watched their interactions curiously for a few minutes. Of all the Doms I'd helped train over the years, Nathan was the last one that I would have envisaged settling down. He'd been wild at first, defiant, angry and rebellious, but I was actually incredibly proud of how he'd overcome his abusive start to life and shaped himself into the man he was today.

Even with the monumental changes to his character, I'd always assumed that Nathan would remain a bachelor like me. He'd seemed too wild to tame, but I'd clearly been wrong, because it was obvious just how smitten he was with Stella.

Stella giggled at something Nathan said, and I watched as her cheeks flushed and posture changed as Nathan swooped down and laid a hard, possessive kiss on her lips before leaning back and staring at her. Taking a sip of my whisky, I smirked at the heated look he was now aiming at her, and suspected it wouldn't be too long before they made their excuses and left, no doubt to go home and fuck like rabbits.

If it were possible for sexual chemistry to be visible, then they were a perfect example of it. The air around them was practically sizzling, and the bond they shared was obvious for all to see. If I wasn't such a hard-hearted bastard it might actually make me feel envious.

The collaring had been good today; it had been nice to see the club so full of likeminded people, and even though I didn't usually scene here anymore, I had really enjoyed

313

sharing the stage with Nathan and Stella. An unfortunate by-product of my participation was the hard-on I'd been rocking pretty much ever since. It wasn't that I was attracted to Stella, as such, but the scene had been fucking erotic, and the atmosphere in here this evening was drenched in sex, which had put me in the mood for a good fuck.

This was a little trickier for me to accommodate, because I was still single. According to my mother, and her traditional Spanish views, I should be married and a *papá* to at least three children by now, but that wasn't the life I had planned out, and much to her worry, here I was at the age of 41, still a bachelor.

The title was exciting. It meant I was free to do as I pleased, fuck who I wanted when I wanted, and not have to think about anybody but myself. It was a selfish outlook, I was well aware of that, but I'd never met anybody who had remotely tempted me to change my direction in life, so I'd simply continue enjoying myself.

Watching as the evening show got underway on the main stage, I settled back in my seat with a smile. This bar had become ingrained in my life. Not that it could technically be called a bar; it was obviously a sex club. A high-class one, admittedly, but still a sex club, and luckily for me I'd ended up as one of the co-owners.

Hijo de puta. My mother would give me a firm clip around the ear if she had any idea I'd invested in this place, that was for sure. Rolling my eyes at how I still reverted to Spanish when I swore, I thought again about my homeland. Perhaps it was time for a visit to my house in Barcelona. I could do with some sun on my skin to revive me, because this so-called summer in Britain had been appalling. I thought about my family and smiled, imagining them sitting on the terrace with plates piled high with my *mamá*'s home-cooked food and the local red wine flowing freely.

Yes, a trip home soon would be good.

Glancing around the club again, I noticed how busy it was now and smiled. This place had certainly been a good investment for me; I had made my money back and then some, while also getting to enjoy the perks of membership and all that went with it. For me, that had mostly meant access to a string of women willing to drop to their knees for me, come to my bed, and leave afterwards without getting attached.

Back in the beginning, I'd come here practically every free night I had. I'd been a young buck with exotic Spanish looks and a talent for fucking, so getting women had never been an issue for me. It still wasn't. I'd aged well, could still fuck like a stallion, and was able to take my pick of whatever woman I wanted, as the extensively female contact list in my phone indicated. I was lucky enough to be one of those men women never said no to, and it wasn't a trait I took for granted. I appreciated my good fortune no end, and would make the most of it until I was no longer able.

I still drank here, and would occasionally get involved in a training scene, but I didn't use the club to pick up women any more. About seven years ago, David had asked me if I'd do the accounts for Club Twist, and as soon as I'd accepted the contract I'd stopped fraternising with the customers. I didn't mix business with pleasure, never had, and probably never would; it was just one of my rules.

I still fucked, of course, but not anyone associated with the club. I had several women on speed dial who knew my tastes and would happily accommodate me for an hour or so as and when I wanted. They weren't prostitutes, as I never paid for sex; they were simply girls I'd known for long enough to trust without any risk of attachments.

As I signalled David for a refill of my whiskey I saw someone approaching me from the corner of my eye. I let

315

out a sigh as my shoulders tensed.

Most of the regulars here knew I wouldn't play in the club and so didn't bother approaching me, but this girl was new. I didn't recognise her, and nor was I bothered about breaking my rules to get to know her.

Another quick glance showed that she was young and pretty, and possibly submissive, if her posture was anything to go by, but I settled into my usual expression of indifference as she approached. My apparent lack of interest in taking sexual partners from within the club had inadvertently earned me a reputation of being supremely selective, which unfortunately seemed to make me into some sort of challenge.

'Hello, Sir. Would you like some company?' she purred, her voice soft and low and adding to my slow-burning arousal, not that I would let her see that. Her use of the honorific indicated that someone had told her who I was, but it didn't make me feel any more inclined to devote my time to her.

Giving her a brief look, I didn't even attempt to be polite. 'No.'

Dios, I was such a bastard lately.

Her expression morphed into one of shock, then hurt, but as she stuttered and fidgeted on the spot I effectively dismissed her by turning back to the bar and taking a swig of my whiskey. 'I'm not interested,' I snapped over my shoulder at her.

The truth was, in recent years I hadn't seen one women in here that had even remotely tempted me to break my "never mix business and pleasure" rule. Yes, there were always beautiful women here, much like the one who had just approached me; women with a submissive side that would no doubt match my needs to perfection, but why would I bother when I could get all of that outside the club from one of my trusted girls?

316

'You're even more of a bastard than I am.' David chuckled from behind the bar as he watched the blonde totter away from me.

I glanced at her retreating figure, then looked back at him and grinned. 'Yeah. Guilty.'

'Doesn't hurt your reputation as a bad boy, though,' he added with a wink, before turning away to serve someone.

Bad boy? I suppose perhaps it might appear that way from the outside, and maybe I was, to some extent. My heart was good, though, I was sure of that; I loved my family, respected my circle of close friends, had high moral values, and never led a woman on. I had just never wanted to settle down.

Adjusting myself on my stool, I decided it was time to leave my ponderings behind and sort out the hard-on I was sporting again. I pulled my phone from my pocket and scrolled through the list of contacts, wondering who would be suitable for my evening entertainment. I smiled as I saw the name "Rosita", before pressing dial and lifting it to my ear.

No more than two rings later and I heard her breathy voice down the line. 'Good evening Sir, this is a nice surprise.' The softness of her tone didn't fool me for a second. Rosita was a switch; she could give as good as she got, and could be a hard-faced bitch when playing as a Domme, but whenever she was with me she submitted to perfection.

'Good evening, Rosita. Are you free?' She also liked to be fucked hard, which for tonight was exactly what I was after. A good, hard, mindless fuck.

'I am, Sir.' Perfect.

'I'll be there in twenty minutes.' I hung up, downed the last of my drink, stood up, and smoothed the creases out of my suit jacket.

Glancing across the bar, I saw Nathan catch my eye and

give a respectful tilt to his head as he realised I was leaving. Returning the gesture, I flashed him a wink, then turned for the stairs. He'd had his kicks for the night. Now it was time for me to get mine.

The End

Author's Note

Thank you for reading!

If Oliver has left you intrigued then keep an eye out for my new book, *Wolfe's Lair*, which features him as the central character.

I hope you enjoyed this latest instalment of the Jackson brothers' story and found the happy endings you were hoping for. Many of you requested a "ten years later" type of ending, so you could see where the brothers were in years to come. I wrote one, but to tell you the truth, I'm just not ready to age them like that yet. I want Nicholas and Nathan to remain young and vibrant and up to their naughtiness! They also feature as side characters in my new Club Twist series, so it seemed wrong to publish a future view of them just yet. Perhaps one day, though.

As always, I love to hear from readers, so feel free to get in touch and tell me your thoughts!

E-mail: **aliceraineauthor@gmail.com**
Twitter: **@AliceRaine1**
Facebook: **www.facebook.com/alice.raineauthor**
Website: **www.aliceraineauthor.com**

Alice xx

The Revealed Series

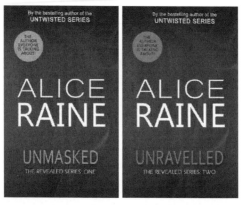

By Alice Raine

For more information about **Alice Raine**

and other **Accent Press** titles

please visit

www.accentpress.co.uk

Printed in Great Britain
by Amazon